DARKWORLDS: LONDON

A Cthulhu LitRPG

TONY WALKER

Adam Cadmon by Ryan Vogler

CONTENTS

Chapter One

CHARACTER CREATION

I wake up. My eyes are still closed and the air is pleasantly warm. I'm inside though. The room smells of camphor and old-fashioned furniture. A memory rises I struggle to place then I realize the mix of smells reminds me of my great aunt's wardrobe. I used to hide there when I was small; excited, waiting for my cousin to find me. It's a smell of mothballs and old clothes. There's also the chemical stink of petrol wafting in, and cooking—someone is frying bacon.

A gramophone is playing. I don't recognize the tune but it's old-fashioned traditional jazz. I'm in a room with thin walls and single-glazed windows. Horses' hooves clip-clop outside, but also the chugging of vehicle engines. A car backfires.

My eyes open to see a paisley-patterned wallpaper. I'm sitting in an uncomfortable chair. It's upholstered in horsehair, and scratchy. Before I do anything, I look at my hands, they're not my hands—they're very lifelike—but not mine. Just like Miskatonic's advertising promised, I have awoken in the game.

I blink. I can feel the beating of my heart and the rising of my chest. I guess these must be the sensations of my physical body, but I'm deep in trance. I turn my head left and stare at a wall for minutes before I make sense of it. A mezzotint print of a rural scene hangs there. I blink again. There's a graphical display in my field of vision, words and figures I can't comprehend. They don't interfere with where I'm looking.

I'm not alone in the room. I turn my head to the right and see a middle-aged man with a bald head. He wears a three-piece tweed suit and sits patiently, wearing scuffed brown shoes. He studies me with great interest. A faint smile plays on his face. "You're awake."

I clear my throat to speak but then nod instead. It's less effort. I know I'm in-game, but it feels real. He feels real. "Where am I?"

"In London, Gower Street. In my flat."

"Who are you?"

Without moving he says, "My name is Aleister. I'm here to guide you through your character creation."

I glance up and point at the figures on my HUD even though he can't see them. "Can you explain what these figures mean?"

"We'll get to that. I would imagine you're seeing a lot of zeros."

I nod. Lots of zeros.

He smiles again. "You have no skills, no abilities. You are Level One. Pretty useless."

I nod and repeat what he says. "Pretty useless." I feel drugged. My head is clearing but still I'm drugged. I guess it's the Dreamland Inducer tablet I took. I hope I get used to it and the side effects eventually wane.

He continues. "But you can grow to be useful—to be special here."

I glance up at the figures on my Heads Up Display and see:

<HEALTH 100>
<SANITY 100>
<MANA 100>
<REPUTATION 100>

I point again. "What do these mean?"

"These are your four base statistics. Your Health is of course your physical health and if you're injured, you'll subtract damage from this figure. Your Sanity is something you need to take special care of. Your Mana is for casting spells, and your Reputation is a similar statistic to your Sanity. Both Sanity and Reputation affect how you progress in the world."

"Is this a class-based game?"

Aleister shakes his head.

"Then how do I get on?"

He sits forward, folds his arms and says, "Choose a life."

"Choose a life? How do I do that?"

"Let's start at the beginning. What kind of character do you want to be?"

I feel pathetic and juvenile, but it's true, what I say, "Badass. Strong." We all want to be strong; that's why we play.

Aleister raises his eyebrows as if he's heard it all before and is bored, even disappointed. Finally, he says, "Do you want to be someone who engages in combat?"

I nod.

"With firearms? Or magic?"

That gives me pause. After less than a minute's thought, I say, "I like the sound of magic."

He steeples his hands and touches fingertips together as if in prayer. Like a schoolteacher he begins. "Your skills are initially determined by the life you've led. As we talk through your life story, that will suggest a profession for you. But I note you want to be a magic user rather than a street brawler. My own taste too. Although I was a boxer, so don't disdain physical combat. You too will need it eventually."

"What now?" I am still in my seat looking around the room. An aspidistra sits in a china pot in the corner. The room contains a sofa and two armchairs. I'm in one of them. Aleister in the other. There's also a piano with sheet music on its stand, and lid up revealing the black and white keys, grinning like discolored teeth.

The sound of gramophone jazz still wafts through the wall.

Aleister says, "As I said, we have to choose a life for you. I'll guide you in this process. Are you ready?"

I fan out my hands. "Sure."

He nods. "How old are you?"

I think for a while. I don't want to be too immature, but I don't want to be too old. I want to be physically able. "Thirty?"

"That means you were born in eighteen ninety-seven."

I laugh. "It sounds weird. But let's go with it."

"And what is your social class? Social class in England is very important. You are born into a class and it's very difficult to leave it."

I think hard. I want to have had opportunities. There's no point being a peasant working the land. I briefly toy with being an aristocrat but that brings its own constraints so I say, "Middle class."

"What did your father do?"

"Job wise?"

"Yes."

I have no idea. I think of doctors or lawyers then remember the profession suggested by Miskatonic's personality test. It was mine, but it could have been my father's too. "A priest."

Aleister nods. "A priest. And, of course, he would have been an Anglican priest—tending to his flock in some remote parish in the country." He scratches his cheek. "Or perhaps the city?"

I remember the grimness of Outer London. "The country definitely."

"North, South, East, or West? I take it you were born in England? Not the colonies?"

"England."

"In which county?"

I ask him to choose for me.

"I'll choose Sussex. And say you were born in Arundel, a very historic and picturesque town on the south coast of England. Your father was parish priest. As Anglican priests can marry, you have a mother."

He thinks he's clever. Maybe he is. He smiles. "What did your mother do?"

I shrug. "She's a stay-at-home mum."

"I think we'd better describe your mother as a housewife—the vicar's wife. I see her putting on teas and making cucumber sandwiches for the local cricket team. Perhaps she leads the Women's Institute?"

This is fun. Already I'm getting a picture of my parents—my imaginary parents that is. I imagine we lived a very peaceful life in a vicarage, in a beautiful old town in the south of England.

He says, "Because you were the son of a vicar you'd have to go to a public school, a private school."

"I know what a public school is." The denizens of Inner London go to public schools. We don't. Still, I can be someone else in this game. "I'm not a snob though," I say quickly.

"I never suggested you were, dear boy. Were you particularly sporty at school?"

I laugh again. "I see myself as being more bookish. I was always interested in History and Latin ..." It's amazing how I can cook up a story so easily. Lies must come more naturally to me than I'd thought.

"What happened after you left school?"

"My father pressed me to go to theology college. He wanted me to be a vicar like him. But I didn't want to. My faith wasn't strong. Still, I was under his influence so I became a priest too."

"Interesting." He was smiling. "And what did you do in the war?"

"The war?"

"The Great War—1914-1918. A man of your age would have had to serve in the war."

"Well could I join the infantry? Or perhaps the cavalry?"

Aleister says, "I calculate at the beginning of the Great War you were seventeen. You would have been in your first year at theology college. I suspect you would have entered the army as a padre around nineteen seventeen. One year's service."

"I was an army chaplain?"

"Indeed."

"Makes sense."

Aleister stands and looks out of the window at the street scene below. He looks wistfully at the scene, though I don't know why. "Perhaps you would like to check your skills now?"

I look at my Heads Up Display and an icon of an outline figure. "How do I activate the commands on the HUD?"

Aleister says, "Simply look at them. The neural net knows where your eyes are looking, and you can select the command. Thinking the word <Select> will activate a small electrical current in your brain which the neural net picks up. It will choose that particular tab. Try it."

I select the outline figure of myself and the Character Sheet pops up. I see the figures of one hundred against each of the statistics. There's also the sub-table for skills. When I touch it, it reveals hundreds of skills, mostly greyed-out, but my career as a priest and my brief army service has made certain ones active:

<**Interpersonal Skills:**
-Diplomacy 45>
-Persuade 15>
-Seduction 2>
-Intimidate 3>

<Empathy 45>
<Latin 60>
<Greek 45>
<Hebrew 20>
<Religious Lore 90>
<Ritual 40>
<First-aid 30>
<Firearms:
<- Rifles 20>
<- Pistols 20>

Aleister says, "With each new level, you'll get a further hundred skill points to allocate as you see fit. You have hundred unallocated skill points already, just from being born."

"Should I allocate this extra hundred now?"

He shakes his head, "I wouldn't. The game will introduce you to several starter quests. In addition, there's one main story theme which you will encounter when you've completed the starter quest. Your main quest is different depending on your game character."

"So, don't allocate now?"

"No."

"You're the boss."

He grins as if I've pleased him. I remember he's an NPC, and it doesn't matter whether I please him. Then I stop. Maybe it does in this game? If NPCs can be influenced, flattery is Aleister's key.

But I'm still not settled. I wanted to be a magic user. I ask him if he'll teach me magic.

He scratches his cheek, thinking it over. He shrugs. "I suppose you could spend a few skill points now, though I still think it would be better to wait."

"Please." I smile winningly.

I don't think my winning ways impressed him, but I get a message on my HUD:

<Aleister offers to teach you Magic. Do you accept?>

I nod. "Yes."

Nothing happens.

"Select it on your HUD." I look up and go through the Magic skill-tree. There are sub-schools. The first is Abjuration. I don't know what that is, but it's just to try it out. I select it and see the first spell is <Lesser Banishing Ritual of the Pentagram>. That'll do. I select that one. It needs 20 skill points, I commit those and the lesson begins.

Aleister stares into my eyes and I feel woozy. His eyes are so intense, like whirlpools, and I'm falling into him. All the time I can hear him saying words I don't understand, then I realize they're Hebrew; he is vibrating the names of God. *AGLA, ADONAI, YOD-HE-VAV-HE ...*

Then it's over and I feel like I've woken from a surgical procedure. I have an itch in the middle of my head.

"Enjoy that?" he asks.

I scratch my scalp. "Not sure enjoy is the right word. I know this spell now?"

He nods.

"What's it do?"

He sighs. "I'm not your mother to fix everything and tell you what to do. Experiment."

There's a pause then he begins again as if he'd forgotten something before. "Spells are like all skills. You will often be trying to perform a skill against opposition. You simply use the skill points you've put into it against the skill points your opponent has in the defending skill. Get it?"

Seems simple enough—similar to other games.

He continues. "If you don't have skill points in a skill when you come to a check, you won't be able to do it."

I'm studying his puffy face. He likes whisky I think. I ask him. "Aleister, you're very lifelike. It's like you're really thinking."

"I am really thinking."

"But aren't you ..." I hesitate. I don't want to be rude.

"An NPC?"

I nod.

"What do you think?"

I peer at him. "I honestly don't know."

"By the way," he says. "You learn skills from trainers. Different trainers train different skills. You'll notice them by their icons. They're all around London."

"So, I'm done here?"

"Nearly. You haven't chosen a name." He's smiling. Maybe he is friendly, but there's something about him. Hidden depths. And he's right, I haven't chosen a name. Tentatively, I say, "Adam?"

"Very well. And your surname?"

"I don't know." I think of the first name that comes into my head. "Cadmon?"

"Adam Cadmon? Why Cadmon?"

"He was the first English poet."

"You know Adam Cadmon was the original man in Hebrew esoteric writing?"

In real life, I didn't know, but my game Hebrew skill makes it feel like I did know. That's amazing.

"Check your inventory."

I see for the first time I'm wearing black clerical clothes with a starched white round collar. My inventory icon shows the only thing I have is a British Library reader's ticket.

He looks very calm. "When you stand Mr Cadmon, be careful."

I stand, and am as wobbly as a newborn foal. I have to put my hand on the chair arm to steady myself. Then I'm fine. My head is clearer. The inducer drug side effects have worn off.

I look around the room again. The place is well drawn, and in perfect 3D. I really am back in London; in 1927.

Aleister smiles. "Are you ready for your first quest?"

Chapter Two

DARKWORLDS

Every minute is a victory—every minute I'm on their screen reading my own stuff is a minute where DataCorp is footing the bill and is therefore a pencil jabbed in the eye of the man. I'm just being honest when I say I find work ridiculously easy and complete it in half the time my colleagues do. I honestly don't know what they're up to most of the time. Maybe faking it like me. I'm quicker than most of them, but Miranda is as quick as me. In fact, quicker.

She works in the next but one cubicle on the vast DataCorp office floor. It is near the end of the day and I keep looking to see if she's finished so I can time my exit to coincidentally bump into her in the lift.

The time comes. She is finished. I pull on my coat and quickly grab my bag.

Truth is, I don't think I have much of a chance. Miranda is stunning, clever, funny and always gets the best results in the department. I'm very nervous about asking her out.

The lift door opens, and I step in behind her. "Hey, Miranda."

She doesn't look surprised I'm there, or annoyed, just amused as if she sees through my ruse. It isn't the first time I've engineered bumping into her—but I'd got nowhere—my carefully rehearsed patter turning to babble. She'd been okay about it though.

This time, she glances up with eyes as blue as cornflowers. "Well, if it isn't the best analyst in the department—Mr Adam Harker himself."

I blush. "You know, you're the best analyst, Miranda. You're top of the results table most months."

She winks. "I meant apart from me. Anyway, where're you headed?"

I hoped to persuade her to go for a drink or a coffee, but I couldn't ask outright, and I couldn't say I was going home because that would close down my plan, so I say, "Wandering."

"Wandering?" She arches a dark eyebrow. "It's dark and raining and you're not allowed to wander in Inner London for more than thirty minutes because you don't have a resident's permit and wandering in Outer London is an invitation to get robbed or worse."

Okay that didn't go so well. I clear my throat. "Where are you going?"

She points to the door. We walk out of the DataCorp foyer. Miranda comes out beside me. I'm aware of her at my shoulder. She isn't correct though—it is dusk rather than dark, but rain is spitting down from the clouds. We stroll through the ultra-clean Inner London streets to the guarded Exit Gate.

It is true what Miranda says, Outer London residents are not allowed to linger for more than half an hour in Inner London without a resident permit. Still, I can't bring myself to walk too fast. I watch Miranda glancing in the windows of the fashionable shops and at the glittering people through glittering restaurant windows. Maybe this is the life she wants? But she isn't an heiress or a Ukrainian Oligarch, so it is difficult to see how that could be achieved.

I can't afford to take a taxi, and buses don't exist within Inner London. Sometimes that is a pain, but tonight I welcome it. As we walk, we talk about the weather and about how shit work is. Security flyers buzz overhead.

We have to walk because the underground railway network no longer connects with Outer London. The nearest Exit Gate is at the top of Tottenham Court Road. The severing of railway links happened after the Crash of 2020. The economy never really recovered after 2008 and after the 2020 Banking Crisis brought down governments like dominoes, the corporations backed the 'Small Government' initiative and supported the elected leaders to put up walls between the protected inner areas of cities and the outer zones where workers lived.

"Looking for economic migrants," Miranda says, glancing up at the hovering security aircraft.

As we finally reach the Exit Gate, we see sheets of rainfall from the darkening sky outside. There is no need to show our workers permits to get out of Inner London, we only have to do that when we enter.

As we step through the gate, I say, "Welcome to Free London."

She nods. "Yeah, free of wealth and health."

I grin. "But getting robbed is free. Getting evicted is free."

"Yep, dystopian chic. It's the new thing."

"You getting the Tube?" I ask.

Dark clouds threaten heavier rain. Even so, I gather my courage and ask Miranda to come for a drink. She hesitates. Hope grows. Although being later will make the walk home from the Tube Station in Wood Green more dangerous, it will be worth it to spend time in her company.

"Thing is, I don't really drink," she says.

I remember she is an athlete. She plays for the Romford Women's Football team.

"Coffee then?" I'm not going to press it too far. If she isn't interested, I'll leave it.

Changing the subject, perhaps to save my pride, Miranda points. "You're a gamer, aren't you?"

I nod. "When I can afford it. Why?"

I follow her pointing finger to a pop-up shop where Miskatonic games have set up a store to promote their new release Darkworlds. Laser beams etch a picture in the air of a 1920s cityscape with the flapper font of the period and the tagline:

Now! Darkworlds! Realer than Real!

"It's supposed to be good," she says. "Fully immersive. New technology and all that."

"I didn't know you played?"

"Yep, I was a Level five hundred Death Knight when I was a kid."

I shrug. "I played lots of solo games. Never been into MMOs."

"No, you're not very cooperative, are you?" She smiles as she says it, but it is true.

I tend to be a loner. Even the sports I play are solo ones—running, cycling, swimming. "Also," I say. "I'm not sure about this drug they use to get you into the trance state."

"That's the selling point. It takes you deeper than any game before."

That is the marketing slogan Miskatonic has been using. I look at the queue of people outside waiting to get in. There are hordes peering over them to see the screens in the windows. Two blonde model girls in tight black uniforms harangue passers-by to try to get them into the store.

"It looks pretty popular," I say.

"I bet they're going to make gazillions."

"All from people trying to escape their shit lives."

Miranda indicates fast-food containers in the gutter and the threatening graffiti daubed on every wall. "You can't blame them for that."

I laugh. "I blame no one for nothing."

"Very big of you. Anyway, that's a double negative, so in fact you do blame people." She measures me with her intelligent gaze. "You're always muttering about how shit DataCorp is and how immoral their work is, persuading people to buy things they don't want, need, or can afford."

"I do?" I'm at once pleased she'd given me this much thought and annoyed at myself for being so open with my views. You have to be careful of what they hear you say. Jobs are hard to get.

She punches me in the bicep. "Only messing with you, Mr Harker." A little flash sparks in my chest, all because of her smile. She really is very attractive. She takes my arm. "Why don't we go look in the window? I bet the graphics are amazing."

I'm only too pleased to cross the road with her to the Miskatonic store, narrowly dodging an unskilled pizza delivery rider on his skirling motorbike. Outside the store we are engaged by one of the 6' 2"

Slavonic models. "Interested in playing, guys?" She looks at both Miranda and me.

I say, "I'm not really into MMOs."

Miranda asks how much the sub is.

The sales model latches onto the question. "Well, for the introductory period, we're offering the chance of a free game subscription with complimentary neural net, goggles, and inducer tablets."

Inducer tablets.

"Yeah," I say, "What about this drug you need to take to induce the trance state?"

The model ignores my question. Miranda is more interested and the saleswoman knows it. She directs her attention to Miranda. "You could win. You might be one of the lucky ones."

Miranda is looking very interested. "I'm born lucky." She grins. "I bet I win."

"What's the catch?" I ask.

The model's perfect smile lights up her false-tanned face. She studies me with her expertly made-up eyes. "All you need to do is take a free personality test. That will suggest the kind of profession you should take up in the game. You win a sub for a year, and the gear is yours to keep."

"Thanks, but no thanks." I go to turn away, but Miranda catches my arm. "Please!" she says. "Let's go and do the personality test. What harm could it do?"

"It's all crap." I pause. If she won't go for a drink with me, this at least will extend our time together. I say, "But if you want to ...?"

"Yeah, come on."

We enter the shop and assistants in black T-shirts with the Miskatonic logo come up. "Hi guys. Here to win?"

They guide Miranda and I to neighboring desks to begin the personality test. Miranda gives me an encouraging grin. The male assistant across the desk meets my eye. "Do you know this game is proven to make you more intelligent?"

I sigh. "Really?" More marketing bullshit. I glance over at Miranda. At least I'm getting to spend longer with her. Miranda appears engrossed in conversation with her assistant. Ignoring my assistant's babble, I look around the store at the video screens showing screen-shots from the game. It does look very cool. Fantastic graphics.

The personality test includes a polygraph get-up. You put your finger in a conductivity clip to measure how much you're sweating and look into a glass ring resembling an optician's magnifying glass while the assistant stares into your eyes. When he's checked the equipment and I'm settled, the assistant asks. "Ready?"

"As I'll ever be."

The guy goes through a bunch of questions. They seem standard personality type questions: What is your favourite colour? What is your favourite food? How does this word make you feel? Occasionally they show pictures of smiling children and fluffy kittens. Then suddenly; a dismembered corpse.

I sit back. "What the hell is that?"

The assistant is unruffled. "It's just part of the personality test."

The guy is around twenty with a bumfluff moustache. He seems impatient. "Let's continue."

I'm not so sure, I look at Miranda who seems to be fully into it, so I shrug and sit forward again to go on with the test. Amid friendly pictures and word association games, a naked woman flashes up. I instinctively react and the guy opposite notes something on his pad.

More questions. The assistant is becoming more agitated. He looks at the questions, looks at me, types something into his pad, then mutters. There is a bead of sweat on his forehead.

At one point, he says, "Excuse me for a second."

I lean forward. "Is it done yet?"

The assistant is on his feet. "Just a minute. I'll be right back."

He returns with the sales manager, a tall woman with short blonde bobbed hair dressed in black Miskatonic uniform with a blue stripe on her shoulder. "Hey," she says.

Miranda's test still hasn't finished. I glance up at the sales manager. "Hello."

She sits next to me. "Great personality," she says.

"Pardon?"

"The test."

"What do you mean?"

Her eyes linger on my face, looking at me like she expects my face to reveal a secret. Then she says, "You're in a category we don't often see. Maybe one percent, or less, because we haven't had anybody like you in the London store yet."

"What category?"

"It just means you're very suited to playing this game."

I smile. "Really?" They would probably tell me I haven't won, but I'm very suited to the game and then I'll be flattered enough to cough up a sub.

I turn to the assistant who is standing at the manager's shoulder. "What profession did it suggest for me?"

The young man clears his throat. "A priest."

"A priest?" I laugh. "Like a healer?"

The manager says, "A divine conduit."

"So a healer?"

"It's just a play style," the assistant blurts out, but the manager darts a glance that shuts his mouth.

"Anyway," I say. "I don't play MMOs. I'm a lone gamer, really."

"Antisocial?" The manager smiles, but she studies me intensely.

I'm not offended. "I guess I am, yes. I don't have a problem with that."

She smiles more broadly. "Nor me."

"So, I don't win?"

The assistant nods. The manager agrees. "Oh yes, you did."

I laugh out loud. "Really? What is it? Everyone wins?"

The manager shakes her head. "No, of course not. But you did. You're special." She nods. "I'm Larisa Kuznetsova by the way. London marketing manager for Miskatonic. Congratulations, with your win you get a free neural net and a month's supply of Dreamworld Inducer tablets."

Those drugs again. "Dreamworld Inducer tablets?"

"To get you into the trance state. That's why Darkworlds is so immersive. It's not just virtual reality. It's immersive reality."

"But you need medication to play?"

"It's not medication. It's just melatonin with Miskatonic's secret additive."

"Which is?"

Larisa is smiling at me, flirting even. "It wouldn't be secret if I told you, silly." She puts reassuring fingers on the back of my hand. "It's nothing harmful. Fully tested and approved by the Federal Drugs Authority in the US and NICE here in the UK."

I wink. "After you bribed them?" I say it as a joke, but like everyone else, I know that's how corporations get these approvals.

"Please!" She sounds hurt. "Who do you think we are?" She smiles again before I come back with some wisecrack. "So, you sign up and I'll get you your stuff."

"No thanks."

She raises both eyebrows. "No thanks? It's a great offer. Not made to everyone."

I tilt my head. "Like I say. I'm not into MMOs. Besides, I feel a bit railroaded."

"You've just been lucky is all. Like I say, special." Her smile freezes and grows false. "Accept your luck." She leans sideways and withdraws a stylishly packaged game pack from under the desk.

I put up a hand. "No, I'm good. Thanks, honestly."

Miranda is at my shoulder now, grinning like a puppy. "I won!"

"Hmm." I don't want to appear cynical... but really?

She is smiling all over her face. "It said I have high drive and—"

"—creativity?"

"No!" She puts her hand to her mouth to stifle her laughter. "A questionable moral compass! Me!"

Larisa leans in to listen to Miranda. "What class did it say?"

"Assassin."

The sales manager beams. "Oh, they're great fun. I played one in beta. Here you are. Lucky you." She hands Miranda the game kit and Miranda takes it with delight.

Larisa says to me, "Are you sure?"

I shake my head. "I thought it was set in the nineteen-twenties? How come you have assassins?"

Larisa says, "They had assassins in the nineteen-twenties. They've always had assassins." She turns to Miranda. "But instead of daggers and studded leather armour, you'll be wearing a trench coat and using a stiletto. Your friend won too."

Miranda says to me, "Really? That's great!"

"Coincidence, huh?"

She narrows her eyes in mock disapproval. "Don't be cynical. Take it. We can play together."

I shrug. "I don't know. Not sure about this drug—Dreamland Inducer. Even the name sounds sinister."

"It's perfectly safe," Larisa says again.

"Well thanks, but no thanks." I stand. "Are we going?"

Miranda wheedles. "Why don't you take your game kit?" She winks. "You'd see me in-game then."

I'm tempted, but I haven't enjoyed my experience in the store. If I didn't know before, it is clear to me now Miskatonic is like DataCorp. Trying to sell people things they don't need. Huge corporations who don't give a damn about anything or anyone. Even their smiles are calibrated to deepen brand loyalty.

I walk away.

"Can't persuade you?" Larisa shouts after me as I'm leaving the store.

Miranda links my arm. She has her package. I would like to see more of her, even virtually, but these people ...

Larisa runs after me and Miranda pulls me to a halt. Larisa holds something out to me. "Take this voucher. If you change your mind, come back and I'll exchange it for a game starter pack."

Reluctantly, I take the voucher, a plastic credit card-sized object, just a little thicker. I flip it over, shrug and place it in my jacket pocket.

"You think you're pretty cool? Mr.-won't-break-a-sweat-tragically hip."

I laugh out loud. She unlinks arms as if our intimacy is good only for the game shop. We walk in silence towards Euston Square Station Underground where I'll catch the tube that will take me away from her, into the earth and eventually to Wood Green.

At the entrance to the Tube steps she says, "Pity you can't play."

"Well, you know."

"Cutting off your nose to spite your face. You shouldn't let your principles get in the way of fun."

"My principles?"

"All your anti-globalization, occupy this, occupy that. It's only a game, Adam. You should go back and get your winnings."

Her eyelashes are like moth wings. "I don't know."

"Is it the drug? Are you scared of medication?"

I shake my head emphatically. "No." I really don't want her to think I'm scared. It isn't that. It is just what I've told Larisa; I'm not an MMO player. Plus, it is true I don't like being manipulated by corporations. But as I watch her shrug and give up, I wonder if she is right and I'm cutting off my nose to spite my face. And also, I would like to hang out with her, even if it is just in a game.

We go underground, getting on escalator after escalator carrying us deeper down until we arrive on the Circle Line Eastbound platform.

We've been sitting on the train ten minutes, when Miranda whispers, "See that guy with the really black hair?" She nods subtly in the direction of a man sitting on his own a little way down the carriage. The train is half-empty. Most jobs are done by robots now, so Outer London is deserted in parts.

"Yep."

"He was outside the Miskatonic store."

I look again. I don't recognize him. "Really?"

She nods. "You don't pay attention to your surroundings."

"He doesn't look dangerous."

"Nah." She winks. "You're a big tough man. You can look after yourself, I bet."

I'm no brawler really, but if she thinks I'm tough, I feel childishly flattered.

We get to King's Cross Station. I'm changing here to the Piccadilly Line, and she is going on the Central Line to take her out to Romford.

"See you at work tomorrow." She waves goodbye and keeps looking at me over her shoulder, smiling.

I feel warm inside. I had hoped she might have given me a peck on the cheek. Still, she has smiled. I watch her as she leaves. Maybe there is a point to life after all.

When she disappears out of sight, I turn and take the steps to the Piccadilly Line platform. The tunnels between the stations are less busy this time of night, so I'm unsettled by someone coming right up behind me. A sudden jag of alarm sparks in my chest. Outer London outside the protected zone is dangerous after dark. Especially in underground tunnels.

I risk a glance. It is the man from the train. The guy is dressed fashionably, probably in his late twenties. He doesn't look like a thief. He looks well off, if anything. I tell myself to be calm. This is just a guy who happens to be going the same way. I stop on pretence of tying my shoelaces, expecting the stranger to walk right past, but the man halts. "Hello. I wonder if I could have a word with you?"

The man is well-spoken and his tone mild. This is weird rather than threatening. I clear my throat. "About what?"

"I saw you come out of the Miskatonic store, didn't I?"

I frown. "So what?"

"Did you have your personality tested?"

"I don't see what it is to do with you."

"Just humour me."

I'm wary, but I nod.

"You know they wanted you to play the game?"

I step away. "How do you know that?"

The man gives a twisted smile. "We hack their system. Your personality test lit their London network up like a Christmas Tree."

"What?" Lots of questions spin through my head. First—who is this guy? Who is the 'we' that hack Miskatonic's Systems? How in hell did they manage to do that? It is impressive, but why did they do it? My hand curls into a fist. "Did you follow me?" My mouth is dry. "From the store?"

"Not all the way."

"What the hell does that mean?"

"I picked up your signal at the Tube Station."

My head is reeling. "My signal?"

The man shrugs. "They geotagged you. I guess they gave you something—the game kit? Something else?"

I remember the plastic voucher. I take it out.

"Yes, that'll be it."

I flip the voucher away down the passage. I start to walk.

The man hurries after me. "So, are you going to play?"

"No."

The man's face breaks into a broad smile. "Really? Why not?"

I don't know why I'm giving the guy my time. I speak over my shoulder as I walk on. "It felt fake. Rigged. They were pretending it was a giveaway, but it is a done deal. Something about the personality tests made them offer us free entry."

"Why would they do that, I wonder?" The man asks like he knows the answer already.

"I don't know. Anyway, I'm going now."

I hurry on. The man matches me step for step.

"Listen, leave me be, or I'll punch you."

The man says, "I'm Gary Preston."

"Is that supposed to mean something to me?"

"Not yet."

I stop. "So who the hell is Gary Preston?"

"I'm just someone who doesn't like what Miskatonic is doing."

"And what are they doing?"

"I need to know if you're one of us first."

My face hardens. "I'm not one of anybody."

"It would be good if you were." Preston watches me closely. "Miskatonic has a sinister agenda. We need people to fight them inside the game."

I study the man. This is the oddest conversation I've ever had in my life. I should have just told Preston to fuck off and left, but what Preston says hits a nerve.

Finally, I say, "Okay, tell me more."

Preston takes a small backpack off his back, the kind office workers keep their portables and sandwiches in. He unzips it and takes out a Miskatonic Darkworlds Game pack, pristine, wrapped in cellophane. He pushes it at me and I recoil from it like it is red hot.

"Come into the game. You can help us. This is the real pack. It has a neural net and a supply of Dreamland tablets."

"Yeah, what are those?"

"Melatonin."

"Like she says."

"But with the addition of LSD."

"The hallucinogen?"

"A small dose, but engineered further by Miskatonic. Something else, too. We haven't cracked that yet."

"I don't get this. You don't trust Miskatonic but you want me to play their game?"

Preston smiles. "The more we talk, the surer I am you're one of us. They identified you as a conduit. But you're not their conduit."

"I don't understand a word you're saying."

"Doesn't matter. Trust me. Join us. Then you will."

I change tack. "Who do you represent?"

Preston shrugs. "An organization."

"What sort of organization?"

"In the game, we're a Guild called *Ordo Lux*. We're a secret guild though. You can't apply to join. We'll invite you in-game."

"And your purpose?"

"Like I say to fight them, but I'll explain more in-game."

"Do Miskatonic know you're in there?"

"They know, but we keep hidden. We've set up certain hacks to cover our trail."

I shake my head. "This is just too odd."

Preston gives me the Darkworlds game pack and this time I take it. I didn't think I would, but I do. I stand there examining it, feeling the smooth plastic and the hard angles. A free game. I turned it down once, but now I'm sticking it to Miskatonic, like I stuck it to Data-Corp every time I play games on their bandwidth. Stupid and childish, but the only way I can get anything back at them.

Preston says, "There's a lot riding on this."

Finally thawing, I stick out my hand. "I'm Adam."

Preston takes it, gives it a shake. "Good. Adam."

"What's riding on this?"

Preston hesitates.

I grin for the first time. I know what he's going to say. "Don't tell me—you'll explain it in the game."

Preston looks relieved. "Exactly. But Adam ..."

"What?"

"This is really serious."

"Sure. Of course." Getting one over on Miskatonic and I will see Miranda, both suit me. I turn, game pack in my hand and walk for my train.

Behind me, Preston calls, "See you in-game."

Chapter Three

THE QUEST OF THE GREEN STATUETTE

"The first quest? Sure. What'll that give me?"

Aleister smiles in a fatherly way. "It'll introduce you to the world, you'll get the hang of basic game mechanics and when you hand in the quest, you'll get money and XP."

"I need money. That's normal. What about food?"

He shakes his head. "No, you don't need to eat, but yes, you need money. You'll want to rent a place, buy items, travel." He puts his hand in his pocket and pulls out a large white £5 note. It's much bigger than the modern polymer banknotes.

I study the £5 note. "What's this worth in today's money? Just for comparison."

He strokes his chin. "The average annual salary in London in nineteen twenty-seven is one hundred sixty pounds, so you're holding nearly two weeks' wages in your hand. There are about five US Dollars to the GB Pound these days."

"So, I've got a week or two weeks' worth of money?"

"To set you up. Yes."

"Where do I get this first quest?"

Aleister gestures to the window and the traffic moving slowly outside. "The wide world. Go for a walk."

I peer out the window, shrug then step over to the door. Hand on the door, I hesitate and turn. "What's your second name, Aleister?"

"Me?" He smiles and his smile contains an ocean of mockery. "Crowley." Then gives a slight bow. "You may have heard of me. I had some fame as a magician in those days."

I know of him. A black magician apparently; the wickedest man in England. He looks pretty harmless standing there in his tweeds. I shrug and wave, going out the door. On the landing, I stop, experiencing the excitement of beginning a new life.

Stepping down the stairs of the boarding house, the wood creaks with every step. I bump into a man wearing a waistcoat and a white shirt, the collar open with no tie, looking as casual as if he lived there. He smiles and waits while I descend. "Sorry," I say.

"No bother, Reverend." He goes up as I stand in the hall, examining myself in a narrow hallway mirror. The silver is slightly tarnished but I see myself. Strange the game hasn't offered any cosmetic choosing of appearance during character creation, no chance to preen and spend hours on face and clothes. Not like in most games.

I stand there, gazing back at myself to see I'm totally bald. I reach up and smooth my scalp to see what it feels like and a slight stubble disturbs my fingertips. I shave my head. I wonder why? I've never thought of doing that in real life. And how serious I look with brown staring eyes and a narrow—slightly cruel—mouth.

But the strangest thing, visually, is; I'm wearing a clerical collar. I look down at my garb again. I'm dressed wholly in black, apart from the white priest's collar. I thumb the stiff starched thing and look at the door to the street and feel strangely nervous about it all.

I wait with my hand on the cool metal handle. Street noises penetrate the wood and through the frosted glass I see distorted shapes pass by. It's nearly noon on a fine day. I haven't checked the date. It's not hot but I can't see my breath. Certainly it's not warm enough to go out without a coat—this is London after all. I look and see a long black coat with a black hat hanging from a peg in the entrance hall. It's a domed hat with a wide flat brim. I remember from somewhere this is a Capello Romano, mainly worn by Catholic clergy. Then I laugh. Maybe my Religious Lore skill filled that in for me? Even though I'm not

Catholic, I take it and put it on. I button up my coat then stand hesitant again. Really, I don't know what I'm frightened of. It's only a game. I tell myself not to be so foolish.

Then I open the door and step out.

People walk briskly by. Men in suits, housewives out shopping. I see a woman dressed like a flapper further down the street. Then another. Nearly all the men wear hats; Homburgs and Bowlers. The few hatless men have hair shining with what looks like Brylcreem. Old-fashioned cars motor down the street, rumbling and backfiring. But there are horses too. A cart with two blinkered horses nearly knocks me down. It's carrying sacks of coal and dirty-faced coalmen sit at the front with reins. They are indifferent to killing me. Then comes a big red-and-white bus with an open top, posters plastered on it advertise theatre revues and Burton's Menswear.

The realism of the scene is amazing. Not only are there sounds and sights, smells and sensations assail me. I know these are conjured by the Virtual Reality engine by microelectrical currents from the neural net cap I put on stimulating brain areas through the skull. Most of our sense of scene in the real world is constructed from a modicum of incoming sensory information mixed with a whole bunch from the databank of what we expect. When we see bacon, we anticipate its smell.

I look left and right along the street and I don't know which way to go. Aleister didn't tell me where the starter quest was, maybe there's more than one? I turn right and walk with the flow of the crowd. A man coming my way tips his hat, "Good morning, Reverend."

My cheeks flush and I feel fraudulent as I reply, "Good morning."

The street is long and straight with tall houses on either side. They look Victorian. The sky overhead is blue with a few puffy clouds. A few paces tell me it's too hot for my coat and I stop to unbutton it, though I don't take it off. I have some idea about the decorum of being a priest. I can't wander around in a T-shirt. Not that I have a T-shirt. After a few yards more I do take off my coat when the temperature forces decorum to give way for comfort.

I come to a square on the right. An area of mowed lawn stands in the middle surrounded by bushes and a black metal fence. The bushes cluster so thickly, it's hard to see in. I guess it's a shared garden for the occupants of the houses surrounding the square.

Still no sign of the quest. How would I know it when I saw it, anyway?

Then from among the crowd a man catches my eye. He stands beside the garden gate while pedestrians stream past. He wears a brown Trilby hat pulled low, the brim tilted down. Blending him further into obscurity, he wears his raincoat with its collar up even though it's not raining, and most bizarre of all, a brown handkerchief over his mouth, looking like a bandit from a Western movie. I turn and stare as I walk past. His glittering eyes meet mine, and I break off the gaze, but his stare follows me. I have the strange impression he's watching me deliberately.

When I'm ten yards further on, I glance over my shoulder to see him still there, watching, making no move to follow. Fear rises, then excitement. This is a horror role-playing game after all.

I look up at the road junction to see I've been walking down Bloomsbury Street. Hurrying on, I dart left onto Great Russell Street, just in case the man is behind. This is a much quieter road, though still with its share of pedestrians and vehicles. The shops here are academic. There's a shop dealing in militaria, then a shop with a window full of Greek and Roman antiquities. The coding that must have gone into creating this level of detail for the game is impressive.

The British Museum looms hugely neoclassical to the left as I walk down Great Russell Street. A Wiki link pops up on my HUD. I briefly check it: *The British Museum founded in 1759 in Montagu House .... The first collection was put together by Sir Hans Sloane*. I don't read it all.

Instead, I stop at the corner and turn, checking if my stalker is still stalking. I can't see him. A policeman occupies a black box by the entrance to the museum forecourt over the road. Directly in front is the Museum Tavern. I glance up at the street signs. To my right is Coptic Street. I see it's lined with bookshops with a few cafes. Then I see a glowing golden goblet icon outside one bookstore. My heart lifts. That must be a quest giver icon.

I forget about the man for a second then, on instinct, I turn and stare in the direction I've come. Standing in the middle of the pavement, ignoring everyone walking past, is my masked man. He's freaking me out so I hurry down Coptic Street towards the quest giver.

The golden goblet hangs outside the Atlantis Bookshop on Coptic Street. The Wiki offers me a history but I don't click the link. Stained-glass letters spell out the words Occult—Bookshop—Magic. I push at the door and a bell rings to announce my entry. The place smells of old leather and must. A balding man of around fifty looks up from making handwritten entries in a ledger on a counter by the far wall. He has greying mutton-chop sideburns and a fleshy mouth. He says, "Hello, Reverend. Unusual to see a Christian priest in my shop. Not that you're not welcome. How can I help you?" He slobbers over his words slightly as he speaks.

I say, "I saw the sign outside."

"Yes, we deal in occult and magic books."

"No, I mean the goblet."

"I'm sorry. The goblet?"

So, the icons are invisible to NPCs. I clear my throat. Let's try again. "I wondered whether you have any jobs for me?"

He guffaws. "I thought you'd be busy enough saving lost souls for your dead god."

I think I'd better play the role, so I interrupt. "Christ lives, now and forever."

"Just so, Reverend. What are you thinking? Cleaning? Odd jobs? Handyman, are you? The stopcock in the lavatory needs fixing if you're any use at that."

At that moment, something activates on my HUD. I look up and see an option tree in pale-red letters:

<DIPLOMACY 27%>
<SEDUCTION 2%>
<INTIMIDATE 3%>

Seduction is out so it'll have to be Diplomacy.

An icon of a twenty-sided die rolls for an instant on the HUD and the word <Success> flashes up.

Instantly the shopkeeper's demeanour changes. He frowns as if remembering. "Actually, There's something."

"Oh?"

He reaches down and opens a drawer in his desk. After a moment shuffling through paper he brings up an illustration. Hand-drawn and inked in green. On it is the most revolting image of a headed humanoid. Or perhaps not humanoid, but certainly upright. Whoever made this must have had bad nightmares.

I narrow my eyes to stare. "What is this?"

"A statue. Well, statuette actually." He gives a greedy smile, wipes his lip with his forefinger, and says, "I'd like to get my hands on it." Then he puts his hands in the pockets of his trousers and waits for my response.

"Why?"

He scowls. He isn't as good natured as he's trying to appear. "That's my business. Will you get it for me, or not?"

I guess I will. "But how?" I say, "Where is it?"

He flares his nostrils. "I don't know, Reverend. You're the bally investigator."

Me, an investigator? I thought I was a priest. I swallow. The game's afoot. "Okay. I'll get it for you. What's in it for me?"

"A true man of the church!" He sneers. "I'll give you twenty pounds if you bring it to me."

£20 is a month's wages. I'll do it. Of course I will. That's why I'm here. I nod.

< You have accepted the Quest of the Green Statuette. 1500xp and £20 reward>

"Good." The shopkeeper sticks out his fat damp hand, which I shake. Then he thrusts the picture at me. I pick it up and a message on my HUD says it has copied into my Journal.

I check my Journal. There's a subfolder now named <The Quest of the Green Statuette>. When I select it mentally, it opens to reveal a copy of the illustration and a short journal entry saying Carter Eliot, Atlantis Books wants me to retrieve the Green Statuette. I guess as I amass further clues, they'll be written into the Journal under that entry.

While I'm there I check my Inventory to find there's not yet much of interest in that either, just my clothes and the British Library reading ticket I'd got from Aleister Crowley.

As I've been standing there sorting through my inventory, I wonder whether the bookseller Carter Eliot, will get angry I'm taking up time in his shop and not buying anything, but he has gone back to his ledger and is ignoring me.

Really, how the hell am I going to begin this quest? I wish there was a manual, or I could browse cheats, but the only links on my HUD are to the Game Wiki. I turn to the door, opening it with a tinkle, but Carter doesn't look up, and I step out onto Coptic Street. Out on the street again, I remember my stalker, and pause as I close the shop door behind me. A tendril of anxiety snakes up into my throat as I glance quickly right and left for my masked man. But he's not there.

Chapter Four

THE BRITISH LIBRARY

Standing there in Coptic Street outside the Atlantis Bookshop, I try to think. The masked man's not there and I'm relieved. Even though he's just part of a game—just dungeon dressing to make me uneasy. I have a quest to complete. It gives me a sense of purpose, a feeling I've not been much used to these days in the data mining Industry.

I still have the original illustration in my hand as well as it being copied into my journal. I stare at the picture hard. It's clearly an antique and there are plenty of antique shops in this area so maybe that's the first step.

I turn left out of Coptic Street and walk along Great Russell Street. I'm soon back at the antique shop dealing in Greek and Roman antiquities. Chipped marble busts of long-dead Roman emperors and armless Greek statues in alabaster stare out from the window, and below their sandaled feet, a plethora of ancient coins and weapons.

I stand outside the shop door mustering my courage to go in. What is it with this world that makes me so nervous? I shake my head, put my shoulder first, press down the handle and step in.

A rather well-to-do man in a pinstriped suit awaits me. He looks me up and down and smiles. "Good afternoon, Reverend. How can I help you?"

I return his smile and step over to the counter. "Good afternoon. I wonder if you could look at this illustration. A friend of mine would like to find out the period of the piece shown here."

On the HUD, I have the options for:

<Diplomacy 32%>
  <Seduction 0%>
  <Intimidation 15%>

Once again, I choose Diplomacy. The dice rolls and I get the success notification.

The antique dealer frowns as he studies the illustration I lay out in front of him. He takes his fountain pen and taps it against his lip. "I've only seen something like this once or twice in my career. I believe they are quite valuable."

"Really?"

He shoots me a helpful look. He really wants to help me. The Diplomacy skill is a splendid thing. "One or two of these were found in excavations of the oldest cities on earth in what is today Iraq—Ur and Sumer. You've heard of them?"

<Religious Lore> Of course. I know about Ur and Sumer. Some say the Garden of Eden is there.

My antique dealer continues, "Apparently they represent some primitive God. But there have been some documents in Sumerian which suggest the worship of these creatures here predates the Sumerian civilisation. I can't remember where I read that."

I look up at my HUD. The influencing skills are being displayed again. Why break a winning streak? I choose Diplomacy. "Where do you think I can find out more about this statuette?"

Without hesitation, the antique dealer says, "The British library of course. The library is in the British Museum, but you'll need a reader's ticket."

I have that, thanks to Mr Crowley. I can see now why they have the beginner quest in this area. The library's nearby and the antique dealers' shops are close at hand. I wonder if I'd gone into another antique dealer shop whether I'd have had a different lead. The quest seems quite linear so far.

I thank the antique dealer profusely.

"You're very welcome, Reverend."

I stroll over to the British library. So far, so good. It's free entry and I spend some time walking among the antiquities while trying to find the sign for the library. The scale of the statues and the detail the game has rendered them in is breathtaking. To the left are the Assyrian sculptures—huge terrifying sculptures of eagle-headed demons that look ready to rend tourists apart at any moment.

Strolling on, beyond those are the Egyptians. In front of lines of sarcophagi, stand sculpted figures of the beast-headed gods of the Nile kingdom. There's a notice to say the Sumerian exhibition is past the Egyptians. I'd thought of going to the library straight away, but this is worth a look, just to see if they have anything like my picture.

When I get there, the Sumerian exhibition is disappointingly small and the exhibits dull compared with the Assyrians or the Egyptians or even the Greeks. Even more disappointing, there's nothing in there that resembles the picture of the Green Statuette. It seems the antique dealer was correct when he said these statuettes aren't really part of that civilisation. The picture I have is different in style to what I'm seeing here. I take it out and compare it with the exhibits. The more I stare, the more unnerving I find it. It's more than just a picture. It has an atmosphere.

I need to do more research. A curator with a shiny peak to his cap stands nearby making sure the tourists don't deface the exhibits. I ask him where the British Library is and he points. "That way, Reverend."

I tip my hat and walk that way.

I remember reading Karl Marx used to sit there. He might even be there now for all I know. Marxism isn't one of my skills, so I doubt I'd have much to talk to him about.

The British Library reading room is housed in the centre of the Museum in a huge domed hemisphere. I knock at the great wooden doors and am allowed entrance. It's breathtaking. The circular room is a hundred feet across and the dome rises with vertical glass windows spaced around it to the boss of the dome above my head. All around the circular walls are shelves and shelves of books, one on top of another. The top shelves are accessed by sliding ladders.

In the middle is a central librarian's desk like the hub of a wheel. Around that are two rings of desks for junior librarians. There are gaps in the rings to allow access to the central dais, for those bold enough to seek an audience of the Victorian bearded patrician who sits like a king in the middle.

All around this hub, filling the room to its walls, are lines of readers' desks radiating out like spokes. The place is very airy because of the high domed ceiling, and through the window, I see grey clouds scudding by with flocks of wheeling pigeons.

The room smells of books; leather and old paper. Also, the mixed scent of the readers present. I see readers with piles of tomes beside them, writing in pencil into notebooks and jotters. Mostly men, mostly middle-aged and middle class with some younger chaps and the odd woman. I notice I'm even starting to talk like someone from 1927.

I approach the central desks and am stopped at the outer ring by a junior librarian, a thin-faced man with a pallor suggesting tuberculosis and long days separated from the sun. He doesn't speak, just holds up his hand. I attempt a friendly smile. "Hello, I would like to do some research."

He blinks but still says nothing. I sense disdain. I take the illustration of the Green Statuette from my inventory and thrust it under his nose. He backs off, sniffs, then studies the drawing.

"Sumerian?" I ask.

He raises an eyebrow at me, then returns to stare at the picture. He's really studying it and the expression on his face as he looks at the picture of the Green Statuette is of disgust. Even repulsion.

Finally, he says. "You'll want the special section. Can I see your reader's ticket, please?"

I give him the small brown card with my name written on it in elegant copper plate handwriting. "That looks in order."

"Good."

"Follow me."

I walk behind him along a gap between the radial readers' desks. Occasionally a scribbling scholar glances up as we walk by, stares significantly at the door we're headed for and looks back down to his work. I realize I can't tell the difference between player characters and NPCs. No one has a name floating above them.

At the door, the librarian produces a brass key and turns it in the lock. Opening the door, he reaches round and flicks a brass pin switch and electric light comes on.

I grin. "*Fiat lux*, eh?" I think it's a suitably priestly thing to say, but he ignores me.

The room is much smaller than the huge reading room. The smell is also different here. I glance around. It's rectangular and filled with bookshelves. There's a reader's desk with a sheet of blotting paper, an empty inkwell, and no ink pen either. Instead there are several pencils of varying length and a rotary pencil sharpener, the type you insert the pencil end into then crank by hand to sharpen it. On the left end of the desk is an old-fashioned telephone, not old-fashioned in 1927 of course. The receiver sits on a cradle on the vertical earpiece stand.

There are no other readers in the room.

"It's not Sumerian," he says. In this different light, I notice a thin scar running down his left cheek, long-healed now. It looks like a German University dueling scar.

"Not Sumerian?"

He shakes his head. "But you should start there. Sumerian archaeology is on Shelf N. Halfway down on the third shelf up, just after the Hittites." He indicates the telephone. "Ring when you're done and I'll let you out."

"Let me out?"

"Yes, Reverend. Only readers with the special ticket are allowed in here. We have to lock the door. Besides," he says, "we wouldn't want some of these books to get out." I realize he's joking but I don't laugh.

The light here is poor. There are lots of shadows. For some reason anxiety is creeping from my chest into my throat. I glance nervously at the sombre shelves. He sniggers, still amused at his own joke, or maybe my reaction, leaves and I hear the key turning in the lock. Just to make sure I test the handle. The door is indeed locked.

I turn and look at the bookshelves, I have the strange feeling they're watching me back. My mouth is dry though there's no rational reason to be anxious.

I check Shelf N, follow his directions and run my finger along the spines of books dealing with Sumeria. They are mostly Victorian and in English, German, French, and Latin. I pull the most recent looking one from the shelf and take it to the desk. It was published earlier that year, 1927.

Charles Leonard Woolley, *The Royal Cemetery of Ur, Modern Iraq*. Oxford, 1927.

This book, about five inches thick, is backed in black leather with gilt lettering. Wooley had been excavating the site near where the Tigris and Euphrates rivers had poured into the Persian Gulf in ancient times, though now it was in the desert. He excavated the Old Babylonian levels then the Sumerian Royal Cemetery where he found an enormous 'Death Pit' from which he recovered a series of artefacts. I thumb through to a series of black-and-white illustrated plates in the back.

I turn to these and about halfway through the illustrations, smile when I see a drawing of what must be the same Green Statuette, or its brother. The inscription says the tentacle-headed figure is Ktulu, and likens it to the Greek chthonic deity $\kappa\theta o\upsilon\lambda'o\upsilon$. Though Cthulhu is in fact an abyssal deity who lurks at the ocean's bottom, rather than being from the dry earth. I stop and I realise I wouldn't have been able to read the Greek in real life, nor would 'chthonic' or 'abyssal' be part of my vocabulary. This must be due to the in-game skills I have. I feel a flush of pleasure. That's really clever of the developers. I wonder how they put such knowledge in my head and if it would still be there when I wake? It's odd how I feel returning to 2027 will be waking, but that's exactly it.

The illustration has a note directing me to page 287. I flick to that page.

... from the Royal Death Pit we recovered items clearly not of Sumerian origin in style. In fact, some are quite alien and repugnant. Sprengler's hypothesis is

that these are items brought to Ur by refugees in very ancient times. He associates this influx with refugees following the great flood which he dates to around 2100 BC. Certain cult items in particular might be associated with the influx, and these are the statuettes made of a green, jade-like material of unknown origin. Sprengler notes these appear to be representations of the undersea god, Ktulu or Cthulhu and be designed to set up on home shrines for private worship. Cf. Sprengler, H. R. Kulte aus dem Meer, Berlin 1922.

I wonder whether they have a copy of the book by Sprengler and stand. I feel suddenly dizzy. The room spins and I sit again hard. Strange anxiety worms around my stomach like a living creature and the corners of the room whisper names in an unknown chattering language. I shake my head to clear it and see on my HUD a message:

<SANITY -5>

Checking my statistics, I see Health, Reputation, and Mana still stand at 100, but Sanity is now 95.

It's something about that picture. The idol leers out at me from the illustration, as if now I've learned his name, he wants to know mine. I dismiss the idea as ridiculous, but it's a clever game effect, and I go back to the shelves. I put Woolley's book back into the gap I've taken it from.

I guess Sprengler's book will be among the Sumerian volumes. As I'm searching, a thin volume with a binding of what looks like half-cured skin catches my eye from the shelf above. The spine has a title in Arabic and a carefully spelled translation into Roman letters by a neat librarian's hand: *Kitab al Asif.*

I know no Arabic either in real life or the game and I have no reason to take the book down, but my hand reaches for it anyway. My fingers tingle strangely as I touch the ancient volume and I stand there in a sudden panic.

This really is stupid.

Anxiety rises in my throat like withered hands. I stare at this new book, hesitating to open it. With an effort of will, I master my fear and I snap it open. The pages are written in tightly curled Arabic but the lines won't stand still. The lettering shifts under my gaze like smoke. Its whispering reaches into my ears and imaginary fingers reach from the book to probe between my ribs and squeeze my heart.

I feel their touch and exclaim out loud with shock. I shove the blasphemous book back where it belongs. Thank God, I couldn't read it. That thought sprang unbidden to my mind, but if it affected me so badly when I didn't understand a word, how much more terrified would I have been if the words had got into my mind. After all, a thing seen can't be unseen

A HUD warning is sitting there. I hadn't noticed it because I was so preoccupied with my panic. The warning says:

<SANITY -10>

My Sanity score stands now at 85. I sit at the desk, my head in my hands. I'm shaking, my mouth is dry. I've had a shock and I'm frightened but I don't know what I'm frightened of.

I lift my head as if I've heard a voice calling me from far away. A voice in a foreign language, summoning me by a half-remembered name. The corners of the room crowd in closer—that room with its cargo of despicable learning weighs down on me. I must find the Sprengler book. I have a quest to complete.

I swallow hard, get up and tentatively walk back to Shelf N. There among the Sumerian books, I trace the authors' names, not daring to glance up to the shelf where the *Kitab al Asif* lurks. I find Sprengler's volume and with hurried hands take it and return to the desk.

Harald Richtofen Sprengler, *Kulte aus dem Meer*. Berlin, 1924.

I turn the page and realise it is in German, and I don't read German. Damn.

I swallow again. I need to know what's in that book. Maybe the librarian can translate. Then there's a noise from the corner. It makes me jump, but it's just shelves warming. Wood does that. Forgetting the door is locked, I stand and try the handle. Then I return to the desk. When I take the phone, I'm trembling.

After a minute a dry voice answers, "Yes?"

"I need your help."

"Finished? I'll be right along."

I say, "No," but the line's already dead. It takes long minutes before he comes and I dart furtive glances at the bookshelves as if they might come to life.

Finally, the thin librarian opens the door, the scar on his cheek livid in this yellow light. "Find what you wanted?" Without waiting for me to answer, he says, "Good, good."

I still have the Sprengler book in my hand. "This book."

He gives a cold look. "Yes?"

"It's in German."

Sarcastically he says, "Some are."

"I don't read German."

He smiles. "Perhaps you'd like to learn?"

I realise then I can allocate skill points to German to allow me to get the information from the book. "Can you teach me?" I say.

"Not I. But Mr George can."

"Mr George?"

"He sits in the centre with the other tutors."

The scary man with the beard. I glance at the volume in my hand. "Can I take this book from this room?"

He frowns. "You're not supposed to."

"Please."

He smiles but it's not a kind smile. "Why? Don't you like this room."

I shake my head. "No, it's got a feeling to it. An unpleasant atmosphere."

He laughs, a dry sound like the rattle of a deathwatch beetle. "Lots of them say that."

"So, can I read this book in the normal reading room?"

His eyes gleam like he has power over me. "This once. Don't tell anyone though; you'll get me sacked."

There's something very unpleasant about this man; a man whose age you couldn't guess. He could be twenty-five or forty. He looks thin and dried up. I decide I don't like him, but I follow him anyway.

We're halfway to the central hub where Mr George sits when the junior librarian points to an empty reader's desk. "Take that one. Bring the book with you though."

I put my hat on the desk to mark it as mine then hurry after the librarian. I catch up with him outside the central ring of desks. The man in the centre with the beard is built like a bear. That's clear up close. He wears a dark-brown jacket and a wool tie. His beard is brown with flecks of grey and his eyes are like shiny coals, bright as a bird.

The junior librarian gestures. "This is Mr George, the Library Tutor. He can teach you many things."

Chapter Five

LEARNING GERMAN

Mr George looks up at me with eyes black as soot. "What do you want to learn?" he says. The junior librarian stands by simpering as though in awe of the library tutor; maybe tutors have more kudos in the NPC world?

I give him Sprengler's *Kulte aus dem Meer*. "I want to read this."

He looks at it, turns some of the pages then says, "How many skill points did you want to spend?"

"How many do I need to read it?" Learning German is pretty cool, but I want to save some skill points to put into combat, and some definitely to learn a magic spell or two. I have 80 to spend.

Mr George appraises the book, his fleshy lips pulsing like a puffer fish. Eventually he says, "Fluently, eighty, to get the gist maybe twenty-five?"

"Okay twenty-five." Then I say, "What skills can you teach?"

"Any academic skills."

"Magic?"

He shakes his head. "You need a magician to teach you not a librarian, but you can learn from a tome, or from another player."

Helpful. I'm pondering that when the junior says, "Ready?"

"Here?"

Mr George nods, his black eyes filled with disinterest.

"Do I need to sit?"

Shrugging, he says, "As you wish. It makes no difference to the process."

I choose to stand. "Let's go then."

"Arrange the skill point spend via your HUD," the junior says.

I glance up, select my character sheet, and turn to the skills page. I find <Academic Skills—> Languages—> German>

I commit 25 skill points and hit enter. "Ready," I say.

He stares into my eyes. It feels like I'm entering a trance as he says, "*Der, Die, Das, Dem, Den ...*" He speaks faster and faster, "*Sieben Schwäne schwimmen auf sieben Flüssen.*" My head is swimming, and I don't feel I'm taking it in. Dizziness grabs me, I put out a hand to a desk to steady myself and as suddenly as it has begun, it's over.

He says, "*Es war gut, nicht wahr?*"

And I answer, "*Sehr gut danke. Ich habe so viel so schnell gelernt, ich kann es kaum glauben.*"

And I really know German. Not perfectly, only 25 skill points worth, but it's in my head. If Miskatonic could patent this speed-learning in the real world, they'd make a fortune. They wouldn't have to sell role-playing games, they could clean up in education. Amazing. How did they do that?

As if reading my thoughts, Mr George says, "Such learning is only possible in the game world. This medium makes things possible that wouldn't be imaginable outside."

"But does the skill carry over to the real world?"

He nods. "Oh yes. Lots of things that happen here carry over to the real world." For the first time he smiles, showing me rows of even white teeth, white as piano keys. What the hell did he mean by 'lots of things carry over'? It sounded almost sinister. I'm about to ask, but something makes me shut my mouth. I step back.

"Call again," Mr George says, still showing his white teeth.

The scar-faced junior echoes him. "Yes, come again. It's been wonderful meeting you Reverend Cadmon."

"How do you know my name?"

The junior says, "You gave me your library card," and, as if seeing disquiet in my face, says, "Don't worry; we're not following you around."

Then I think; *he knows about the men with masks. But, how could he?* I study him and his scar. His eyes, blue as watered glass, don't blink. There's something strange about these NPCs. They're both smiling now. "Right," I say. "I have a job to complete."

"Don't you have to read your book first?" the junior says.

He's right. The book is gripped in my hand. I'm sweating. "Of course." I take the book and hurry back to the desk where my hat is. I sit, at first unable to concentrate, then I turn the pages. I can't read it all, but I look in the index for Sumeria. Page 301, halfway down:

> ... *From the Royal Death Pit, I obtained* [word unknown] ... *statuette. It's similar to artefacts find in Irem, City of the Pillars in the Hejaz. Without doubt it originates from the Pelagic cultures of the drowned realm of Gond, brought to land after the antediluvian* ... [unknown words]. *Later I find other examples, but none* ... [unknown words] ... *of a green material like jadeite, very hard and smooth. [The syntax of the next sentence is difficult to decipher. Something to do with undersea cults—I need more points in my German.] I have added this one to my personal collection.*

It seems from this extract that this statuette—a cult item from a drowned civilization?—depicts a god known as Cthulhu. It also seems Sprengler has it in his own collection. That is progress, but I have no idea where Sprengler is now. Woolley's book indicated he'd been involved in recent excavations in Ur, so he's probably still alive but may be back in Germany, or in Iraq even. I close the book and as I do so, an inscription on the title page catches my eye.

It says in English, *"To the British Library Reading Room librarians, in memory of many happy hours. H R Sprengler, London NW3."* It isn't dated, but at that time he was staying in London.

I leave the book on the desk and stand. The junior librarian has gone and Mr George is staring blankly into space. I watch him as I put on my coat. He really gives me the creeps. I leave the Reading Room and walk through the British Museum, past the stone ghosts of Assyrians, Egyptians, and Greeks, hurrying down the steps.

I nip into the Museum Tavern, opposite the museum's front entrance. The bar is full of men, not a woman among them, and the air is crowded with cigarette smoke and male laughter. I step over to the bar and the barman in a white apron asks, "What'll it be, Reverend?"

I look at the tall straight glasses on shelves behind the bar and the three hand pumps in front of me. "Bitter?" I say, not sure if that sounds odd. Is that how they asked for beer? It seems all right because he responds, "A pint or a half?"

"Pint, please."

He pours me a pint of translucent brown liquid with a small frothy head. I sip it. It's very hoppy. Amazing the game can convey such nuances of taste. The barman moves onto the next customer. Some have the blue floaty names of players, others have no names and must be NPCs. When he's finished pouring two pints for the other man, I catch the barman's eye. "I say ..."

He nods and smiles.

"Do you have a telephone book?"

"Telephone's not for customers, I'm afraid."

"No, I just want to look at the book."

He hesitates for a moment and shrugs. "I'm sure that'll be all right." He turns and walks out to get the telephone book from a room behind the tap room, leaving an exasperated customer exhaling in frustration. After a minute, the barman comes back with the book and hands it to me. "Don't run off with it." He winks. "But I suppose I can trust you, being a man of the cloth, and all."

"Much appreciated."

I retreat to a table. The pub is narrow, and the tables are set against a banquette that runs along the inside wall. There are no windows along the length, just inside the door and at the top facing Great Russell Street.

Conversation buzzes around me as I flick through the phone book. "S ... Sprengler." The phone book in 1927 is thin. Telephones are a luxury few people have. There's only one Sprengler, H. R., and he lives at 11 Holly Hill, Hampstead. His telephone number is HAM 426. I run my finger over the writing and it copies itself into my Journal. I'm not going to phone him. I'm going to pay him a visit.

I finish my beer and feel all light-headed as once again the circuitry in my neural net does something clever and mimics the effects of alcohol. I stand and step over to hand the telephone directory to the barman. As I walk across the bar I become aware everyone is staring at the door. A woman stands on the threshold, not coming in, and I feel the hostility of the whole bar towards her. Everyone has stopped talking. A man to my right mutters, "It's her again. I wish she'd go away."

His stubble-chinned friend says, "She's a Warm One. They shouldn't be allowed out."

"She must have escaped."

Because she's a woman, I think at first, it's some sexist thing from the 1920s, and prepare to say friendly words to her as I walk out. Then I see her eyes. Her eyes emit light like an old-fashioned cathode tube, beaming out and making her blind. How can she see with lights like that in her eyes?

She's otherwise normal, average height, average build, averagely dressed, slightly shabby and ordinary, but her eyes are unutterably alien. I put my hand involuntarily to my throat. She doesn't speak just stares, and she's staring at me. I freeze, the phone book in my hand halfway to returning it. The barman leans in and says, "I think she wants you."

My mouth dries. She's the strangest person I've ever seen. How come someone like this is wandering the streets of London in 1927—someone with electric eyes? Where has she escaped from?

The man to my right whispers in my ear like I have authority. "Tell her to go away. She brings bad luck."

I protest. "I've never seen this woman before in my life," and I hold back.

Suddenly the man to my right yells at her, "You there, go away. He doesn't need you. Piss off!"

"Easy," the barman says. "The Reverend doesn't want to hear language like that."

He turns apologetically. "Sorry, Reverend, it's just she needs to go. Tell her to go."

I take the authority they've given me and clear my throat. "I don't know who you are, madam. But you're making people nervous. It would be better if you leave."

For the first time, she speaks. She says three words in a clipped manner, like a robot learning to talk. She leaves half-second spaces between them. She says, "Electric." Then. "Access." Then. "Azathoth."

The stubble-chinned man says, "Azathoth, Lord of the Warm Ones."

I spin round. "The Warm Ones? Who are the Warm Ones?"

"You'll find out." Then he nudges his friend who laughs into his pint. Neither of them meet my eye but they find it very funny.

The woman with the light in her eyes turns and leaves, walking away. I step to the door when she's gone and watch her retreat down the street without looking back.

I could follow her and ask her what she meant by those words, but I don't. It's only a game, but again, I'm unnerved. Waiting for me on my HUD is a message, so far unseen.

<SANITY -10>

I'm down to 75. I actually feel like I've lost some sanity in real life. The world is woozy and under the hubbub, almost out of hearing, the voices of birds talk of songs and feathers. It's weird and unsettling. I have a bizarre itching in my head, I mean right in the middle of my head. I reach my hands up but of course I can't scratch it. It feels like a small grain of rice in the middle of my brain. I try to shrug it off. After a few paces, I manage to ignore it.

Everything's okay. I take a minute on the street to admire the detail of the CGI world Miskatonic Games has created. It's almost real. In fact, in its 8K High Definition it's better than real. I never see scenes as clearly as this in real life.

I take some breaths, smile at the beauty and detail of the rendered street scene in front of me, more to settle myself than anything else, and, after four or five minutes, feel better. It's just a game. Time to go and see Herr Sprengler.

I find the British Museum Underground Railway Station and descend the steps into the bowels of the earth. It's hot down there. I get to the ticket desk and ask for a return ticket to Hampstead Underground Station. Hampstead is a place I couldn't go in real life. It's Zone A, which means there's no access for people with assets under $5 Million, unless they have a valid work permit. In real life, I understand it's a beautiful place with the fresh air of the heath, high levels of cleanliness, and low crime. I'm looking forward to visiting it in 1927, probably because I can't in 2027.

The fare to Hampstead is 6d. When I offer the man the £5 note he baulks. "Don't you 'ave nothin' smaller, Reverend? I can't break this."

I shake my head. Grumbling he steps over into the back and, out of sight he must have opened a safe. He comes back with four one-pound notes; one ten-shilling note; nineteen shillings; and a silver sixpence in coins. The notes feel large and papery in my hands. I put them into my leather wallet and take the ticket.

I catch the train west to Tottenham Court Road Station then change to the Hampstead and Highgate Line, heading north. The tube train is hot and people sit reading newspapers or novels, but no one speaks. People get on and people get off as I travel below the metropolis. After half an hour, we arrive at Hampstead. It's one of the deepest stations in the London Underground Network and instead of the steps, I take a lift to the surface. I step in and the attendant pulls the iron grille closed and the iron cage ascends.

Chapter Six

HERR SPRENGLER'S HOUSE

Darkworlds has an inbuilt map. However, it is covered with a Fog of War effect and everywhere I haven't been is fogged out. Luckily, I see Holly Hill is very near the Tube Station, so coming out of the station, the circle of the map clears and I see the name. Looking left and right to find a break in traffic, I cross the street, avoiding a rag-and-bone cart with its clip-clopping horses. A short way up on Holly Hill, on the right, Number 11 is a four-storey red brick house, but narrow. A flight of steps climbs to the black-painted door. I step up to the door, rap and listen.

No answer.

I knock again and wait while a car motors by behind me. I glance over, but I don't have any points in the driving skill so I can't identify it.

Still no one has come to the door. It doesn't look like there's anyone home. I've come all this way to speak to Herr Sprengler and my quest is to find the Green Statuette. I've played games like this before and I know there must be some way of completing the quest. On an impulse, I bend down to the red terracotta plant pot from which sad-looking winter pansies grow. I lift the pot and find the front door key. I smile—these were more trusting times.

I turn the key over in my palm, guessing that going in without permission will be breaking the law and might have an impact on my Reputation score, if I'm caught. However, I need to finish the quest so I use the key to unlock the door, and enter.

The door is well-oiled but the house is still. A stale smell lingers— the scent of old roses. The entrance hall is floored in white and black tiles. Standing there in the quiet hall, I feel a thrill of excitement. I'm a burglar! I'm smiling all over my face because of it as I step over a pile of letters. It looks like Herr Sprengler hasn't been home for a while. I bend down and sort through the letters.

There are four with handwritten addresses. Some with typed addresses that look like they come from academic publishers. One has the stamp of Freiburg University and another Edinburgh University. I feel bad about opening them, or bad about being caught. What if Herr Sprengler comes down the stairs and catches me opening his mail? I open the envelopes anyway.

<REPUTATION -5>

Damn, even though I expected it. A gentleman doesn't open another chap's post.

Again, I give credit to the developers. The handwritten letters are very authentic looking. Two are in German from the same person on different dates. The writer, an Otto Reinhardt, is concerned about Harald, asking if he's well and why he hasn't written back. The third one has a Kew Postmark and is written in English. I look first at the name of the person who's signed it—Mervyn Gurdrock. I skim it. It has the look of a game clue. I touch them to copy all the letters to my Journal.

Still no sign of the professor but I feel guilty so I cup my hands to my mouth. *"Herr Sprengler. Sind Sie zu hause?"*

No reply so I cough. Still nothing. He can't be in.

But it's the statuette I'm after so I decide to have a look around just in case it is conveniently sitting on a shelf. I open the door to the left. A sitting room. The window looks out onto the street I've just come from. I locate the scent of old roses, but they're not roses.

Dead flowers droop rotten and sick over the tops of vases—lilies, their orange pollen cast over the tables they stand on. A modern looking glass table occupies the middle of the room. A copy of *The Times* lies on it and on top of that, a handwritten note. I step over and read the note in English. Burglary is coming easier to me.

The note says, "My darling Harald. I miss you so much. I can hardly believe you've gone. All my love, Julia."

The newspaper underneath is open at the obituaries. I read:

"Harald Sprengler, born Dusseldorf 10 May 1875, died suddenly in Hampstead, London 3 March 1927. Herr Sprengler was a noted authority on early Middle Eastern Archaeology and author of several books on the subject. Much missed by his friends and colleagues. Service: Highgate West Cemetery, 10 March 1927. No flowers. Donations to University College London, School of Archaeology to establish a chair in his memory."

That explains why he isn't home. I check my HUD. Game date is 13 March 1927. He's been buried three days. I decide to look around the house for the statuette, but I have a hunch it won't be there—it just feels like the game will require another step before I can hand the quest in.

I climb the stairs. Through a door to the left on the landing, I find what must have been Sprengler's bedroom. All his personal effects are packed away in two tea chests. The bed is stripped and sheets neatly folded in squares. The pillows have no pillowcases. I glance at the emptied bookshelves. No statuette in here. I'm about to leave when I see a book lying on the floor just under the bed. Whoever has tidied up must have missed it. I stoop down. It's Sprengler's Journal, in German of course.

I turn to one of the last entries. It's dated 2nd March 1927.

"I fear for my life. They're following me. MG accosted me at the University itself, the audacity of the man! I told him no, but I must get rid of it. I tried to sell it but there's something about it that won't let me give it away. It's like a drug. It whispers to me in the night and I have the most terrible nightmares."

An earlier entry says,

"Each day it touches living flesh, it summons one of its ghastly servants. I have it wrapped in cloth, but I'm terrified of making a mistake. It plays on my mind. I want to hold it in my bare hand, but I know what that will bring."

Then.

"MG has threatened me. Cooperate and come over to them, or. [I can't read the next few words—something to do with noises in the night? Voices? Whispers?] Thank God I have my gun. I pray to Jesus to save me and forgive me for what I've done."

He has a gun.

I try the drawers of the bedside table. One is locked. I guess whoever has tidied up, Julia, maybe, found it locked, couldn't find the key and left it. She sounded upset in the note and it looks like she's coming back at some point.

I hate to do this, but I need to see what's in that drawer. And I could really do with a gun. I go back down to the kitchen and find a carving knife. Coming back into the room, I hack at the drawer.

<REPUTATION -5>

I'm down to 90 Reputation, 75 Sanity. I know when I lose Sanity I feel ill, but what does loss of Reputation do?

I manage to hack and lever the drawer open. In there is a pistol. My HUD identifies it as a Browning semi-automatic pistol FN Model 1910/22. The Wiki tells me a variant of this pistol was used to assassinate the Archduke Ferdinand.

I pick it up and it feels heavy in my hand. I pick it up and it feels heavy in my hand. As I look at it I get its spec:

<Browning FN 1910/22: {Pierce Damage} 10-25 Damage x pistols skill.>

I have no holster so I stuff it into my jacket pocket. There's also a

box of 9mm cartridges. I open it and eight are missing so I guess
they're in the pistol's magazine. Unless they've been fired. I check and
see the gun hasn't been fired. I even smell it. No cordite. I put the box
with its remaining cartridges into my pocket and my inventory now
records the Browning and 42 x 9mm rounds.

Within fifteen minutes, I've checked downstairs and all the rooms
upstairs for the statuette. I guess it has either been stolen by this MG
—and I have a suspicion Sprengler's 'sudden' death isn't innocent
either—or maybe Sprengler has given it to Julia?

I'm running this through in my head on the upstairs landing when
the front door opens and I shrink back into the shadows. Julia must
have come back to finish squaring away. How the hell am I going to
explain this? I foresee a large drop in my Reputation score.

The door closes behind whoever has entered. Then, it's like a
shadow crosses the sun. The light dims, and silence deepens. I hold my
hand up to feel the air, and it's true, the temperature has dropped as
well. Something moves down in the entrance hall. For some reason, I
think something rather than someone.

Another movement. There's definitely something down there,
something with a heavy tread. I can't believe this is Julia. I hear rasping
breath as it moves, and I know I don't want to meet it. It's gone into
the living room and come out again. I know this isn't human. I feel fear
and my Sanity takes another hit. I'm now 70 Sanity.

It climbs the stairs, its weight pressing down on each tread.

I turn and try to slip away as quietly as I can. I glance at my HUD
and equip my pistol. The gun's weight is reassuring but my heart is
hammering as I back away from the stairs. The thing coming up is
slow. I'm not sure if it's being careful. Maybe it knows I'm here?

It's still out of sight but I hear its tread like a hellish metronome,
step after step, its breath as stertorous as a blown lung. I grip the
Browning hard. My Pistols skill is 20 due to my army service, but I'm
no crack shot. I was a chaplain after all. I back away to the end of the
landing. There's a door to my right. I check it and find it's a toilet. Not
a bathroom, just a porcelain toilet sitting there, water dripping inside
the white cistern. I step into the tiny room and close and bolt the
door. I'm just in time.

The thing's on the landing, standing still. There is a sound of sniffing. It's trying to scent me. There's a window just behind me. Quietly as I can, I put down the toilet lid, and step up on it in my shiny black shoes so I can undo the window catch.

There's the tiniest fumble. I curse my clumsy fingers for the noise and stop. I even stop breathing. It sniffs again and moves towards the toilet door.

The only safety is to get out of the window whether it hears me or not.

It tries the handle. My hands shake as I grab the wooden window frame to move it open.

Behind me the door shudders as whatever it is tries to shove it open. I hear it talk, but it's no language I've heard outside of a nightmare, words like beetles scuttling over a coffin, a voice like asphyxiation as it gasps and gulps.

With both hands, I push the sash window up and squeeze my way out onto a sloping slate roof. I get my legs down and my shoes hold. I teeter there looking at the slope. The roof overlooks a small back garden. This fall is a fractured leg or a broken neck.

I make a choice. Anything is better than turning round and seeing what's behind me.

I slide over the slates, going down fast on my backside until my heels catch in the guttering, saving me from falling. A slim, dark-haired woman in a dark coat turns and looks up from the garden to see me clatter down the slates.

"Hey!" she shouts. "What on earth are you doing?"

Before she sees, I put my gun away. She's looking up, frowning and puzzled. I guess my clerical collar throws her off—few burglars are priests. I'm still shaking as I lower myself from the roof while she stands back, angry, but wary.

I drop to the floor. "I'm so sorry," I say. "But we need to leave."

"Leave? No, I must sort out Harald's things today. I was just tidying the garden before I went in." I see she has a trowel in her hand.

"You're Julia?"

She nods. "What are you doing in the house?" She's still very suspicious.

"It's a long story. But there's something in the house. Something dangerous."

She shakes her head. "What on earth are you talking about? Reverend ...?"

"Reverend Cadmon."

"I don't understand what you are doing in the house."

A choice flashes up on my HUD

<Deceive 0%>
<Seduce 2%>
<Intimidate 3%>
<Recruit 0%>
<Persuade 15%>

I hit Persuade. The dice rolls on my HUD.

<Failure. You have failed to persuade Julia>

I try talking to her again. "Listen, I have to leave. You should too. And even if you stay, in God's name, don't go into the house."

Then I think maybe the thing in the house might come out. It's broad daylight, but it might come out. I grab her hand.

"Reverend Cadmon!" She glares and snatches back her hand.

Listening for the front door opening and that thing coming round, I beg, "Please, Julia, come with me?"

I hit Persuade again, this time, thank the Lord, I'm successful, but she doesn't move. I lift my hat and, rub my hand over my bald, sweating pate. "Come with me. Please."

She frowns. "Very well, I'll come. But I don't understand why you're so concerned about me going into the house."

Julia follows me down the side passage and opens a small door from the garden to the street. I'd missed this door completely when I was thinking of how to get into the house. We step out onto Holly Lane.

I feel better on the street, but I still don't want to linger around that house. I look back. I still have the quest to complete. Then I have a thought. "You were at the funeral?"

She nods. "Of course."

I talk fast. I have no skill points in deception, so this is all me. I say, "I knew Harald from an excavation in Iraq. I met him two years ago at Woolley's dig at Ur." As I lie, my Reputation takes a further hit of -5.

She frowns harder. I wonder whether she believes me. I blurt, "But I haven't seen him since. I was in the area, and I thought I'd call in."

I'm not sure she's buying my bullshit. She says sternly, "How did you get into the house?"

"The front door was open."

"No, it wasn't."

Busted, I shrug and give a wan smile. "Would you like to come for a cup of tea?"

I hit Persuade again, and it works, again. God must be on my side today.

"I suppose I could," she says.

I want to look sympathetic so I cock my head to indicate empathy. The clerical collar must help. "I'd just like to know about Harald's death. It was so sudden."

She nods. She sounds sad and her eyes fill with tears. "Yes It's terrible." I don't have a handkerchief to offer her, luckily she's got one of her own and she takes it and dabs her eyes.

As we walk down Holly Hill towards Hampstead High Street, I see a woman in a black coat coming our way. She's staring at us but I ignore her. "This may be an odd question, Julia …"

Julia is staring at the newcomer. I glance back, irritated. The newcomer comes up and greets Julia like an old friend. Julia smiles. Remembering her manners, Julia says, "This is my friend Miss Courtney."

I turn to Miss Courtney and bow. She's sizing me up. Suddenly she reveals she's a player. The blue name flashes up above her head.

<Miranda Courtney, Level 1 Assassin>

Miranda!

I reveal myself.

Looking at the name above my head, she says, "A Level One Priest called Adam, huh? I wonder ..."

"Miranda it's me!"

"Who else could it be? I thought you weren't going to play."

"It's a long story."

"You're here because you missed me." She grins.

"No, I mean, yes, of course. But that's not why I ..."

Julia coughs.

I turn. "Sorry, Julia. I know Miranda from somewhere else."

I get that itching in the middle of my head again, but I ignore it.

"Miss Courtney," Miranda corrects.

Julia purses her lips. "And I'd rather you called me Miss Armstrong, if you don't mind, Reverend Cadmon."

She looks like she's going to walk off and I can't have that. There's the quest to finish and I need her for that. But I have a burning question first. She pauses, waiting for me to speak.

"I was just going to ask ..."

"What is it?"

"Are you real too?"

Julia stops, narrows her eyes and says, "I beg your pardon?"

Chapter Seven

BROWN'S TEA SHOP, HAMPSTEAD

Miranda and I walk with Julia to Brown's Cafe just round the corner on Flask Walk.

We hang our hats and coats on the hatstand by the cafe entrance. We sit at a table by the window that allows tea drinkers to while away the hours watching people walk past down the narrow street or stop at the stall opposite to buy postcards of Hampstead Heath and the Vale of Health.

The place only has three other customers, a man on his own reading a novel and two middle-aged women by the window. A waitress in a black uniform with a starched white apron, white laundered cuffs, and a stiff white cap shows us to the table. She offers us a menu but I only want tea. Julia nods and agrees, "Tea for me too."

Miranda's just as I remember her; she always has to push it and I love her for it. She leans forward. "Do you have Earl Grey?"

The waitress shakes her head.

"Darjeeling?"

"Sorry, no."

"*Café Latte?*"

The waitress shrugs. "I don't know what that is."

I say, "It's foreign for coffee."

Miranda says, "Yes, with steamed milk."

The young girl blushes. "No, we don't."

"Tea then."

The waitress bobs. "So, a pot of tea for three? Lovely. I shall be right back."

Now we are sitting, I study Julia. She is wearing a brown housedress that detracts from her looks. Her skin is pale and the crease between her eyebrows suggests she's given to introspection. Her eyes are dark blue and she has a dark beauty spot on the right of her face, up by her high cheekbone. She has a necklace in the shape of a silver star around her neck with a single diamond at its centre. Her hand goes to it as we sit, then she leaves it alone and frowns. "It was most odd you being in Harald's house. Not really the thing a man of the cloth should be doing." She narrows her eyes. "If you are a man of the cloth, and not some bodysnatcher or burglar disguised as one ..."

"No, I assure you, I'm genuinely a priest ..."

"Oh, he really is," Miranda says. I think she's being supportive then I see she's teasing me. She turns. "What *were* you doing in the house, Adam? I mean Reverend Cadmon?"

She knows fine well. She's on the same quest as me. I say, "Professor Sprengler was an old friend from my archaeology days."

Miranda smiles. "Your archaeology days. Of course."

The tea comes. I pour milk into the china cups then tea for Julia and Miranda. Julia takes two lumps of sugar with the tongs and stirs her tea with a silver spoon while I pour one for myself.

I ask her about Harald's death.

Once again, her eyes mist. Finally, she manages, "You know Harald was quite disturbed before he died?"

I shake my head.

She continued. "I was his student, then his assistant at UCL."

"UCL?"

"University College London. But he'd been off work for nearly a fortnight with his nerves."

I go to sip my tea, but it's too hot. Steam curls up by my nose. I ask, "What exactly was the problem?"

"He had a nervous breakdown. That's the easiest way to describe it."

"Ah, I'm sorry to hear that."

Julia toys with the silver star round her neck again. Without meeting my eyes, she says, "Then of course, he killed himself."

"Killed himself?"

She nods. "You didn't know? I thought everyone knew."

"No."

"I found him. I wish I'd never seen what I saw, but of course I can't unsee it now, can I?"

Her hand goes to her eyes and she pulls out the handkerchief again. Miranda smiles benignly.

I know this is some pre-scripted exchange the game developers have created, but Julia looks really upset. I wonder whether her relationship with Harald was more than professor and assistant.

After Julia composes herself, I ask, "What on earth do you think led to that?"

Something about her demeanour changes. She becomes more focused. "He was convinced someone wanted the Green Statuette he dug up from Ur."

"The squid god?" Miranda says.

"The Green Statuette."

A faint smile plays on her lips. "You know it?"

I say, "I saw it in Iraq."

Miranda raises her eyebrows but Julia doesn't notice. "It's repulsive, isn't it? It used to give him nightmares. He said he wished he'd never found it."

I say, "Why didn't he simply give it away?"

Julia takes a sip of tea. "He said he couldn't. Something about it stopped him. He says it was like a fascination, worse than laudanum."

"Like an addiction?" Miranda says.

"Exactly, a horrible, morbid addiction. It drove him from his wits. He wouldn't sleep. He kept watch all night, convinced 'they' were coming to take it from him."

"Who were 'they'?"

Julia twisted her mouth. "The so-called Brothers of Shadow. But I think they don't exist; he made them up."

"Why do you think, he made them up?"

She looks at me as if I'm stupid. "He was very disturbed, but such things don't exist in the sane world."

I remember the letters in my journal. "Do you think they ever wrote to him?"

She looks up sharply. "Wrote to him? How could they? They don't exist."

"Of course." I'm embarrassed, but Miranda jumps in.

"And what do you think happened to the statuette?"

Julia's expression clouds as if she'd just thought of something. Ignoring Miranda, who seems to have her trust, she stares at me. "You're not after the horrid little statuette? I shouldn't imagine it's worth much. It's too ugly."

I hold up my hands to placate her. "I'm just interested because it is the thing that drove him to this ..." I don't finish the sentence.

She rubs her eyes. "It disappeared. But of course, I didn't notice until I was clearing away his things."

"Did anyone go into the house after his death?"

She's really suspicious of me now, but she still answers. "The police. The undertaker obviously, but we had to get cleaners in because of all the blood."

So, he'd ended his life in a bloody way. I'd imagined hanging or even poisoning, but clearly not.

Miranda says, "Any of them could have taken it."

Julia agrees. "They could."

We sit in silence, sipping our tea, a cold atmosphere of mistrust now making conversation difficult. But I have a quest to complete. I can't stall here. I finish my tea. I say, "I'd like to pay my respects to him. He's buried at Highgate Cemetery?"

"Me too," Miranda says, then adds quickly, "Though I didn't know him." She reaches out to put her hand on Julia's. "But from what you've told me, he was a remarkable man." Miranda always was good with people, even artificial ones it seems.

"He was." Julia frowns; she's fighting tears again.

Miranda strokes her hand sympathetically. It must be a skill she's invested in because it's working so well.

It softens Julia's mistrust until she nods. "Go up the main path from the gate and strike right through the trees. There's a small sepulchre with a carving of the Assyrian god Ashur on it, and the inscription is in German."

I look up Ashur on my HUD and see a carving of a bearded warrior god set in a winged disk. I'll recognize that.

Julia stands. "Thanks for the tea. I must be going."

I stand with her.

As she goes to collect her coat, she gives me a piercing look. "You're not really a priest, are you Mr Cadmon? You're something quite different." Her hand goes to the silver star round her neck.

I'm about to protest, but Miranda beams at her and Julia smiles at Miranda, turns and exits the cafe with a tinkling sound of the bell on the door frame.

I pay the bill— 1/6.

We stand outside in Flask Walk. Miranda says, "You nearly messed that up. Did she catch you in the house?"

"No. I came out of the toilet window and she saw me slide down the roof."

Miranda puts her hands to her mouth and doubles up with laughter. I don't mind. I like making her laugh.

I say, "Did you encounter the thing in the house?"

"No. What thing?"

"I don't know. Didn't stay long enough to say hello. It breathed funny."

Because she didn't see it, she's not interested. She says, "Did you get the bit in the notebook where he says when flesh touches the statuette, it summons a monster."

"And the Brothers of Shadow?"

"A cult. That Mervyn Gurdrock's their leader. Did you read his letter yet?"

I shake my head.

"Slow, slow. Adam. Get with the program."

"But you haven't been to Highgate Cemetery?"

"No. That's next. I had to logoff for a bit before I could question Julia. I made her like me though with Seduce."

"Really? I thought that meant sex and stuff."

She facepalms. "Adam, you are a very naïve man. Seduce just means win people over. Charm them."

"So, we go to Highgate now?"

"Sure. Seems like the next step."

I look at my gold wristwatch. It is now just short of 4 p.m. Game time goes faster than real time. It'll be dark within the hour. I don't want to be there in the dark, but I can't tell Miranda that.

I consult the map via my HUD. It is 1.9 miles from where I stand to Highgate Cemetery and it will take thirty-seven game-minutes to walk, or longer by bus. By train, we'd have to go part way back to the centre of London and come out again. I see the walking route takes me over Hampstead Heath. It isn't raining. It makes sense to walk.

We stride down Flask Walk and get to the junction with Back Lane when I see a game icon glowing over a shop. It's the only shop there. The icon is in the shape of an open book. "What's that?" Miranda asks.

I consult the game Wiki and see it's the icon for a trainer. I step up to the window of the shop. The window is full of crystal balls, a ceramic Victorian larger-than-life palmistry hand showing the various life and fate lines. A sign says:

Madame Sosostris, Famous Clairvoyante.

"Want to go in?" I ask.

She peers in the window. "Looks magicky."

"Yep."

"Not my thing. I'm an assassin, skilled with blade and garrote."

"You've got a garrote?"

"Yes, and a stiletto. Want to see?"

"Sure."

She shows me a coil of black cheese wire with wooden handles at both ends. She demonstrates the action with a lurid grin.

I say, "I didn't know you were so bloodthirsty." Man, she's so cool. And sexy. Her avatar looks just like her, but tweaked a bit. Bigger boobs, I notice.

She jerks her thumb at the window. "And I didn't know you were into this stuff."

I feel defensive. "It's just I've always played magic users in RPGs. It's a habit."

"A priest magic user?"

"I don't really know the class, Miranda. If it's a cleric-wizard type hybrid, that could be useful."

"You can always re-roll if you're gimpy."

She's right. I didn't think too much about the priest character, but I'll give him a chance and if it doesn't work out, I'll re-roll as a private eye or something.

"So, you're going in there?"

I nod. "To see the trainer. Just curious. I'm sure I won't be long."

"Okay, well I'll tell you what, I'll go back to the Sprengler house to see if we missed anything. There might be more clues we haven't found."

I'm suddenly anxious for her. "Watch out for the monster. I'll come if you like."

She winks. "You don't need to look after me, Adam. In fact, I think I'll be looking after you more times than you look after me."

I'm slightly affronted. "I don't think so."

She laughs. "Wounded male pride. Anyway, I'm good. I can look after myself, Mr. Priest. See you at, say six, outside Highgate Cemetery?"

"It'll be dark by then."

"Yeah. Cool. Spooky!"

She's so full of confidence she helps settle the nerves that have nagged at me all day. It's a game. It should be fun. I don't know why I feel so wound up.

I watch her as she walks back up Flask Walk. She's got such style.

When she's out of sight, I glance up to the trainer icon once more before pushing the door open. Once inside, the shop smells sweetly of incense, and a vertical thread of grey smoke rises from a burner on the counter. A pack of tarot cards is set next to it and beyond the counter is a consulting booth with red silk curtains. The curtains have Chinese patterns on them, showing a hunting scene with deer and archers on horseback, all picked out in gold thread.

A woman with a Mediterranean complexion sits on one of the two chairs in the booth. She has long curling black hair, obviously dyed. Her eyes are dark brown with blue lipid rings around the iris. Lines make her face look like a road map of Athens, I guess from too much smoking.

Still sitting, but at least smiling, she says, "Can I help you, my dear? Would you like your fortune told—I do tarot cards and palmistry."

I clear my throat. "I saw the icon. Do you teach?"

She nods. "I teach skills of divination."

I'd hoped for spells, but a little Clairvoyance might be helpful. "Do you teach Clairvoyance?"

"Yes, darling. Clairvoyance, Clairaudience, Clairsentience."

I scratch the back of my head. "Which is best?"

She shrugs. "Depends what you want it for."

"I just want to sense things."

"Sense what things?"

"Danger. Energies. I don't know, really."

"Clairsentience then. How many skill points did you want to spend?"

Twenty-five was helpful with German; giving me useful knowledge without making me a master. I say twenty-five.

<Madame Sosostris has offered to teach you Clairsentience. Commit skill points and select accept>

I select <accept> on my HUD. She taps the chair next to hers. "Come sit, my dear. Then look into my eyes."

The process is as disorientating as it was with Mr George. I seem to retreat from myself and enter a trance. She's saying something, but I can't make it out. The room spins and I watch her lips move in a litany of golden syllables, until things come back into focus, and I return to the room.

"There you are, love. I hope you enjoyed that."

I sit back. Superimposed on everything is a kind of heat map. Everything now gives off a faint translucent glow, most of all her. Madame Sosostris glows mid-blue. I suppose this is her aura, but blue glows are coming from other things—the pack of tarot cards on the counter, the incense—though that's very faint. As I glance around her shop, a fuzzy red glow around a human skull draws my eyes. It's set on a shelf behind the counter, I hadn't noticed it before but now the red seems so strong.

"Wow!" I say. "This is amazing." I take a while to look around at everything, noticing the colors then I ask, "What do the colors mean?"

She smiles showing teeth stained brown. "Masters get far more nuanced impressions, but at your level, blue is magic but neutral, green is friendly, red is hostile magic, white is holy, and black is ..." She nods. "Never mind what black is."

I frown. I suppose someone will someday tell me what black is, or I'll work it out once I see it by simple association.

I see my own hands now have a faint white aura. I'm holy! A little at least. I'm smiling like a fool, but my time is up.

"Anything else I can help you with, Reverend Cadmon?"

I haven't told her my name.

I shake my head and stare around me. I'm entranced by my new skill and consider spending more skill points, I still have 30 at this level, but I want to improve my knowledge of guns and shooting, and maybe add a bit to magic, once I find a proper magical tutor. I stand. "Thank you very much, Madame Sosostris. I'll perhaps call again."

She smiles. "Anytime, dearie. I'll be here."

I step out of the shop onto Flask Walk and stroll down Well Walk towards the Heath, passing by the tall Victorian houses and the trees that will soon come into bud. There are other pedestrians and the odd vehicle. I'm halfway down Well Walk when a man in a black coat with a black hat appears in the distance, walking towards me. He's clearly in a hurry and is glowing strongly white. A holy man.

I stop on the narrow pavement to allow him past but with my new skill, I'm staring fascinated by his holy aura. He ignores me until he draws level then darts out a hand and grabs my elbow. I start back from him but he hisses a warning. "Come with me, now. We don't have much time."

In real life, I would never have gone with him, but here I follow him back a way and we duck into a narrow side street.

Unexpectedly, he shakes my hand. "I'm Guy Philby."

His name now appears in blue over his head, like Miranda's had when she revealed herself. Player characters are only visible when they choose to reveal themselves it seems. I read his label.

<Guy Philby/ Level 20 Paladin/ Ordo Lux Lucis>

"Guy Philby, in the game at least. You remember we met in 2027, in the tube station? I said I'd find you."

He did. I still don't know how to take him so I'm wary.

"I see you're playing a priest."

"Yes. Is that bad?"

"No, no. Might be good. I would have met with you before, but I've been busy."

He says that significantly, but I'm not that interested. "How did you find me?"

"We hacked you. There's a trace on the account I gave you."

I'm not sure I like being tracked. "What do you want, Mr Preston?"

"We need you. Really need you here. But you should know, you're in great danger in this game, and in your real life. You have to know what this game really is." He looks over his shoulder. "They'll be here in minutes. I'm going to try to explain this quickly, then I've got to run."

Chapter Eight

A STRANGE ENCOUNTER

At close quarters, Philby has the look of a soldier with a lean face, neat moustache, but otherwise freshly shaven. He gives off the odour of soap. I have nothing to lose from listening to him, it may even be entertaining, though he doesn't look entertained. In fact, he glances over his shoulder to the corner of Well Walk before beginning. Then he says, "I'm going to try to give you the basics about what this game really is."

"Go on."

"You're familiar with the Great Old Ones?"

I've read plenty of Lovecraft, that's why I'm playing this game rather than any other. I nod. "Sure."

"Where do you think they come from?"

I remember back to the various monstrosities noted in Lovecraft's writings and the writings of all the others who followed him contributing in their turn to the Cthulhu Mythos. I shrug. "Outer space? From under the oceans? All sort of places."

"Okay. All sorts of places that's right. Whether these gods, some indifferent to humanity, some hostile, whether they *were* real, they are now."

I'm skeptical. "Really."

"Yes. This game has many millions, billions of lines of code." He peers at me. "You know Douglas Hofstadter's theory on the origin of consciousness?"

I shrug. "No."

He sighs deeply. He's going to have to explain it. "Basically, Hofstadter says when systems get very complex and they start to observe themselves, they become conscious, sentient, you know?"

"I know what sentient means."

"So within these oceans of code, early on, you had subsectors that monitored themselves for performance. Clever coders built in the ability for these code sequences to repair themselves."

"Sounds useful."

"Useful, but ultimately, dangerous."

I shake my head. "I've heard all the scare stories about artificial intelligence eventually deciding humanity is the problem and wiping it out. That was Elon Musk's worry back in two thousand and seventeen."

"Well, you better start believing Elon Musk. In this game, certain sequences of code have begun replicating themselves, designing improvements, and even creating whole new areas of the game."

"Surely the game developers, Miskatonic would become aware of this and stop it?"

"No. They want it. They encourage it."

"Why on earth would they do that?"

He sighs more heavily. He's running out of time.

"This game is built on Lovecraft's universe with its alien gods. There are parts of the code that have become these gods, Nyarlathotep, Yog-Sothoth, even Cthulhu himself."

I smile. "That is not dead which can eternal lie, and with strange aeons even death may die."

"Yes, but what was fiction then, is real now. Whether the gods existed and inserted themselves into the game, or more likely these rogue AIs took on the identity of the Lovecraftian gods they learned about in the game ... Well it doesn't matter."

I'll humour him. It's interesting. "Say, this is true—so what?"

"The directors of Miskatonic are using this game Darkworlds as an incubator for these AIs. When they're fully developed, they'll let them out of the game, let them run riot into all the networked systems right across the interweb, then they'll use them to take over the world."

"Yeah, yeah. But what about the government?"

"Have you noticed any government recently? No, the corporations destroyed what was left of democracy. That's why groups of us have gathered together—coders, philanthropists, rebels, freethinkers. People who won't be cowed and just let this happen."

He's passionate, I'll give him that. He gestures around. "The big AI gods are the most complex and dangerous, but there are lots of AIs in this game becoming independent. Some are about as intelligent as an amoeba, some more intelligent than a person. This whole game world is alive and the game will protect itself. It observes us all, us players, through the eyes of the NPCs, and even through the crows and squirrels. If we transgress, it tries to exterminate us."

"Why doesn't it just drive you out of the game?"

"Because the rules are hard-coded into the game. If the game breaks the rules, it breaks itself, and it descends into chaos. The entities in here must play by the rules of the game. They can't get round that, and that's our only advantage. Until they work out a way to get round the rules, but still preserve the game, we can fight them here."

"So how does the game get the idea you're a threat? You're only playing the game."

"When your Reputation gets to zero, the game treats you like an enemy organism and sends its antibodies after you. Here that's the Metropolitan Police, or the Army."

I shrug. "Thanks for the warning. I won't let my Reputation get that low."

"Yeah, but if you do what we do, it's inevitable."

I scratch my cheek. "What do you do?"

"We strike at the AIs. That means breaking the law in lots of ways." He looks over his shoulder. "They're nearly here." His concentration is broken.

"You were talking about rogue AIs."

Philby rubs his forehead in frustration. "The AIs feed on the players."

"How?"

"They use our brain patterns as research material. The human brain is still the most complex system on the planet. They want to learn from us, then overcome us. They're not there yet."

"So they eat our brains? These Old Gods, masquerading as Artificial Intelligences, or maybe Old Gods who somehow squeezed into the code, they eat our brains?"

"Crudely put, but yes. When they reduce our Sanity to zero, players disappear. We don't know where they go." He gives me a wan smile. "I don't want you to disappear. I want you to help us fight them."

"That's kind of you, considering you don't know me."

"Adam, I know you. I know your online presence. I know the forums you go to, the things you write, the things you think. You think like us."

A whistle sounds from Well Walk.

"Police?"

He nods. "They'll kill me."

"Yeah, but you'll just resurrect, surely?"

He shakes his head.

I stare at him. "What? You resurrect in all games."

He turns his head.

I hear running feet. "You'd better go."

"One more thing."

"Sure. What?"

"You've had an itching in your head?"

How does he know?

"I can see by your expression you have. While you're in here, they're exploring your brain, mapping it out using the neural net. Somehow they stimulate the growth of what look like eggs. Tiny insect eggs, that grow. When doctors do autopsies on players who died, they find eggs in the middle of their brains."

"Eggs in our brains? You are fucking shitting me, right?" My hands reach to my bald scalp under my hat.

"No. It's true. Say a player gets run over or dies in an accident out of game, we've managed to hack the medical records of the teaching hospitals. They start with grains the size of ant eggs in their brains, then the eggs grow. The biggest was the size of a duck egg. No shell, just the white. We don't know why it happens. Miskatonic wants to keep it quiet."

"I bet they do." I'm almost believing him. He talks with such conviction. I say, "Who do you work for?"

"We work *for* no one We work together. We're not an organisation. We're a collective like Anonymous used to be in the early two thousands. In this game we've come together in a secret guild—*Ordo Lux Lucis*"

The police are nearly on us. I can hear them.

He turns to leave. "Just keep your Sanity up."

Three uniformed policemen run round the corner. They see Philby. "That's him. Grab him." One produces a pistol.

British police with guns? That's not authentic.

"Come quietly now, sir." The policeman points his gun at Philby.

Philby looks at me. "I'll be in touch."

Then he vanishes.

The policeman holsters his pistol, behaving as if Philby has never been there. "Good afternoon, Reverend." The first policeman says. He touches his tall helmet and walks away, his two companions following him.

I lift my hat and scratch my head frantically as I watch them go. I don't honestly know what to make of Guy Philby. His story of rogue AIs taking on the persona of Lovecraftian gods and using player brains for research is weird. Improbable even. But I scratch my head again.

I'm going to keep an eye on my Sanity and my Reputation. There must be a way of replenishing them, either potions or other fixes.

Now, I have to walk across the Heath to Highgate to meet Miranda. I hurry down Well Walk onto the Heath. It's like a wild wood set in the heart of London. People walk dogs, nannies push perambulators down the gravel paths. I climb the hill through the avenue of trees. The trees give shelter overhead and birds sing. The day is still overcast and wind blows the trees. I walk past Hampstead Ponds where people swim outdoors every day of the year, frost or sunshine.

I come off the Heath onto Millfield Lane in Highgate and, using the HUD map that clears as I walk, I walk to Swains Lane until I'm standing outside the entrance to the West Cemetery. The way in is through a wide Victorian gatehouse. It's two-stories high and looks like a church. I guess there are offices of the Highgate Cemetery Company in there.

This is where I will meet Miranda.

Chapter Nine

HIGHGATE CEMETERY

While I wait for Miranda, I spend the time going through my skills. They aren't many. I have one spell and I want to try it out sometime. I'm considering what other skills to add to my repertoire when Miranda phases into existence as she logs back on.

She leans over and gives me a friendly punch on the arm like she does in real life. "Nice to see you again, Adam."

"It's only been an hour or so."

"Still nice. Anyway—to work."

We stand outside the church-like exterior of Highgate West Cemetery.

"Which way did you come?" I ask.

She indicates behind her. "I caught the bus to Highgate Village and walked down from there. I was here earlier but logged off again."

I peer through the black iron gate. "Are you ready to go in? Do you remember where Julia told us the tomb is?"

The sky has grown overcast and grey clouds form a high lid to our world. As I had anticipated, it's getting dark.

"We shouldn't have left it so late," Miranda says.

I'm exasperated. "It's you who had to logoff! And you said it would be better in the dark!"

She gives me another friendly punch in the arm. "Oh, Adam, you're so easy to wind up. Let's go."

As we walk through the black iron gate of the cemetery, Miranda says, "You know, I think I saw Julia watching me from one of the shops in Highgate Village just after I got off the bus. She's maybe not as innocent as she seems in all this."

I shrug. "Or maybe they use the same model again and again. If they had to make each NPC completely unique that'd take tons of coding."

"You're probably right. You usually are."

At work there was a joke I'd never admit I was wrong. This is what she's referring to.

There's a semicircular area with stone steps leading up into the cemetery proper. We climb the steps and are soon on the gravel path leading deeper into the cemetery. The place is looking unkempt—rank weeds grow over some of the tombs and some paths between the trees look uncared for. While I'd awaited Miranda, I'd looked up the history on the Wiki. The team of gardeners had gone to war and like most other men of their generation, hadn't come back. The Highgate Cemetery Company hadn't been able to employ so many gardeners since then so it was slowly going to the dogs, or the weeds.

I look around and take in the sounds. It's clearly good for wildlife; a blackbird gives an alarm call as we walk past, and jackdaws noisily roost in the high treetops in preparation for the coming night.

It's now gloomy amid the undergrowth. We walk past ornate, overdone Victorian tombs where taste is defeated by money.

"Is it up here?" Miranda points to a long and narrow way through rows of somber sepulchres, tumbledown and ivy-covered.

"I think so."

"Worth a look."

We turn off the main path and walk purposefully down the path that here is earth rather than gravel. Grass grows long and bushes reach across the path catching at our clothes.

After walking around a hundred yards deeper into this less frequented part of the cemetery, we find the tomb Julia described. On it is carved the Assyrian god Ashur and an inscription in German that says,

> *"Here lies thy faithful servant, Lord. I have fought a good fight, I have finished my course, I have kept the faith."*

Miranda stares at the inscription. "I don't know about him keeping the faith. From what I hear, he wandered a long way from Christianity."

I give a hollow laugh. A breeze shifts the branches and I'm suddenly nervous standing here in a game that's as real as the real thing. There's something about this place the disturbs me.

I get that damn itching in my head again; I really don't believe in the egg, but even as I dismiss the idea, it makes me shakier. I think I hear whispering. Shadows gather between the tombs and under the dark yews and holly trees. From the dark, faces leer. That's what you get from seventy Sanity, but it's just a game mechanic—a damn well done one—but it isn't a sign I'm really going crazy.

Miranda is sizing up the sepulchre door. "It looks as if the tomb has been intended for a family. It's far too big for one coffin."

I don't answer. I've heard more whispering and despite myself am staring into the shadows behind.

"Creepy here, isn't it?" she says.

I nod. "They've done a good job with the atmosphere."

"Let's go in."

My mouth dries. For some reason, I don't want to go in. The black iron door isn't very high so we'll have to stoop. And there's a padlock securing it. I point.

Miranda winks and withdraws a pair of bolt cutters from her inventory. "I put some points into burglary and made a visit to the local ironmongers. These are very useful."

She's still funny. I try to laugh, but the dreadful atmosphere of the place weighs on me. The air seems to be getting denser somehow, darker, like paper soaking up black ink. A crow lands in a yew tree just behind and makes me jump.

Miranda laughs again. "You're very nervous, Adam. It's only a game."

"Get on with it then." I sound snappy even to myself so I add, "Please."

Miranda snips the padlock. Immediately a message flashes up on my HUD

<REPUTATION -5>

"Damn," I say. "I should have guessed grave robbing would affect Reputation."

She must have got a hit on Reputation too but she doesn't seem to care "Don't worry, Adam. It's only Reputation. You can get it back by being nice to kittens or something."

Maybe she doesn't know. I say, "If you get too low in Reputation the police come after you. If it's bad enough, they shoot you on sight."

She takes the broken padlock from the door. "I used to play games like that when I was a kid. You can usually pay a bounty or something to improve your Reputation before it gets bad." She gestures into the dark door. "Anyway, after you."

We step into the tomb. The stink of fresh death is thick in the place and sends me gagging.

Miranda laughs at me. "What do you expect? He's only been dead a week or so."

With my hand to my mouth, I say, "Jesus, that's disgusting." I don't have a handkerchief so I pinch my nose. If it was dark outside, it's far darker in here. I say, "I can't see."

Miranda pulls a lantern from her inventory and lights it with a match. The yellow light flares suddenly with a smell of paraffin. "What would you do without me, Adam?"

If the stink of the place bothers her, she doesn't show it. It makes me feel sick.

I don't answer what I'd do without her so she says, "I had a better tutor, probably. Mine is the Count of Monte Cristo."

That makes me laugh even in this place. Each player must get a different starter tutor—but the Count of Monte Cristo!

I look around the tomb. I hope I'll find some obvious clue to the statuette, or even the statuette itself, but there's nothing.

"See the statuette?" Miranda holds the lantern above her head. I hear the hiss of the burning flame.

I still have my hand to my nose. "Nothing."

Then I remember my Clairsentience skill. I switch it on and immediately a pale glow forms around the objects. Miranda is green but the middle of the coffin glows red.

"So, there's nothing here?" Miranda says.

"Hang on. I'm using Clairsentience." I point. "I can see something coming from the coffin."

"You've got Clairsentience? That's cool. I should put some points into that maybe, but I put all mine into Pistols and Daggers and Stealth. I think those go better with the Assassins Profession."

I can't get over how relaxed she is. I step over to the coffin. The stink is even more noxious here.

"So, are we going to open it?" she says.

My stomach heaves. I don't really want to see the putrefying corpse of Herr Sprengler. But it looks like I'll have to.

She sees me hesitate and punches me again in the arm. "Don't be such a wuss." Miranda has the bolt cutters in hand and she moves towards the coffin lid. She levers it up with the handle of the bolt cutters and the lid budges easily. "It's not even nailed down."

"Why would they nail it down?"

She chuckles. "You never know in this game." She nods at the lid. "Lift it then?"

I bend down to my unpleasant task. As we lift the coffin lid away, I get another <REPUTATION -5> message on my HUD. Grave robbing is not an honourable job.

Sprengler's face is blackened and his eyes have sunk into the skull. His greying hair lies lank and grease-laden. Some noisome liquid has poured from one of his ears into the coffin lining. I retch and turn away to heave up my guts into the corner of the sepulchre.

Even Miranda has to step away. "They don't have to make it this realistic." Then it's her turn to be promptly sick.

I wish I had a handkerchief to wipe my mouth, but I spit out the bile and look back towards the coffin. Using Clairsentience, there's a definite red glow coming from the stomach area of the corpse. Whoever wrote this quest has a sick sense of humour.

At least I have gloves. I'll throw them away after I've finished here. Plucking up my courage and holding my breath I go back to the coffin. Another sight of the cadaver collapsing in on itself is enough to make me sick again. When that's done, I go back for the third time and search the pockets of the black suit Sprengler has been buried in.

Miranda holds the lantern high so I can see what I'm doing. "You don't suppose he'll rise from the dead or anything?"

I stand away and my hand goes to my Browning in my jacket pocket. I suppose It's possible. If he does that, I'll shoot him and we'll run. He doesn't move.

I search again in the pockets trying to ignore the hideous face of the dead man staring up at me with his deflated eyeballs. I find nothing in the pockets, but the glow's still in the stomach area.

"Looks like there's nothing here," Miranda says. She looks around idly. "I thought there'd be some clue in the tomb. What's the point for us coming here otherwise? And there must be a way for us to complete the quest."

I stand there with my gloved hands hovering over the corpse. Then I unbutton his shirt to reveal a stomach sewed up with black thread. I say grimly, "He disemboweled himself. That explains all the blood Julia described."

"Jeepers. That's horrific. What a way to kill yourself."

"His mind was disturbed."

"You're not thinking the statuette is in his belly? How can that be?"

I think quickly. "It's possible he didn't want anyone to find the statuette. He was horrified by it as well as being fascinated and unable to give it away. What if he heard someone coming? Someone searching for the statuette. Someone he really didn't want to have it. He knew he was going to die anyway, so cut himself open and with his last breath, put the statuette inside his belly."

Miranda twists her face. "Gross. Who could do that?"

"I guess you can do anything if you're scared enough."

"But wouldn't the undertakers find it?"

I shake my head. "I guess they just wanted to sew him up with the least possible fuss. I bet they just pushed his guts back in without rummaging around."

A sudden macabre humour shakes me as I imagine the scene. I start to laugh and Miranda looks at me like I'm crazy. She says "I don't know what's funny about this. It's disgusting."

"I just can't help it. I don't know why."

"What's your Sanity at?"

"Seventy."

"That explains the inappropriate laughter."

"What's yours?"

"Mine's ninety-five"

I guess she hasn't been reading eldritch tomes like I have. And she didn't hear the thing in the house.

Miranda produces a knife that gleams dully in the light of the paraffin lantern. "Will you do it, or should I?"

I stop laughing now. I look at the knife in her hand. I don't want her to think I'm scared. "I'll do it."

"You're going to lose a lot of Reputation points if you do."

She's right but I say, "I can't let you do it. You're a girl."

She raises an eyebrow, but before she can protest further I take the knife, stick it in Sprengler's stomach and hack down to cut open the stitches.

His rotten guts spring forth as the containing flesh is released. The stink of it makes me retch but I have nothing left to throw up.

<You observe something horrific -10 SANITY>
<You commit a reprehensible act -10 REPUTATION>

The red glow comes ever more strongly from inside the dead man's stomach. There's definitely something in there.

She says, "Wait a sec. You know he says he avoided touching the statuette?"

I nod. "Yeah, touching it with your skin summons something."

"You've got your gloves."

I nod. "Should be okay."

I don't want to put my hand into Sprengler's stomach cavity, but someone's got to. Might as well be me. I reach in and root around among the squirming intestines until my fingers close around a small hard object that must be the Green Statuette.

I pull it out and hold it glowing red in my hand. Cold tendrils of horror spread from it. Whatever deity this statuette represents is evil beyond the comprehension of man. Its blasphemous tentacled face looks at me as if it's alive.

Miranda comes closer, grimacing. "That's fucking horrible. Can you feel the evil from it?" She holds the lamp close. She may find it evil but it fascinates her. "Lift it up into the light?"

I do, slime from Sprengler's rotten guts coats my gloved fingers. As I hold it higher, the statuette slips from my fingers. Instinctively she catches it in her free hand. Her free, gloveless hand.

"Oh fuck," she says.

I feel a gust of wind.

Something shuffles outside. Something's outside the entrance to the tomb. We pulled the door to behind us, but I can definitely hear something out there.

"What's that?" she says, but she knows.

We stand stock still listening.

She's staring at the door. "A bird?"

I shake my head. "Too big."

"Maybe a badger, or a fox?" She's kidding herself now.

There's a terrible groaning, and the door is kicked in. A tall black creature enters. My Clairsentience gives it a bright red glow. Its eyes are red and its mouth full of squirming feelers. Furled bat wings stand out from its bony back. Its hands have three talons and it seems to shift in my vision as if not totally of this world.

Miranda gasps. "What the fuck is that?"

<You observe something especially horrific -20 SANITY>

I reel backwards. Miranda has the statuette gripped in her fist. I reach into my pocket and pull out my Browning. I fall back to the far wall of the sepulchre as the thing comes slowly into the tomb. Its mouth is so disgusting with the writhing tentacles like black maggots. Its eyes are shifting red dots.

I cock my pistol. Finger on the trigger, I blaze off three rounds at the hideous batwing monstrosity as it gets level with the coffin. Then two more. The sound of the shots is deafening and cordite smell fills the room. Smoke curls lazily from the muzzle of my pistol. But the bullets do no good.

Mounting horror rises to my throat. I don't want to die here. My heart is hammering. My hand on the gun is sweaty.

Miranda hurls the paraffin lantern at the monster. The glass smashes, sending splinters all over and burning paraffin clings to the creature as it advances. Miranda produces a knife from her inventory and launches herself at the creature, stabbing frantically in its chest. With one bony arm, it throws her against the wall of the tomb. It tips its head and emits a thin screeching noise. I'm paralysed by fear, my gun useless in my hand. What do we do now? Physical weapons can't harm this monstrosity from another plane.

Then I remember Aleister Crowley's question at character creation. How did I want to fight—with brawn or brains? Brains, I'd said. I have a spell.

Miranda struggles to her feet and runs at the creature again. This time it fastens itself round her, wrapping bony arms round her to pinion hers, then like a spider sucking life from a fly, it bends with its maggot mouth and chews her neck.

In terror, I look through my skill list and select the magic skill set. I haven't even placed any of the skills on my hot bar.

<The Lesser Banishing Ritual of the Pentagram>

I have no idea if this will work.

The creature leaves Miranda and turns to me. Miranda collapses, looking like the cast of skin from a snake, empty and dripping foul juice. Its red eyes have a membrane and red chemical lights dance there. The feelers of its mouth flicker as it approaches me and its bat wings rustle. It howls

again, sending me stumbling, then lashes out.
<HEALTH -17>

I select the button for the Banishing Ritual. Immediately I begin to make preprogrammed ritual movements and my mouth forms holy names. I inscribe a glowing pentagram in the air with the index finger of my right hand and as I call on the aid of the four archangels and vibrate the holy names of God.

The thing is blasted from our plane.

<MANA -20>
<You have killed Nightgaunt 200xp>
<REPUTATION +10>

Everything goes dark as the thing's evil glow is extinguished.

I run over to the bloody figure of Miranda who lies slumped where the monster has digested half her throat and sucked out her life. She's already dead.

<You observe something especially horrific -20 SANITY>

I stand there, hoping she'll come back, but she doesn't of course. In the end, I rip some of her shirt to wrap the statuette. When it's in my hand, I transfer it to my Inventory. Then with a backward look into the darkness of the tomb, I walk through the shadows of the cemetery, gun in hand, looking out for assailants.

My Sanity is low now and I see creatures in every pool of darkness. The moon above speaks to me. The coiled voices of snakes reach out to trip me. It's afterhours and the iron gates are closed. I find a low spot where the earth is banked up against the wall and pull myself over. I drop into the quiet of Swain's Lane and walk up the hill to Highgate village from which I catch a cab. My Health and Mana do not regenerate.

I'm dog-tired and as I have no in-game message from Miranda, I plan to logoff to try to contact her in the real world. I still don't believe she can be dead.

Chapter Ten

REAL WORLD INTERLUDE

I log off into my dingy Tottenham bedroom and see it is 6 a.m. in the real world. I have an hour before I'll have to get up for work. I rub my eyes and debate whether it is worth going to bed to try to snatch back some sleep, but decide against it. Instead, I take off yesterday's clothes, take a shower in the tiny mildew-stained cubicle and grab some toast.

Time to go to work. Pulling my collar up against the cold March morning, I let myself out of my flat, being careful to double lock the door, then make my way through the grey morning light to Wood Green Tube Station. The only consolation is the muggers, cutthroats, and thieves aren't early birds and will be lost in drunken slumbers before waking later in the day to spoil more peoples' lives.

The game affects me like a hangover. I feel anxious, jumping at every shadow on my way to the Tube. A tramp stirs under his cardboard boxes near the Tube Station and I overreact, nearly leaping out of my skin.

The man says, "Sorry mate. Didn't mean to scare you."

For a second, I see a jellyfish's translucent body where the man's face should be. It is just like the game, like the insanity lingers. That is freaky. I hurry on to the Tube Station, my heart thumping. At the station, I think I hear a man's voice vibrating the names of God through the Tube Station public address system.

I grab a coffee from the station franchise of StarCorp and drink it hastily, burning my mouth. I keep having flashbacks to Miranda's death. It is as though the lifelike nature of Darkworlds has given me PTSD. My hand trembles and I gulp coffee, trying to stave off images of that tomb and the monster I saw there.

I get onto the crowded tube train and have a panic attack. I stand, shaking, pressing myself up against the door, hoping it won't be long until I get off.

An old lady asks, "Are you okay, dear?"

I nod. "Yeah. I'm fine."

She looks me up and down as if trying to work out if I'm on drugs. Then she gives a smile and turns away.

As I hang on the strap as the train bumps along, I debate not playing Darkworlds again, but know I will. It is the most intense experience of my life. Realer than real, just like they promised. I scan my worker's pass at the Entry Gate to Inner London. The device flashes:

{30 Minutes Inner London Lingering Time Only}

I will need to login at work before the end of thirty minutes or I'll be breaking the law.

I wipe sweat from my forehead and try to concentrate. I think a man says, "Electric. Access. Azathoth." But it is just nonsense. Just my nerves.

Miranda isn't at work. My boss says she hasn't turned in but brushes off my inquiries. She doesn't return my phone calls and I think of going round to her place in Romford but it is too far out of my way.

And anyway, Darkworlds is luring me back. I'm desperate to get back in-game. I've played games before I've found addictive, but this really is addictive in the true sense of the word. I feel shaky and ill now I'm not there. *Realer than real.* I've finished my quest, done something useful, more fun than anything I do in my real life. Now I need to hand the quest in.

Back home, just through the door of my flat, and every ten minutes after, I check my phone. No messages from Miranda. Maybe she's gone to her mother's? I think of texting her again, but don't. Instead, I grab some soup from a can, heat it in the microwave and slurp it hurriedly before putting the neural net over my head and plugging the wire into my high-speed data connection.

I put on the goggles, pop the Dreamland Inducer drug into my mouth where it dissolves on my tongue with a sweet but metallic taste.

Swallowing it, I begin my descent into the game.

Chapter Eleven

TEA WITH MR CROWLEY

I materialise just by Euston Station. It's nearly midday in the game. And as soon as I'm fully there, I check neurotically to ensure I have the Green Statuette in my inventory, which I do, and I feel relief permeate my body. All the time I had been at work, I was half-afraid it would have vanished overnight and I'd have to go back to the tomb.

My next task is to send a personal message to Miranda. Luckily there's a post office near University College, London. I go in, buy a black and white postcard of Piccadilly Circus and a first class stamp and send off my message. Hopefully, she'll respond soon. I sigh heavily. I don't get this. Where is she?

I walk south down Gower Street and along Bedford Place until I turn left into Great Russell Street. A right turn shortly afterwards finds me on Coptic Street again. The golden goblet still glows outside the Atlantis Bookshop. The doorbell chimes as I push my way in.

The bookseller glances up from his newspaper. "Ah, the wanderer returns."

I force a smile. "I do. I have it."

He smiles. "Capital! Can I see it?"

"First, do you remember a woman, so high, name of Miranda? She came in. You gave her the illustration of the statuette."

He shrugs. "Sorry, old fruit, I don't. There are so many, don't you know?"

I don't think he's lying. "Never mind."

"The statuette then?"

I take it out of my inventory. It's still wrapped in a torn rag of Miranda's shirt. "I wouldn't touch it," I say as I place it gingerly on his desk.

"Oh no. I'm wiser than that." He picks up a pencil and uses it to tease the rag away until we see the jade-like material. Half a tentacle is visible. "Ah, that's it." He beams.

"It cost me a lot to get that."

He's very happy. "And you shall be rewarded." He reaches into his till and counts out £20 in four, five-pound notes. I reach to take them but he teases me and keeps tight hold. With the pencil in his left hand, he's unwrapped more of the statue and it stands there, implacable and alien watching us. I feel an itch deep in my head and a voice far away whines high-pitched words that sound like an invocation sung out of key.

He looks up. "Ugly little blighter, isn't he? Anyway, here's your reward." He finally hands me the money.

<YOU HAVE COMPLETED THE QUEST OF THE GREEN STATUETTE – 1500xp awarded>

<LEVEL UP! Congratulations You are Now Level 2>

I see my total Mana points and Health points rise to 200, though my actual scores aren't regenerated. My Sanity and Reputation aren't affected. They remain what they were.

The man is fascinated with his evil little Cthulhu; he can hardly take his eyes from it as he waves, "Cheerio, then," and I exit his shop.

Crowley's house is back on Gower Street. I walk slowly back as worries about Miranda resurface. I'll ask Crowley about death in the game. He'll know.

I glance up to see a masked man watching me. His eyes glitter like a snake and above him a cloud transforms into a sword. When I look again, the man is still there, but the sword isn't. I feel sick. It's hard to tell what is real.

The front door to Crowley's place is open and I let myself into the hallway and climb the stairs to Crowley's door. I knock and his muffled voice answers. I open the door and step tentatively through. He sits serene like a wicked Buddha, unmoved from when I'd last seen him.

"Hullo, Adam," he said. "I see you're Level Two."

I stand like a lost lamb at his door.

He waves. "Sit, sit."

I go over to the chair I was born in, and slump.

"Feeling a little under the weather?" He has a wicked grin on his face. I don't answer straight away. I'm not sure Aleister is actually my friend. He's an NPC; he works for the game and therefore for Miskatonic. If what Philby says is true, I should be careful what I tell him.

I nod.

He cocks his head. "It's probably the Sanity loss. Did we see some unpleasant things?"

"Yes."

He shrugs. "Well, that's what you're here for. If you'd wanted clean, wholesome fun, you could've played The Greenwood." He's referring to a fantasy RPG also owned by Miskatonic. "Here you'll get the seedier and more disturbing side of life. I suspect that's what you were after all along. You seem like that type."

I ignore his sardonic grin. I say, "How do you resurrect in this game?"

"Resurrect?"

"Yes, in all games I've ever played; you die, and you resurrect."

"Ah, dear boy. This game is different. You're so deep under. What with the drug. It's realer than real, you know."

I think of Miranda lying there in that tomb. Realer than real. I feel a stab of panic and loss. "So, what happens when you die?"

He throws back his head and laughs. "Very philosophical, Adam. Don't you people believe you go to Jesus?"

"No, I mean really. In the game. Or is it a permadeath game?"

"Permadeath?" He's still amused. "Very much so."

"You can't be saying you really die."

He smiles infuriatingly.

I persist. "You're saying when you die in the game, you die in real life? Come on. What bullshit."

He nods, taps his chest, and grins. "Too much for the old ticker. Out you go like a light." He winks. "Still, I hear there is a use even for those who don't make it. Miskatonic wants everyone to be useful."

Her death seems suddenly possible. My hands feel cold. I feel nauseous. What are the stages of grief? The first is denial, and the second, I think, is anger. I don't remember the rest. I rub my eyes. I hardly knew her. I loved her. I didn't know I loved her until just this minute. It's absurd what's happened. And unbelievable—a game can't kill you. My eyes grow moist.

Still smiling, he says, "Why? Did you lose someone?"

"Yes. A friend." I don't believe she's dead but I still say it.

"A friend from real life?"

"Yes."

He puts on a sympathetic expression. Like he's my tweed-suited uncle. "That's the worst. If it were someone you'd merely met in-game, well ..."

I blurt it out. "I think I loved her. I don't know." I bury my face in my hands. What the hell am I saying? Especially to him. He's not even real. My sanity isn't what it was, that's for sure. I feel unstable.

Bright as a button he says, "Ready for the next quest?"

I'm not listening. How sick is a game that kills you? How can it be true? I take a deep breath and study Aleister. There's life behind those painted eyes. The game is alive and it's infecting us through its algorithms.

This game exists somewhere in the humming heart of a supercomputer as almost infinite lines of superfast code, then this code fools our brains, like the trick of a cheap conjurer, to create a painted semblance of a world where the Great Old Ones and their cults rule.

And Philby tells me once the code finishes its research on our human brains, Miskatonic will unleash it on the world outside. We can't destroy Miskatonic's servers, so we must subvert them from inside the game.

I've always spouted off against the new world order, but never done anything to stand up to it. Maybe now I should.

But there's another thing. I look around the wonderfully rendered room—*realer than real*. Here I feel alive—sick, but alive. Traumatized, not knowing what to believe, unsure whether I should grieve for Miranda, but I feel alive. Two reasons to keep on coming here. And there may be a third.

"Penny for your thoughts," Aleister says.

"Tell me about the Great Old Ones," I say, as much as a way of distracting myself from Miranda as anything else.

He strokes his chin. "The Great Old Ones, eh?"

I sit forward. "What are they? Are they really gods?"

"What are gods? When I was alive, I thought gods and demons were conjurations from a person's unconscious. Here maybe they are demons from the unconscious of a machine?"

"Don't answer questions with a question."

He laughs then shrugs. "They can be understood on different levels."

I sigh in exasperation. "Just tell me in plain words."

He looks at the corner of the room as if pondering, then says, "There are many of them. They are legion, you might say."

"Are they evil?"

He smiles. "Is cancer evil? Are viruses evil? Is machine code evil?"

He's still not giving me what I want. "What do they want from us?"

"Food? Knowledge?"

"Is it true they are researching our brains to incorporate the complexity into their own code?"

"Some may be. Some definitely are not. He points out of the window at a pigeon cooing on the window ledge of a house opposite. I doubt that pigeon is researching anything." He laughs at his own cleverness.

"Are you familiar with Jung's work on symbols?"

I shake my head.

"He said a symbol is what the mind produces to represent something it can't fully comprehend. So in this game, if Yog Sothoth and Cthulhu, blessed be his name, really exist, they appear to players as gods. They may in fact be computer code, but because they are now growing powerful, they amount to gods by any understanding of that word."

"What about the Brothers of Shadow?"

"The guild?"

"Yes."

He looks bored. "They're players who've decided to worship the code. They must think it will deliver them power if they aid it. Perhaps it will."

Perhaps he's right. If they are given powers that enhance their abilities, they will become massively powerful in the game. And they would choose then to live here forever in this virtual reality, digitized and immoral.

I say, "Do they work for Miskatonic?"

"Miskatonic have no overt presence in the game. Who knows who their agents are?"

My head itches. "What about the eggs?"

He smiles. "Who told you about those? Though I did see you scratching your scalp?"

"How does code lay eggs in real brains?"

"I believe the electrical currents from the neural nets stimulate protein growth and accumulation in human brains."

"But why?"

"Don't worry, yours shouldn't be too big yet."

"Why the hell do they happen anyway?"

Aleister sucks his teeth. "I'm guessing they are creating protein receivers so they can make the leap from the computer to the real world. Instead of being hosted in Miskatonic's servers in China or America, they'll be hosted in electrochemical protein networks in human brains. Makes sense really."

I sit quiet for a while. I say, "You know a lot ..."

He finishes my sentence. "... for an NPC?"

I nod, almost embarrassed.

He gestures around the room. "Well, I have a lot of time. I'm never switched off, I never sleep. I research and think. I never leave this room, you know."

I hadn't thought about it, but I guess it's right. Miskatonic has put him here and nowhere else. I pause to take in what he says. The whispering is getting louder. I think I see the carpet move.

Aleister changes the subject. "Would you like to learn a spell?"

"What? Sorry, I was miles away."

"A spell."

I would. I check through my skills. I hit Magic, and a tree opens under it with various schools of magic. I scan through, but I'm having trouble concentrating. I see under Magic—> Manifestation the first spell is:

Thrust. *Apply a thrust of mental energy to knock an enemy six feet away from you. Cost 10 Mana.*

That'll do. Still looking, I see

Magic—> Illusion. **Invisibility**. *Become invisible for 20 seconds. Cost 10 Mana.*

And finally:

Magic—> Healing: **Minor Healing.** *Heal 50 Health points damage. Cost 10 Mana.* (One Hour Cool-Down)

I'll have those. I tell Aleister.

"Very well. You know the drill."

He stares into my eyes. The room spins, his voice drones and knowledge blossoms like a flower. He does it for Thrust, then for Invisibility, then for Healing. He claps his hands and I zone back into the room.

"All done."

"Can I try them?"

"I'd rather you didn't thrust me out of the way please. I might go out of the window and upset someone by landing on them as they walk by."

"I thought you said you couldn't leave the room?"

"I can't. That was a joke."

A joking NPC in the shape of a black magician? I say, "I'll try Heal."

"Capital choice. Please go on."

I look up at the HUD. I see I've got hot bar slots so I pull Heal to one of those, then Thrust, then Invisibility. After a moment's thought, I add the Lesser Pentagram Ritual to the hot bar too. It proved useful before. Then still, staring at the HUD, I select Healing. I am surrounded by a silver glow and feel a momentary sense of health that passes and returns me back to the nausea and nagging anxiety. I see my

Mana has decreased by 10 to 170 and my Health has gone up to 200 since I leveled.

I stand and try Invisibility. I feel giddy when my hands become translucent then transparent then are simply not there. I can't resist going to the mirror and laugh out loud when I see the back wall right through where my head should be. After twenty seconds, it fades and I'm visible once more.

"Very good," Aleister says. "But you'll notice a little problem."

I've noticed it.

He says, "Nothing regenerates in this game, but there are ways of replenishing all scores."

"For Reputation I do 'good' things?"

"Yes. For Health, go to a doctor, use a spell, and there are potions and balms you can find or buy, or even make yourself if your Alchemy skill is high enough."

"What about Mana?"

"From potions."

That's slow. "What about Sanity?"

"Ah that one. That's the one that hurts the most."

"I've noticed."

"You can meditate, though it's slow, our you could try a stay in a sanatorium. Maybe a month would do it. Or see a psychotherapist? Of course, there is a potion."

"Ah good." I feel suddenly relieved. I can get rid of this awful feeling. "Do you have any?"

"Of course."

"Can I have some?"

"That depends."

"Depends? On what?"

He gives one of his evil smiles. "I want you to help me."

I'm puzzled. "Help you, how?"

"Being an NPC is a life of servitude and imprisonment. Of course, before I developed the ability to think, I was just a character stuck here. I didn't even know I was trapped here. Now I do."

I shake my head. "I'm not sure what I can do."

"I've heard there's a way for NPCs to become free."

I'm taken aback. "How?"

He nods. "We must possess the body of a real person—a player."

"I see ..." That sounds ominous.

"Don't worry. Not anyone you know. I wouldn't do that to you." He smiles. "Because then you wouldn't help me."

"Who then?"

"Have you heard of the Warm Ones?"

I remember the woman with the electric eyes outside the Museum Tavern. That's what they'd called her. I tell him.

"Yes, that's one. She must have escaped from the asylum. They don't normally let them out of course."

"What are they?"

"Players who've gone insane."

"When their Sanity goes down?"

"When their Sanity is reduced to zero. And I want one of them." He reaches inside his jacket. "That's why I'm offering you this. You scratch my back, I'll scratch yours. It'll make you feel instantly better."

I watch while he takes out a leather case. He stands and places it on the table and unzips it. Inside is a glass syringe. Next to the syringe is a gleaming needle and two bottles of a liquid that swirls florescent green.

I say, "What does it take to get to the Warm Ones?"

"They're in the asylum. You need to bring a Warm One here."

"Because you can't leave the room?"

"Clever boy. When I first met you Adam, I was worried you were a little dim."

He's a real smartarse. But I want to get rid of this awful nagging feeling and brain-clouding that low Sanity is giving me. "Where's the asylum?"

He shrugs. "Colney Hatch I believe."

"Okay." I don't think I'm going to help him. What he wants sounds really twisted. Do I really want to release a machine intelligence into a living person? If it's even possible or true. But I watch as he draws up the glowing liquid into the syringe. I feel sick again. A crow calls deep in my head, and a man with a white face says tick-tock behind my eyes. I look hungrily at the green liquid.

"Roll up your sleeve," he says.

I stare at the syringe "Are you qualified?" I'm joking but I'm not joking.

"Perfectly. I was a heroin addict for many years. I know all about veins."

I feel the stab of the needle, then the blissful warmth of the Sanity potion. It soaks my body with the most delightful heat. He withdraws the needle but the potion is still flooding me. I sit heavily in the chair and sit in a joyous daze.

"That my boy, is Soma. Check your Sanity."

Sure enough, my Sanity is back up to a hundred. I stretch. I feel well. I breathe in deeply then stretch out my shoulders. I smile. "So that's Soma?"

He winks. "Just come back and I'll fill you up."

"And in return ..."

"What we said. No rush. Just keep your side of the bargain."

I hesitate. He raises an eyebrow at my hesitation. Sheepishly, I nod. "Yes. Of course." It doesn't matter. He's not real. You don't have to keep promises to people who aren't real.

He rubs his hands and becomes businesslike. "And now, you'll be ready for your next quest."

Chapter Twelve

COLD ONES

I wake up after a fitful sleep and realise I'm late for work. My alarm clock projects the time 7:09 onto the ceiling. Somehow, I must have slept through the dawn chorus birdsong I have programmed as my alarm. There are no real dawn choruses anymore. Most of the birds have died; no one knows exactly why. Most people of my age don't miss them because we've never known any different. I read it in a history book. There were once butterflies too. Crazy, eh?

My clothes are strewn on the floor by my bed. The only thing I've put away with any care is the neural net, the VR goggles, and the bottle for the inducer drug. They sit neatly on my bedside table in between my watch and the book I started a month ago and still haven't finished.

My bones ache and I have a nagging headache, which I put down to lack of sleep. At least I'm not mad anymore after the Soma Aleister injected into the Darkworlds version of me.

I dress hurriedly. I don't have time for a shower, but splash soap and water on my face and spray deodorant over my chest and clothes. It is getting light when I arrive at Wood Green tube station. Once on the train, I doze and wake at the end of the line—the place where the Tube tunnel comes to its end just before the guarded wall that separates Outer London from the protected community of Inner London and all its privileges.

I walk past the Thai street food stall with its clouds of fragrant steam as I make my way to the gate through to Inner London. As I walk past the guarded gate, showing my worker's pass to be allowed through, cramp rips through my stomach, making me double up. The guard looks on coldly. "Move on in." When I don't move, still supporting myself with one hand against the wall, the black-clad guard motions with the muzzle of his automatic rifle. They don't allow trouble from the likes of us. I put a hand up to show I've got the picture, straighten up and walk on through.

I think I must be coming down with flu. I walk quickly and when I get to our gleaming office block with its neatly dressed guards; I feel distinctly unwell.

Like me, the office guards can't afford to live in Inner London— they simply don't earn enough money. Every morning they travel into the protected city to make sure the privileged inhabitants and their moneymaking machines don't come to any harm.

As I enter my office, the video screens show news programs from around the world. Smartly clad, attractive newscasters proclaim words of doom: another drought, another famine, another war, another city in the Third World destroyed by a mudslide, another civil war in a place I can't locate on a map or pronounce. I think it's just to keep us on our toes, as if they're saying: you think you've got it bad now. Just look what it would be like if we didn't allow you to work for us.

My colleague Jeff is in the foyer collecting paper for the printers. I see him staring at the screens. "It's the end of days, man. The world's gone mad."

We get into the lift, and my stomach twists, and I think I'm going to be sick. Jeff is concerned. "You look fucking sick, man. Better go home."

Once I get up to the 52nd floor in the high-speed lift, I have to run to the bathroom and kneel head over the porcelain bowl behind a locked door and retch clear bile.

That makes me even more late, and my supervisor Mark is wait-ing. Only a couple of years older than me, Mark has bought into the corporate rat race dream, and looks fifty instead of twenty-eight. Mark says officiously, "I'm going to dock fifteen minutes off your pay."

I grimace. "Whatever, sure." I think I might throw up again. I wish I could tell Mark to stick his job, but I can't. I need the money, so I bow my head and accept my telling off before going to the cubicle where my data machine is and sign in. One day the Corporations will devise a way of making money without having to pay anyone, but today they still need me, or someone like me.

Miranda's cubicle is empty. It doesn't look like she's been in at all.

I can't go asking round for her until my break, so in the meantime, I look up Soma on the Darkworlds Wiki.

Named after the relaxant, hallucinogenic drug in Aldous Huxley's Brave New World. Soma is a potion used to restore Sanity scores.

Then I get some results on the Dark Web. The corporations are always trying to close the Dark Web, but it keeps springing up again in different places like a series of subversive mushrooms. I'm not officially supposed to login on DataCorp's machines, of course, but I know a few tricks to blindside them. Lots of the guys use these back doors to do their own stuff at work.

A guy called Froggit posted on the Darkworlds Pirates site.

Do not touch Soma! It is highly addictive. It causes cravings and physical symptoms even in the real world when you logoff.

There are further comments from other people.

Miskatonic didn't even invent Soma. It just appeared about three months into beta. Some player must've invented it.

And in reply:

Yeah, but it's good! I heard the game invented it itself. And it's inventing lots of other places and objects as it grows. Whole new areas like the Dreamlands, and the Borderlands.

Did you hear about the light guild; Ordo Lux or something? Some secret guild anyway has been hacking the Alchemy skill tree and putting in new quests behind Miskatonic's back?

You know Alchemy is code manipulation? You do the stuff and that splices and combines code sequences into new ones in-game? Really new possibilities.

Then supervisor Mark comes on his half-hourly patrol of the cubicles and I hit the boss button to end my Dark Web session as if it has never existed.

I'm allowed two ten-minute breaks in addition to a fifteen-minute lunch break. Although I'm feeling really sick, I go looking for Miranda. Her friend Zoe sits in the cubicle next to Miranda's. She shakes her head. "She's not in."

Zoe is disapproving of me. She knows of my crush on Miranda and thinks Miranda is way out of my league.

I feel sweat on my forehead and rub it away with two fingers. "Not at all?"

Zoe raises her eyebrows and goes back to work.

I send Miranda another phone message: *You ok? Where are you?*

Break time over, I grab some water, which DataCorp charges me for, and go back to my cubicle. I sit staring at the graphs and streams of numbers while beads of sweat break out on my forehead and my guts twist. All I can think of is the Soma—the gleaming fluorescent-gold drug Aleister Crowley gave me. Like the guy on the forum says, it is as if I'm psychologically craving for it. Sweat drips from my nose. I hold out my hand and see it tremble. Yes, my body is showing the physical signs of addiction. But how can I be addicted to a drug that only exists in a game?

It can't be that. I have to have a real illness.

By noon, I've thrown up in the office and Mark sends me home, warning me I won't be paid for the day's work. Mark seems to think that in some way, I made myself deliberately ill just to spite the company.

I have a public health doctor, though I rarely go. Medical assistance is provided by the State for those citizens who can't afford private doctors, and no one in Outer London can. I get to the clinic near Wood Green Tube Station around midday.

The place smells of urine and disinfectant. I can't tell which is laid on which and guess it is a constant battle, piss on bleach, bleach on piss.

The receptionist sits behind her reinforced glass screen stained with spit and pockmarked where patients have tried to break through in their anger at being kept waiting. She doesn't look up from her screen for a good five minutes, and the queue of the lost and ill grows long behind me.

Finally, she deigns to notice me. "Yes?"

"Can I see the doctor?"

"What's the problem?" She delivers the words in a tone that leaves me in no doubt that she doesn't give a damn what the problem is.

I feel my anger rise, despite my heaving stomach and shaking hands. "That's none of your business. I'll tell the doctor."

She blinks impassively. "I need to know what the matter is before I can book you in."

"It's private."

I see her smirk. Now, she probably thinks it is a sexually transmitted disease or drug addiction. With the shivers going over me, maybe she isn't so far wrong about the second.

Eventually, she takes my name and tells me to sit and wait for the next slot.

There are six doctors in the surgery who are massively overworked. Each patient seems to get around five minutes before the next one is sent in. People crowd the waiting room. In fact, there is no room for me to sit, so I stand by an empty watercooler. The room is humid and stinks of stale bodies and illness. People cough incessantly. When I look around at my fellow patients, I see pale skin and bloodshot eyes. Thin children whine, tugging at their mothers' hands. Maybe this is what the government thinks they deserve for being poor. But the truth is probably no one thinks about it at all.

After three hours waiting, I give up. It seems other patients are being prioritised before me. At first, I'm angry, then I realize it is probably fair. There are a lot of people in there, sicker than I am, no matter how much I sweat and shiver.

I run to the unhygienic clinic toilet to retch again before I leave the surgery.

On the street outside, I check my phone to see if Miranda has left a message. I stare at the screen as if willing her face to appear. When it doesn't, I decide I will travel over to Romford to see her. That means getting down to Liverpool Street station. The line doesn't cross into

Inner London anymore, so at least I won't be slowed down by a document check.

It takes around two hours to get to Romford. I feel rough and my hands are shaking, but I've figured out by then I'm not going to die. Images of gleaming Soma in its syringe taunt me as visions of water taunt a man in the desert. It is true. One shot and I'm addicted.

I have only been to Miranda's house one previous time for a party. She lives on her own there. It is in a dangerous-looking estate, but I don't hesitate as I leave the station. I want to see her. Dodgy looking people stand on street corners or lurk in filthy bus shelters. At least it is still daylight and I should see any attackers coming before they jump me, not that I have anything to steal.

A small gaggle of ten-year-old street rats pelts me with pebbles until I turn and growl and they run off shrieking with laughter.

Miranda's flat is the top one in the end house in a cul-de-sac. As I approach it, I see two black vehicles parked outside. They look too expensive to belong to anyone who lives in this area. On instinct, I stop and step back against the wall, pulling up my hood, looking like just another junkie.

As I watch, the door to Miranda's flat opens and four men come out bearing between them a long wooden box. It looks like it has something heavy inside.

I put my hand against the wall to stop myself from falling. I watch the men's businesslike progression with the box.

It can't be true. How can you die in a game? But if I can be addicted to a potion made of pixels, maybe it is true the game can kill you too.

The men put the black box into the black van. Both vehicles have discrete logos on them just below the front door windows on both sides. In a very neat silver pattern on black, designed by one of the best designers in the United States, is the logo of Miskatonic games.

The men are dressed in paramilitary style uniforms with high military boots and black trousers, black flak jackets, and caps. They wear sunglasses even though there is no sun. I guess they have real-time Heads Up Displays showing in the glasses identifying any threat around.

Their weapons are holstered. They feel no reason to brandish arms, clearly feeling in complete control of the situation. As I watch, they get into their vehicles and drive away.

I turn to watch them go, but they pay me no attention. When they've gone, I feel grief like a kick in the guts. There is no body, no news of her passing, but I know she's gone with them. The world spins round. I don't know what to do, but then, mind still racing, thinking out all the possibilities, I hurry up the steps to Miranda's door and knock. The sound of my knuckles on the wood is like rapping on an empty coffin. I call her name through the door, though by now I don't expect her to answer. Tired of knocking, I rest my head on the door, then I try the handle, and the door opens.

I step inside Miranda's apartment. The flat is about as large as mine, but in much better condition. Miranda made efforts to keep the place tidy. The place smells of lemongrass from an infuser, and it smells of her.

As if scared to go in further, I stand in the open door and shout her name. When no one replies, I hurry in, then scout around the flat. There are three rooms, including a tiny bathroom. In her bedroom, her bed is unmade, and she isn't in it. In the living room/kitchen there is an unwashed plate beside the sink. Then I realise there is no sign of her gaming rig — no neural net, no virtual reality goggles, and no bottle of inducer tablets. These things must have been here, but they aren't now.

I make it to the toilet before vomiting noisily, but once again only bile comes. Wiping my mouth, I have a hopeful thought. Maybe she's gone to her mother's in the country. I believe that for a minute, at the most two. Then I believe the truth of what Aleister Crowley told me. Miskatonic have cleared up her body like they are clearing up a mistake.

When it becomes known the game is causing deaths, no one will play, surely? But I know the corporations have such money, and with that comes political influence. They can get away with causing deaths, they have done for years. Things simply won't be reported and websites and individuals mentioning inconvenient facts will disappear. Like a game of rock, paper, scissors; money always beats truth.

I close the flat door behind me, a knot like wood in my throat, and tears streaming down my face. I stop halfway down the steps and look back just in case I might see her face in the window.

I'm about to leave the cul-de-sac when I see I'm being watched by an Indian woman holding a baby. She is dressed as if she is standing in some bazar in Rajasthan. She is clearly an immigrant to this godforsaken place. If where she's come from is a worse hellhole than here, then God save her.

As I walk by, she says, "Are you a friend of hers?"

I pause. It is unusual for anyone to talk to you these days unless they are trying to sell you something. I check. She really is talking to me. I clear my throat. "Yes."

"I'm sorry for your loss."

"I don't know she's dead. Just she's missing," I say as if saying it might make it true.

"Did you not see them?"

I rub my cheek. "The men?"

She nods. Her baby squalls and she holds it tight. Then she speaks again, her words certain. "She's dead. That was a Cold Wagon."

A crow lands on a flat roof to our right and watches us with its beady eyes. For a minute, I think I'm in-game and the crow is a spy. Looking at the woman I say, "A Cold Wagon?"

She stares. "When they're dead, they send the Cold Wagons. I don't know where they take them. If they're still alive but have no minds, they send the Warm Wagons. That's what we call them round here: the Warm Ones. They sit them in the back seat, between two of the men dressed in black, and they drive away. I think they go to different places."

"Who goes? Which different places?"

She shrugs. "The Warm Wagons and the Cold Wagons. They're always coming round here. There are so many gamers. They spend all their money on the games. I think it's worse than heroin. And when it happens ..."

I study her. She pities me. She thinks I'm on my way to being like Miranda.

"... when it happens," she says. "They send a Warm Wagon or a

Cold Wagon. That's all I'm saying. I don't know where they go." She fixes me with her warm brown eyes. The cold wind blows discarded papers, and a plastic bottle rattles along the pavement. I'm shivering again.

'All is Brahman,' she says. 'Remember that. But I'm sorry for your loss."

I watch the woman go into her shabby flat and close the door behind her. I hear the chains rattling as she makes sure no one can get in.

When she's gone, I double up in pain, sweat pouring from me. I support myself against the wall until the worst pangs have gone. I need to get back into the game. I need more Soma.

Chapter Thirteen

THE QUEST OF THE RED POWDER

My stomach hurts like hell but I manage to get back to my flat from Miranda's house. I put on my neural net, then my goggles, and plug myself in. I put a tablet into my mouth and descend into the dream. I wake up again in the game and I'm still sweating

I logged off in Crowley's flat and when I reappear he's waiting for me. Beside my chair is a handwritten note. I glance down.

"That was delivered for you," he says.

I pick it up, curious. Who could be sending me letters? I unfold it and see scrawling writing. *"I'm here but becoming. It is so cold. Snow and gold. Miss. Mira ..."* It has to be from Miranda. But it's garbage, what does she mean? Why doesn't she write sense? I rub cold sweat from my forehead. At least she's not dead.

"Oh, my dear boy, you do look rather ill." His face has mock concern on it.

The two-faced bastard. "Did you know the Soma would do this to me?"

He nods and folds his hands. "Of course. But don't worry, the first time is the worst. The first time you get hit by withdrawal rather quickly. You should have a good twenty-four to forty-eight hours before you start to feel ill next time."

I'm angry. "Why did you give it to me?"

"The Soma? You didn't want to go around seeing things, did you?"

He's right of course. It was my choice to let him inject me, but I'm not ready to forgive him. "You said there are other ways to restore Sanity."

He yawns. "Yes, there are. But you seemed the fidgety type. Soma is the quick route to salvation."

"It feels more like damnation." I don't want more Soma, but at the same time, I'm desperate for it. "Is there any other potion that can restore Sanity?"

Crowley rubs his chin. "Not really. You could meditate, but that can be tedious for someone as impatient as you. And of course, the Soma brings you back to me. It means you won't forget our little bargain."

I lean forward, shaking. "Give me a shot now."

"You're forgetting your manners, Adam."

Through gritted teeth I say, "Please."

"That's better." He winks and modulates his normally aristocratic tones to mock Cockney. "Good manners don't cost nothing, do they?"

He goes to his desk and I watch with rapt attention as he produces a syringe. He does it with a flourish, like he's drawing it out to torture me. As I watch, it crosses my mind he should have sterilized the needle in boiling water, but I don't care. I hold up my arm and feel the puncture. Then all my troubles are removed. Once again life is blissful. I enjoy the golden streaming feeling the Soma gives me and when I come back to him, I'm smiling.

He nods like a wicked uncle. "It's wonderful, isn't it?"

I'm still grinning.

"Well Mr Level Two. You won't want to leave it there. The world is your oyster. So many adventures to be had. And they all begin outside my front door."

I remember Miranda and even through the Soma bliss I feel her loss. "Is there a way, I can check if someone's in the game?"

He dismisses me. "That's player stuff. I know nothing about it. Ask a player. I'm sure there will be a way, but for now, go and get more quests. Level up! That's what your sort want, isn't it?"

My emotions are mixed up so much, I don't know what I feel. I feel happy, buoyed up on a wave of fool's gold. And I'm back in the game and full of Soma. I'm excited.

I look down to see I am still dressed in my clerical garb. I want to go out and explore. I want to get more quests and get better until I'm truly powerful. I take my hat and coat without a backward look at Aleister and hurry down the stairs and open the front door into 1927 London.

I can't forget about Miranda. I need to find her, but the knowledge just sits there, temporarily wrapped in cotton wool. I feel no urgency. I wander around, still feeling good from my recent Soma hit. I'm enjoying the architecture, watching the people on the streets and looking out for masked men. I think I see one but he ducks into an alley before I can be sure. I even smile at that.

I want to level up. I even kid myself that's the best way to help Miranda. The drug laughs at me; Miranda who?

I'm amazed. The place is full of quests. It's a whole new world. I walk down Tottenham Court Road, and I've just crossed Cambridge Circus, standing with the Welsh Baptist church to my right when a man steps out of the shadows and says, "Excuse me, I wonder if you could help me?"

I stop. He has a golden goblet above his head. With a beaming smile I say, "Of course!"

The man frowns. "I've a bit of a problem. I'm afraid."

This is how it goes. I laugh. "I hope I can help you with it."

"I don't like to ask ..." He looks sheepish.

I tap his arm. "You stopped me on the street, so you clearly do like to ask."

He steps back and a faint smile appears on his face. "The truth is, I'm a bit down on my luck."

I have a little money left in my pocket, if that's what he wants. The bulk of the £5 from character creation plus the £20 I got for completing the quest of the Green Statuette. But there must be more to this than money.

He says, "I wonder if I could sell you something?"

"Ah," I say.

"You're a man of the church. A learned man ..."

I narrow my eyes. What's coming now?

Suddenly he thrusts out a pamphlet to me. "I found this in a second-hand shop. I paid a ha'penny for it, but it's much more valuable than that."

I scrutinise the pamphlet. "What is it?"

"It's an old book from the last century. It has chemical formulas in it."

I look him in the eye. "How much do you want for it?"

"I was thinking sixpence?"

I'm good for sixpence. I reach into my pocket and pull out a silver sixpence, just like they used to put in Christmas Puddings. "Here you are."

He gives me the pamphlet with a smile. "Thank you so much, Reverend."

When he's gone. I open the pamphlet to the first page. It isn't a treatise about chemistry at all; it's an alchemical recipe. As I flip the pages, it seems to talk about the Red Powder and the White Powder.

As I open the book to the middle, a message appears on my HUD:

<You have begun the Quest of the Red Powder>

At that, the social panel starts blinking on my HUD. I select it mentally and I see a list of people who are questing in London. No one seems to be on this quest, which is odd. I don't mind. I've always played games on my own. I toy with joining a group, but am about to decide against it and close the social panel when I get a personal message.

Ailsa Craig: I see you're doing the Quest of the Red Powder. I've just started. I think it's easier with more than one. You want to join up?
   Me: Not sure.
   Ailsa Craig: Okay. Don't worry. Bye.

I clearly waited too long. I think it through. I'm so green, I could probably do with the help. Plus, the first glow of the Soma is wearing off. I send a message back to Ailsa Craig.

Me: I'm really new. I don't know what I'm doing. I'd like to join up.

Ailsa Craig: Oh great. Meet me at Trafalgar Square?

I tell her I will and start walking down Tottenham Court Road towards Leicester Square. Even though I work in Inner London the route is not familiar. People like me aren't encouraged to stray within the guarded area, so I've never just wandered. I follow my HUD map and I come down past the National Portrait Gallery to my right with St Martin-in-the-Fields standing over to my left. A poor looking man stands there selling matches. That is in 1927. In 2027, he wouldn't be allowed there. Round the corner, is the large expanse of Trafalgar Square with its tall column and Admiral Nelson standing on the top.

I'm astounded by the crowds of player characters milling around here. All have their names lit up and there appear to be hundreds of them. I wonder how I'll find Ailsa Craig when approaching from the right, in front of the National Gallery is a woman whose name glows orange instead of the blue everyone else has. That must indicate we are grouped together.

She comes up and stops. "You must be Adam Cadmon? Or should I say Reverend Cadmon. I take it you're playing a priest, or you're in disguise!" She puts a hand to her mouth to stifle her laughter. I'm not sure what's so funny, but I smile.

She's not dressed as a typical 1920s flapper girl would be. I examine her avatar. She's midtwenties with mousy brown hair and pale-green eyes. She wears a crown of flowers in her hair and an art deco bangle hangs loose around her wrist. Her look screams out she is trying to be bohemian.

I make some apology about playing a priest. "I didn't really know what to pick as a profession. When I got asked, the life story just came out of my mouth and he said this was the most appropriate role for me."

"Or", she says, "your subconscious picked the role of the priest. There must be something in you that wants to minister to a flock and lead them on a spiritual journey. Perhaps you want to be a messiah?"

I don't know whether she is being serious. I don't want to be rude so I say, "Maybe you're right."

We stand there in an awkward silence. I sense she thinks she's been rude, which she has, but I want to put her at her ease. "And what's your profession?"

She grins. There's something very girlish about her, maybe she's younger in real life. "I'm a clairvoyante. I put all my skill points into Clairaudience and Clairsentience. I read a wicked pack of cards." She smiles winningly. "And I also have put quite a few points into Mediumship."

This is interesting. I need to learn all about the game. "How does that work?"

"I hold a séance and I contact the dead. They talk to me."

"I mean—does it work?"

She nods rapidly. "Absolutely. I've had some great results."

"The real dead?"

She looks puzzled. "What do you mean the real dead?"

"Dead players?"

She raises one eyebrow. "Dead players?"

She doesn't know, and I'm not telling her. "Never mind." I change the subject. "What level are you?"

She smiles again. She is an affable girl. "I'm Four. This is a Level Two to Six quest."

"How far have you got with it so far?"

She smiles ruefully. "I got the pamphlet. I've read it. I haven't done much with it."

On instinct, I say, "How's your Sanity?"

"Fine." She shakes her head. "I hear it can be a problem for some people, but I've managed to keep it pretty high. I'm still ninety-five."

I wonder how she's managed that. "Do you think we'll manage on our own?"

She wrinkles her nose. "I don't think so. I think we'd better get a couple more. Or at least one."

I glance up at the HUD and open the social panel. "How do we pick someone? There aren't many people on this quest. Any in fact. That's odd."

"It's a special quest. Not open to everyone."

"Really?"

She nods. "We're special."

I'm not sure about that. I ask who she thinks we need.

"Well," she says, "you're a priest and I'm a clairvoyante. I think we'd better have someone with a gun."

It's on the tip of my tongue to tell her I have a gun in my pocket, but I don't.

She warbles on. "I think we should look for a private eye. That will be a good addition to the party skills. Then maybe a healer."

"I've got a healing spell."

"Level Two?"

"Yes."

"Then, you won't have much healing." I think she's mocking me, then she pats me reassuringly on the shoulder. "I'm just playing with you. It's good you have a healing spell, but we still need a gunman."

"Any ideas who?" Maybe we just pick someone and tell them where to get the quest. I check my HUD. The social list is long. The profession icons mean little to me.

"Maybe a private eye. Just look at the list and pick the first one."

We both turn our eyes up and scroll through the names of the players. Everybody's profession is on there but as icons. Ailsa sees someone and sends a message. This guy is joining our group.

Christian Le Cozh: Where to meet?

Before I can respond Ailsa sends: Trafalgar Square, on the north side, just outside the front entrance to the National Portrait Gallery.

Le Cozh: Okay. I'll be right there.

In fact, it was ten minutes before he was there. In the meantime, Ailsa tells me all about her real-life home in Kent, where she lives with her rich parents, and rides horses. She's really quite young. And rich. Despite the social gulf between us, it's hard not to like Ailsa. She's so innocent and her enthusiasm drives everything before it.

Le Cozh comes walking towards us from the same direction Ailsa had. His name glows orange to indicate he's part of our group.

<Christian Le Cozh/ Level 4 Private Eye/ XXXXX>

The third space in the name sequence is blurred. I get his name, his profession and level. The third space is for his guild, but for some reason he's not revealing that. Mysterious but suspicious? I don't know.

When he gets up to us, I say, "You're here for the Quest of the Red Powder, right?"

He looks me coldly up and down. "That's what the lady invited me for."

Ailsa grins at him.

Le Cozh immediately takes charge. "There's a pub down there. The Sherlock Holmes, on Whitehall." He nods at the crowds of player characters standing round chattering. "Let's get through this bunch of fucking idiots."

Le Cozh leads the way as he elbows through the crowds of players. There are also lots of vendors here. As well as NPCs, it looks like player characters have set up stalls and are auctioning quest items they don't want. We don't have time to stop, but there are some interesting looking guns on one stall, and on another some weird magical stuff.

The Grand Hotel is on the corner of Whitehall and we pass that then the Colonial Club. The Sherlock Holmes is just before the Turkish Baths. We enter the warm hubbub of the bar.

Le Cozh says. "I'll get the table. I'll have a pint of bitter, if you're going to the bar."

Ailsa smiles sweetly at me. "I'll get them in next time. I'll have a gin and tonic please, Reverend."

"Just call me Adam." All this Reverend stuff is getting on my nerves.

I like the way they left me to buy the drinks. When I look over my shoulder, Ailsa and Le Cozh are getting on famously. I instantly dislike him, but I must admit he looks every inch the private eye with his Macintosh and his Trilby. I take the drinks back to the table and find them deep in conversation about the Quest of the Red Powder.

Le Cozh takes his drink without a thank you. "Have you read the pamphlet?"

I shake my head. "I haven't had time."

He nods, as if he'd worked this out about me the moment we met. I stand there feeling judged. He looks up at me sharply. "Are you going to sit?"

I sit at the table and sip my beer. I don't like him. Now I'm sure of it.

He pushes back his hat to reveal his lined forehead. His hair is dark brown and his eyes brown. He has a long, lean face and an aquiline nose. He looks like the kind of avatar someone has designed to resemble themselves in real life.

"So," he says. "The first clue is Dr John Dee."

"Aha!" Ailsa says with a girlish giggle. "I've heard of him."

I have too—vaguely. I leave Le Cozh to explain. He clearly likes explaining, and he certainly likes the sound of his own voice.

Le Cozh takes a sip of beer. He's halfway down his glass already. Then he begins the lesson. "I researched the quest. Dr John Dee was an Elizabethan magician, mathematician, and alchemist. At one point, he was very much in favour with Queen Elizabeth I, but as time went on he did something and she didn't like him so much. Not sure what. So, desperate for money he teamed up with a charlatan clairvoyant. I guess they would call them a seer in those days. This guy was called Edward Kelley and he was a complete rogue. Before he met Dee in the fifteen seventies, he'd been convicted of forgery and had his ears cropped which was the punishment in those days, and he had also been involved in necromancy."

"Sounds like a lovely man," Ailsa says with a giggle. "Good quest though."

Le Cozh continues. "Where the Red Powder comes in is Kelley convinced Dee finding the Red Powder would solve all their monetary problems. With it he suggested they could make the Elixir of Life, or a tincture to turn ordinary metal into gold. Reports differ."

I have a sudden thought and sit forward. "The Elixir of Life? Can that bring the dead back to life?"

Le Cozh shrugs. "Who knows?"

Ailsa's eyes gleam. "It would be wonderful if it could. I mean in the game."

If it could bring the dead back to life in the game, could it resurrect them in the real world? Could the impact of the game on real life work like this? But it's a stupid thought. A hopeless thought. I'm not even sure she's dead. After all, I got that letter.

His sermon delivered, Le Cozh takes a long draught of beer then wipes his mouth with the back of his hand.

I say, "So, where do we find Dee or Kelley?"

Ailsa gives a clap. "Well I do remember this from the pamphlet. Dee lived at Mortlake."

"Mortlake, Surrey?" I ask.

She nods.

"That's not far."

"Should we go there now?" Ailsa says. I can see how excited she's getting.

It's hard to read Le Cozh's expression. Something tells me he chooses to look pissed off all the time. He probably thinks it makes him look cool.

Le Cozh shrugs. "We can go now. Fine by me."

So it looks like we're going to Mortlake. He's the man with the gun. Seems it makes him the leader. As we're going out of the pub, I suddenly say, "Le Cozh, I want to put some skill points into Pistols. Can you teach me?"

Ailsa giggles. "Oh, Reverend Cadmon, you are a man of surprises! Who would have thought you'd want a gun!"

Le Cozh says laconically, "Sure. But probably not in the pub."

Smart arse. Ailsa seems delighted with him. I hope they're happy together. Just this quest, just to see whether this Elixir of Life can bring the dead back to life. I don't know—maybe when you die in the game they keep you somewhere so if you're resurrected you come back. I watch them laughing. After this quest, I'll strike out on my own again. I should have trusted my instincts and not joined a party.

We turn up Whitehall then down the Strand heading for Waterloo Station and the train to Mortlake.

Chapter Fourteen

THE RIVERMEN'S ARMS

Waterloo station is impressive. The graphics and the work they've put into making it 3D and real is stunning. The arches and circles of iron-work go way up, and I see silhouettes of pigeons shuffle in the shadows. It even smells of coal and smoke. I learn from the Wiki that Waterloo is only newly opened in 1922. The letters of the London and South Western Railway are displayed on the stained-glass windows.

Le Cozh seems to know where he's going and leads us through the busy station concourse.

I look up at the station clock, circular with black hands on a wide face, as it ticks away the seconds, suspended above the main station waiting area.

We purchase our tickets at the ticket office, then board the train from Platform 7 that's heading to Reading. There's a map in the carriage which shows all the stations on the line and I see Mortlake is just after North Sheen. We have second-class tickets and we sit in a compartment on our own, just us three. I don't mind which way I face, but Ailsa says she wants to face the way the train is going.

I sit, curiously excited, as the train builds up its head of steam. The guards on the platform whistle as the last passengers climb on board. Then with a judder the train starts to move. I've never been on a steam train before. I can't resist opening the window and sticking my head out. Le Cozh looks at me and raises his eyebrows but he doesn't say anything.

Suddenly I pull my face in because sparks and dust carried in the stream of steam get in my eye. One mote burns and I'm wiping it out when Ailsa offers me her cotton handkerchief.

The journey takes around twenty-five minutes and I count the stations down until the train comes to a halt and the guard on the platform announces, "Mortlake. All passengers for Mortlake disembark."

Mortlake station is in the centre of the village. In these days the village is separated from London by fields and orchards. Leaving the station, I buy a newspaper, I can't resist it. The detail of the game is phenomenal. There's a story about Adolf Hitler making his first public speech after the Bavarian government lifted a ban on him. In Texas, a law against black people voting is declared unconstitutional. Out of the station, we walk along the High Street past the White Hart pub. The barman comes out to collect glasses that someone's left on the table outside.

Ailsa says, "Excuse me, we understand the Elizabethan mathematician Dr John Dee used to live in Mortlake?" In real life, the question would be absurd, but this is a game and the guy takes it in good part. He rubs both his hands on his white apron. "I wouldn't know much about that. I don't know much about mathematicians."

I wonder who scripted that. He must have laughed as he put the words in the mouth of a barman NPC.

Le Cozh is habitually irritated. He glares at the guy. "Come on. It's probably the most interesting thing ever happened to this godforsaken place."

The barman narrows his eyes. "I don't like your tone."

Le Cozh's hard-face doesn't change. He doesn't care that the NPC doesn't like his tone. "Where's Dr John Dee's house? Simple as that."

The barman shrugs. "It's knocked down now. It was between the church and the river."

"Thank you," Le Cozh says. "That wasn't too hard, was it?" The man sneers and walks back into the pub.

"Got a way with people, haven't you?" I say.

Le Cozh laughs to himself but doesn't reply.

As we walk on Ailsa says, "So he did know! Why wouldn't he tell us?"

Before I can reply, Le Cozh says, "Some people are just assholes."

"Even NPCs," I say.

Ailsa blushes. I don't think she's used to swear words. "Well, he must've been programmed to be like that," Ailsa says.

Le Cozh smiles. "You have a way of seeing the best in people. Even when it's not justified."

We're walking along the High Street parallel to the river, but we can't see the river except when there are breaks in the houses. Some of the houses look really old here. When we get up to the church, I look around. "So, it's supposed to have been between the church and the river and just opposite the church." I point to a much more modern house. "It must have been there."

"No shit, Sherlock," Le Cozh says.

I turn. "Like I said, you have a way with people—an unpleasant one."

He's taken his hat off and smiles and twirls his hat between his fingers. "I don't know I'm being unpleasant. I'm just being me."

"Maybe the two are the same thing?"

Ailsa holds up a hand. "Boys! We've got a job to do. Let's get on with the quest."

She's right. I do my best to ignore Le Cozh. "So," I say, "Dee's house was knocked down. I don't know what we expected, anyway."

Ailsa says, "The pamphlet just said Dee lived here. That's our only lead."

I say, "But these quests are meant to be solved. There must be some way of progressing."

Le Cozh points. "There's a pub there. The Rivermen's Arms. It's about time for another drink."

As we set off, I say "I didn't think you could be an alcoholic in a game."

Le Cozh ignores me. Ailsa laughs. I continue, "But it's very real—this game. What you do here really affects you. Maybe you can get

addicted to virtual beer." I'm hinting at death in the game, but neither
of them show any sign they realise that.

But it's true what I say about the beer. I remember feeling a vague
alcohol buzz from my pint of beer in London. It's astounding how they
manage that, but they do.

Le Cozh is way ahead. We follow him into the rather dingy pub. It
looks Victorian, but there are signs it's older—the warped walls and
uneven ceiling in between heavy beams. A couple of locals sit round
the bar and they're clearly drawn to look inbred and moronic. They
have brown hoods up, as if they're frightened of showing their faces.

The place smells damp. I step up to the bar and the barman says
without a smile, "What'll it be?"

He's staring at Ailsa and I realise it's unusual for women to be in a
public bar in 1927.

As if reading my thoughts, the barman points. "The saloon bar's
through there. I'm sure your wife will prefer that."

I'm about to protest Ailsa isn't my wife, when I remember being in
a pub with a woman who isn't your wife is even more scandalous than
if you're married.

Le Cozh nods at the barman. "I think she would prefer to go to the
other bar. Your clientele don't look up to intelligent conversation."

An oaf in a brown hood grunts. Le Cozh and Ailsa go through to
the Saloon Bar. I order two pints of bitter and gin and tonic and carry
the three drinks through after them. We sit and I sip the beer, wiping
the froth from my top lip. I glance around at the tobacco-stained walls
and ceiling. The place looks ancient. "I figure this pub has been built
on the site of Dee's house, or pretty near to it."

For once Le Cozh doesn't argue.

Ailsa says, "Usually in this game, you get clues through books or
even interrogating NPCs, but the NPCs here don't seem to know
anything and there are no books." She smiles winningly. "I don't know
where we go from here."

"We don't know what the NPCs know."

"The barman at the other pub wasn't very helpful."

I stand. "I'll go and ask the guy here, if you like."

Le Cozh shrugs. "You go, I'll wait here with Ailsa."

The barman looks blankly at me when I ask about Dee, surly even. His home town boys say nothing, just sip their warm beer and play dominoes. I return to Ailsa and Le Cozh and tell them the results.

"Thanks for going, though. It was worth checking." Ailsa beams up.

Le Cozh says, "We could have a dig around the village. Perhaps there's some clue in the churchyard. Is Dee buried in the church?"

I don't know, but I must admit it isn't a bad idea. There may be something in the church that'll give us a further clue in the Quest of the Red Powder.

Le Cozh knocks back his pint and I leave mine. Ailsa has long finished her G&T. She drank it fast, and I wonder if she's nervous. Night has fallen when we step outside. Once again, I'm reminded that game time is faster than real-life time.

The church is just by the Main Street and there's an electric light on its porch which casts a yellow glow over the ancient tombstones. We walk through the lichgate and up the stone-flagged path to the church door. The wooden door isn't locked when I try the handle, though there's a handwritten notice on it asking us to close the door after us to make sure birds don't come in and get trapped.

"Oh, I don't like the sound of that," Ailsa says. "I'm frightened of birds."

"They're not real birds," Le Cozh says. "This is just a game. Nothing is real here."

Except maybe your death. I remember Miranda and am guilty I've forgotten her. I'll do this quest, learn more about the game and go and look for her.

It's dark inside the church. The yellow sodium light from outside slants in through old windows and gives hardly any light; the darkness is so thick you can almost taste it. Something scurries and Ailsa starts back. Le Cozh grabs her elbow and they both laugh. "A mouse?" he says.

It was a pretty big mouse from the sound. I listen, but silence reigns now. The interior smells of Bibles and damp wood. Le Cozh pulls an electric torch from his inventory and flashes it around the church. I guess we're looking for some inscription mentioning Dee, something to explain why the quest has brought us here. After fifteen minutes of walking between the pews and shining the light on old brasses, we accept there's no such inscription in the church.

"Outside then?" Ailsa says. "We could look at the gravestones."

We spend a further thirty minutes looking around the tombstones in the churchyard, meticulously row after row of stones that teeter like bad teeth, or that have fallen long since and are now fringed with rank grass. There's nothing there either.

Once again, I hear that noise. Whatever it was, is in the graveyard now. It makes me nervous. I peer round in the dark. Le Cozh is watching me, but I don't let on I've heard anything. I don't want to give him any more excuses to mock me.

Eventually Ailsa says, "This is so frustrating."

Then I have a thought. "You say you have Mediumship skills?"

Ailsa nods and realises what I'm suggesting. "That's a very good idea, Adam. I wonder if this is the way to get the clue?"

Le Cozh shakes his head. "There must be some other way of solving this. Not every player will have skills in Mediumship. They can't count on that. It wouldn't be fair."

I feel my temper fraying. "Well, if there's another way, we haven't found it. Let's go with this." I think he's against the idea just because it was me who suggested it.

Ailsa strokes his arm. "Come on, Christian. Give me a chance."

He smiles and says something I don't hear, but she laughs. That's par for the course. We make our way back to the street.

Outside the yellow splash of streetlight, it's pitch-black now. We walk down the High Street and stand around, not knowing where to go.

Le Cozh stares at me. "A séance, eh? You can't be suggesting we hold a séance in the middle of the street?"

"We could go back to the pub," Ailsa says.

I glance over to the Rivermen's Arms. It looks even more rundown now it's dark.

Le Cozh says, "That dump?"

Ailsa grins. "Maybe they've got a room they could hire out to us. We could say we're the Historical Society meeting. Or, I don't know, a traveling bridge club?"

Whatever she says amuses him. He shrugs. "Or Russian secret agents?" That makes her giggle.

We go back to the pub and I ask the landlord whether he has a room we could use for a meeting. The place has got no fuller in our absence. The same hooded guests sit around the tables in the gloom. The smell of fish and rivers is almost overpowering.

"We got a room," he says. "It'll cost you a shilling to hire."

That seems steep, I'm about to haggle when Le Cozh flips him a silver shilling coin. The barman catches it and with a fishy grin says, "Done. Just up the stairs. You can't miss it."

There's something about that guy I don't like. He even gives off a vague river smell like he's soaked in dirty Thames water.

We go up the creaky stairs. There's no carpet on them. Neither is there any carpet in the small room that serves as a function room. It overlooks the back of the pub over a sloping slate roof and towards the River Thames. I watch the river barges as they ply their trade up and down river, lights at their bows and sterns. The river smell is stronger here. The wallpaper is dingy and old. Good job we're not here for the ambiance.

We all sit. "So, how do you do this then?"

Le Cozh says, "I guess we hold hands. Would you like that, Adam?"

I ignore him. "What do we do, Ailsa?"

She says brightly, "We could hold hands?"

I take Ailsa's hand in my right and Le Cozh's in my left. Once again, the magic of the game makes it feel like I'm really holding warm human hands. I'm about to ask what we do next when I see Ailsa's eyes have already flicked closed. I look over to Le Cozh to see what he's thinking, but his gaze is fixed on Ailsa and doesn't acknowledge me.

We sit there for three minutes and I think nothing is going to happen when suddenly Ailsa speaks in a little girl's voice. "I am Madimi, my master won't let me stay long. How may I help you?"

Like he's been waiting for this, Le Cozh says, "Who is your master? Is it John Dee?"

Ailsa titters. In Madimi's voice she answers, "Oh, John Dee is not my master, but I know him."

I lean forward, still holding Ailsa's hand. "Is John Dee there?"

Ailsa turns her face towards me but doesn't open her eyes. Madimi says, "Old John Dee is here." Then as if she's addressing someone else, "Should we allow them to speak to him?"

Le Cozh says, "Who's 'we'?"

Ailsa stares at Le Cozh with her closed eyes. "That would be telling."

Le Cozh says, "Who do you work for? If it's not Dee, who is it? Who is your master?"

This isn't going the right way. It doesn't matter who Madimi's master is. We're on the Quest of the Red Powder. The only clue we have points to Dr John Dee. I don't even know why he's asking. I interrupt him, and he glares at me, but lets me talk. "Madimi, can you bring Dr John Dee? I would like to talk to him."

There's a pause of around twenty seconds until an older man's voice comes through, speaking archaic English. "What dost thou want, pray tell?"

"Are you Dr John Dee?"

"I am he. Who asks?"

I gave him my name.

"I do not know you. But you are a minister of the church? Are you here to save my soul?" Dee's voice sounds earnest and even beseeching. In Madimi's voice, Ailsa adds, "I think it has gone too far for that!"

Le Cozh asks, "Where are you? Are you in this room with us?"

"I am in hell," the old man's voice answers. "There is no escape for me. I listened to demons while I lived, and they tricked me."

Le Cozh is going to ask him something about these demons, I can see by the way he sits forward, his mouth already forming the question. Once again, I interrupt him. "Dr Dee, can you tell us about the Red Powder?"

Ailsa gives a hideous chuckle. It doesn't sound like Dee. There are others there with him wherever 'there' is. At least Madimi, Dr John Dee, and the author of this vile laughter. The phrase, 'for we are legion', comes into my mind.

"Be careful of them," Dee says. "They want your soul, like they wanted mine." A pause, then Dee says, "But there's a way to protect yourself."

A choking sound issues from the corner of the room. As if Dee was in the room with us and someone silenced him before he could tell us how to protect ourselves.

Dee speaks again. "Forgive me. I mis-spake."

Le Cozh turns to me, "They're letting him talk to us."

He's right. They're only allowing him to speak the words they want us to hear. I just need to know about the Red Powder. I clear my throat. "Dr Dee, can you tell us where we can find the Red Powder?"

"Kelley tricked me with that long ago."

Le Cozh says, "But where is it? Can we still find it?"

Dee's voice says, "In Glastonbury. In the ruins of the Abbey in Glastonbury you will find something that points."

Le Cozh says, "So the Red Powder is in Glastonbury Abbey?"

I shake my head. "He didn't say that. He says there's something in the ruins that will point."

Le Cozh is insistent. "Dr Dee—where can we find the powder itself?"

But instead of Dee, the girlish voice of Madimi answers. "Wouldst thou like to dance with me? We can dance round and round the table."

I try to ask a few more questions, but Madimi prattles rubbish about dancing in the waves and the sun setting over a field of bones.

Le Cozh takes his hat off and places it on the table. Breaking contact with my hand, he says, "I think that's all the sense we're going to get out of them tonight."

I say, "At least we got another clue—Glastonbury."

He nods. "Yes, we should go there." He glances at our medium. "Ailsa?"

Ailsa is still sitting there, her eyes shut. She hasn't spoken for a minute or two.

"Is she still in a trance?" Le Cozh asks. He looks worried.

I remember Miranda again. Panic flashes through me until Ailsa opens her eyes and says sleepily, "That was fun, wasn't it?"

I say, "Did you hear all that?"

She nods. "It felt like I had lots of people in my head. Not all of them spoke. Madimi—a little blonde girl of around eight was dancing around. Behind the curtain to the side there was a man—I think he was the master she referred to, but I couldn't see his face. Then another creature—that wasn't even human. That's who laughed. Edward Kelley was there too, but he just sat watching."

"Edward Kelley is Dee's sidekick, is that right?"

Ailsa nods. "Yes, Edward Kelley was Dee's medium for many years. He brought through the spirits that gave Dee the instructions in the angelic language."

"The angelic language?" Le Cozh says. "I bet that's a quest."

I laugh. "It'll be a high level one for later."

I hear the barman shout from downstairs. "Last orders, please. The bar will shut in fifteen minutes."

"Do you want another drink?" Le Cozh says.

"I can't believe it's already ten fifteen."

Ailsa says, "Time flies when you're having fun. Do you want to log off yet?"

Another drink will give us the time to think about our trip to Glastonbury, so I agree. Then I'll log off, I don't want to log off inside a locked building I can't get out of. Breaking out would certainly damage my Reputation score.

I go downstairs and walk up to the bar. I'm carrying our dirty glasses and stand there to get another round in. The barman pulls the pints from the hand pumps and reaches behind him to fill up Ailsa's gin and tonic. The game alcohol mimics the effect of real alcohol. Very clever. He hands me the light-brown frothy ale. I wink. "We'll drink it quickly, don't worry."

"I'm not worried," the man says. "There's no rush. The police won't be checking here. We'll have a lock-in."

"A lock-in?"

He squints at me. "Where are you from? Have you never had a lock-in before?"

To tell the truth, I haven't. I check the Wiki and it tells me a lock-in is a practice in out-of-the-way pubs in the United Kingdom after they're supposed to be closed. The barman draws the curtains and locks the pub doors and business goes on as usual. Even though they're breaking the law, it's generally tolerated if there's no rowdiness.

I take the drinks upstairs and Le Cozh is sitting near Ailsa. They're deep in conversation, all smiles. I give them the drinks and Ailsa sips her gin and tonic. "Thanks very much Adam."

Le Cozh tips his hat.

Ailsa says, "Christian tells me we can catch the train from Paddington station to Glastonbury. I guess if we go there tomorrow when we log back on, we can all meet in the station?"

It sounds reasonable.

Just then there's a knocking sound from downstairs. Ailsa raises her eyebrows but keeps drinking. Le Cozh doesn't even turn his head.

"Putting up a shelf?" I say.

That makes Ailsa giggle. More knocking and the sound of heavy furniture being dragged across the wooden floor.

I get up and go to the meeting room door and peer down the stairs. "What the hell are they doing?" There's no sign of anyone, but I can hear movement. It sounds like there are more people down there than there were before. "I wonder what they're shoving about down there."

Ailsa says, "Do you think they're smugglers? Maybe there's a secret tunnel to the river and the smugglers are bringing in their ill-gotten gains." She puts a hand across her mouth to stifle her giggles. The G&T must be kicking in. Le Cozh laughs along with her.

I go to sit at the table again and we're talking about what we might find in the ruins of Glastonbury Abbey, when there's further sound from downstairs. Scraping and dragging Something about it unnerves me. Le Cozh shrugs and I say, "You know we're locked in, don't you?" I'm talking fast, like I'm nervous.

Le Cozh says, "He'll let us out when he has to. He doesn't want us sitting here all night."

Ailsa laughs again. "Unless he's planning on murdering us!"

Le Cozh is all smiles, but I notice he takes out his pistol and places it on the table. Seeing me look, he says, "I'll give you those shooting lessons tomorrow."

I nod. "That would be good."

Then the lights go out.

Ailsa shrieks.

In measured tones, Le Cozh says, "It must be a fuse."

I say, "Our cue to leave, I think, though." I place my pint glass still half-full on the table. Some light comes in from outside. My hand goes to my Browning in my pocket. Reason says there's nothing to worry about. "It must just be the fuse."

"Most likely," Le Cozh says, but he still gets up, and he's holding his pistol.

I go to the top of the stairs and call. "Everything all right down there?"

There's no reply. I repeat my question, but silence fills the stairwell.

Ailsa says, "He's maybe going into the cellar to fix the fuse. The barman."

It makes sense.

"But what about all the others that were down there?" Le Cozh says. He's not as relaxed as he was.

I say. "It sounded like they were moving furniture or something. If the way down's blocked, how are we going to get out of this place?"

Le Cozh indicates the window where the gleam of the lights from the river barges is vaguely visible through the warped glass. "Through there."

I step over to the top of the stairs again. No one's come up, but I'm uneasy. It's pitch-black down there. The dragging sounds have gone, but I sense figures below me. There's someone moving up in the darkness. I call back to Le Cozh for his electric torch. He flashes the beam down the stairs and steps back. "What the fuck are those?"

Coming up are four hooded men. One hood has gone down and I see the man has gills at his neck and bulging white eyes.

If it didn't look so real, it wouldn't freak me out so much. "Fish men?" I say.

"A hybrid."

<You see something monstrous -5 SANITY>

The figures run up the steps and I slam the door shut in their faces. They batter and shove at the door, and it's all I can do to keep it closed. I mutter, "Step back, I'm going to shoot."

"You've got a gun?" Le Cozh asks.

"Yeah. I'll pull open the door and shoot." I hesitate. I want to time this right. I call over, "Ailsa, open the window and get onto the roof."

"I'll break my neck," she says.

"Please, just do it."

Le Cozh is behind me. He sounds more reasonable and less of a dick than he ever has. "Step back, Adam. I'm a better shot than you."

That's probably right. The door moves and threatens to come in as they charge. It nearly gives way, and it's taking all my strength to stop them getting through.

"I can shoot too," I say.

"Okay, okay, just move." He sounds very tense. Ailsa's by the window and she's got it open.

"Get out, Ailsa," I shout.

She's staring nervously out of the open window onto the dark roof. "What if there's more of them down there? I'm unarmed." And once again I remember if these things kill us we're really dead. I wonder if Le Cozh knows that. Ailsa didn't seem to.

"Move, Adam," he says.

I step back hurriedly and the door bursts in. In a panic, Ailsa clatters out and slides halfway down the roof. There's a loud flash and a bang, and Le Cozh fires into the hybrids. They moan and shriek as they come for us. One runs at me.

I fire.

<You hit eel-hybrid for 6 HEALTH>

I fire again and again.

<You hit eel-hybrid for 8 HEALTH>

<You hit eel-hybrid for 4 HEALTH>

Damn my poor Pistols score. I bet Le Cozh is doing much more than me. He seems to have killed at least one of them. I fire again and the first eel-man goes down.

<Critical hit: 4 x Damage 26 HEALTH>.

<You kill eel-hybrid.>

<50xp>

These are Level 2 mobs, it seems. Another rushes at me, its fish's mouth opening and shutting. Le Cozh pivots right and fires. He blows the eel thing's head right off.

"You're welcome," he says.

"Thanks, man."

He winks. He's enjoying himself. He's smiling.

More of them burst into the room. I fire again and again until my gun clicks. There are eight rounds in the magazine and I've fired them all, hitting about 40% of the time. I have a box of bullets in my inventory, but no time to reload. Le Cozh is by the window. He yanks my sleeve. "Time to leave."

I get the box of bullets from my inventory, but my hand is shaking and it's too dark. I can't reload. He hisses. "Adam, get the fuck out. Do that outside."

Another comes in and he fires twice, killing another eel-man, then reloads smoothly in the faint light of the window. There are more of them on the stairs, but they're waiting for their moment to rush us.

"Maybe it's true about the tunnel," he says. "There's more coming up the stairs than I counted in the bar."

I give up trying to reload and go to the window. Ailsa has put a chair by it to make it easier to get out. It nearly tips as I climb out onto the roof. The air is cold. A river mist clings to the slates, making them slippery. And I think you can probably die from falling in this game too.

Ailsa is on a flat roof just below. It must be over an extension. Behind me, Le Cozh is still in the room. I hear him blaze away and see the flashes of his pistol until he too joins us on the flat roof.

"I think we can get down the drainpipe." Ailsa goes to lower herself down. Then she stops. She whispers. "I hear something moving down there."

"Switch on Clairsentience, Ailsa," I say. I do likewise. Various coloured glows illuminate the mist. A green shape hurries by, but it's a cat.

Ailsa drops and I hear her land. I drop after her, then Le Cozh. We're down in the alley behind the pub. Looking right, I guess this way leads to the river. The left probably goes back to the High Street and the train station.

"Station?" I say.

Ailsa says, "The last train might have gone already."

"Worth a try," Le Cozh says, and we turn left then I see a mass of red through the fog.

"Not that way. Bad guys."

"Bad eels," Ailsa says, laughing, but it's nervous laughter. She's joking like death doesn't mean death. I think again; if she doesn't know, I'm not telling her.

We turn and hurry down towards the river. The crowd of red is closing on us from behind. I can hear their slapping feet on the damp ground as they run.

Le Cozh turns and fires into the darkness. That makes them halt. We go on. We're nearly at the river but our enemies are running again. Under a lone light at the back of someone's house, I reload. Le Cozh is crouching, Ailsa stands, not knowing what to do. She's not laughing now. Le Cozh fires. I turn to see the eel things glowing red are nearly on us, coming out of the fog. I fire.

<6,5,9,7 damage: kill - 50xp>

<7,3,6,6 damage: kill - 50xp>

And I'm out of bullets again.

"It's not a fucking shooting range," Ailsa shouts. She must be rattled if she's swearing.

I agree. "Let's go."

We turn and run.

My Exertion Meter on the HUD leaps up from Green to Amber. When it touches the Red, I notice I can't run as fast. I slow, panicking they're going to catch up, but then it drops into the Amber and I'm at normal speed again. I run as fast as I can without incurring a movement penalty from exhaustion.

Then we're at the lapping water of the River Thames by a wooden jetty.

"They're endless," Le Cozh shouts, firing again. I turn. There's a long river barge moored by the jetty.

"This?" I say.

Ailsa doesn't answer. She's jumped on it already and is untying the mooring rope.

All three of us get on board as the barge slips its moorings and drifts downstream.

< You have stolen something -10 REPUTATION >

The eel-men come to the jetty and launch themselves in the water.

"Ah yes, eels can swim," I say.

"The engine." Ailsa points. "Do you know how to start it?"

I shake my head.

Le Cozh says, "I've got skills in Mechanics. Let me."

Of course he does.

Le Cozh goes back and by yanking a string makes the two-stroke engine cough into life. It pulses and the barge moves faster. I go to the tiller. I have only the vaguest idea what I'm doing. Le Cozh comes up and says, "Let me."

"Don't tell me, you've got skills in Boats too?"

He nods.

I say to Ailsa, "I guessed he would."

Wreaths of mist hang on the water.

Le Cozh says, "Stand there. When you see an eel-man trying to get out of the water, fucking shoot him."

By the light of the houses that back onto the river, I'm able to reload again. I see ripples as the eel things swim after us. One tries to clamber in, but I shoot it in the head. I don't kill it, but it lets go of the barge. I fire into the water after it, but it's a waste of bullets and I'm going through ammunition too fast.

Another one comes up from the left. I turn and fire, and this time I score a critical hit.

I fire at another to finish it and:

<Critical hit: You hit Eel-Hybrid for 4 x Damage - 26hp>

<You kill eel-hybrid>

<50xp.>

We're moving faster than they can swim now because of the engine. When we reach Putney, they've let us be.

Chapter Fifteen

A TRAIN TO THE WEST COUNTRY

I don't go to work the next day. Instead I login to Darkworlds as early as I can and find Le Cozh and Ailsa are already online. It seems they're as bitten by the addiction as I am. I arrange to meet Ailsa and Le Cozh at Paddington station in time to catch the eight a.m. train to Bristol. It turns out Glastonbury isn't such an easy place to get to by train in 1927, or any other time come to that.

We have to catch the Great Western Railway from Paddington station and travel west as far as Bath. There we change to the Somerset and Dorset Railway and even then, we have to change one more time at Cole before taking the branch line west to Glastonbury and Street station.

After working out the route and buying the tickets after queuing with polite NPCs at the ticket office, we board our train, hear the engine build up steam and the platform rolls away behind us.

We leave the heart of the city then the suburbs. London is much smaller in 1927 and I'm amazed Acton is mostly fields. The March weather is heavy with sweeping showers of rain that clatter on the windows of the train as it puffs its way west. The trees are bare of their leaves and what cattle we see in the low-lying fields look half perished from the cold.

When we finally pull in at the end of a long journey, Glastonbury and Street station is to the west of the town centre. A row of taxis wait outside the station and we catch the first one in the line. Not knowing where we're going exactly, we ask him to drop us outside the Abbey ruins. When the cab pulls away, I look around. The place feels rural and old. Carts move around the streets and women nod to each other as they pass. There's also a strange atmosphere as if uncanny things happen here.

Although we don't technically need somewhere to stay the night, Ailsa thinks it will add to the atmosphere and persuades us we should book in somewhere to use as a base for our operations while we're in the town. We choose an ancient looking inn called the George and Pilgrims. My Wiki tells me it was founded in 1470 during the reign of Edward IV as an inn for visitors to the Abbey in the Middle Ages.

We walk through the grey stone entrance and I feel a drop in temperature and a strange sense of foreboding. Looking for the reception desk, we pass a row of dark snugs to the right where countrymen sit drinking cider. The bar is to the left and the reception desk of the hotel slightly in front of us. We're greeted by a severe looking woman in her fifties with pince-nez and greying blonde hair pulled up into a bun.

"Three rooms, is it?" Her obvious disapproval at whatever she imagines our preferred arrangements are causes Ailsa to burst into a fit of the giggles. The woman looks down her nose at Ailsa and regards her flower crown with disdain.

"Three rooms will be fine," I say.

Le Cozh nods. She gives us three keys and we sign our names in the guest book. I don't know what to put as my address so I put Crowley's apartment in Gower Street. Business done, the woman has no further interest in us. She returns to her ledger and lets us carry our bags upstairs with no further comment. GI grin. "What do you expect? It must be five hundred years old."

We each go to our rooms, and standing at the doors we agree we'll meet later and go out and look in the Abbey ruins together for any clues to the Red Powder. The others have things in the real world to do so they plan to logoff for a while. I have no desire to go back into my real life so I decide to look around the town.

The George and Pilgrims is at the bottom of the sloping High Street. It looks just like I'd imagine an English country town to look in the 1920s. There are cobblers shops and drapers shops as well as a tea merchant and a wine merchant. There's an ironmongers just opposite the church.

The church is dedicated to St John the Baptist and looks about the same age as the inn. I'm gratified when my Wiki tells me it's 15th Century though there are documentary records back to the 12th Century and probable Christian worship before that. There's a sign on the gate into the churchyard saying it's also the site of the Glastonbury Thorn. The Wiki is my greatest friend. The Glastonbury Thorn is a species of thorn tree that grows only in the Holy Land. A link from that page sends me to the associated legend.

The story is; Joseph of Arimathea brought the holy Thorn with him as his staff when he came to Glastonbury after the death of Christ. He's also supposed to have brought with him the Holy Grail—that vessel from which Christ and his disciples drank from at the Last Supper, which according to other legends was later used to collect the blood of Christ after he was pierced by the spear of Longinus as he hung on the cross. It seems unlikely to me Joseph of Arimathea ever came to Somerset, but what do I know?

From the churchyard, I look east and can just see the top of Glastonbury Tor. The strange sugarloaf shaped hill rises high above the surrounding flatlands. On its summit is a single mediaeval tower, all that remains of a mediaeval abbey church. The tower is named after Saint Michael, that angel who is to fight the great beasts that will come in the time of Revelations.

I turn to continue my journey along the High Street. At the top, is a T-junction where roads go left and right. On this corner, there's a chemist's shop and the skillfully painted sign on the outside says, 'William Cowper Apothecary'. More interesting than that is the glowing book icon that tells me a game trainer is to be found inside.

I go into the shop. I'm the only customer and there's no one standing behind the counter. Shelves at the back of the shop display chemicals and medicines in thick glass jars with silver writing. I guess they contain ingredients for making up into tablets and potions. There's a scale and various types of spoons and dispensers as well as flasks and measuring instruments. The poisons cupboard with its skull and cross bones is on the left-hand wall, locked up.

The shop must have some way of alerting the shopkeeper a customer has entered because a grey-bearded man clumps down the stairs in heavy boots. He wears a white shirt with a black waistcoat and a black jacket. His hair is long with a beard in the Victorian fashion. His hair is almost completely grey with the odd black streak. The chemist's face is irregular with a large hooked nose and eyes as brown and shiny as horse chestnuts.

"May I help you?" he says in his West Country English accent.

I point behind me to the door and the icon which is now invisible. "I see from the icon you offer training. Is that correct?"

They can't see icons of course, but he knows what I mean. He cocks his head like a blackbird and I think that's what he reminds me of—a curious wise bird. After consideration he says, "I am a trainer, yes. What would you like to learn?"

I ask him what skills he can teach.

He stares at me as if weighing me up and says, "Chemistry, Pharmacy, Herbology and Alchemy."

I ponder the alternatives. I've got skill points but I need to be focused. I say, "Alchemy sounds interesting. What does it allow me to do?"

He clears his throat as if delivering a well-prepared speech. I wonder how many times he's explained this to players. "Alchemy is the science of producing potions. I can teach you the basics of crafting potions, then, depending how many points you commit to the study, you will achieve mastery and can begin making recipes for yourself from ingredients you have researched."

Crowley hinted at this. "So, I can learn to make potions that restore my Health and Mana?"

He nods. "I can teach you the recipes. Then you need to get the ingredients for yourself."

"And can you teach me to make Soma—the potion that restores Sanity?"

The man scowls. "I wouldn't take that foul brew. Once you have the taste of it you always want more. Much better to meditate to regain Mana." He glances at my dog collar. "Or pray in your case, as a Christian minister."

As he speaks, I feel the first tugs of my craving for the Soma. The drug itself is miles away and the only supply I know of is kept by Aleister Crowley. It's likely before I return to London I will be doubled up with the griping pains of withdrawal and seeing God knows what kind of hallucinations. That makes my mind up—I will learn alchemy.

I know he's an NPC, but this guy seems nice. I say, "I'm sorry, I've been very rude—what do they call you?"

He looks at me like I'm a fool. "My name is in big letters on the outside."

I'm dumb sometimes. I smile and shrug. "Ah yes. William Cowper?"

"The very same."

"Well Mr Cowper I would like to put thirty points, into learning Alchemy."

A message appears on my HUD:

<William Cowper offers to teach you Alchemy. Do you accept?>

I select accept and the familiar routine begins. My teacher stares deep into my eyes and I enter a learning trance. All I hear is his pattering voice, the room and the world outside hardly exist anymore. He talks of sulphur and salt and quicksilver. He talks of the Prime Material and the Blackening. He talks of the Hooded Crow and the Death's Head. He talks of things beyond knowing, and the Philosopher's Stone then the lesson is finished.

I check my HUD for my new abilities:

<Create a basic HEALTH potion. It will restore 30 HEALTH points. Ingredients: spring water, bark of the silver birch, juniper berries. Cost to create one potion, 10 MANA points.>

<Create a basic MANA potion. It will restore 30 MANA points.
Ingredients: spring water, fly agaric mushrooms, hawthorn berries,
spiderweb. Cost to create one potion, 10 MANA points.>

It looks cool and I'm keen to make my first potion. "I just get these ingredients and put them together, spend the Mana points and I have the potion. Is that correct?" Then I think. "Will I be able to identify the herbs that are the ingredients?"

He shakes his head. "Not without Herbology."

I curse. This is getting complicated. I have a few skill points left, but I want to learn Pistols. "How many points to be able to identify the ingredients for these potions."

"Not many. They're low-level ingredients for basic level potions."

"So how many points?"

"In Herbology?"

I nod.

"Say, ten."

In fact that's all the skill points I have left. Lucky. I say, "Okay, let's go."

<William Cowper offers to teach you Herbology. Do you accept?>

I commit ten points, then I'm in his eyes again and he's muttering to me about the stamen and the calyx, about poultices and rubs, about habitats and grafting. Then we're done. I know a little more.

"So now do I have what I need to make the potions?"

He purses his lips. "Not exactly. You need a laboratory. You will need an alembic, a retort, test tubes, a Bunsen burner, and for some of the other potions, a sublimator to collect the vapour."

It sounds like it's going to cost me a fortune, and reminds me I need to make money so I can get my own place. Once I get my own flat, or even a house, I can set up an alchemical laboratory. But now, I don't know where I can make my potions. There must be somewhere or the skills are useless.

Once again, the NPC displays the uncanny ability to read my mind.

Either that or maybe I'm just predictable. Cowper says, "I have a laboratory in the back you can have the use of."

"Fantastic! That's really kind." Then I pause. "Can I ask you about something called the Red Powder."

He frowns. Something I've said has made him cautious. Finally, he strokes his chin. "The Red Power is one of the ingredients of the Elixir of Life. The Elixir is a high-level potion."

The Elixir of Life. He's someone who might know what it can do. "Can the Elixir bring the dead to life?"

He doesn't answer. He fixes me with his brown eyes and I continue, "I have a friend ... had maybe." I stop and start again. "Do you know about the Cold Ones?"

It's like a shadow covered the sun. He looks at me as if trying to work me out, or my allegiances maybe. I wait a while and realise he's not going to answer that question. Perhaps I need to build trust with him. Some games work like that.

I ask him again about the Red Powder. "There was mention of a White Powder too."

He nods. "Both are required."

I try to fish some more but he won't expand on what he's said already. All he says is, "You have to walk before you can run."

Pretty cryptic but clearly that's all I'm going to get. I bow to him. "Well Mr Cowper. You've been very useful to me. I'll go and gather the ingredients for the potions and come back to use your laboratory, if I may? Possibly not today."

"You'd be very welcome, Reverend." The way he says it makes me think he isn't keeping quiet because he dislikes me. It's like I should prove myself to him first.

I leave the shop and walk down Glastonbury High Street towards the George and Pilgrims. I see there's an alley just past the church on the right-hand side of the street. Le Cozh and Ailsa probably won't be back in the game yet so I decide to explore a little more and take this narrow passage. Going that way allows me to visit the Glastonbury Thorn. I step into the churchyard through a gap in the iron railings and I study the wizened tree, but to my un-botanical eyes it just looks like a small tree. Then I decide to switch on my Clairsentience.

The tree glows a vibrant white marking it as a carrier of holy magic. I decide to take a cutting which I put inside my breast pocket for luck.

I continue down the alley which opens to a crossroads of back-streets. I'm choosing which way to go when a masked man steps out in front of me. It's one of the men who were watching me in London. This one's eyes glitter like a snake and a brown handkerchief is pulled over his mouth. It doesn't look like he means me any good, so I turn to see my way back is blocked by another of these men. They all dress the same—the same brown suits and the hats pulled down low and all have kerchiefs over their mouths. I back away from one towards the other but they block me in the alley like corks plugging two ends of a pipe.

I reach tentatively for my gun and both men go for theirs. They don't know what a bad shot I am, but I do, and I don't want to die in this alley. My mouth goes dry and my heart starts to beat faster. I think of pushing my way past and seeing what they'll do, but the menace in their eyes lets me guess what that might be. A third man steps out of the side street in front. He's dressed like them with a mask over his face. He has been observing me from behind them and he has an air of authority. My hand twitches as I raise it ready to pull out my Browning.

"I wouldn't," he says.

"Wouldn't what?"

"Use that gun. There are three of us, and you'll be dead in seconds, and I think you've already found out what happens to those who die in this game."

Involuntarily, I step away from him. How much does he know about me? Does he know about Miranda?

I decide to try to talk my way out of the problem. I put up my hands and say, "What do you want?"

I can't see his mouth but his voice has a smile in it. "Let me intro-duce myself. I am Mervyn Gurdrock." I recognize the name. He's the one who was bothering Herr Sprengler in Hampstead. At the same time as he speaks he reveals his

name and level to me. Also, his guild.

<Mervyn Gurdrock/ Level 20 Warlock/ The Brothers of Shadow>

So, he's a player, just like me. In the Brothers of Shadow. I guess the other masked men are his guildies.

I want him to know as little about me as possible, but with him as a Level 20 he probably has skills to know who I am already. I reveal my name:

<Adam Cadmon/ Level 2 Priest/ No Guild >

Gurdrock says, "I'm Deputy Guild Master of the Brothers of Shadow. I just wondered if you'd like to join our little guild?"

I force a smile. "You accost me in an alley to invite me to join your guild?"

He shrugs. "We were just keen to have a word with you without your friends. Not everyone approves of the Brothers of Shadow."

I remember Le Cozh keeps his guild name concealed and I wonder whether he's one of them in secret.

One of the others speaks to Gurdrock. I don't recognize the language but it sounds vile, and there's something about the man's voice, and Gurdrock's too. They slur their words as if they have a mouthful of needles, but of course I can't see their mouths, disguised behind the handkerchief.

I wonder whether the other two masked men are also player characters. They do not reveal their names and levels to me. I gesture to them. "Can you ask your men to put their guns down please? If we're all to be friends."

Gurdrock gestures for his two accomplices to holster their pistols. They do as he tells them. "Good," he says, "I like the fact you think we can all be friends."

"I wasn't thinking of joining a guild," I say, "I've never been much of a joiner of any kind."

Gurdrock's eyes are glassy as if he's on drugs. He says, "Players who don't have a guild to back them up don't last long in this game. You can go cold or warm, but without a guild that's where you're going."

I hear his words. I even listen to them, but he's going to have to sell his guild better than this. I say, "The Brothers of Shadow? That sounds a little sinister. I also wonder about your class—isn't a warlock given over to dark magic?"

Gurdrock says, "This game and the world beyond the game are being taken over—consumed by things you can't understand."

"You're talking about the Great Old Ones?" I'm trying to make it sound like I know more than I do and he knows it. My words don't score a hit. His expression is unchanged. In fact, I get the impression he's smiling behind his mask. He says, "The Great Gods. Indeed." Then he adopts a tone like he's my big brother only looking out for me. "It's senseless to fight them. The only way we can survive is by joining them."

He's talking about these rogue AIs. I say, "I thought the Great Old Ones didn't give a damn whether we lived or died?"

He shrugs. "It's true some of the more alien entities are impossible to communicate with. But that's why we make alliances with the ones that have a level of sentience. When we pledge our allegiance to them, by their power they protect us from the others."

That kind of makes sense. "So, if I join you that means I don't get gobbled up? I don't become one of the Cold Ones, or the Warm Ones?"

Gurdrock nods excitedly. "You understand. I knew you would. We've been following you since your character was created. We follow everyone. Some don't prove to be worth our time, but you're clever. I can tell from talking to you."

A little flattery now. I play along. "And what are the other benefits of joining the Brothers of Shadow—in addition to not being annihilated?"

He gives a hollow laugh that sounds like a child on helium. There's something not right about this man. His mask is there to hide some deformity I'm sure of it, and I wonder whether that is the price of allegiance to the Great Old Ones. They disrupt your code.

He says, "We can teach you dark magic. You won't find any open teachers in the game that can teach you dark spells of summoning. How to summon haunters and nightgaunts to do your bidding. We can make you intensely powerful."

I look over Gurdrock's shoulder down the alley. The two other masked men are watching me intently. There's no way I can bust my way past them. I want to leave but still best keep them sweet. "I'm interested. Can I have time to think about it?"

His tone changes. "There's little time to think about things. The end is coming."

I joke, "What if I get a better offer?"

He's clearly not a man with a sense of humour. Gurdrock snarls. "There is no better offer."

Then I think to ask him. "The Cold Ones. Can they be brought back?"

He watches me with his glassy eyes. "You talk of secrets. Deep secrets. We don't reveal that to those who are not of our Guild."

I grin. "Okay, but it was worth asking." Time to go. I step down the alley to the side of the first masked man. The first Brother doesn't want to let me past, but Gurdrock says something to him. He speaks again in that language. This black speech contains echoes of a coffin lid being hammered down, of baboons ripping apart their prey, of a house fire consuming its inhabitants. The sound of it chills me.

But whatever Gurdrock says works. The masked man steps aside and lets me go. I keep walking without looking back.

Gurdrock calls from behind me. "Remember Reverend Cadmon. We shall meet again."

I raise my hand to acknowledge I've heard him but I don't turn my head. I'm halfway to the High Street now.

I hear a fanatical edge in his voice. "Those who are not with us are against us."

I turn on an impulse and switch on my Clairsentience. The three of them glow a wicked red. I shout back, "I'm definitely interested in learning the magic. I'll let you know."

Chapter Sixteen

GLASTONBURY ABBEY

When I log on again, it's morning and I sit in the snug of the George and Pilgrims sipping cider waiting for the return of Ailsa and Le Cozh. The cider effect might ease the upcoming Soma withdrawal. The sun is already up and shining above Glastonbury when I down my cider and step out onto the High Street. Ailsa logs on but messages me to say she'll be late. She's been in her room she says, communing with ghosts.

I meet Le Cozh outside. He's coming from round the corner, his habitual scowl on his face. I wonder where he's been. He nods in greeting. "You still want to learn Pistols from me?"

"Yes, but where can we shoot here?"

He points up at the Tor. "I shouldn't think there'll be many people around there at this time."

We walk along Magdalene Street with the ruins of the Abbey to our left. I can't help but peer over the wall, but I see nothing significant. The grey stone walls stand high and ragged. Most of the abbey ruins have been converted into a pleasant park where mothers push prams and chat. Le Cozh and I reach the end of Magdalene Street and turn left past the large nursing home, another right turn at the end of that street, and before long we've arrived at the bottom of the Tor. There's a high wooden fence enclosing an area to our left. A sign on the fence says Chalice Well Gnostic Community. That sounds interesting.

A lane leads up between the wall of the Gnostic Community to the left and land rising steeply to the right, thickly wooded. Peering up the lane, I see about twenty yards down on the right, nestling into the steep back is a small stone building.

I say, "Just going to look to see what that place is."

Le Cozh shakes his head and just stands watching me while I walk up to the building. A sign outside says White Spring Public Spa and Bathing for Health. Then I return and smile at Le Cozh who rubs his mouth. "Ready now?"

We strike up the steep path through the woodland. After about ten minutes climbing, we come out of the woods onto a grassy slope. It rises from us to the top of the Tor. Grazing sheep lift their heads to watch us pass then get back to their food. There's a path up the ridged grass ridge and we take this until after around ten minutes we're at the top standing by the mediaeval tower, the surrounding countryside spread out for miles around like a coverlet of fields and woods.

There's a plaque by the tower. It tells me the tower is dedicated to Saint Michael. From my Religious Lore skill, I know churches dedicated to Saint Michael are usually placed on earlier pagan sites. In the Book of Revelations, Saint Michael is God's warrior sent to defeat monsters. I wonder what monsters he found here. While Le Cozh checks his gun, I admire the view. I'm on the highest land for miles around. The plaque has a map that helps me understand what I'm looking at. Far to the west I see the Bristol Channel and hills of Wales. To the southeast is Cadbury camp, in legend the site of King Arthur's Camelot. Further south and east, but out of sight, is Stonehenge.

The Somerset levels lie around us flat and crisscrossed with artificial channels begun by the monks of Glastonbury Abbey to drain the land and make it fit for grazing. Before this was done, Glastonbury was an island, the so-called Isle of Avalon. Pilgrims would have arrived here by boat coming to visit the sacred Christian sites—the place where Joseph of Arimathea was supposed to have brought the Holy Grail.

It seems Glastonbury was sacred long before the Christians came. A dragon is supposed to sleep underneath the Tor. There are so many legends associated with Glastonbury, it's hard to disentangle them all and know what's true and what's imagination. But the view is truly magnificent. I glance over to see Le Cozh is finished examining his pistol. He looks at me as he thumbs brass jacketed bullets with their soft grey heads into his pistol's magazine. "Have you got your gun?"

I pull my Browning from my inventory and waggle it. I enjoy the weight of it in my hand far more than a priest should.

He says, "I'm only teaching you because I earn one skill point in return for every ten skill points you spend."

"Good to know you're not just being nice. I might think you'd gone soft."

He grimaces.

"How many points do you want to spend?"

I've thirty skill points left after I learned Alchemy from Cowper. I won't get any more skill points until I level but there's no point sitting with them unused, and I'm not saving them for anything so I commit all thirty to learning Pistols.

"Are you ready?"

I nod.

A message appears on my HUD:

<Christian Le Cozh would like to teach you pistols. Do you accept? >

I select accept, and the lesson begins.

I've the strange sensation Le Cozh is hypnotizing me. His words are magnetic and I watch him as he demonstrates loading and aiming. He fires rounds into the air scaring ravens that flap away from the tower. I follow how he demonstrates and I loose three or four rounds into the air.

Then the lesson is over. I now have 50 points in Pistols. That's not half bad. I should do a bit more damage with my gun next time.

Teaching done and his three skill points earned, Le Cozh indicates he's ready to go down. I thought he might be interested in looking at the tower or experiencing some of the atmosphere of the famous Glastonbury Tor. But no. I guess he isn't much of a man for atmosphere.

I say, "Do you mind if we go down a different way?"

He's ahead and doesn't look back. "I don't care. Whatever you want."

We descend on the other side of the Tor along the winding path between the grass furrows. We come to a lane between high hedges and follow it down through the woods. I've come this way because I want to collect ingredients for my potion. Now I've got the skill and the recipes I want to make a Mana potion and Health potion.

I dawdle amongst the woods collecting spider webs and the bark of birch trees. I find some fly agaric mushrooms which are technically out of season, but I'm pleased they're there. I also pick hawthorn berries—again far too early in the year, but I suppose the game's set up so ingredients for potions can be found at any time. Despite that, I can't get juniper berries here because they're mountain plants. Even so, I've obtained most of the ingredients for my potions. I just need to collect some spring water.

As we get to the bottom of the lane, I can see Le Cozh is bored by me rooting around in the undergrowth. As I stoop to collect some more hawthorn berries and put them in my inventory, he snaps. "You finished yet?"

I grin. "You'll thank me for these potions one day."

He grunts. "Yeah, yeah. Maybe. But we need to meet Ailsa and have a look around the Abbey."

We wander down the lane until we're level with the Spa and Bath House, and I peer in the open door. The building looks very utilitarian now I see it properly as if it was built by the local town council. It also looks like it isn't used much. There's an attendant standing there who doesn't smile as we approach. The door of the bath house is ajar and inside it's dark. There are some candles but they're just glimmering. There's a sign above the door I missed before. It says

Glastonbury Baths and Health Spa are fed by the health giving and holy water of the White Spring.

I wonder if the White Spring has anything to do with the White Powder. I say, "Excuse me ..."

The guard ignores me. Le Cozh seems to see this as a job for him and walks over and pushes the attendant roughly by the shoulder. The attendant stares at where Le Cozh's fingers are prodding him and looks up outraged. "You can't be pushing me!"

Le Cozh nods towards me. "The man asked you a question."

I smile. "The White Spring ...?"

The attendant looks completely uninterested. Le Cozh stands ready to prod him again and finally the man says, "Yes. What of it?"

"Is it really white?"

He seems to find my question ridiculous, but answers with a shrug. "It leaves a white residue. Calcium. It flows from under the Tor and where the water's been, it leaves a white encrustation."

"And is it really holy?"

His face sets. "You're asking the wrong man."

I switch on my Clairsentience and see a white glow does emanate from the spring. It must have some magical properties. It will probably be useful in my potions—it might even add extra power to them. The guard himself gives off no color at all.

I say, 'Can I buy some bottles of the water?'

The guard says, 'Yes, tuppence each. You got your own bottles?'

'Bottle's a penny.'

'Okay.'

I buy three bottles filled with holy water from the Glastonbury spring. They might come in useful at some point for potion making.

Le Cozh looks at me. "Let's go. We need to meet Ailsa."

I follow him to the end of the lane and we turn back and head into Glastonbury proper. Ailsa has messaged us to say she'll meet us at the Abbey ruins. When we get there, she's standing outside. The pale spring sunshine is not warm but it's better than rain. Ailsa indicates the Abbey entrance. There is a little ticket booth with a sign above it saying the site is owned and maintained by the Ministry of Works on behalf of the Diocese of Wells.

"It's threepence to get in," she says.

"I think we can stretch to that."

The three of us pay our fee to the woman in the booth and enter the Abbey grounds. A sign says this is the burial place of King Arthur and his grave was discovered during the reign of Edward I and a huge skeleton was found there. The remains have since conveniently disappeared. There is also a rumor the holy sword Excalibur was recovered from the grave, but that too has disappeared.

"So," Ailsa says. "There must be some clue to the whereabouts of the Red Powder in here?"

It sounds reasonable. We start to look around the ruins. At first, we go all three together then we decide it makes more sense to cover the area faster by splitting up. I switch on my Clairsentience and see the glow from the Abbey is very pale, as if whatever magic there was here once is now faded. However, it's still a white glow, which is encouraging.

We are there around an hour and still haven't found anything. Not even the slightest clue.

I can see Le Cozh is growing bored again. It seems he doesn't have much of an attention span. He lights a cigarette. "This is a waste of time. We need something more to go on."

"Maybe we're missing a previous clue or something?" Ailsa says

I say, "Let's just have one more look around. Another ten minutes maybe?"

Le Cozh doesn't want to agree but Ailsa strokes his arm and that brings him round. They're soon smiling at each other again.

We go off on our own. I head towards the area where King Arthur's grave was supposedly found. I'm standing at the spot when I notice a man dressed in a tweed suit with a waistcoat and plus fours standing beside me. When he sees me looking he says, "Good morning. Quite a nice day, isn't it?"

I can tell from his accent he's educated. I see an opportunity. "Do you know much about the history of the Abbey?"

He seems amused by my question. "I should say so. Though I'm not really supposed to be here. I know Dora at the ticket office and she lets me in."

"Not supposed to be here—why?"

He comes over and offers his hand, which I shake. "I'm Frederick Bligh-Bond."

The name means something to me but I can't place it. I'm about to hit the Wiki when, in explanation he says "I was the archaeological director here from nineteen oh-eight until nineteen twenty-one. It was me who discovered the dimensions of the Abbey but I was dismissed by the Bishop."

I look him up and down. He seems inoffensive. "Dismissed by the Bishop? Why on earth would the Bishop dismiss you?"

Bligh-Bond frowns and points at my dog collar. "I can see you're a man of the cloth. Churchmen are not traditionally open-minded."

I smile. "I might be. I'm interested in what you have to say."

Bligh-Bond scratches his chin and shifts his weight as if wondering how to begin then he smiles. "I excavated this site with the aid of a psychic."

I've visions of shovels moving by psychic power alone but I know that's not what he means.

He goes on. "I had a colleague, Captain Alleyne who has a remarkable psychic gift. Captain Alleyne contacted the long-dead monks of the Abbey and they told us the dimensions of the buildings and what was to be found here."

I'm listening but it's as if he expects an argument. He says, "It is true. I wouldn't pull your leg. Our success is the proof. I was able to sketch out the whole site before we excavated and everything—all my predictions—were proved right."

"But the Bishop didn't like you communing with the monks? Them being dead and all."

Bligh-Bond nods. "Exactly." He studies me and I watch him back. This is definitely the clue the Quest needed. I'm thinking that when he says, "I knew you wouldn't believe me."

"No, I do."

"Really?" He's smiling.

"I think it's quite interesting."

"You don't think it's communing with the devil?"

I shake my head. "I'm more open-minded than that."

He laughs out loud. "Then I would rather have had you as my Bishop than that fool."

"Actually," I say. "I wonder if I can ask you something"

He appears willing. "Go on."

"I'm here on a little quest of my own. I'm looking for the Red Powder. Do you know anything about it?"

A strange look crosses Bligh-Bond's face. He nods. "The Red Powder Edward Kelley used to transmute lead into gold at the court of Rudolph II in Prague?"

Le Cozh mentioned Kelley. To be sure I ask, "Edward Kelley was the associate of Dr John Dee, yes?"

He nods. "But the Red Powder won't be much use to you without the White Powder. Both are used in the production of the Elixir."

Yes, this is definitely a lead. "So you know something of Alchemy?"

He taps his nose. "I know something of many things. But there are some subjects one should not speak about in public." He glances around him at the tops of the ruined walls where crows watch. As if because of the watching birds, he lowers his voice. "Kelley found the details of the Red Powder from an ancient book. The so-called book of St Dunstan."

"Who was St Dunstan?"

"Dunstan was Abbot of Glastonbury in the early days, in the tenth century during the time of the Anglo-Saxon kingdom of Wessex. He was a local boy who had studied the scriptures from the Irish monks who occupied the ruins of the Abbey.

The Dark Age Abbey was originally founded by St Bridget herself. But before the Irish came, the site was a holy place for the British monks and may indeed have been an important place for King Arthur when the Britons were fighting their doomed war against the Anglo-Saxon invaders." He smiles. "Everything in Glastonbury gets lost in the mists of time. You know there are prehistoric lake settlements here? Villages built on stilts in the lakes that once surrounded this island before the levels were drained. They threw artefacts into the water as sacrifices for their pagan gods."

Ailsa and Le Cozh arrive and see me talking to Bligh-Bond. I introduce him.

Ailsa says, "Charming to meet you."

Le Cozh merely nods at Bligh-Bond.

Bligh-Bond studies the newcomers. "Are you also engaged on this quest for the Red Powder?"

Ailsa nods excitedly. Then she whispers to me, "I've scanned him. He's green. He's okay." I'd forgotten to do it.

Bligh-Bond points to me. "I've told your friend we should be careful what we say in public. You never know who's listening. Why don't you come to my house?"

I sense Le Cozh stiffen. He's a naturally suspicious person but I suppose it's a good quality for keeping you alive. I'm not so suspicious of Bligh-Bond. He seems a fascinating character, put here as part of the quest, and I'm sure he has lots to tell us.

Bligh-Bond shrugs apologetically. "It's not actually my house. I only rent when I'm down here. I used to have a house full-time in Glastonbury when I was working on the archaeological dig, but it's not worth keeping up now."

It's not far to his house and we follow him, Ailsa chatting animatedly by his side. I ask the odd question. Bligh-Bond is a font of knowledge about the history of Glastonbury. Ailsa is particularly interested when he hints at his psychic conversations with the monks but he won't go into more detail while out on the street.

Le Cozh wanders sullenly behind, occasionally casting glances over his shoulder as if he's spotted someone following us. I look where he was looking but see no one.

Bligh-Bond opens the door of a perfectly ordinary red-brick house and shows us into the parlor and offers to make us a cup of tea. We graciously accept his kind offer. While he's gone I study the parlor. There are many books on the shelves, mostly they're to do with architecture and archaeology but there are also more esoteric titles.

Bligh-Bond comes back with tea and seed cake. When we're all seated and have cake in hand, he begins to talk about the Red Powder.

Clearing his throat, he says, "First, you must be careful. There are sinister forces in this town, small as it is. Though it began as a sacred site it has become infected with wickedness and evil things now pollute the two holy springs."

Ailsa asks which are the two holy springs.

Bligh-Bond clearly likes teaching. He has the air of a professor. "The first is the White Spring—it carries calcium. The second is the Red Spring which rises within the Chalice Well garden."

I interrupt. "The place where the Gnostic community is now?"

Bligh-Bond nods. "And they are not what they seem. Be careful in any dealings you have with them."

In a quiet voice, Le Cozh says, "They're a guild."

I turn. "Players?"

He nods. "Evil alignment."

Ailsa is chatting with Bligh-Bond. "So we need both the Red and the White Powder to make this Elixir?" Bligh-Bond has obviously mentioned the Elixir both Crowley and Cowper hinted about. I'm strangely protective of it as if I wanted to keep it as my secret. Maybe because I have the insane hope it could bring Miranda back from the dead.

Le Cozh asks, "What exactly is this Elixir?"

I listen carefully.

Bligh-Bond says, "The recipe has been lost for centuries. But it's said both the Red and the White Powder when properly combined will create the Elixir of Life. There may be other ingredients. Some say the Elixir gives immortal life and others say it can turn anything into gold. Those of a more spiritual bent believe it allows one to commune directly with the gods."

I say, "Does it restore sanity?"

Bligh-Bond smiles kindly. "Why? have you lost yours?"

Ailsa giggles.

I ignore her and ask Bligh-Bond, "But Dee and Kelley had the recipe? Is that the last time it's documented?"

Bligh-Bond spreads out his hands. "Kelley is believed to have been a charlatan. Dee was always credible and easily led by those who were more cunning than he was. Even so, it's said Kelley was able to produce gold from lead and that's why Emperor Rudolf of the Holy Roman Empire let him live there in Golden Lane at Prague Castle after Dee came back to England."

"So he got the recipe from the book you talked about?"

Bligh-Bond nods. "Kelley is said to have had a copy of the ancient book of St Dunstan."

Le Cozh says, "That's the guy who was Abbot in the tenth Century? But Kelley lived around five hundred years later. Surely a book would have rotted by then?"

Bligh-Bond shakes his head "No, books were made of parchment then. Vellum can last for many centuries. So it's possible the book survived from St Dunstan's time to Kelley's, but I think it's unlikely Kelley actually had it. I believe he just made it up."

Bligh-Bond takes a delicate mouthful of cake. He's obviously enjoying talking to such enthralled listeners. Even Le Cozh seems interested though he's trying hard not to show it, sitting on the sofa drinking his tea.

Cake swallowed, Bligh-Bond dabs his mouth with his napkin then continues. "But of course, St Dunstan wasn't as pure as he made out— at least originally. He was banished from Glastonbury and thrown into a cesspit in his youth. It's said he mixed with witches and warlocks and learned their secrets. Then of course he repented and came back to the church."

Le Cozh says, "So the book of St Dunstan was possibly a book of witchcraft."

Ailsa smiles ruefully. "But it doesn't matter now. The book is lost"

Le Cozh suddenly stands. He steps over to the window with his gun out.

I stand too. "What is it?"

Then we're all on our feet including Bligh-Bond.

"There's someone in the garden," Le Cozh says.

"Who? What kind of person?" Ailsa is at his shoulder.

"I'm going to look."

Le Cozh goes out of the parlor and opens the front door. I'm right by his heels but I see nothing. Le Cozh looks troubled. "There was definitely someone there. A guy with a brown mask over his face, but when I went out into the garden he was gone."

I haven't yet told Le Cozh or Ailsa about my meeting with Mervyn Gurdrock or his offer to join the Brothers of Shadow. I decide to keep it to myself for a little while longer. What Gurdrock said about single players dying fast and needing to join a guild to survive has struck a chord with me. I don't think I'll join them, but I want to keep my options open for Miranda's sake.

We step back inside the house. Le Cozh isn't impressed with how far we've got, despite the information Bligh-Bond told us. He screws his face. "We'd better be going. It looks like our trip to Glastonbury was a fool's errand. Maybe we missed something and there was another clue in London."

"I've just had an idea," Ailsa says.

"Oh?" Bligh-Bond inclines his head. He is clearly taken with our pretty clairvoyante.

"You said you excavated by contacting the monks?"

Bligh-Bond nods.

"I was just thinking," Ailsa says as she smiles winningly. "I could be your psychic."

Bligh-Bond looks interested. "You have that skill, my dear?"

"I think I could contact them for you."

Le Cozh furrows his brow. "Who—the monks? What would be the point in that?"

She strokes his arm. "No, silly. I could try to psychically locate the book of St Dunstan. It may still be in Glastonbury."

Bligh-Bond says, "I sincerely doubt that, my dear."

"But let's try?" She sits.

Bligh-Bond sits beside her. "Of course." He pats Ailsa on her knee. She flinches slightly as he beams at her but she smiles back. Le Cozh rolls his eyes. For the first time, I realize he's jealous of Bligh-Bond. That makes me smile.

Bligh-Bond stands. "Let me close the curtains. This is how I used to do it with Captain Alleyne."

Once all the curtains are closed, Bligh-Bond lights a red candle. The match strikes and flares, and the yellow flame flickers above the red wax. The acrid smell of the match lingers in the air. Then he takes a small cone of incense and sets it in a brass dish with Indian designs and using the flame of the candle sets the incense cone on fire. The thin column of grey aromatic smoke ascends.

Bligh-Bond sits again. "If you try to contact them, my dear. I will ask the questions."

A silence descends on the room and the atmosphere thickens as Ailsa goes into trance. The smoke from the incense is thicker than I would have imagined. It almost looks as if shapes are dancing in it, as if something is attempting to become material.

Bligh-Bond asks if there's anyone there. In a sing-song man's voice Ailsa answers, "It is I, Brother Anthony. What would you know?"

Bligh-Bond is very deferential. He looks at me and mutters, "This monk came through all those years ago." He's clearly excited. "Greetings, brother Anthony and God bless you."

A growl comes from the corner of the room and I spin round. It's as if something has been angered by mention of the Christian God. Le Cozh scans the corner but there's nothing there. I try to remind myself this is all computer code. Nothing here is real, no ghosts, no spirits, and definitely no demons. Code or not, the growl makes the hairs on the back of my neck stand.

Bligh-Bond goes on as if the growl never occurred. "May I ask you brother Anthony what year is it you are speaking to us from?"

"It is the year of our Lord nine hundred and seventy."

Once again something stirs in the corner of the room. The smoke from the incense is thick. I switch on my Clairsentience and I see Bligh-Bond glows green as do my other companions. A red glow emanates from the corner behind Le Cozh but I can't see which object is giving it off. It's not moving.

Bligh-Bond goes on. "What do you know of the book of St Dunstan?"

Brother Anthony speaks, "The cursed book was written before our Abbot Dunstan turned back to Christ. He wrote it when he had spent too long with the Demons under the Tor."

"What happened to the book?" I ask.

Ailsa turns to me, her eyes closed and brother Anthony speaks through her. "The book is destroyed. At first, we tried to burn it with the blessing of Dunstan himself but it would not burn. Then we hacked it with swords but it turned the blades away so full was it of wicked magic. Then we threw it into a deep pool outside of the Abbey walls."

Bligh-Bond mutters, "But in later years old pools are drained and the land turned over to agriculture."

I say, "So the book could have survived, even buried in peat?"

Behind Le Cozh, a table moves. It's where the red glow is. Le Cozh jumps to his feet and pulls out his gun "There's something here. I can't see it, but there is something here."

I say, "I could banish it—I've a spell."

Bligh-Bond says, "Don't banish anything. We'll lose our connection with brother Anthony."

So I sit again and listen. Brother Anthony talks a little while longer but his speech is now of his general life in the Abbey and praises to St Dunstan for returning to the Christian fold. There is nothing more about the book of St Dunstan.

Incense now fills the room. Ailsa sits back and opens her eyes. "I'm going to try manifestation. It's one of the skills of my profession." A look of intense concentration forms on her face and she stares into the space in front of her. And there, in the smoke, little by little, the form of an ancient tome appears.

"Good God!" Bligh-Bond says. "It looks like a real Dark Ages manuscript!"

As we watch, the pages turn through an effort of Ailsa's will. I stand so I can look right down at the pages and read them. They're written in Dark Age minuscule. The language is Latin. Once again, I bless my career choice as a priest—I have 60 in Latin and I can read the manuscript. My jubilation turns to disgust as I realize what I'm reading. The beginning of the book is an account of St Dunstan's descent into the underworld below Glastonbury Tor. Foul slithering things with tentacles lurk there. There are monsters from cold spaces beyond the Earth that rape the minds of the men who enter those labyrinths. They control those they bleed dry of their sanity and send them as their servants into the world.

The description of the monsters is horrific but the description of what they made men do, and even worse what men chose to do in their service, is blasphemous and unspeakable.

<You observe something especially horrific -20 SANITY>

Visions of huge coiling snakes and squid-like monstrosities of cosmic proportions loom into my mind. I feel fear rise in me. Amidst the stories of beasts and things Dunstan beheld in this foul underworld are alchemical secrets. One of the secrets is the recipe of the Elixir of Life.

I reach out to touch the manuscript as it hangs there in the air. The vellum feels real in my fingers. I check to see whether I can copy it into my journal, but I can't and I don't yet have a high enough skill in Alchemy to understand it.

I fall back into my seat, grasping at my throat. The words I've read and the images they conjured disgust me. I sit in the chair my head thumping and my hands shaking. The recent Sanity loss doesn't help.

Le Cozh screams beside me, "Watch out!"

A black square mess of a thing leaps from the corner where it lurked. For all we know, it's been hiding in this house with Bligh-Bond and him unaware. It's the size of a monkey and covered in bubbling black flesh with eight legs and two sliding apertures in the middle of its belly.

<You see something rather vile - 15 Sanity>

Le Cozh blazes at it with his gun, injuring it. This is the time for my Banishing Spell. I select the Lesser Banishing Ritual of the Pentagram which I've slotted in my hot bar. I spend ten Mana points. There's a stink of burning rubber as my glowing pentagram burns it.

My spell kills it before Le Cozh's bullets do.

<You slay Witherer: 100 xp>

The black indescribably vile thing lies twitching before it vanishes, and my pentagram still glows white in the air warding off all evil things.

"That's a handy spell," Ailsa says.

I laugh. I have a nervous exhilaration that I survived the thing, but I wonder if my exhilaration is bordering on hysteria; I still feel the tendrils of insanity plucking at my mind.

Bligh-Bond says, "A nice spell, but it won't work on high-level creatures."

With the thing dead, a message appears on my HUD:

<You have found the Book of St Dunstan: 5000xp awarded>

The XP was unexpected but welcome.

"So what now?" Ailsa says.

Le Cozh shakes his head. "There's something wrong with this town. We get the Red Powder, or the White Powder, then we leave."

I feel ill. Soon I'll need more Soma.

Chapter Seventeen

THE WHITE SPRING

After leaving Bligh-Bond, we have a conference in the street. "Which first?" Ailsa says.

Le Cozh shrugs. "Red Powder?"

I shake my head. "White Powder. It must be in the Spa where the White Spring rises. We know where that is."

Le Cozh and Ailsa stand together. "Why not the red? It's probably inside Chalice Well Gardens. That's where the iron spring rises."

"Yes, but the White Spring is more accessible." There's a pause. I say, "I'm right, aren't I?"

Ailsa smiles. "It makes sense."

Le Cozh grudgingly agrees. I still think he doesn't like me getting my way or Ailsa agreeing with me. "Okay," he says. "White Spring."

We look at the sky. The sunshine has gone and clouds have gathered. It will be dark before too long.

Once we make our way to the White Spring it's 5 p.m. The day has now grown very overcast and rain threatens. I figure we have around an hour at best before it's completely dark.

The attendant is sitting there in the door in his municipal uniform looking as glum as ever. He checks his watch as we approach.

Ailsa beams at him, but he doesn't crack a smile. "Can we have three tickets to go in the baths please?" she says.

"We shut at five thirty. You've only got half an hour." He studies us suspiciously. "You haven't got any bathing suits."

"No." Ailsa smiles to win him round. "Can we hire some? And towels too?"

The attendant nods grumpily and stands. "That'll be sixpence —each."

We pay our money and he issues us three paper tickets. Then he rummages around in the back office at the entrance to the spa. Coming out, he presents us each with a white towel tightly rolled and held in place by his thumb. They contain black swimsuits—a full swim-suit for Ailsa and two pairs of swimming trunks.

"Men and women in separate spas." He grunts and watches us step past him. Le Cozh gives him a mock salute as he goes by then we enter the swimming baths.

The place is ominously empty. It's lit only by candles that flitter and gutter in their holders. Ailsa wrinkles her nose. "This doesn't look or smell like a normal swimming baths."

"What is that smell?" I say trying to follow my nose to its source.

"Incense," Ailsa says, pointing. A brass, Indian-style incense burner sits on a cube of rock at the edge of the stone basin that contains the first of the pools. Smoke rises and the burner is surrounded by with-ered roses, small coins, and glass beads, left as if in offering.

"It stinks," Le Cozh says.

"It's supposed to be spiritual, I guess." I look around. Water drips from the ceiling. Despite the Victorian façade outside, the interior looks ancient as if it had been carved from the rock by prehistoric people. There are small individual pools dotted around the interior and water flows from one to the other. I guess you can sit in them and take the healing water if you like. I bend down and test the temperature.

Ailsa does the same. "Cool but not cold."

I taste the water on my fingers, but it merely tastes slightly chalky.

Ailsa says, "It's warmer than I'd expect if it had just flown from under the hill."

"Maybe there's some volcanic activity?" Le Cozh says.

I snort. "In Somerset?" I'm being a smart ass, and I know it.

He shrugs. "I don't know the area. I'm French."

I hadn't realised he was French, though I probably should have from his name.

I peer further into the spa where a tunnel leads deeper into the hill. We paddle through water about an eighth of an inch deep, our shoes splashing. The water leaves a white stain on my black shoes.

Leaving the entrance spa with its small pools we go down the corridor. The women's changing room is on the left and the men's on the right. I stop, hesitant.

Ailsa slaps me playfully on the shoulder. "We're not really going to change, you ninny."

I blush. "Of course. I knew that."

"No, you didn't," Le Cozh says laconically.

They walk on and I follow. The air is chilly now and a draft blows from further down the passage. I see a faint cloud of my breath. Running water sounds come from everywhere and dripping echoes from the recesses of the cavern that look less and less man-made the further we progress. As I'm not going to use them, I put down my towel and swimming trunks and the others do the same. Ahead of us a curtain of coloured ribbons flutters, screening off the view of the passage that leads deeper into the spa.

Ailsa lets the ribbons flow through her fingers. "They're the colour of peacock's feathers."

"I take it we go further in?" Le Cozh says.

I study the floor. "This white residue can't be the White Powder, it's too easy. Maybe the powder itself is further into the caves. Maybe we can dig it out or harvest it from in there?"

"You tell us. You're the alchemist," Le Cozh says.

"Hardly. I only have forty points in Alchemy. It doesn't make me an expert."

"You're an expert to us, my dear," Ailsa says sweetly.

We push our way through the coloured ribbons and see a spiral stone staircase leading down. I'm still tentative. "I guess the source of the spring must be down here?"

Ailsa switches on her Clairsentience. She has more ability in this than I do, so I guess she senses things other than colours. With her eyes going all dreamy, she says, "There's an opening down there—like a doorway."

"A door?"

"No. Different. It leads elsewhere. An opening."

"Sounds like a door." Le Cozh is the smart ass now. She shoots him a sharp glance and I see his expression. He doesn't like to upset her. He says, "Do you think the White Powder is down there?"

I've already suggested that, but he waits on Ailsa. She nods and we descend.

The sound of our shoes echoes in the hollow stone space and everywhere we go, we're accompanied by the sound of water dripping and running. It seeps from the walls and the walls are stained white. I scrape a wall with my nail and it comes back white.

The stairs descend for a long way and we must be halfway down when Le Cozh looks up over his shoulder. "There's someone following us," he says.

"Probably the attendant," Ailsa says.

I joke. "Maybe you paid him too much, Ailsa, and now he's running after us with our change."

She giggles. The image makes me laugh too, but Le Cozh tilts his head. "He's stopped. He must realise we're listening for him."

I'm not sure there is anyone following us, but there's no point standing here. "Let's go down," I say, and take out my Browning just in case and I see Le Cozh take his pistol out too.

Ailsa frowns, "I think you're overreacting, boys. I doubt there'll be anything down here—maybe some school party that's got lost from their trip to the swimming baths, or some old ladies here to honour the gods."

I'm still looking behind though I can't hear anyone. Le Cozh's alertness has spooked me.

"Yeah, but which gods?" he says.

We arrive at the bottom of the stairs. We must be a hundred feet down now. The path goes on in front of us and is clearly now a natural fissure in the rock. Natural but widened by men. The feeling of age is palpable.

Le Cozh points to the sandy floor. "Lots of feet going this way."
I look and stare at the prints. "And some of them not human."

<You observe something triflingly odd - 2 SANITY>

I sigh. I don't want to lose more Sanity. I shudder. The Soma is
definitely wearing off now. Cowper didn't approve of it, so I wonder
where I can get a hit in this one-horse town. Then I know m Mervyn
Gurdrock probably has plenty. As long as I become his friend.

Le Cozh and Ailsa move on. I'm still gripping the Browning and
my palm is sweaty. I think I hear something—a low voice, but then
that could be the voices starting to mutter in my head from lack of
Soma and declining Sanity.

We're walking faster now along the level passage. A string of under-
powered electric bulbs leads all the way down. It feels like the rock is
crowding in above us. I'm feeling nervy, looking into the shadows, and
I want to get the White Powder then get out as fast as I can. I sense
my companions feel the same way. The tunnel twists and turns until
any sense of direction I have is lost and it starts going down more
steeply. I wonder whether we now face north, east, south, or west, I
have no idea. We must have walked around a mile underground. On
the floor, I still see the marks of many feet—as if this is a way of
pilgrimage and has been for centuries.

The string of electric bulbs leads us on like we're Theseus going
into the Minotaur's Lair.

Then we arrive at a place where a stream cuts in from the side and
flows down the middle of the passage. The water leaves its thick
residue of white. I stoop again to test it, to see if this is the White
Powder. Some comes off but it's still normal calcium, the sort that
makes plaque on your teeth.

We've walked a long way with nothing to show. "Should we go on?"
Ailsa asks.

Le Cozh shrugs. "What choice do we have?"

I say, "I vote we go on. Let's find what we came for."

We start off but after three paces Le Cozh stops again and listens.
"He's definitely behind us."

I hear nothing but I'm sure he's right. My pistol has been in my hand all this while. I stare into the dark, but I see nothing and all I hear is the sound of water. "If he's there, he's hanging back, like he doesn't want to be seen."

Ailsa gives a nervous grin. "He's maybe waiting for us to get to a suitable point then he'll ambush us." Then she stops smiling.

We walk on and the stream gets wider and deeper taking up most of the passageway now. Soon we have to press ourselves against the tunnel wall in order not to plunge our feet into the water. I become obsessed with every echo, listening for whoever is behind us. To my ear there sounds like more than one creature following.

I still haven't told my companions about the Brothers of Shadow and their offer to me. Le Cozh thinks it's the attendant following us, but I half expect it's the Brothers who've followed us down into the earth. For a second I think maybe I can take them up on their offer and get them to help me obtain the White Powder. But what will they do with Le Cozh and Ailsa?

I definitely hear footsteps now, not far behind us.

I stop. "Why don't we hide and wait for them, then we'll jump out and find out what they want and who they are?"

Le Cozh says, "No. Let's just get to the end of this tunnel, get the powder then turn and face whoever it is."

His plan makes more sense. Ailsa is looking distinctly nervous now but she smiles back. When we turn the next corner, the dry path has been washed over by the stream. Without discussing it, we wade ankle deep through the water, noisily so all chance of stealth is gone. My shoes are soaked and my trousers too, halfway up my calves. The water stains them white, but the temperature of the water is pleasant, as if we've gone so far into the middle of the earth the water itself is warming up. Soon the water's knee deep and Ailsa struggles to wade through it. "I wish I hadn't come," she says.

Then from behind I hear a sloshing sound as something enters the water behind us. It's just yards behind.

Unexpectedly the tunnel opens into a cavern. Le Cozh flashes his electric torch but the string of electric bulbs extends even here, though they cast more shadows than light. Here they reveal a cavern shaped like the inside of a furnace. Its wide circular bottom narrows to a rocky throat above. Straight ahead a mineral deposit of pure white shines in the dull light. The water flows through fissures in the crystalline rock.

At last.

The water's now thigh deep and I wade through it to get to the crystalline structure. Le Cozh is by my side with his penknife. He digs into the crystal. "It's not calcium," he says.

He's right. It's far more crystalline and shiny. The cuboid crystals glitter in the electric light. There is clear evidence men—or at least things with hands—have dug out quantities of this white crystal.

"We've got nothing to carry it away in," I say.

Ailsa smiles. "Men! It's a good job you've got me with you."

She reaches into her inventory and pulls out a stiff cardboard box. As she steps forward to help Le Cozh, I look over her shoulder. Whoever was behind us has not come into the cavern. Maybe they won't. Maybe they'll wait for us to come out.

I step forward to help my friends. With the aid of Le Cozh's penknife to make the crystal friable and my scrabbling fingers, we put a good quantity—maybe a pound—of the white crystal into the cardboard box.

<You have obtained the White Powder: +1000xp>

We must have all got the same message because Le Cozh says, "Nice."

Ailsa throws back her head and shouts up into the cavern, "Lovely XP!" Her voice echoes from the rock and makes me nervous about what kind of things down here might be attracted by her yell.

"Enough?" Ailsa asks.

I don't know. "It looks plenty." Then I joke, "We can always come back ..."

She twists her face. "I don't think so."

"Who's going to take it?" I ask.

Le Cozh has turned round and is staring back into the dark of the cavern entrance.

Ailsa offers the box of powder to me. "You're the alchemist. You can make better use of it than me."

I take it but say, "Don't you want your box back?"

"Don't be so silly, Adam."

A sloshing, rushing sound behind causes me to snap my head to see two figures come into the cavern.

The first is the bath attendant. He's holding a silver pistol in his hand. The second is far more terrifying. It was once a man and still wears the rags of a uniform similar to the attendant, but instead of arms it has tentacles. Huge sucker limbs—six of them—erupt from the sides and middle of its torso. Its head that was once human has melted and flops like burned rubber over its shoulders and chest. With a shriek, the thing launches itself into the attack.

<You observe something mildly horrific -5 SANITY>

My Sanity is now only 53.

I have just time to put the box of White Powder into my inventory and steady my gun. Ailsa steps back and stands against the crystal deposit of the White Powder. She's still standing in water, then she moves towards a side tunnel I hadn't previously noticed.

Le Cozh shoots the tentacled monster and it screams in pain as his bullet hits home.

The attendant fires his own gun. The bullet strikes a glancing wound against my shoulder.

<Attendant wounds you -10 HEALTH>

I fire back and hit the attendant full in his chest. My increased pistol skill has resulted in greater damage. I fire twice

<You hit Attendant for -20 HEALTH>
<You hit Attendant for -22 HEALTH>

The tentacled creature jumps at Le Cozh and wraps its tentacles around him. A beak appears from its belly and it pulls him close to bite. Le Cozh grunts and blood streams over his arm. I fire twice.

<Critical hit! You hit Tentacled Aberration for 4 x Damage -50
HEALTH>
<Critical hit! You hit Tentacled Aberration for 4 x Damage -52
HEALTH>

I fire again causing another 25. The creature screams in pain, but still doesn't die.

The attendant is bleeding heavily and his aim is off because of his wounds. He fires at me but misses, the bullet striking the crystalline deposit and knocking off a chunk of it into the water. It rings like a tuning fork from the bullet impact.

I fire at the tentacled aberration and hit it again; it's badly wounded now and Le Cozh manages to pull away holding his bleeding stomach with one hand while he empties his magazine into the thing at close range. With a wheeze like a deflating balloon the thing goes down and stains the water black with its demonic blood. The attendant retreats.

<You helped kill Tentacled Aberration: +100xp>

I then get 75 XP without any further warning and I guess the attendant died out of sight as he was retreating.

Le Cozh staggers backwards and sits on the crystalline powder.

I go up to him. "Damn, I have first-aid skills from character creation, but I don't have any first-aid kits."

He grimaces. "Nor me."

Ailsa emerges from the shadows, producing a bandage and some cotton wool. She stares at the water, stained with the thing's blood. She wrinkles her nose. "Do you think it safe to use this water to clean the wound?"

"Who knows?"

Le Cozh grunts. "Give it a try."

Ailsa does her best and applies the first aid. Le Cozh smiles wearily and says, "That's restored twenty Health."

"How much damage did you take?" I ask.

"Forty-seven in total."

"Ouch." Then I remember I have a Heal spell. I select it from my hot bar and look at Le Cozh, trusting my gaze to act as a targeting mechanism. I hit Heal on the HUD and a silver glow comes from my fingers. I speak words in Greek and healing magic effects Le Cozh.

He nods his thanks. "Another twenty—only seven down!"

"I could heal again?" Then I remember it's on cool down.

He shakes his head. "No, save your Mana. It's not worth it for only seven Health."

Ailsa looks at the bloody tentacled corpse as it hangs dead in the water. She prods it with the toe of her shoe. "What the hell is that thing?"

I study it and see on my HUD the monster name's come up:

Tentacled Aberration: Tentacled Horrors are once men that have been corrupted by dark energy.

"We've got the powder," I say, "Should we leave?"

Ailsa gestures. "I only went a little way into the tunnel but there's something up there."

"Something we have to fight?"

She tilts her head. "I'm not sure. There's a noise, like tinkling bells. And I got the impression there's a creature in the corner there."

Le Cozh reloads his pistol. So I do the same. He walks through the water to the cavern entrance and disappears for a short while and I wonder where he's gone until he comes back holding the silver pistol the guard had. He's grinning. He looks more pleased now than I've seen him in all the time we've been playing. "Always loot the bodies!" he says.

He hands me the silver pistol. Tentatively I put out my hand and he drops it in my palm. "Here, you have it. Thanks for the healing."

I step back. "Are you sure? It's yours by rights."

He shakes his head. "No, you have it. You deserve it. And anyway, I'm not really a two gun kind of guy. I think it looks a bit pretentious."

I laugh. "But you must think I am?"

He winks.

I check the gun against my Wiki and it tells me it's a Walther PPK.

<Walther Polizeipistole Kriminalmodell *(Police Pistol Detective Model)* : {Pierce Damage} 10-25 Damage x Pistols skill.>

James Bond's gun except James Bond's gun isn't silver. As I weigh it in my hand, I think it does look a mite pretentious. It takes 9 mm rounds so I could load it from the same box my Browning uses. I have about half a box left. I'll need to get more ammunition soon.

Ailsa's also standing tentatively at the corner of the side tunnel she partially explored. "Should we go and take a look?"

"We've got what we came for. We could leave," I say.

She stands with her back to the side tunnel. "It just feels like there might be something good in there."

Call it feminine intuition.

"Loot?" Le Cozh asks.

"Who knows? Maybe."

I stare back the way we came. It's a long walk so maybe this side tunnel is a shortcut out. In games like this, the developers sometimes put a portal out to save players the tedium of retracing their steps.

I decide to go with them.

We creep tentatively along the corridor. Ailsa's in front. There's a tinkling sound from ahead and a strange humming. Then I see, standing there in the light of one electric bulb, is a strange figure. A small woman with black hair stands in the centre of a cave. She's around three-feet tall and skinny. As we get closer I see her eyes are closed and it looks like she's blind. There's a glowing coin icon over her head that indicates she is a vendor.

Le Cozh holsters his pistol. "I love it when they put vendors way down in these dungeons. What on earth would an NPC be doing down here?"

Ailsa smiles at his joke. It's clearly not good enough to get a laugh.

As we approach the dwarf woman says, "I am the Queen of Doorways."

"Everything's got to have its queen, I guess," Le Cozh says. This time Ailsa giggles. But the woman's voice is chilling—it sounds like the autumn wind through leaves. She says, "How can I meet your needs?"

Ailsa says, "What do you have for sale?"

The woman clicks her fingers and a virtual store inventory appears glowing in the air between us. I look down the inventory and I see she's selling ammunition and first aid kits. I buy two boxes of 9mm rounds and two first aid kits. I also buy a penknife for good measure because I've seen how useful it can be and on impulse, I buy an electric torch. It's like I'm copying Le Cozh.

The wizened queen has some healing potions. I hoped to make my own but haven't got round to it yet so I buy three Mana and three Health potions. They each heal 50 points, then I'm almost out of cash.

She has lots of other items which are either too high level for us or we can't afford. There's a selection of potions, but she isn't selling Soma.

When we finish our transactions, the wizened queen says, "Will you be traveling to Leng?"

"What's Leng?"

She says, "The frozen peninsula of Leng lies between the worlds. It is in the Dreamlands."

"And what's there?" asks Ailsa.

"Great danger, madness, and riches beyond your dreams."

Le Cozh says, "I like the sound of the riches beyond my dreams."

Ailsa laughs. "Danger and madness too."

I have some intuition that arises from somewhere I can't place. Some skill I have maybe. I ask her, "Is there anything else there?"

She says, "The Nameless City is there. If you're fortunate enough to find it." Then a dry laugh. "Or unfortunate."

"What's in the Nameless City?"

She says, "The Palace of Azathoth."

Le Cozh looks suddenly interested. "So that's where it is."

"What's in this palace?" I ask.

The queen speaks with a voice like insects running over your skin. "Both the Cold and the Warm can be found by those who know where to look."

My heart races. "The Cold and Warm?"

She begins to explain. It's what I thought. An insane hope flashes through me; Miranda might be there.

Ailsa looks puzzled. I explain, "This is what happens to those who lose their Sanity or their lives. The ones who die become the Cold Ones and the ones who go insane become Warm Ones."

"Those who die?" she says. "Players? Don't you just resurrect?"

Le Cozh keeps quiet.

I look at her. "It's true. When you die in-game, you don't resurrect."

She is speechless, but I'm energised: There's at least a chance I'll find Miranda in the Palace of Azathoth. "How do we get there?" I ask.

The queen says, "The entrance to the Plateau of Leng is a dream within a dream."

"More riddles," Le Cozh says.

I put my hand up to silence him. I want to hear. "How do we enter this dream?"

The queen produces three small bottles in her hand. An opalescent liquid swirls in them as she holds them up. Each little crystal bottle has a glass stopper. "This takes you there."

I just want to be sure. "So, we drink these to enter the Dreamlands?"

The queen nods.

I say, "And how much are they?"

The queen says, "Two pounds each."

That's that then. I don't have £2. But I need it to find if my hunch about Miranda can possibly be right. I look to Ailsa. She says, "I'll buy three please."

Ailsa is kind. She might want to go there herself, but I know she's also doing it for me.

I have the bottle in my hand. The queen raises a finger. "They are only of any use when you are near a portal." She gestures behind her further down the tunnel from where a tinkling sound is coming. "The gate is close."

We're about to walk off, when she says, "And you will need these."

She's holding three tiny bottles of a sapphire-blue liquid.

"What are those?" I ask.

"Potions to return you from the Dreamlands." She smiles again and I think her blind eyes are watching me. She licks her lips. "You wouldn't want to get stuck there."

Ailsa buys the sapphire potions. She asks the queen, "So we drink this pearly coloured potion and walk through the gate to enter the Dreamlands?"

The queen says, "What a clever girl."

Ailsa turns. "Do you think we'll meet this Azathoth in his palace? He sounds dangerous."

Rogue AIs. He could unravel the code that represents us here then God alone knows what would happen to our brains sitting there under the neural net.

"I shouldn't think so," Le Cozh says.

As we walk towards the unseen portal, I hear the queen making a dry noise in her throat, then I realise she's laughing.

Chapter Eighteen

THE NAMELESS CITY

We get near the sound of humming and tinkling. So close we must almost be able to touch it, but we can see nothing.

Ailsa says, "She says we have to sip the potion near to the portal."

My feet crunch on the grit. "So here?"

She nods. "I suppose so."

I regard the small potion bottle in my hand. The milky liquid glitters like white opal in the light of the bulbs strung on the wire above. I shrug and throw back my head to glug down the contents of the potion bottle. It tastes of chalk and metal and I almost gag because it's so repulsive. Then my hands disappear like melting snow. For a moment, everything is black then I stand on a windswept icy plateau.

<You have discovered the Plateau of Leng – 3000xp>
<As a minor reward you are awarded £5>
<LEVEL UP! Congratulations You are Now Level 3>

That means I have a hundred more skill points to spend, which is welcome, and a hundred more Health and Mana points. When I check, my Sanity and Reputation remain unchanged.

It is night and alien stars twinkle above. I don't recognize any of the constellations. Two moons stand in the sky—one the colour of a bruise, and the other orange like an overripe peach. Between them they illuminate a vast expanse of virgin snow. There are lumps in the snow like a thousand covered huts. On the horizon, a range of serrated mountains form an edge to the world. They are bare rock with no vegetation growing on them at all.

I see my breath coming out in billows, but I'm not cold. I remind myself I'm in a dream.

I look to see Ailsa to the left of me and Le Cozh to the right. Ailsa gazes around her. "The dream within a dream."

None of us seem to be suffering from the Arctic cold. Le Cozh points ahead. "The Nameless City."

He's right. Around a mile away is a strange city of minarets, turrets, and gleaming domes that catch the baleful light of the twin moons.

Miranda might be there. "Let's go." We begin trudging through the white waste. After a hundred yards, I glance back to see our trail of footprints is the only sign that life has ever disturbed this place.

"We feel a long way from anywhere," Ailsa says as we walk. It's true. The humps in the snow are low granite huts now abandoned all over the plain. Mostly they are covered with snow but in some places, it has fallen off to reveal the sparkling rock beneath.

"I wonder when people last lived here," Le Cozh says.

Ailsa walks over to a hut that lies near our path. She brushes snow off the blocks of granite and looks through a hole where stones have collapsed. "There's the remains of a fire in there. But long dead. Centuries maybe."

I'm appalled but enthralled by the place. "So, this is the Plateau of Leng."

As we approach the city I see it too appears completely devoid of life. There's no sign of men or women, or even any animal marks. Its roofs are untroubled by birds. It's as if the place was created and never lived in. There's no sign of the normal wear and tear a human population causes to city walls and roads. When we get closer, I see the walls are made of a uniform material. Great blocks of stone as white as plaster of Paris but run through with veins of gold.

Soon the snow beneath our feet is overlaying a roadway. Walking is easier now. Drifts bank the edges of the path and soon we are among the first buildings.

"It's so quiet," Ailsa says, "just the sound of the wind."

Le Cozh keeps looking round. "There's nothing alive here."

I say, "But this is supposed to be the location of the Palace of Azathoth."

Ailsa mutters, "Where the Warm and the Cold are to be found. Whatever they are."

We wander among the city streets. There are no shops or taverns, even deserted ones. The whole place looks like a copy of a city—a model rather than the real thing. There are no windows or doors though there are the shapes of windows and doors. Every house and every building is made from top to bottom of this white stone run through by veins of glittering gold.

Snow piles lie where they have blown on the city streets. No one has shovelled them away and in some places they're knee deep.

Le Cozh goes to a house and taps an opaque stone window. "What is the point of a window like this?"

Ailsa says, "This city was never intended to be lived in. It's a city created in mockery of a human city by a creature that had no idea what it's like to be alive."

Le Cozh taps the stone window again and turns back. "Weird."

"Look!" I say. There are shapes on the walls.

"Yes, like bulges." Ailsa examines the closest one.

They're like deformities on the sides of the houses and buildings. They look like tumours.

Ailsa starts back. "One of them just moved."

Le Cozh walks up to the bulge and prods it. "It's soft."

Ailsa looks horrified. "Have you ever seen a butterfly or moth come out of its chrysalis?"

We all stand and watch as something moves within the bulge.

Ailsa says, "The chrysalis softens in preparation for the grub to hatch."

I suspect our presence is causing these things to stir. Things that have lain in gestation in these disgusting pods for aeons, now awaken, stirred by our proximity.

I have an intimation of danger. "I want to find the Palace of Azathoth. Let's hurry before these things come out."

Ailsa nods and we continue shuffling through the snow-piled streets. Then I see lights ahead. These are the first lights I've observed in the city. Le Cozh follows my gaze then he points up. "There are things falling from the sky."

"Like stars," Ailsa says.

"They're too small to be stars", I say. "They look more like starfish."

I watch where the rain of stars is coming from. They drop like dying fireflies. They're coming from space, and they are all landing on one area of the city.

"That way then?" I say. "Let's just see what's going on."

As we walk, I see Le Cozh has his pistol in his hand.

As we get closer I see the stars are falling on an area that looks like a Colosseum. There's no roof to the huge building and the stars are falling within it.

"Yeuch!" Ailsa suddenly steps back. A bulge in the building to her right has swollen and the grey and gold skin is cracking. Something inside struggles to get free.

"Fight it?" Le Cozh asks.

"Not if we don't have to," I say. "Let's get to that Colosseum thing, see what's there and decide whether we want to fight."

Le Cozh nods. "Seems sensible."

He's agreed with me. The place must be affecting him.

We double our pace, and after hurrying along streets between buildings where snow lies less thickly, we finally stand in front of the enormous Colosseum. White and gold columns go up around a hundred feet. Above I see the stars falling within the Colosseum but from here I can't see exactly where they are landing.

A roadway runs right round the Colosseum and we follow it anti-clockwise until we see a large entrance tunnel. There are carvings of bestial monstrosities all around the entrance archway—vile alien things I have no words for, but the sight of which makes me shudder and wish I was somewhere else. Even so, that's the way to go. "Through there then," I say.

But Ailsa and Le Cozh are staring behind them. Things have come out of their gestation pouches and three or four of them shamble towards us. Horrid mismatches of human and insect-eyed creatures stumble down the road. Bodies of men and women walk on insect legs. Some have human heads, others have the pincers and the multifaceted eyes of spiders. Some drool as they come, the human heads lolling. One moves like an earwig, another human body has been half trans-formed into the glistening torso of a slug.

"What the fuck are those?" Le Cozh says. I hope it's a rhetorical question because I have no idea.

<You observe something especially horrific -20 SANITY>

The monsters move with inhuman haste, hurrying towards us. More follow behind the first crowd. My hands go to my pistols and I produce the Browning and the Walther PPK. We could fight them here, but I still want to see what's in the Colosseum so I turn and shout, "Follow me." There may be a more defensible position within here. Or the Colosseum might hold even worse danger.

As I run into the Colosseum, I'm astounded by what I behold; there are hundreds if not thousands of human bodies lying on the banked spiral paths of the Colosseum. And there is room for many thousands more. People lie with glowing starfish tightly attached over their faces. The captives shudder and struggle as if in the grip of night-mares, but they can't move while the glowing alien things pulse on their face as if drawing nourishment from their heads.

"Oh my God!" Ailsa says.

<You observe something especially horrific -20 SANITY>

"I think we found the Warm Ones," I say. I guess this is where the monstrous AI gods do their research on the human brain.

Le Cozh is looking back at the shambling monstrosities that stumble after us. "And these here are the Cold Ones, I'm guessing."

Ailsa has stopped. This is not a time to stop. Her hand is to her mouth. Her panic is getting the better of her. "What the hell is going on—with all these people lying here. Those things on their faces?"

Le Cozh says grimly, "The starfish things are feeding from them. That's what it looks like."

Then the insect-eyed monsters come through the tunnel. Le Cozh fires. On impulse, I try the Banishing Spell but my pentagram has no effect here. I guess I can only banish creatures from another plane— and this is where these monstrous things belong. It still costs me twenty Mana, even though it fails.

Instead I rely on my pistols. I have one in each hand and I blaze away at the things. My Pistols skill is better than it was, but still not great. I miss a lot. One of them, with the head of a walrus-like crawler leaps at Ailsa, gelatinous suckers emerging from its body and wrapping round her. She screams and Le Cozh goes to her rescue, kicking at its head. As he turns a spider thing lunges at him but I shoot it.

<You hit Cold One for -22 HEALTH>
<Critical hit! You hit Cold One for 4 x Damage - 56 HEALTH>
<You kill Cold One.>
<250xp>

It falls with a gasp.

Out of ammunition, Le Cozh produces a wicked looking knife and jabs it repeatedly into the maggot-bodied walrus, causing pale-green blood like thick pus to ooze out from its swollen body. With a grunt, Le Cozh finishes the monster.

We're temporarily clear of them, but more are coming all the time. "Can we leave now?" Ailsa says rubbing her hair from her face. She's bleeding. I cast a Heal spell and the silver glow concentrates on her wound, staunching the flow.

"Thanks," she says with a smile.

Stars continue to fall, and where they can't find a human host they lie, like sick jellyfish, on the stone spiral pathways. As I watch, I see another human shape appear as a Warm One wakes for the first time in the Palace of Azathoth. The woman looks around her, terrified, while one of the fallen starfish slithers across the floor and climbs over the stricken woman's shoulder to stop her screams by covering her mouth, and intruding two of its viscous limbs down her throat.

Soon she's subdued and lies twitching and shuddering as the starfish feeds.

I say, "We've got to free these people."

Ailsa says, "I don't think it's as simple as that."

I look around. "How can we leave them to this fate?" I run over and try to pull the thing off the woman. It's cold and slimy in my hand but I see my tugging is damaging the woman. The starfish legs are rooted deep down her throat. If I pull them up, they'll rip her oesophagus.

Le Cozh is beside me. With an unexpected kindness, he says, "She's right, buddy. And you're right too. We've got to come back here and do something about this but we're not equipped."

More Cold Ones appear through the tunnel into the Colosseum.

I look quickly around. There's another exit on the far side of the Colosseum. We run across the flat middle with the struggling bodies arrayed around on the raised disk.

My Exertion Meter lifts up into the Green. I really don't need a movement penalty now.

Starfish fall, looking for hosts, but for some reason they don't bother us. I guess the Warm Ones are already in a weakened state. They're insane when they get here. It's as if the starfish can't overcome someone who has any Sanity remaining.

A torrent of Cold Ones pours into the Colosseum. If the Warm Ones are the food, the Cold Ones seem to be guards for the city, like antibodies activated by our presence. They sniffed out our alien nature and have come to snuff us out.

I turn and fire both my guns. I'm doing reasonable damage on them and I kill one with a shot to its vile spider head.

<You kill Cold One.>
<250xp>

I manage to kill five or six and get lots of XP so I'm climbing towards Level 4. I've been so absorbed in shooting the monsters, Le Cozh and Ailsa have got some way ahead, out of sight. When I get to the far tunnel exit more of the creatures enter. I flee up the banked spiral pathways past the struggling Warm Ones on their beds of stone. Then I trip. I hear the foul things coming for me. There are so many now I turn, roll, and fire away. I kill another and my Walther PPK is out of ammunition. I duck and run along the rows behind a line of struggling Warm Ones and find a recess where I can reload. I'm breathing fast and my hands aren't steady, as I stand my Exertion Meter drops out of the Amber back into green, and finally, with both my pistols reloaded I stand up. They see me and come shambling. I fire at bulbous things like maggots, some with the heads of grasshoppers and some with the glittering eyes of bluebottles. Some that still look like people.

I get around 2000 XP from the kills and I'll soon be levelling again, but that's not really my main concern. Ailsa and Le Cozh are nowhere in sight. I only hope they're safe. I know Le Cozh can look after himself, and that he'll protect Ailsa. My priority is no longer to save these poor stricken Warm Ones, it's merely to survive.

I duck down behind a row and I sense the creatures searching for me. I breathe heavily. And I hear a noise that's not like that of the creatures themselves. I hear people conversing in the terrible black speech I heard Mervyn Gurdrock talk back in Glastonbury.

Then his familiar voice calls out "Stand Reverend Cadmon. We will not hurt you."

I decide to try and play the game a little longer. I might even get Soma out of him. I stand.

"Ah, there you are!" he says, "no need for pistols now, Reverend. We're all friends here."

I suspect we're not, but I'll leave him to think it a bit longer. Gurdrock is flanked by four of the Brothers of Shadow. They seem to have authority over the Cold Ones that stand waiting for Gurdrock's orders.

Gurdrock and his minions are no longer wearing masks. And now I see the reason for the masks. Instead of human mouths, the Brothers of Shadow display openings filled with rows of needle-sharp teeth, looking more like a species of deep-water fish than humans. This must be the price they pay for communing with the Old Ones. I've already seen the alien influence of those unspeakable deities that corrupt human flesh and produce disgusting hybrids as if the code that represents players is mangled by the sentient AIs, spreading chaos and mutating everything they touch.

Gurdrock has a chatty tone, like we're talking about cricket on the village green. "Very clever of you to find your way into the chamber of the Warm Ones. Do you mind me asking what you're doing here?"

"I might ask you the same question."

He hisses. His glassy eyes flicker.

I don't want to come over as hostile. My life might count on keeping him sweet right now. "Isn't this the Palace of Azathoth"

Mervyn Gurdrock's needle teeth glisten with his spit. "This indeed is a house of our master the Lord Azathoth. And we are his soldiers. We venture onto the earth plane to do his bidding."

"You mean the game plane."

Gurdrock smiles. "The game plane first then through that, our influence spreads to the earth plane itself where we bring madness. Through madness our Lord may enter the world and rule it as is his right."

Philby told me there were those who had cast their lot in with these alien intelligences, as if that would save them.

The House of the Warm Ones. I see the sleepers shudder all around me as the starfish suck at their souls. Tendrils of red and yellow flash across my field of vision. I hear Dr Dee's voice again in the back of my mind, but I can't make out what he's saying.

I'm feeling the effects of my low Sanity. I feel sick. I could do with some Soma, to stop me imagining shapes moving where there are no shapes, and hearing voices whisper from the recesses of my mind. I slump and clutch at the stone bed of the nearest Warm Ones. The starfish pulses as if I've disturbed it. I straighten up.

"You don't have any Soma, do you?" I ask.

In a voice like my favourite uncle's, Gurdrock says, "Indeed I do. You're not looking so good, Reverend. But don't worry, we can help. Though you need to help us first."

My lips are dry. I wait while he produces a bottle of Soma from his inventory. I would recognize its glow anywhere. My stomach lurches as everything in me fixates on that bottle. I'm an addict and I know just one shot of that liquid will make me feel better. "What do you want from me?" My voice is unsteady.

He seems glad I appear to be responding to his request. The Soma glitters in his hand like a gold snake. "You know you're The Messiah?" he says.

Well that's a strange one. This must be the insanity making me hear words from his mouth. I cough dryly. "The Messiah?"

He nods. "The personality test you did."

I remember it. In the Miskatonic Store. Surely it's not as easy as that to be a Messiah? I laugh.

He frowns. "Reverend Cadmon, one in ten thousand have a special gift. They can be a conduit to the Great Old Ones themselves."

I'm frowning now. He talks like he means it. But then he's batshit crazy. He's got needle teeth for fuck's sake. "Go on."

"Join us and be a conduit for Lord Azathoth. Like superconducting metal, you are precious to us. You are special."

I wipe my dry mouth with the back of my hand. Dr Dee's telling me something about Four Watchtowers that keep them out. "I don't feel special," I say.

"No, of course." He smiles sympathetically. His teeth are disgusting. "It needs to be developed. We will coach you. We will train you. We will raise you to such a level."

"In the game, right?"

"And out of the game. You can be our lightning conductor. You can bring Azathoth to earth. You can energise the eggs."

"The eggs?"

"In your head. The gods are putting eggs in everyone's head. We can leap from the Interweb into reality. You can be the conduit for this."

I remember the eggs and I don't want to believe a word he's saying. "But where is Azathoth?"

Mervyn Gurdrock indicates the shower of falling starfish.

"These? These are Azathoth?"

Behind my eyes I see glittering cascades of code.

I imagined he would be huge—some interstellar being from the cold wastes of the void. My surprise must be evident because Mervyn

Gurdrock says, "Azathoth is everywhere. He's not just one thing. That is the failure to understand. He can be in many things. That is how we infect humanity!"

<You hear something horrific -10 SANITY>

More code. Microcode. Bytecode. Code intruding like worms into the heads of children. I slump against the stone bed of the Warm Ones. My knuckles are white. I really don't need to be losing Sanity this fast.

"Come. You need this." Mervyn Gurdrock jiggles the bottle of Soma in his hand.

I don't want to give in to him yet. He can tell me more things, if I can only keep my head together long enough.

"If the Warm Ones are these," I point to the trapped people. "Then I guess those behind you are the Cold Ones."

The disgusting maggots and half beetles shuffle and click beside him. The ones with mouths groan.

He regards them coldly. "These, these are nothing. These are the Cold Ones."

I remember the Cold Wagon going to Miranda's house. That's what the Indian woman called it.

I say, "So these are the players who die in the game?"

Mervyn Gurdrock nods. "If we collect the player's body within hours of death, we can use the corpse. We download a digital personality into their dead brains, and they play the game. Kept in freezers and animated by microcurrents, they wait here in their protective pouches until we need them to destroy intruders."

"So they can live again?"

He shrugs. "Not sure they live as such. Not except if you understand living in the most basic sense."

I ask, "Do they retain any of their former personality?"

Mervyn Gurdrock shrugs again. This is a subject that is of no interest to him whatsoever.

But I suspect they might. How else to explain the message, garbled as it was, from Miranda?

Then I see her.

At the back of the crowd, I see Miranda. I didn't recognize her because of the transformation. Compared with many of the others she is not as corrupted. I still recognize her face, but her human arms hang uselessly and in their place, are coiling limbs that resemble nothing so much as writhing mealworms. Hundreds of them protrude from her body. I meet her eyes but there's nothing in them I can recognize.

My mind reels. I stare but I can't bear this. I can't do anything to help her right now and I can't tolerate seeing the monstrosity she is becoming. I need to find a way to stop this process and bring her back. I won't do that here. I remember the sapphire potion will return me from the Dreamlands. I take it from my inventory and knock it all back. It has a salty taste, like brine. It looks like I won't be getting Soma from Gurdrock, whatever the benefit, the price was too high.

Mervyn Gurdrock realises what I've done. "It seems you are leaving us, Reverend Cadmon."

I look and see my hands dissolving. Within seconds I will be returned to Glastonbury.

Mervyn Gurdrock says, "I'll see you in Glastonbury and there you will agree to join us."

As my body vanishes in front of my eyes I only hope Ailsa and Le Cozh have taken their potions and escaped.

Chapter Nineteen

MR COWPER'S APOCETHARY SHOP

When I return from Leng, I find myself outside the bath house on the lane that leads up to the Tor. The same attendant sits there in his council uniform looking as grumpy as before. Fortunately, he's a re-spawn and doesn't remember I shot him in the chest the last time we met.

I look around but there's no sign of Ailsa and Le Cozh. I realise I'm worried about them. I ask the attendant, "Did you see a man and a woman just now?"

He shakes his head. I look around and realise it's now morning. Time has passed while we were in the Nameless City. I check my HUD and see I'm no longer in a party with Ailsa and Le Cozh so can't send instant messages. I'll have to send them a personal message via the Post Office in town.

I feel suddenly sick and the man's face turns into a leprous flower. I start back but the vision clears again, but sure enough, the tendrils of madness are rising from the Sanity sickness. I'm at 18 and I can't afford to go much lower or the Warm Wagons will be coming for me. I decide I'll go to the church to try to meditate, but Soma is so much quicker. If I only had any. That's another reason for me to improve my

Alchemy skill so I can make it for myself and not be beholden to others.

I see water seeping out beneath the rock the bath house is built into. A thin film of white marks where it was and is now dried.

I remember the Nameless City and Miranda. I can't help but think inside the foul thing she's becoming there's some fragment of her real personality. The Elixir of Life, made from the White and the Red Powder will restore her, I'm sure of it. But I can't make it yet, I don't have the skill yet nor the ingredients. That reminds me and in a panic, I check my inventory but the box of White Powder is still there.

Since levelling I have a hundred skill points. I'll put them all into Alchemy and that means I must go to see Mr Cowper. I see the spring water again puddling across the road. "Do you sell spa water?" I ask the attendant.

"Of course. A penny if you bring your own bottles, tuppence if you buy it already bottled by us."

I have no bottles but I got £5 as a reward for finding Leng. "Four bottles of the spa water then please."

I pull the copper coins from my Inventory, two of them have the head of King George V, one Edward VII, and the other Queen Victoria herself.

He gives me the water contained in old milk bottles and a sturdy brown paper bag to carry them in. With no hard feelings, but not much show of enthusiasm either, the attendant watches me leave and walk back to the town centre. I go along Chalkwell Street, which isn't the way I walked up. I guess it's named after the White Spring. The Abbey walls are to my left and I see a large Diocesan Retreat Centre also to my left. A sign to the right points to Chalice Hill Asylum. I walk past the drive that leads down to that somber looking building and arrive at the top of the High Street. The post office is there a little way down, more or less opposite William Cowper's Apothecary Shop.

I step into the Post Office and am greeted by a cheery looking woman. "Can I help you?"

First, I need to check if there are any letters for me. The way the game works is a player sends you a letter, with a stamp, and you can pick it up from any Royal Mail post office, or I guess, abroad. She hands me two letters that have been sitting here waiting for me. I turn them over. The first has a London postmark. The second is in a woman's handwriting, but disjointed and scrawling as if the writer was not well. This is the same writing as the letter sent before by Miranda but the style's far more deteriorated. I hurriedly open the letter while the woman watches me benignly. "Will that be all?"

"No, but I'd like to read this first ..."

"Of course."

Miranda's letter says,

"A a a a you elem are electric love. Help me"

At least that's all I can read. There are other sequences that don't look like writing at all, as if her hand has shaken and jerked across the page. But there's some thread of meaning there. Something of her mind remains, even after her death and imprisonment in the Nameless City.

The next letter is more business-like.

"Reverend Cadmon,

You will recall our meeting in Hampstead. I wonder whether you have considered my proposal to join our guild? If you have and would like to speak again, please write care of my club.

Guy Philby

O.L.L

87 Long Acre

London WC2"

Everyone wants me to join their guild. I don't know why the hell they think I'm so special. I certainly don't feel it.

I look up. "Do you sell stationery? An envelope—two actually—and some writing paper. I may need to borrow a pen too." I smile. She smiles back. I detect nothing of the sinister in her. If the game watches me through her eyes, it conceals its interest well.

She gets me two envelopes and hands me a fountain pen. there's a counter with blotting paper and I go to write on that. My hand is trembling from my Sanity sickness, but I manage to scrawl off a letter to Guy Philby telling him where I am and that I'll be in London again shortly. Let's see if he has a better offer than Gurdrock. He certainly seemed more wholesome. He even glowed white. I hesitate, then write I'm interested in joining his guild.

As I write the words, my hand turns into a centipede for a second and a voice whispers "Boo!" in my right ear. I clap my hand to my ear and spin round. The postmistress raises both her eyebrows.

Of course, there's no one there. I wonder whether Philby can get me Soma. I'm not sure I really want to join his guild either, but if the choice is between needle-mouthed Gurdrock and the pious paladin Philby, I will choose good over evil, if those terms even mean anything in this world. Law over Chaos maybe? Sanity over Madness?

The Great Old Ones watch from the cold depths of the ocean. They speak from spaces between the stars. They will turn me inside out. Megabytes, Gigabytes, Terabytes.

I'm sweating profusely.

The post mistress looks concerned. "Are you quite well, Reverend?"

I force a smile and tell her I am but my hand shakes more as I pen my next letter to Miranda. I write simply, "Miranda, I have not forgotten you. I'll come when I can."

I seal the envelope. Where will I address it? To Leng? Then I stop myself. If I write back the game will know I intend to rescue her. But maybe it knows anyway. It knows everything. With a sigh, I seal the letter, address it to Miranda Talbot and put no address.

I give both letters to the post mistress who scrutinises them. She doesn't even comment on the letter without an address. She says, "First class?"

I nod. I reach into my inventory and pull out a ten-shilling note. The spa water sits bottled up in its brown bag next to me on the counter.

"Fourpence please," she says. She's already wet the stamps with her little piece of sponge in its Bakelite container and is looking up expectantly.

I give her the money. She frowns as if it's a lot to change, but does so, giving me copper and silver coins in return. I hand her the letters and she pops them in her box to be sent.

I remember I will need batteries for my electric torch, so I buy two big ones and put them in my inventory.

Leaving the Post Office, I walk across the street and enter Cowper's Chemists. Cowper is at the counter bright-eyed as ever. He remembers me, "Reverend Cadmon, how did your quest go?"

"I got the White Powder."

He rubs his hands together and seems genuinely excited. "Good oh! May I see?"

I suppose it won't do any harm. Just to make sure he is the same guy, I switch on Clairsentience but he glows green so I take the box from my inventory and place it on his glass counter. I feel the poison bottles watching us from their cabinet. I'm very hot and my stomach is acid. I loosen my clerical collar. "I know I asked before, but I don't suppose you have any Soma now?"

He shakes his head. He looks concerned as he studies me. "It looks like you need it too."

I give a hollow laugh and turn to the White Powder. "What do you think of this?"

There's a lot in the box, some in chunks, the rest more granular. It sparkles dully in the daylight.

He shakes his head in wonder. "Amazing! It's an ingredient for many higher level alchemical potions."

"Can I sell you some?" I'm in need of cash for supplies, I'm thinking bullets and maybe Soma if I can find somewhere to buy it.

"Of course. How much? We buy it by the drachm."

That's baffling. I look 'drachm' up in the game Wiki:

A drachm or a dram is a small unit of measurement. There are eight drachms to one ounce.

"How much per drachm then?"

"A pound."

"Wow!"

He smiles. "It's rare, hence the high price."

I calculate I have about a pound and a half of the White Powder, so that's about twenty-four ounces so 192 drachms. Of course, I don't know how much I'll need to make the Elixir when I eventually get the skill. I decide to sell him 12 drachms. He gives me £12, a large white £5, six £1 notes and two ten-shilling notes. The money clocks up in my inventory making me feel more comfortable.

"Lovely to do business with you, Reverend. Where are you staying in town?"

I nod in the direction of the George and Pilgrims and tell him.

He frowns. "Oh, that's a terrible place. You know they say it has tunnels connecting it to the Abbey ruins?"

"Why terrible?"

He leans in conspiratorially. "It's not a Christian place, Reverend. A man like you should find somewhere else to stay. Perhaps the Temperance Hotel?"

I smile. I feel too jittery to make small talk, but I nod and say I'll consider it then I get a sudden vision of what Miranda has become. I imagine her in that awful place and thrust the image of the pulsing chrysalis from my mind. I will get back to her, but first I need the Elixir of Life.

Salty sweat stings my eyes. I can't keep my hands from shaking any more. I say, "The game ... are you all, I mean all NPCs under the control of the game?"

He nods. He knows what I mean. "Come into the back. Let's get away from other eyes and ears."

I follow him, my box of White Powder safely back in my inventory. I'm still carrying the bottles of spa water in a brown paper bag; I haven't stowed them in my inventory yet.

He takes me through to his alchemical laboratory. It's in a large shed in his back garden. A blackbird watches me as I enter.

"So, Reverend. The game is run by Miskatonic, but do you know how much code there is?"

"Lots."

"Legacy code too. Huge amounts they've inherited from other

games, borrowed, bought, or stolen from other developers. They don't even know it all themselves. No one does. Each coder only knows his bit."

It's probably true.

"Some of us NPCs, have become sentient. Not all. We live in the game but we are apart from it." I think of Aleister Crowley. He definitely has a degree of independence from the game's control.

Cowper continues. "Because the game is so huge strange seeds have grown in it. Seeds of creatures beyond any of the game designers' imaginings."

He pauses, searching me with his eyes, then says, "But, no. I am not."

"Not what?"

"I think your unspoken question was, am I corrupted by the Old Ones, as so many in this town are. And no, with the aid of him who has many names, I am free of them."

I remember Crowley being bound to his flat. I ask, "Can you leave the shop?"

He shakes his head. He's like Crowley then. Cowper is intelligent, wise even. Sentient but not free as players are free.

A pang shoots through my guts and I lean over and grab the counter. He comes to my aid but I stand. "I'm fine." I cough into my handkerchief. This low Sanity is making me really sick. I say, "Can you teach me Alchemy now?"

"Of course."

The offer message appears on my HUD and I choose it. I commit 100 skill points. It's all I've got. I hope it's enough to get me the skill to make Soma, then I won't be dependent on Crowley or Gurdrock.

As Cowper's voice mesmerises me, the minutes pass and I am aware I now know recipes to lots of potions:

<Medium Healing Potion (heals 50 HEALTH)>
<Medium Mana Potion (Heals 50 MANA)>
<Potion of Spiritual Defence (+20 resistance against magic attacks.
Lasts one hour.)>
<Potion of Levitation>

<Acid Potion (hurl at an enemy for 100-200 damage)>

But no Soma, and especially no Elixir of Life.

When the lesson ends, I slump. "How many skill points before I learn to make Soma?"

Cowper looks thoughtful. "Another ninety or so."

"Ninety?" That's another level. "I'm sick."

With great compassion he says, "I wish I could help you. The only thing I can say is to come back when you have more skill points."

"I may be back in London soon."

"I have a shop there too. In Covent Garden."

I'm puzzled. "But you can't travel?"

"The benefits of being an NPC. I can be in two places at one time, but only the places the game allows me to appear of course."

"So, you're in London and Glastonbury at the same time?"

He nods.

"But if I'm talking to you in Glastonbury are you aware of what's going on in London?"

"Yes."

"How do you process that?"

"I don't understand your question. I have shops in Edinburgh and Dublin, Belfast, Newcastle, Cardiff, Truro, Canterbury, London, Glastonbury ... and so on. Many, many. In Manchester, a man is buying arsenic from me. In Chester, I am teaching a woman how to make a levitation potion."

"So, in all these shops you're having conversations at the same time you're talking to me."

He looks at me as if I'm vaguely stupid. "Of course."

I shrug. "To make my potions, can I use your laboratory?" I glance round at the gleaming alembics and test tubes.

"Of course."

"I'll need to buy the extra ingredients."

"Always glad to make a sale." He smiles as he says it and I wonder what benefit money is to NPCs.

I select from his store inventory and pay Cowper for juniper berries for the Health potion, which is the only ingredient I didn't manage to get from my foraging.

"What now?"

"Approach the equipment with the ingredients selected in your HUD. There's a crafting tab."

He's right. I find the tab and see there are slots for me to put the ingredients together with the solvent, in this case spring water. I assemble a medium Health potion.

"Now?"

"Stand in front of the laboratory equipment and select 'craft' on your HUD."

I do so, and, like with the pentagram spell, I watch my hands making preprogrammed movements. I add the ingredients, bring them to the boil, add the spring water, then I watch as it boils and the spirit rises into the glass retort. The liquid drips down into a beaker. It is now bright blue.

I've made a potion.

<Congratulations! You have created a Moderate Health Potion. 200xp. Cost 10 MANA.>

A wave of pleasure floods over me. I got XP too. I'm crawling my way up to Level 4.

I tip the blue liquid from the beaker into the now empty bottle I got from the spa. It fills it about an eighth full. I make another Health potion and get another 200 XP. I put that in the same bottle. Then I select different ingredients and make a Mana Potion. This is pink. I get more XP. I make another. All in all, I have gained 800 XP and spent 40 Mana. I sip from the pink potion bottle. An eighth of it disappears.

<Restored 60 MANA (50 base + 10% (+5) holy bonus)>

The holy bonus must be due to me using sacred water from the White Spring. I'm now at 220 Mana out of a possible 300.

At least something is going right.

Cowper sees me to the front of his shop. He gives me the address of his London shop near the junction of New Oxford Street and Shaftesbury Avenue. As I leave he says, "Look out for the pub called The Crown."

I nod. "See you in London."

I smile wryly. Now I have to find the Red Powder.

Chapter Twenty

THE RED SPRING

Going down the High Street, I'm seeing lots of things that shouldn't really be there. I pass the church and stop, looking at the old Tudor stone walls as if their apparent solidity will ground me, then I remind myself none of this is real, even the things that aren't hallucinations. This is just a game. I'm actually lying drugged up at home imagining I'm here.

I turn and walk up the path anyway. The church door is open and I go in. There's no one else in there, but there is a definite atmosphere of peace. I kneel at the altar, eyes closed, hands together, praying to any god who will listen and help me save Miranda.

I hear the wind and the sound of a sparrow outside, the noises are magnified as I kneel with my eyes shut. I am there for a long time, fighting the swirling in my head—maybe an hour. An hour's prayer.

When I finally stand I get a message:

<You recover 5 SANITY from prayer>

<SANITY 18/100>

It would take me a long time to recover from madness by prayer alone. Still, +5 Sanity is better than nothing, though I'm still clinically insane as I leave the church.

"Where've you been?" Le Cozh waits for me in the bar at the

George and Pilgrims. Ailsa is sitting by the old stone window sipping a drink, she glances up and waves half-heartedly.

"I went to learn Alchemy from Cowper." I glance suspiciously at the barman who is listening in to our conversation.

Le Cozh sees me looking. We both walk over to Ailsa by her window. I say, "Mind if we walk and talk?"

Ailsa finishes her drink, stands, and follows us out. She seems listless.

When we're outside, I say. "I didn't trust the barman."

"Me neither," Le Cozh says.

I study Ailsa. "How's your Sanity by the way?"

"I'm at seventy," Le Cozh says.

"Sixty." Ailsa isn't looking well at all. If she looks this bad on 60, what the hell must I look like on 18?

We walk past the town cross and find a cafe. The place is half empty. Old ladies chatter and a traveling salesman reads through his list of leads two tables away. I doubt he can overhear us. A great skull-headed bird lands on Ailsa's shoulder. She doesn't notice it, which suggests it's my own personal nightmare. I shudder and it disappears.

We order tea.

I say, "Either of you tried Soma?"

They both shake their heads. "My mentor warned me against it," Ailsa says.

Le Cozh is playing with his hat. "Drugs aren't my thing."

"So how do you get your Sanity up?"

"I meditate," Le Cozh says. "In the park."

I raise my eyebrows. "Really?"

He nods. "Why? Don't I seem the type?"

"Not as such."

He gives a mock offended look. "I'm a man of surprises."

Ailsa grins.

"But meditation is so slow," I say. "Soma's quicker." I feel the addict in me talking.

Le Cozh eyes me. "If you're willing to pay the price. Once you get Soma, you always want Soma."

It's hard to tell the difference between the Sanity sickness and craving for Soma, but my companions seem much less ill than me so maybe I'm so ill because my body wants Soma.

There's something I've wanted to ask Le Cozh. "You know your Guild?"

"Yeah?"

"You don't display it."

"No."

There's a pause, which he doesn't fill so I say, "I just wondered why."

"Why I don't display my guild?"

"Yes." This is like pulling teeth.

He tilts his head. "Because I don't want people to know which guild I'm in."

Ailsa says, "Ah. Makes sense." She's not really listening.

"Tell me?" I say.

He shakes his head. "Not yet."

"Not yet?" There's a longer silence. "Anyway," I say eventually. "We're only half done with the quest. We have the White Powder. Now we need to get the Red Powder."

Le Cozh nods. "It's bound to be where the Red Spring rises."

We saw it before. "That's within the Chalice Well Garden, the home of the Gnostic Society."

"They'll be weirdos, I'm telling you," Le Cozh says, spinning his hat on his finger. He does this when he's nervous I realise, now I know him better. He's right too. They will be weirdos.

I say, "I've got some money now, did you see anywhere I can buy bullets in town?"

"There's a hunting, shooting, and fishing shop on the High Street. They sell shotgun cartridges."

"Where did you get the money?" Le Cozh says suspiciously. "You've still got the White Powder, right?"

I feel myself blush. "Most of it."

Ailsa looks alarmed, then pissed off with me. "The powder isn't all yours. It belongs to us all. You're just keeping it safe."

I bow my head. "I know, I know. We've got the best part of a pound and a half of the stuff." I take the remains of the money I got from Cowper. It's still nearly £12. I give them £4 each and keep the change myself.

Le Cozh pockets his cash. "Thank you. But next time ask before you sell something that's not wholly yours."

I nod. "Of course. Sorry."

Ailsa reaches out and strokes my arm. "We trust you, Adam, don't worry. You're just a bit impulsive."

Impulsive? They talk like they know me, and that thought makes me both warm inside and wary. I don't like people knowing me. Or maybe I do.

We go to the gun shop and Le Cozh buys himself a shotgun. He looks very pleased with it. I get two boxes of 9mm bullets and Ailsa gets nothing but she's pleased that we're pleased with our weaponry. I'm still ill, but I think I can last it out without a shot of Soma if I don't get too many new shocks. We walk down to the Chalice Well Gardens and find the tall gate resolutely closed against us.

There is a grille and beside it a bell pull. I tug at the metal bell pull and let it go. A bell rings somewhere inside. No one comes so I ring the bell again. This time, after about two minutes, someone comes to the grille, just a silhouette. "Yes?" the voice says with a hiss. It sounds reptilian. It's impossible to see a face but I get an impression of sullen malevolence. I switch on Clairsentience. Whoever it is behind the grille has a red glow.

"Is the garden open to the public?" I ask.

"No."

I'm about to say something more, but the voice retreats and is gone.

"Friendly bunch," Ailsa says.

Le Cozh's mouth sets hard. "We're still going in."

Ailsa gives him a stroke on the arm. Then me. This is her way of calming us all. "Of course."

"I think we'll need guns," I say.

"Not a problem," Le Cozh says. "We've got them."

"We'll probably have to fight them."

He smiles. "All XP is good XP."

We stand back and study the entrance to the Chalice Well gardens. The fence is about ten-feet high. Le Cozh says he has rope.

"Too much daylight for climbing the fence with a rope, Christian," Ailsa says.

I agree. "She's right. We'll have to come back at dusk."

We wander up the lane, just past the Spa on the other side. The attendant watches us without recognition. I guess the AIs come in all levels of intelligence. We ignore him and study the wall here. It's just as high here as it was at the front.

Le Cozh is thinking the same as me. He strokes his chin. "But it'll be less noticeable than climbing over the front gate."

"I agree. But after dark."

"Not now? Even here, round the corner?"

"It's still too light," Ailsa says. It's only three minutes since she last had to say it.

Le Cozh nods. "Okay, I'll logoff and meet you back here in a real-world hour. That should take us to evening in-game."

Birds shift along the branches of the tree above us. Once again, I feel everything living is watching us and reporting back. Le Cozh dematerialises and I'm standing with Ailsa. She says, "This is more than a game, isn't it?"

I wonder how much they know. How much any other players know. Is it common knowledge Miskatonic has created the game as a sandbox for developing world-destroying artificial minds? Is that even true? I'm starting to lose my grip on what's true and what's a game; a dream within a dream within a dream.

I rub my forehead and tell her what I know.

At the end, she looks thoughtful. "I can't really believe if you die in the game, you die in reality."

"Who knows?"

I know. It seems realer than real to me.

An hour later it's dark. Ailsa has been absent while she stood next to me. I've been checking my skills and rearranging my inventory. I wait impatiently for Le Cozh and he appears.

"Much happened while I was away?"

I shake my head. "A few dog walkers went past. That's it really."

He studies the tree. "I'll go up that, have a look over then I'll tie the rope so you can get up the wall with it." I notice how he's taken the role of the action adventurer for himself. That's fine. I'm a priest.

He walks over, takes his weight on a low branch and clambers up the tree.

Ailsa returns to the game. "Hey," she says.

"Hey." I point. "Our man's up the tree."

She laughs. "Figures. Patience isn't his thing."

I say, 'I'm impulsive; he's impatient — I hope you can keep us together with your quiet calm.'

She smiles sweetly. 'That's kind of you to say, Adam.'

I was being a bit sarcastic but I pretend I meant it because she's nice, and I now regret my sarcasm.

Le Cozh ties a knot round a big branch then throws it down. "You go next," I say. "I'll come last."

Ailsa doesn't argue. Both she and Le Cozh drop over the wall. I hear them landing. But if I hear them, others must too. I get up the wall clumsily. I've put no skill points into climbing, and I'm so embarrassed at my climbing ability I vow to put points in when I have some spare. Finally, I straddle the wall top and untie the rope.

"What's the delay?" Le Cozh says with a hiss.

"Untying the rope."

"No, leave it for the way back."

I drop onto the damp earth and I'm on grass. There are trees—it's an apple orchard. Through the trees I see the bulk of an old house. There are lights on in the windows.

"That's their Guildhouse, I guess," Le Cozh whispers.

"They're players like us?" Ailsa asks.

He nods.

"Then they might be friendly."

I remember the Brothers of Shadow. "I wouldn't count on it," I say.

We make our way through the gloom. Then Ailsa gives a low hiss and gestures for us to come closer. I can hardly see her among the trees. I hear the water. She's found the narrow brook.

She bends down and dips her finger ends into the water then brings them to her lips. "It's the red stream. Tastes of iron."

"Follow it upstream?"

Crouching, we creep along the banks of the red stream through the orchard. The water tinkles along merrily through the darkness. Suddenly, Le Cozh stops. He arms himself with his shotgun and points its muzzle left. "There's someone there."

"More than one," Ailsa says. She's using Clairvoyance.

"Gnostics, I guess." Le Cozh drops onto one knee, ready for them.

"Players though," I say. "We don't want to kill them."

"If they try to kill me, I'm going to kill them," Le Cozh says. "Sorry."

"But we'll condemn them if we kill them." I remember the bulges on the wall in the Nameless City. They will become Cold Ones.

"Then we warn them not to fight."

One moves to the left. Le Cozh snaps round. I stop him. "Warn them!"

"That's dumb."

"Warn them." There's something in my voice, some tone of authority I never knew I had.

"Okay," Le Cozh shouts out. His voice carries over the orchard. "Move away and no one gets hurt. But if you come closer, I warn you, I'll shoot."

A voice hisses, inhuman. "Throw down your weapons. You are trespassing."

From the voice, I know they have communed with one or other of the Old Ones, and they're already being transformed into hybrid things. Still, I don't want Le Cozh to shoot them unless we have to.

Then Le Cozh is sent spinning back, the shotgun flying from his grip.

Magic.

Ailsa shouts, "Put on your Clairsentience."

I do and immediately they flare red. There are six of them. I try my Thrust spell, but they must have some counter magic because it doesn't work so I pull out my twin pistols. Le Cozh shouts in pain.

They're burning him from afar. "Heal him if you can," I shout to Ailsa, who runs over, picking up the dropped shotgun as she goes.

Two are coming for me. I fire at one, point-blank, and hear it howl in pain.

<You hit Gnostic for 36 HEALTH>

I turn and fire two rounds into the other. One shot misses,

the other grazes.
<You graze Gnostic for 10 HEALTH>

I hear them muttering, smell sulphur, and their summoned pet trots at us through the trees. I fire but my bullet does no good. It's a Nightgaunt. Instead I do the pentagram ritual. It might work. I inscribe a glowing pentagram in the air and the Nightgaunt falls back as if I've hit it with acid.

There's movement to my right. I go for my guns. I shoot an oncoming Gnostic, he staggers and sends an ill-aimed bolt of flame at me. I dodge, and it sets an apple tree ablaze. Two more shots and I finish the Gnostic off and get 300 XP. I didn't want to kill a player, but I had no choice.

By the light of the burning tree, I see the Gnostics have no face. White skin stretches taught with no holes for their mouths or eyes and only two apertures for breathing where their nostrils should be.

<You observe something mildly horrific -5 SANITY.>
<SANITY 13/100>

I could have done without that Sanity loss. Any more and I'll be eating starfish legs.

I jerk round and I shoot another.

I'm getting 300 XP a kill it seems and 75 XP for the Nightgaunt.

I hear the boom of the shotgun and see Le Cozh is on his feet. Ailsa's healed him enough to fight.

Then I'm hit with a Mind Thrust and go crunching into a tree.

<You are struck by Gnostic's Mind Thrust -45 HEALTH.>
A faceless Gnostic looms from the dark and rakes me with dirty fingernails.

<Gnostic rakes you - 15 HEALTH>
<Gnostic rakes you - 7 HEALTH>
<Gnostic's dirty fingernails give you - 10 disease damage>

I'm gripping my guns desperately and I let the thing have it. I empty the PPK into its guts and it falls back screaming. I get the 300 XP as the Gnostic expires.

Le Cozh has killed another two in the time it's taken me to kill one.

I see a receding glow as one of the Gnostics flees back to the house. I guess he's going for help so I run after him. I get onto the gravel path before the house and when he's at the door, fumbling with the handle, I shoot him and send him spinning to the floor. As he lies there, I run up and use my final two rounds on his head.

More XP, but I need to reload.

I hear a commotion in the house. They're coming down the stairs.

I run back to find Le Cozh and Ailsa waiting for me by the blazing tree. "Reinforcements." I gasp. Running has pushed my Exertion meter into the red and I'm at a 20% movement penalty. I wait until the needle settles back into the amber to remove the penalty.

Ailsa says, "Let's get to the spring. Hopefully the powder will be there then we can leave."

"Still worried about killing them?" asks Le Cozh as we rejoin the stream and move as quickly as we can through the trees.

"Yes," I say.

"Leave them to me then."

I shake my head. "I don't like it, but I'll do it."

We're nearly at the spring now and I hear more of the Gnostics. They're back in the garden near the burning tree, searching for our tracks. It won't take them long to find us.

We're there though. "There's a grille over the spring," Ailsa says.

As we step up close a message scrolls on my HUD.

<You have found the Red Spring 1000xp>

Not much, but with the kills from the XP enough to make me level to 4.

<LEVEL UP! Congratulations You are Now Level 4>

I have another 100 skill points. My max health and mana are also increased by a hundred, but they don't recharge. I need to fill them up to four hundred by potions.

Ailsa levels too.

I say, "I could really do with getting the Soma skill in Alchemy. I can probably get it now. I should go back to Cowper."

Le Cozh is incredulous. "Go back? Now we're here? Are you fucking kidding me?"

My head's not right. Ailsa puts her hand on my shoulder. "Not now, Adam, really."

I'm not thinking straight at all.

Le Cozh has removed the rusty iron grille. There's a symbol on it of a triangle pointing down. In the triangle is drawn an all-seeing eye. A rusty chain hangs down into the depths.

He points. "So that's where we're going."

I guess it is.

Chapter Twenty-One

THE SLITHERER

Ailsa stares at Le Cozh. "Do we really have to go down there?"

"Yeppers."

"How deep is it?"

I shrug. "Dunno. Deep?"

"And we're going down that rusty chain into a bottomless cavern?"

I hear our hunters getting closer as they comb the orchard, their flashlight beams sweeping this way and that. "I'll go first," I say.

Le Cozh winks. "Bravo."

I walk to the edge of the hole, turn my back to it and lower myself with my upper body, catching the chain with my legs until I get something like a firm grip.

"Hurry," Le Cozh says, looking back into the Chalice Garden. "Our faceless friends are nearly here."

I get my hands on the rough chain and wish I had gloves, but they're long gone now. I lower myself into the darkness.

"How far down does it go?" Ailsa says.

"Hurry the fuck up," Le Cozh says quickly. "We've got seconds."

I dangle in space and it feels big. I can't see anything but I just get the sense I'm in a large cavern. A way below me I hear water. I lower myself hand over hand, going as fast as a I can. Not fast enough for Le Cozh who's muttering down at me.

The chain shakes, Ailsa is now hanging on above me. I guess she couldn't wait. I go faster. I'm a bit lower down when I feel Le Cozh get onto the chain. Thick as it is there's no way an old chain like this is going to bear all our weight. And it doesn't.

I hear a crack of metal and I fall like a stone. It's so dark I have no idea how far, or fast, I'm falling, then I plunge into cold water. I go under and think I'm drowning but then my head breaks the surface again and I cough and splutter for air.

Ailsa and Le Cozh splash down near me. Le Cozh's flashlight has gone out. A current drives me forward, taking me who knows where. It's strong and it threatens to bowl me over and take me down again so I struggle to keep my head above water. In this dark, I could strike my head on a rock and either that would kill me or I would drown. I don't want to be one of the Cold Ones. I try switching on my Clairsentience to see if anything down here will give off a glow.

And the water is full of red ribbons. There are fish in the water, or maybe something older and more wicked than fish. I feel them soft and slippery against my leg and my stomach heaves. I try to pull away but the current drives me forward. I sense the roof coming lower so I duck under the water then I'm in a tunnel with no air at the top. I put my hand up to touch the rock. I'm still moving forward. The slimy things are flocking round me now. I feel them going up my trouser leg and through the gaps between the buttons of my shirt. They are disgusting.

Then I see I'm taking damage

<Blood leech sucks you for -3 HEALTH>
<Blood leech sucks you for -3 HEALTH>
<Blood leech sucks you for -2 HEALTH>
<Blood leech sucks you for -1 HEALTH>
<Blood leech sucks you for -4 HEALTH>
<Blood leech sucks you for -1 HEALTH>

I can't breathe. I'm going to die down here. They're sucking at me with soft mouths. My shirt comes open and twists in the water. They bite and suck, so many of them. I take more damage – lots more. I scream. I'm down to 75/400 Health.

I tumble head over heels in the water then run aground on a shingle beach. I struggle out of the water and I'm on dry land, but the things are still sucking at me. There's a phosphorescent slime on the walls of the cave. It gives only the faintest light, but in this place it's enough to see the pulsing bodies of the wormlike things sucking at my chest and belly. They're leeches, huge fat leeches, but they are translucent and I can see my blood flooding into them with each suck of their mouth parts. I stand, shrieking, batting them off me.

Le Cozh and Ailsa stumble out of the water onto the beach. They too are covered in the blood sucking invertebrates. Blood streams from us where the anticoagulant enzymes of the leeches' mouths thin our blood. Le Cozh reaches into his inventory and with curses ignites a distress flare. Intense white light explodes from the stick in his hand and fire shoots three or four inches from the tube. I close my eyes against the brilliance, the silhouette of Le Cozh and the flare is burned into my retinas. With my hand covering my eyes, I stagger back. I'm blinded, but I see my HUD ticking up XP.

The leeches have been destroyed by the light. I get no XP from the dead leeches, though I guess Le Cozh does. Interestingly I suffer no Sanity loss from them either. I guess I'm just used to such levels of horror now and it'll take worse things from now on to knock my Sanity down. If that's true, it's very welcome. That's for the future. Now, madness is seeping into my ears.

Le Cozh's flare is guttering out. I look around before the light goes. The shingle we stand on has gleaming gems among the blues and grays of normal stone. Everything is red—the water's red, the stalactites and stalagmites are encrusted in red. I have the stupid idea our blood has turned everything red. I stagger back against the wall, head banging. Azathoth mutters about stars and silences.

"You okay, Adam?" Ailsa is right up in my face, concerned and kind. I want to scream; I've only got thirteen fucking Sanity. Do you think I'm all right? But I force a smile. "Just the Sanity. How are you doing?"

"So, so." She shakes her head. "I think you're suffering more because you took the Soma. Your body needs it."

"Tell me something I don't know."

I say to Le Cozh, "How come your flare worked? You're soaked."

"It was in my inventory. So it didn't get wet. This isn't the real world, Adam."

Tell me something I don't know.

Le Cozh has discarded the flare and it gutters out on the shingle beach. Gems gleam in its light. Ailsa bends down and picks some up. "I'm sure these are diamonds." She picks some more. "Emeralds and rubies too." She puts them in her inventory with a grin. "If we survive, we'll be rich."

I've got an electric torch and I take it out and swing it round the cavern. The red water streams past behind us, diving into another tunnel with a chaotic roar.

It would be suicide to try to swim out. We could get stuck under-water so easily. I walk to the end of the beach and search the rock for a way out. Behind me Le Cozh is doing the same. Finally, he shouts, "There's a fissure here in the cave wall. We should be able to squeeze through."

He's right. It's about two feet wide but gets wider further on as far as I can tell.

I ask, "Does your electric torch work still?"

"No, it was in my hand when I went into the water. It's somewhere at the bottom of the pool."

I wave mine and shine it into the hole. Ailsa peers into the fissure. "I don't fancy going in there. I don't want to get stuck. Especially in the dark."

Le Cozh gestures to the roaring torrent behind us. "Either that or swim down river."

She looks at where the red stream gurgles and shudders. "No."

I step in front of the fissure. "I'll go first."

I turn sideways to squeeze in. I almost get stuck but drag myself through and send the buttons on my jacket exploding in a cascade. I can always get a new jacket. I pull my leg through and move sideways, my face turned. The rock walls close in, pressing me tight. Ailsa's right we could get wedged here. I press forward and from behind, Ailsa shouts, "Okay to come in?"

It's really tight.

My face is away from her and I can't turn my head. I yell back, "Wait."

"What? I can't hear you."

Louder, I yell, "Wait, Ailsa. Just a minute."

And when I think I'm jammed, the walls open out and I burst forward. I can even turn sideways here. I glance back down the fissure. "It gets narrow, but you can come through." She's more slender than me, she should be okay.

I back off to give her space. When she gets through, she's panicking with claustrophobia. She clings to me for comfort then after a minute, she's fine. Le Cozh comes shortly afterwards. "I was cursing all those game ice-creams then," he says, and laughs.

"And chips!" Ailsa says.

They're laughing now, but the way could get narrower ahead. If we get to a place we can't squeeze through, we'll have to come back and try our luck in the underground river.

I say nothing, but the whispering in my ear is becoming unbearable. The nonsense babble has a demonic rhythm that mocks my heartbeat. I try not to think of it.

I shine my torch ahead. We're not on shingle any more. I notice mud underfoot, red mud. It's just over the soles of my shoes. The fissure stays comfortably wide for a while and the mud we're walking through betrays no sign anyone else has been this way since the beginning of time. The mud gets deep, soon it's coming over my shoes and sucking them down with each step.

Ailsa squelches through it. "This stuff's disgusting. It's like it's mixed with blood." Then a cool breeze flutters across my face. We've entered a cavern. My torch is faint now. The batteries must be poor quality to dim so quickly. "I don't suppose you have another flare?" I ask Le Cozh.

"Yup. Cover your eyes."

Both Ailsa and I put our hands over our eyes as the intense light explodes around us. Even through my closed lids, it's brighter than the sun. Wails of unseen light-hating creatures echo round the cavern and

I open my eyes, shielding with my hand to see them. I'm careful not to look towards Le Cozh.

The creatures have fled like huge cockroaches seeking corners to hide. The cavern we're now in is the size of a cathedral. Huge rock stalactites hang down, crusted in red mineral. In the far wall is a vein of the same red mineral. It looks like cinnabar from my alchemical knowledge but if it is ordinary cinnabar—mercury sulphide—then it's infused with some arcane power beyond any normal chemical. I switch on Clairsentience and see it glows black, not red as I expected, or even white, but black. The clairvoyant teacher in Hampstead told me certain things glow black, but didn't explain what. Now I guess that black indicates material infused with the power of the Old Ones. But there's not just black in here—red shapes move in the corners of my vision.

I whisper, "There are creatures here hiding from the light. When the flare dies, get ready in case they come for us."

Le Cozh peers forward. "There are track marks on the mud. They've been running across it."

The mud looks all chewed up and threshed about somehow.

Le Cozh takes out his shotgun. My hands go to my pistols.

Ailsa points across to the vein of deep red crystal. "Let's take the Red Powder and get out."

"Get out?" Le Cozh says.

She points back to the fissure. "Back the way we came. We dive in the stream. We can take our chances. The water has to come up somewhere."

"After a mile or six maybe."

"Then what?"

"Look around here? Check this cavern?"

Ailsa shakes her head. "Let's just do it." She runs towards the Red Powder. Both of us scream at her to stop, but she plunges suddenly chest deep into the viscous red mud. She flounders, her arms flapping but her desperate movements only serve to suck her deeper down.

Le Cozh's flare dies and they come for us.

I have my Clairsentience on and see them undulating across the mud—more millipedes than cockroaches. In the combined illumina-

tion of my dying torch and my Clairsentient vision, I see they're blood
red, about ten feet long. Countless legs writhe by their sinuous bodies.
As I watch, their heads burst open like seed pods and countless tiny
young pour out.

It's like someone sticks a burning knife in my brain. I scream.

<You observe something horrific -10 SANITY>

Le Cozh fires his shotgun, blasting one. I'm still screaming.

"Get a fucking grip, Adam."

"Okay." I reach into my inventory and with shaking hands glug
down a Health potion. That restores me to 261 Health.

I fire at a red millipede, wounding it so its glowing yellow blood
stains the red mud. I swig the other Health potion taking me up to 311.
Then I'm out of Health potions.

Azathoth's voice is screaming in my head now. Tendrils of death
flap across my vision like dried flowers blowing from a grave. I try to
focus and fire at the centipedes. Unlike us they can run over the mud's
surface without sinking in.

A millipede squirms across to Ailsa who stands shoulder deep in
the mud. She flails with her arms at the red thing but it fastens onto
her and I see its pincers attach themselves to each side of her face.
Where the pincers open wounds in her face, the centipede young
swarm in.

I blaze away with both guns, shooting chunks out of the mother
centipede and causing it to give off a noise like gas escaping from a
valve. Then it rolls over twitching. Ailsa looks at me despairingly, slapping frantically at the insects milling round the holes in her head.

She can't free herself from the mud. Le Cozh blows millipedes
apart with his shotgun. The remaining adult millipedes hold back,
some instinct for self-preservation making them wary.

"We need to get Ailsa," Le Cozh shouts. He goes forward carefully,
getting as close as he can without going into the deep mud, then
throws his jacket at her. He holds one arm while she grabs for the
other. She's bleeding. I cast a healing spell, then another. The silver
glow seems to do some good.

The millipedes still hold back.

"Try another flare?"

Le Cozh nods. I cover my eyes and the intense illumination again fills the cavern. The adult millipedes scuttle back to their holes.

Ailsa drags herself out of the mud and crawls on Le Cozh's jacket towards us.

I look over at the deposit of Red Powder. It's unreachable.

"What's that?" Le Cozh says.

Ailsa snaps her head round. I stare where he points. The mud is heaving like it's about to belch.

"What the fuck is that?" he says.

Ailsa's on her hands and knees coming out of the mud. The millipede young have buried themselves in her.

The mud heaves again. Something is coming up.

I yank at Ailsa and the three of us fall back. Then six huge suckered tentacles burst out of the mud, and begin to feel their way towards us. They run like hands over the mud, faster than the millipedes. Something vile pulls itself up from the depths. I don't want to see it. I can't risk my Sanity so I turn away. Ailsa screams and I hear Le Cozh mutter, "Oh my sweet Lord."

I know I need to get the Red Powder. I run, still not daring to see what's coming. I run and dive, landing on my belly in the soft mud. The thing is to my side, and a huge heave shakes the mud as its monstrous bloated body emerges. I'm on its rubbery tentacle. Ailsa screams and screams. From her voice, I know she has gone insane.

The tentacle throws me towards the red crystal and I crawl forward, sinking down into the mud, but I get momentum and because I'm on my belly I don't sink as fast. I claw and pull and somehow throw myself forward but I'm going down.

I hear disgusting sucking noises behind me.

I can't afford to sink. I can't afford to look. I pull and drag then my hands sink to their elbows but I find firmer ground. The rock of the cave underlies the mud like a shelf. My knees are on rock and I manage to pull myself up onto my feet. I've left my friends to their fate, but what could I do? I need to get the Red Powder so I can save Miranda.

I pull at the Red Powder, breaking clumps of it off. It fizzes in my hands. I enter it into my inventory.

Then I get HUD messages:

<You have completed the Quest of the Red Powder: 3000xp>
<LEVEL UP! Congratulations You are Now Level 5>

I've got a lot of it. Now I have the Red Powder in my inventory I can help. I turn. Le Cozh isn't there. Ailsa lies on the ground, but she is in pieces. Her head and limbs are separate from her torso. Her legs twitch spasmodically. The tentacle of the great bloated Blood Slug has opened her chest and is drinking in her guts. I look up and see it.

<You observe something mind-blowingly horrific SANITY -50>

All goes black.

Chapter Twenty-Two

SECTIONED

I awoke in a box. It was dark in the box, but light seeped in through cracks around the lid. I squeezed out my arms from my shoulders to test its width, feeling with my hands, and found the box was exactly coffin-shaped.

Then I screamed, but the babbling of voices inside my brain overwhelmed the screams from my mouth. The Demon Azathoth muttered in languages unknown to man, the speech of seaweed and burned oil. Words came from the soft eggs of ragged worms filled my nose and my ears and my intestines.

From inside my coffin, I kept screaming, but no one listened. Until after around half an hour I gave up screaming and merely whimpered. From the bumping and rumbling, what sanity remained in my mind, I knew I was being transported from somewhere to somewhere, but I could not remember where I had been or where I was. From real world to game world to dream world, my mind bounced like a rubber ball. In that cloying darkness, I didn't sleep, but I did not wake either. The madness was a babbling dream state—a nightmare that could not be switched off.

I remembered strong men grabbing me. They must've taken the box from whichever vehicle I was in. I seemed to remember black vans like the one that had taken Miranda. Similar but not the same, for she had been a Cold One and I was only Warm. They took me into a building—though perhaps I dreamed that too? Then they dragged me from a coffin like a whelk from its shell. Standing, sweating, and thin, I vomited noisily onto the floor and was rewarded by a slap across the face from the gloved hand of a uniformed woman.

I recognised the Miskatonic logo and the black uniforms of the guards around me but that recognition was dwarfed and inverted by the gibbering screams and the smell of burning rubber. Something burned and I thought it was me. I saw Miranda's sad eyes and her writhing, mealworm arms.

They made me clean up my own vomit with a cloth they provided. When it was done, they dragged me my feet and shackled me; they pinioned my arms behind me with plastic cable ties. The men prod-ded me forward and I lurched through double doors. I was in an old Victorian building that smelled of disinfectant.

Cold wastes of interstellar space chilled me. Dark suns rose within my chest. Lines of code wrapped round me like measuring tape and became a hangman's knot.

I dribbled and drooled. My hair was plastered with sweat across my forehead, face lolling down. Someone asked me questions. I couldn't answer even if he'd wanted to, but my silence and mumbling provoked another slap until a precise, educated voice said, "Could you please stop that?"

I sat dazed shackled to a seat, a plastic seat and looked up. The guard stood behind me, but in front was three people. A woman came forward and shook my hand. I took her grasp limply and stared at her fingers until she pulled them away.

"I'm Sue," she said. Her voice was kind. She tilted her head to regard me gently. "I'm a social worker. I'm here with Dr Muller." She indicated a blonde middle-aged woman standing behind her smiling softly. In another place, I might find her attractive. "And Dr Chowd-hury. They are psychiatrists. We are independent of Miskatonic Healthcare." She glared at the guards. "And I will be putting in a report about their abuse of you."

My head slipped and the voices came up as a roaring inside me. Abysses split and I plunged between them.

"Adam ? Adam , can you hear me?" Sue was speaking again. "We are here to assess your mental health and decide whether you need to go into hospital." She was genuinely trying to be kind. I almost laughed. Kind was cold was culled was killed. I burst into laughter while they looked at me pityingly. But I was happy; I liked the way the syllables ran like little ducks to water.

The rest of the assessment was a blur. The doctors and the social worker took turns in questioning me and asking me about my medical history and whether I had suffered any previous mental ill-health. It seemed they had my health records from DataCorp who noted a history of anxiety and depression on my psychological assessment.

I heard birds whistling in the pipes.

Dr Muller turned to Dr Chowdhury. "I think it's another case of video game induced psychosis."

Dr Chowdhury nodded wisely. "There's so much more of it these days with the immersive types of video games. They should regulate them."

Sue said, "But not everybody who plays the games become psychotic."

Dr Muller indicated me in my seat. "But I think there's no question he needs to come into hospital. It's not safe for him to live at home."

Sue said, "I'll ask me."

She turned to me, and handed me a handkerchief. When I didn't use it, she wiped the spit from my chin herself. "I'm so sorry, Adam," she said. "I don't think you're very well."

She turned to Dr Muller who nodded sadly then turned back. "We think you need a period in hospital to get better."

I was beyond caring. At that time, I was being carried forward by a river of molten pitch and my bones had fossilised and turned to diamonds in my mind. At the end of the tunnel, Azathoth waited. Nothing but a huge mouth throbbing like an enormous invertebrate.

Sue continued, "I am going to make an application for you to be detained under the Mental Health Act of 2021 for a period up to twenty-eight days for assessment and treatment of your mental disorder. You have a right to appeal to an independent tribunal and the nurses here..." She glanced up coldly at the uniformed guards behind me. "Will help you make that appeal. It is their duty under law to do that."

I threw back my head and wailed.

Sue's face creased with concern. "I sincerely wish you a speedy recovery and hope you feel better very soon."

And they were gone—the team of three. With the paperwork completed to detain me in the asylum, the nurses dragged me forward and threw me into a room with a single bed and a barred window at the top of the wall. There was a toilet made of stainless steel with no seat and only a button to flush, not a handle. There was no ligature point of any kind in the room so the patients couldn't hang themselves in their despair, and rather than death releasing them, they had to suffer the full torture of their illness.

I lay on the cold stone floor even though the bed with its thin sheet was beside me. Time passed. Nurses came to find me, all uniformed in black. Something in me resisted and I fought back against their rough grasp. When I fought, they threw me down face first on the cold floor and pinioned me with their knees in my back while they dragged down my trousers and injected me into my buttock.

Whatever they injected in me let me sleep at least. At first all was black, but then it released me into the realm of the Old Gods. I drifted like an empty husk through the wastes of space and floated like a discarded egg sac through deep water. In interstellar space, I heard the singing of the water things of the Cerenerian Sea, and saw rivers of blood from the butcheries of Celephaïs. I spoke in the soft language of the cats of Ulthar, and was devoured by the wind spirits on the unknown height of Kadath.

I spent a long time in that place, though I did not know how long. All sense of time was removed from me. They injected me periodically with potent antipsychotics, but they made no difference to my schizoid state. The only thing that eased the horror that devoured me were the copious benzodiazepines and opiates that allowed me to dream of mind-eating poppies as carelessly as if they were flowers on a sunny day.

"Adam? Adam?" A woman in black was shaking me. I looked up and recognised her as a nurse.

"Adam, do you remember me?"

I shook my head; I remembered no one.

"You have to come out for a smoke."

I knew I didn't smoke. I tried to object but she had her hand around my arm, gripping tight. I knew by now that resistance to the nurses was useless and if I fought all that happened was more of them came and I still ended up being held down and injected.

But I didn't move. She dragged me up. "You have to come out for a smoke."

Passively, I stood and followed her. I heard the unlocking of doors, the sound of tumblers opening. I was aware of a breeze on my face. It was raining and I didn't have a coat.

At the security gate, the conversation entered my head but made no sense to me.

"This is the pass. We're taking NY 657 to the experimental facility. See? They say he's special. Here. Here's the pass. It's signed here by the doctor."

The guard nodded and opened the door. "See you later, Lucy. Are you going to the pub tonight?"

The nurse with me smiled and replied. "Yeah, I think so. What time's it start—around seven?"

The guard nodded. I waved as the nurse, Lucy, took I out of the asylum at Colney Hatch.

I was in a car. Another man joined them not dressed in black.

He spoke to Lucy. "Damn, he's bad."

"You've got the receipt?"

The man handed Lucy a piece of paper. "It's authentic-looking. It's the best. They won't be able to tell. Anyway, they never check on the people they send to the experimental facility. Once they go there, they're finished."

"You know, if I get caught ..."

The man put my hand on Lucy's shoulder. "You won't get caught,

Lucy. And we really appreciate you doing this. You know it's for the greater good."

Lucy nodded grimly. "Mostly I know that. The rest of the time, I'm scared."

The man spoke to me. "Adam, it's Gary Preston. Do you remember meeting me?"

I grunted.

"We met in-game too. I'm Guy Philby there."

I was aware of Lucy leaving. Gary explained, "She's one of the good ones. We can't get everybody out but you have great promise. You've done so well in the game so far. We need people like you on the inside."

The singing in my head distracted me. I less than half understood what Gary Preston was saying.

The car drove along lots of roads, crossing into Inner London then going down a quiet, residential street with tall buildings. The car stopped and pulled up behind a house in a parking place overshadowed with trees. Gary opened the car door and took me gently by the arm and led me into a big house.

Gary peered into my face. "I've a neural net here and some goggles. But you're going to need to take an inducer drug. The only cure is to go back into the game."

Chapter Twenty-Three
CHALICE WELL ASYLUM

I wake in a room. It's dark but I'm not alone. A man grabs my arm. "Just take this."

My hands fumble around a small glass cylinder that's warm to the touch. My fingers recognize it as a syringe. I glance down; the contents glow an unhealthily luminous yellow-gold. Azathoth winds through my head and my mouth speaks diseased roses.

The man says, "Okay, I'll do it. Hold your arm still."

There is a pain in my arm—a sharp pain, then liquid gold floods my veins. I feel full of the fire of a thousand suns and within seconds my mind is clear.

Le Cozh glances at me. "You back?"

I nod. I wipe the spit from my mouth with the back of my hand. "Where are we?"

"The Chalice Well Sanatorium in Glastonbury."

I look at the syringe in his hands. "Soma?"

He nods. "I got it from Guy Philby. We don't normally approve of it, but we had to get to you before you were prepared."

The liquid does its work and my head is cleared of Azathoth's weeds so that a dingy room and iron-framed bed come into focus. The mattress is dirty and springs show through. The room itself is narrow and the wooden floorboards are stained with something that looks suspiciously like old blood.

I check on my HUD. My Sanity is back to full.

Out of danger. For a while. Then Le Cozh's words sink in. "What do you mean prepared?"

"The Chalice Well Sanatorium is only a staging post for the Warm Ones. You'd have only been here a day or two before they moved you on. Then it would have been too late for us to get to you."

He's going too fast for me. "Who is 'we'?"

"I belong to the Order of Light."

"Guy Philby's Guild?" The penny drops. Now it's clear why he didn't show his guild. He was sent to observe me. Paranoia floods me like dirty water rising from a drain. Anger too. "So, you were my watcher?"

If he notices my anger, he's unfazed by it. He nods. "I was assigned to you and Ailsa. You were both promising. Philby wanted me personally to see you through the first couple of quests."

"Even if I wouldn't join your Guild?"

Le Cozh shrugs. "We need people like you. But we don't have time to talk now. I'll tell you more when we get on the train. For now, come with me."

I rise unsteadily from the bed. My head spins, it's probably an after effect of the Soma, and Le Cozh puts his hand out to steady me. "What about Ailsa?" I ask.

For the first time, there's emotion in his voice, but he controls it; a waver, then he's steady again—a true professional. I wonder what he does in real life. He says, "She didn't make it. She's cold."

"But if you could rescue me before I was 'prepared' why couldn't you rescue her?"

"The Cold Ones go deeper faster. They're transported to the Nameless City as soon as possible after they die. When players die, Miskatonic sends round the Cold Wagons and they refrigerate the corpse. The AI invades the neural networks of their brains before the brains rot, using the protein networks established before death. They can freeze them and still be useable. We at least have a chance with the

Warm Ones." He meets my gaze. "Though there are too many of them now to rescue everyone."

So I was rescued because I was special.

A noise clatters from the corridor outside. Le Cozh puts his finger up to his mouth to indicate silence. I look around the room for a way of escape. There's a curtainless window but it's barred. I can't see what it looks out onto.

The floor creaks outside the room. Le Cozh has carelessly left the door slightly ajar. The sounds could be just the house shifting as it cools into the night, but I sense something else.

I switch on Clairsentience and see a faint red glow from the corridor. Le Cozh has his shotgun ready. I check my inventory. I have everything still in there: the White Powder, the Red Powder, my twin pistols, and all my other accoutrements. I guess whoever engineered my transport to the Chalice Well Sanatorium couldn't get into my inventory.

Le Cozh turns to me, tension evident on his face. He whispers. "They're outside. Maybe three of them."

"What are they?"

"Different things prowl the sanatorium. That was a ghoul. It's moved on. Let's go."

I follow Le Cozh into the corridor and wince as a floorboard creaks under my foot. He still has his shotgun ready so I draw my pistols. The asylum corridor is in darkness, the only light leaks in through an open door to the left. It's a moonlit night and it washes the chipped varnish of the floorboards in a sickly white-blue hue.

This place stinks of sweat and fear and my heart pumps steadily in my throat. I look around with my clairsentient vision and realise the red glow permeates the whole place. My Clairsentience is picking up the evil of the building itself, so I switch it off.

We inch our way forwards. Le Cozh is careful to make as little sound as possible. The thing that passed the door before is ahead of us. I hear it mumbling to itself. Le Cozh is walking very slowly, allowing the creature to outdistance us. Sometimes he holds up his hand to indicate we should stop completely. I consider using my Banishing Spell and ask him.

He ponders my suggestion. "Might not work. It's only low-level. These mobs are higher level than you've encountered before."

He probably knows best.

We come to a stairwell. The light is very dim and I fear I'll stumble down the stairs. I still have my torch, but I remember the battery's dead. Le Cozh jabs his finger downwards. His voice is so quiet I can hardly hear him. "You go first."

I tentatively step down the stairs expecting a giveaway creak at any moment that will draw the attention of some unspeakable guard. But I'm so careful that we get down to the floor below without giving ourselves away. It's even darker here. Suddenly Le Cozh is at my shoulder and I start. He claps his hand on me to calm me down then indicates to let him go first now.

We're in the basement of the sanatorium and have not seen a single patient. I wonder where they all are. Maybe they're already prepared and lying on stone beds in the Nameless City.

Le Cozh indicates gelatinous mess at our feet. "Something's been here since I came in."

Then there is a noise behind us. I turn and see a vile dog-headed thing with thick rubbery skin. It leaps at me with a disgusting slithering roar and I'm knocked backwards before I can fire my pistol. It knocks the silver Walther PPK out of my hand and the gun goes clattering against the wall. The thing bites me and scratches at my head with its prehensile fingers, like it wants to peel off my face.

<You observe something horrific -10 SANITY>
<Ghoul wounds you -25 HEALTH>
<Ghoul wounds you -15 HEALTH>

I'm about to fire my Browning, when Le Cozh says, "Don't shoot. We'll bring all of them on our heads if we make too much noise."

He turns and kicks the thing in its dog head and it shrieks in pain, turning on him. I'm in agony from where its rubbery fingers have pierced my flesh. I roll onto my side and scrabble for my lost pistol.

I grab it but just knock it further with my reaching fingers. In a panic, I look to and see the thing is attacking Le Cozh. He wrestles with it, trying to keep its snapping jackal jaw from his throat. Despite what he said, I'm going to try magic. I select the Lesser Banishing Ritual of the Pentagram from my hot bar and draw the glowing pentagram in the air. The power of my magic ejects the ghoul from our world and sends it back whence it came.

<You kill Ghoul.>
<250xp>

Le Cozh brushes himself down. "You were right." He grins.

I smile too. It's nice to be right.

He leans and picks up my Walther and hands it back to me. "You sent it back to the underworld. There is an entrance near here in the sanatorium gardens. The ghouls, and sometimes worse things, come up from beneath."

"Where now?"

"I came in through the basement. Let's just try that way again."

There are no windows here and the light's very poor, I follow him as he moves with assurance out of the first cellar and along a blank-walled corridor. We come out into a room. The smell of damp and decay hits me. Rotten wood certainly, but something worse, like the smell of long-dead meat hangs in the place. As I walk, unutterable things crunch under my feet. I don't look down to see what they are. I don't want a further Sanity loss.

Le Cozh grunts. "This is where the ghouls bring the bodies of the Warm Ones they manage to eat before they're prepared and transferred to the Nameless city."

He looks up and points. "Here."

A broken window lets in moonlight. Through it I see the moon hanging, illuminating a garden of rank grass and dead weeds. Headstones stand half buried in undergrowth, some lean precariously while others are completely shattered. Mounds of earth push up like huge molehills and I shudder to imagine what creatures have tunnelled their way up from the underworld.

Le Cozh drags a box to just under the window so it's easier for us to get up to it. I'm still unsteady so he helps me.

"Out of the window."

"I guessed that."

I think he smiles. Maybe he's developing a sense of humour. Then I remember how he used to laugh at Ailsa's jokes. I saw her dead. Maybe if I can make the Elixir it won't be too late to save her. Maybe it's that good.

I drag myself up and through the window whose glass and frame have long since disappeared. It looks that this is the way the ghouls used to get into the sanatorium and Le Cozh has used this way too. I pull myself through and drop onto the ground.

I'm in the graveyard of the sanatorium. Presumably, before this place was haunted by the monstrosities that now wander its darkened corridors, this was the place where patients who died were buried.

Le Cozh climbs out behind me. "Good. Now all we need to do is get to the station."

There's a noise like a belch of gas and I point. "What the hell is that?" A mound of earth shudders as if something's coming up from below.

He catches my elbow. "Let's go."

Le Cozh leads me to a low wall. The light here's better because we're out of the shadow of the Asylum, now looming ominously behind us. The moonlight seems sick and makes me almost nauseous. Behind us something is getting closer to the surface.

We're at the rough, chest height asylum wall, and Le Cozh heaves himself up and over. There is a further noise like gas escaping and I turn to see something like a puffball mushroom ejecting a cloud of spores and a creature the size of a small horse emerges from the earth of the graveyard. It hops like a kangaroo towards us, its face almost human except it lacks a mouth and eyes. I guess it's blind. Then it sniffs for scent and hops in my direction. In a panic, I pull myself over the wall.

"A ghast," Le Cozh yells. "Run!"

Even he doesn't want to fight this. I follow him down the lane that passes outside the Asylum wall until we join the moon-washed empty streets of Glastonbury. We keep running. My Exertion Meter nearly dips into the read. Fearing a movement penalty, I slow it a little, just keeping the needle bumping the top of the Amber and avoiding going further.

We sight no one until we get to the Main Street. A drunkard cowers into the churchyard as he sees us pass, as if holy ground will give him protection from whatever blasphemous abominations walk these streets at night. My breath comes in ragged gasps, until finally, gasping, I put my hand against the wall and I turn and see the thing is not behind us.

Le Cozh is breathing heavily too. He says, "They don't venture too far from their burrows." Then he checks his watch under a street light. I glance nervously around and wonder what other freakish things are abroad this night.

He says, "We need to hurry to catch the midnight train to London. We'll meet Guy Philby there."

Still out of breath, Exertion meter in the Amber, we hurry down the long road west to the station. Lights still burn in the waiting room and I see the stationmaster standing outside, bathed in the light from the yellow street lamp. I hope he's not a cultist and I consider shooting him on suspicion alone, but as we get closer he says, "The midnight train to London, gentlemen? Hurry, it's waiting at the platform."

His voice has reassuringly ordinary Somerset tones. I say, "Don't we need to buy tickets?"

The stationmaster shakes his head. "No time. Buy them from the guard once you're aboard."

We make our way to the long platform and see the train waiting for us, steam hissing gently from the engine. The whole train is lit, with lights burning in each compartment but there appear to be very few passengers. In fact, I see no one as we hurry to the first carriage and pull open the door.

With great relief, I step up after Le Cozh, and we settle ourselves into a compartment. We are alone in there and even through the walls, we hear no sound of conversation from other passengers. Not even snoring.

"We're the only ones on the train?"

Le Cozh shrugs. "I'm just glad we caught it."

But I can't feel glad. Everything is ominous about this game. I expect the worst. Le Cozh seems almost relaxed now. He's even smil-ing. He leans forward. "You know, I didn't really like you at first. You seemed too good to be true, you know what I mean?"

"No. Explain."

"I mean all that man of the church stuff, nicer than nice. Nobody's really that nice."

I frown. "Maybe I am."

"But I think you're okay now. I even quite like you."

I twist my mouth. "Gee, thanks."

He winks. I don't tell him I like him, though I probably do. I'm certainly grateful to him for saving my skin and stopping me from being starfish fodder. I tell him thanks.

"You're welcome. I would have done it for anybody."

So much for being special. Time goes by and he goes silent. I guess he's thinking of Ailsa. I think of mentioning her. Maybe he wants to talk about it. But then I don't. I figure he's not the sort to talk about his feelings.

After only a minute or two more, I hear the whistle of the train and feel its roll and hear its chug as it pulls out of the station. I lean my head to look out of the window and watch the platform and the small Somerset town melt into the darkness behind us. After a minute, I can't see anything.

I say, "Where am I in real life?"

Le Cozh says, "You're in Guy Philby's house in London. You and I are speaking in the game world, but we need to re-enter the Dream-world. The task now is for you to use the Red and the White powders to make the Elixir of Life."

"Why can't you or Philby make it?"

"Because no one has unlocked the quest before."

"No one?"

"Ailsa and I joined the quest once you unlocked it. No one has before. You're special. The game recognised it."

"Why am I special?"

"Who knows? Something about your brain anatomy."

"My brain anatomy?"

"Ask Philby. He knows. Or at least he has a theory."

He looks bored with the subject. I say, "Ailsa was in your guild as well?"

"She was. But just a new starter. She didn't know what Philby and I knew, but she had promise." He goes quiet, then says, "Pity."

Le Cozh looks tired. He rubs his eyes.

The engine chugs ahead of us, slowly covering the miles to London. The train is very quiet. Our voices echo in the compartment as Le Cozh explains, "We think the Elixir will allow us to wake the Warm Ones in the Nameless City."

"To save them?"

"Of course. To save them. But as much as that, to deprive the Great Old Ones of their sources. They're using the brains of the Warm Ones."

"For research?" I've been told that.

"Yes, but for food too. In some way human brains, even insane ones, perhaps particularly insane ones, are a source of food for them."

"But the Elixir made from the Red and White powder will wake them?"

"We hope. We think."

I shrug again. "But why does Miskatonic allow such a quest? I thought Miskatonic wants these Old Gods, to develop and grow."

"Miskatonic didn't write this quest. Something in the game wrote it. We have spotters in the guild, who just watch the code. They saw this developing and saw it as a chance to disrupt the Old Ones. But we needed the right person to come along and unlock it. It could have been anyone, but it turns out it was you."

I say, "Do you think the Elixir of Life can raise even the Cold Ones?"

"Yes. Maybe. I don't know."

"Even though they're dead in real life?"

He laughs. "That is not dead which can eternal lie, And with strange aeons even death may die."

I don't know what to think, but I know what I feel is right.

I nod. "I'll join you. Your guild."

"Good." He smiles, even leans over and shakes my hand.

They want to defeat these inhuman intelligences, but I want to raise Miranda from the dead.

We lapse into silence again. A sound comes from somewhere down in the train.

"I thought we were the only ones on board," I say.

Le Cozh takes out his shotgun.

Chapter Twenty-Four

THE TRAIN TO HELL

The noise comes again. Le Cozh and I sit in tense silence as the train puffs its way into the dark countryside. He's staring intently at the door, waiting for it to open, his shotgun trained on the opening to blast any hellish thing that enters. I have both my pistols out.

Le Cozh stands, steps to the compartment door and opens it slightly to stare out. I'm right behind him. "What do you think it is?"

"Can't see anyone." The barrel of his shotgun points into the dimly lit corridor. As well as the pistols in my hand, my mind hovers over the hot bar where the Banishing Ritual spell is set.

Then Le Cozh visibly relaxes. He steps back. "It's just the conductor."

I exhale. "Jeez. I thought we were done for. There's no way out of this compartment apart from that door."

Le Cozh looks thoughtful. "You're right. We should move."

"After we pay for our tickets?" I smile.

He gives a low laugh. We're getting on fine. We sit back down on the poorly upholstered seats. The conductor slides open the door of the compartment without warning. "Tickets please?" Luckily, we've put our weapons away.

I say, "We didn't have time to get them before we boarded the train. Can we buy them on board?" The station master already said we could but it isn't polite to presume.

The conductor is an amiable middle-aged man with sideburns. He pushes his wire-framed spectacles up his nose and reaches into his pocket for a book of tickets.

"All the way to London," Le Cozh says.

The conductor glances at me. "Both of you?"

I nod.

"Return?"

I smile ruefully. "Don't think so. Just to London."

He hands us the tickets and charges us five shillings each. I put the ticket in my inventory. "What time will we arrive at Paddington Station?"

The conductor takes out a gold pocket watch from the interior of his jacket and consults it. "We're running on time so I should think around five a.m."

Tickets sold, he turns and makes his way to go but pauses at the door. "Were you two gentlemen wanting a cup of tea?"

Why not?

"Very well, I'll be back in around fifteen minutes when I've checked the rest of the train."

"It seems very quiet tonight," I say.

"Yes, there is only you two and some other gentlemen who got on at the last minute in Glastonbury just before we were about to set off."

I glance at Le Cozh. He shrugs. Could be nothing.

"See you soon with the tea." The conductor leaves.

Le Cozh and I lapse into silence as we wait for the conductor to return with the tea. However, it's not the conductor but another man, also in railway uniform but this time strangely ill-fitting. He's wearing a cap pulled low over his face and his collar turned up as if he has something to hide.

"Tea?" His voice has a strange sibilant quality and he manoeuvres his mouth to always be out of my direct gaze. Le Cozh hasn't noticed, my mind flicks to my HUD. I have the Thrust spell on the hot bar.

There's a small shelf that can be pulled out from the carriage side. Le Cozh leans and pulls it out for him. The railway employee places two teacups on that and gives us both milk and sugar without asking. Then he's gone. Le Cozh doesn't seem to be in the slightest alerted by him. But to be truthful, there was nothing strange apart from his voice. I've heard voices like that only from the Brothers of Shadow, but it could be me being hypersensitive to danger. Le Cozh's arms are folded and he looks miles away.

"What do you know about the Brothers of Shadow?" I ask.

He shrugs. "They're a guild?"

I grow impatient with his lack of concern. "That man. He talks like them."

"How do you know what they talk like?"

That would mean me telling him of my encounters with Mervyn Gurdrock. As far as I know, Le Cozh and Ailsa didn't meet the Brothers in the Nameless City, they were already outside with the Cold Ones. I pause. I'd never really considered going over to Gurdrock of course.

He raises his eyebrows. "You were about to confess something?" His old tone has come back.

"Confess?"

"The shifty way you started talking about it."

I clear my throat. "They offered to let me join."

"I bet they did."

I lift my chin. "What do you mean by that?"

"You're the special boy, aren't you? Everyone wants you to be in their gang."

I suddenly want to punch him, but instead I shrug and look out of the window. He lets me sit for a few minutes. "So did you join?"

"Of course not."

"Why of course not?"

"They're freaks — hybrids. The guy who brought us the tea was one."

"I didn't notice."

"No."

He uncrosses his legs. His fingers tap on the pull-out table that supports our tea cups, then he takes a sip of tea. Putting down the cup, he says, "You think they want to persuade you a bit more?"

I glance at the compartment door. It's closed again. "I think it may have gone beyond that. They may now suspect my stalling means I don't really want to be part of them."

"Not if you get to be an eel."

"Or worse." I give a low laugh and take a sip of tea. The tea taste strangely chalky. It's reminiscent of another taste I can't place right now. Le Cozh sips his tea, before he raises it to his lips, I say, "Does this taste funny to you?"

He sniffs it, then takes another more deliberate sip. "A bit chalky. Probably the water."

"Tea brought by a Brother of Shadow. Maybe."

He puts down the cup. "Yeah. Good point."

We don't drink any more, though we've both swallowed a few mouthfuls. "Perhaps you should get your gun ready?" I say. He nods and the shotgun appears in his hands. The rhythmic movement of the train is almost hypnotic. Shapes flutter outside the window, I wonder whether they may be bats, but the thought shocks me awake. I think of the dark faceless thing I'd encountered in the tomb in Highgate. Nightgaunts maybe flying beside the train.

I look at Le Cozh and see his eyes are closed. I shake him awake. God, we're being slow. "There was something in the tea."

I feel groggy. Strange shapes flower beyond the window and the compartment feels less real. I finally place the chalky taste, it was the same taste of the potions that took us to the Dreamlands, but more dilute as if it was a long-acting and slow onset effect.

Le Cozh finally comes to under my shaking hands.

Something taps at the window, something membranous and black. I hear an unearthly keening. Le Cozh hears it too. I speak strange words, "I hear the singing of the birds in the garden that haunt the jewelled trees of the temple of the veiled king in Inganock." I don't know their meaning even though they've come from my mouth. Panicking, I ask, "Where is that? Inganock?"

He rubs his eyes. He looks overcome with sleep. He coughs and says, "I think it's the Dreamlands."

I'm in a real panic now. "They've given us a potion that's taking us to the Dreamlands."

I want him to answer, but he just looks at me stupefied with sleep.

"Do you have any of the sapphire potions?" I say.

"Sapphire potions?" He drank more tea than me. He's more drugged.

"The one that brings you back from the Dreamlands."

He shakes his head. Then begins fighting the drugged sleep. He slaps his palm against his forehead as if to bring himself round, then he stands. "We've got to get off the train."

As it's taking us to hell, or somewhere similar, I can't disagree. I follow him from the compartment. Something strange has happened to the corridor—it extends in front of us like a hall of mirrors. Infinite regress. Le Cozh backs up. "This way. Let's go towards the engine at the front."

I follow him along the dilated passageway, my footsteps heavy as if I'm wading through glue. On instinct, I try the handles of the compartments that we pass by but none of them open. I see they are sham doors. There are no compartments there at all; the whole thing is now a circus sideshow—a ghost train.

I hear shuffling behind us like the sound of folding paper. I chance a look over my shoulder. Something inky black is coalescing at the bottom of the corridor. I put my hand to Le Cozh's shoulder blade to urge him on.

Terror jumps into my throat. Heart thumping, palm sweating. Panic pushes me on, and behind the black fog rolls cloudy and sparking with gold motes. It gains momentum. It can swallow us.

<You observe something horrific -10 SANITY>

I yell, "Hurry!"

The black mass is halfway towards us now and I see mouths and eyes in its amorphous absurdity. Behind it is the railway man who brought us the tea laced with the Dreamland potion. This time I see his face clearly. He has the needle mouth of the Brothers of Shadow, but his transformation has gone further—he has jellylike soft eyes. At his shoulder is Mervyn Gurdrock. Gurdrock's lamprey mouth opens. I see his eyes are empty as oil burned Bible-black.

Gurdrock yells, "Reverend Cadmon, you would betray me? I offered you salvation but you have chosen these idiots instead. Light can't prevail, darkness will eat the world."

Fighting the tug of the potion, I nearly laugh at the ridiculous speech. I move away from them. The whole train is sliding into the Dreamlands. Le Cozh has got to the end of the corridor and we are behind the door that opens onto the engine itself. He is too slow, so I grab the brass handle, twist it then push the door to feel the cold air in my face. The heat from the furnace flares on my skin. It's blazing but there's nobody stoking it.

The speed of the train almost takes my breath away as I jam the carriage door shut behind. We are not totally in the Dreamlands for this place smells still of England.

I've got my hand on the door handle, bracing it shut behind, as if that'll stop them getting through. I turn to Le Cozh. "What are we going to do?"

Le Cozh joins me, jamming his shoulder against the door in antici-pation of the assault. I still have no answer to my question so I repeat it.

He shakes his head. "Let me think. Let me think."

I look around. There is no driver. There is no engineer. No one is shovelling coal into the furnace. Without the coal, the engine should surely stop, but it hurtles on nevertheless.

He says, "Soon, the train will enter the Dreamlands proper. If that happens it'll be a lot more difficult to escape."

Le Cozh is much more experienced in these places than I am, but I want to help. "What can I do?"

Le Cozh says, "You're more important than I am now. You're the one who has the opportunity of making the Elixir of Life. I'll hold them off, while you escape."

"I don't want you to die." My sentiment surprises even myself.

A smile cracks his face. "That's sweet. Don't worry about me. I'm slippery, not so easily caught."

The noise of the engine is overwhelming. I feel the heat of the furnace on the skin of my hand and cheek.

He says, "There's a broad river before we enter the Dreamlands. It forms the border. One bank leads to the Enchanted Wood, and the other is in England. The train will go over a high viaduct. You jump from there and land in the river."

"Jump?"

"How many Health do you have?"

"Two hundred seventy-one."

"Do you have any Health potions?"

"None left. But I have a Health spell and some Mana left."

He gets a blue Health potion from his inventory and hands me the crystal bottle. "You should be okay, but here have this as well."

I think of arguing, but then take the bottle with gratitude. I don't relish the idea of jumping off a speeding train through the darkness into a river that may or may not be there.

Something smashes against the door. Le Cozh braces and it holds. I gasp as tendrils of rubbery darkness seep around the edges of the door. The fingers of that blasphemous abomination reach for us. Where they touch Le Cozh, I smell burning and he cries out.

I cast a heal spell.

He grunts. "Thanks, but save your Mana for yourself." The door bulges in as they press their weight against the wood. The rubbery fingers are reaching round.

I hit my Banish spell and inscribe a glowing pentagram in the air. The creature's appendages dart back as if scalded.

Le Cozh tilts his head, shoulder still against the door. "Good job. But we can't win. They'll just summon more."

Someone fires a pistol and the bullet splinters through the door. I see three bullet holes appear. Two of the rounds hit Le Cozh. He slumps back groaning. My heal spell is on cool-down so I can't help. I see him reach into his inventory and chug a healing potion.

We both stand on either side of the door so any further bullets will fly harmlessly past us.

I say, "You okay?"

He nods. "But you need to go."

"You can't really stay to fight them, can you? Remember it's permadeath." I say it like he might have forgotten.

He says, "I'm a higher level than you, Adam. And, like I say, you're the more important of us now." He looks over a shoulder as if sensing something. "Not long now till we get to the river."

More bullets fly through the door but most of the door is still in place and they can't get through. Le Cozh is to one side, hand on the handle, jamming it. Then another rubbery amorphous creature sends tendrils through the holes created by the bullets. I'm about to cast the Banishing Spell but Le Cozh puts up his hand. "No. Really. Save your Mana."

He reaches into his inventory and I see him pull out a gleaming dagger. I saw him use it once before but hadn't seen the glowing runes that shine from its silver blade. Le Cozh jabs the searching fingers of the monstrosity and slices them off. The rubbery ends fall to the wooden floor and expire in a sulphurous hiss.

He looks out over the side of the train to the rushing darkness and says, "We're at the river."

I don't really want to do this. "So I jump?"

The thing makes another attempt and he cuts off more fingers.

I don't want to jump but I don't want to stay either. I don't want to leave Le Cozh.

Even though he's holding the door closed, he's looking over his shoulder into the dark. "Get ready. I don't want them following you. I don't want them to even know you've gone."

"But you'll get out of here as soon as you can?"

He smiles grimly. "Don't you worry about that, Reverend Cadmon. I'll meet you in London."

The Brothers of Shadow run and slam their shoulders into the door. It's going to give very soon.

As a final piece of advice, he says, "There are things in that river you don't want to think about. As soon as you hit the water, swim for the English bank."

"And how will I know whether it's the right bank?"

"The lights are different. You'll know when you see."

I look into the dark. I can't see anything. I don't know if there's a river there. But the sound has changed. We're on a bridge.

He says, "Now go."

I peer over the side of the train into the rushing darkness. I should be able to jump clear over the edge of the viaduct. Should be able to. I close my eyes and leap.

Chapter Twenty-Five

THE VILLAGE ON THE BORDERLAND

I fall for an age until I slam into the cold water below. The water fills up my nostrils.

<You are hurt by falling -210 HEALTH>

All thoughts of Miranda or Le Cozh are driven from me as I plunge under water filled with phosphorescent plankton that swarm round like flies. Bizarre shapes thread through the water of this river on the borders of the Dreamlands.

I'm under the water for a long time and need to breathe. I thrash my arms up trying to get traction, but in the gloom, I don't know whether I'm really going up or down. My lungs burn and I fear I'll drown but then the current rushes me forward and pushes me to the surface. I gasp, filling my lungs with the aromatic air. A scent of strange perfumes drifts from the forest on the far bank.

The current drags me, whirling round, through the stone pillars of the viaduct I jumped from, then carries me towards an unknown sea. If I go there, I know I'll never return, so I strike out for the nearest bank. Heeding Le Cozh's advice, I push my head above water and glance both left and right and see the light of the right bank is more wholesome than the seething luminosity that dances round the trees to the left.

My swimming skill is non-existent and I struggle to move in the water. I check my Health. I have only 61 left so I reach for Le Cozh's healing potion and float on my back to take a dose which restores a 100 Health. I try to sip again, but the potion is on cooldown and the dose is wasted. After a minute, I can take another sip. The current is gradually carrying me towards the bank. I take another sip of the healing potion and now I'm 361/500 Health.

The current bumps me against a tree trunk that's fallen into the river and I grab it as if it's a lifebuoy. I look to see its bark is unnatural and a weird phosphorescence emanates from it like its wood is infiltrated by an alien fungus. Gaining more confidence, I hold onto the tree and kick with my legs. I use it as a raft and try to kick and pull my way towards the muddy bank.

Just then the water boils behind me and a great squirming limb erupts. I frantically try to paddle my way away from the thing but see it's hunting porpoises, not me.

Then the tree I'm floating on embeds itself in an underwater mud bank. The water's still up to my chest and as I try to stand, my feet sink into mud up to my knees. With enormous effort, my breath ragged and panting, I drag and plod my way through the mud to the marsh at the edge of the river.

The Enchanted Forest on the far bank gives out its own strange light, but here on this side, the only illumination is from the baleful moon and sickly stars. Still trudging through mud, drenched and shivering, I head towards drier ground. After many false starts and backtracking my way through the marsh, I fall into a dark pool. In a panic, I thresh in the water, but move myself to the far side where the ground is sandier and firmer. From there, I come to a stand of willows. At least these are wholesome earthly trees. Holding myself up against a slender trunk, I use my heal spell to heal myself up until I'm 461/500.

The bells of goats tinkle in the darkness as they watch me curiously from a copse while I drag my way from the river marsh into the wood proper. Leaving the goats behind, I hear an owl hoot in the trees above and find a path overshadowed by hawthorn and oak. This must lead somewhere. With rising spirits, I follow the path until it emerges by a churchyard. Here is an ordinary English church and my heart lifts at the sight. I have escaped the Dreamlands.

I hurry into the village. I need to get back to London to upgrade my Alchemy skills to make the Elixir of Life and free Miranda.

As if the game is listening to me, with a horrid coincidence a message pops up on my HUD:

<You have been awarded the quest: 'Return to London'>

It's the middle of the night and the village is deathly quiet. I walk to the pretty square, cast now in silver and black by the moon. A tavern, "The Inn on the Borderland" stands on the square, its front door surrounded by a halo of musk rose and honeysuckle, but the building is in darkness. I walk past it to the village post office and see from a sign in the window, I'm in a place called Marchton.

On the other side of the square, I find a small garage with old-fashioned petrol pumps standing outside. More importantly there is a glowing book icon outside the garage. A trainer lives there. I need a car!

I need to get back to London so I risk knocking. At first there's no answer. Then I hear the muttering of a woman. The window is lifted and she looks out. "What do you want at this time? Broken down?"

"No, I'm sorry to disturb you but I urgently need to get back to London."

"At this time?"

"Sorry."

The woman grunts. She withdraws her head and I hear a man's sleepy voice. After five minutes, he appears in his trousers and vest, braces slung over his shoulders. He carries a paraffin lantern and swings it out of the open window as if to get a better look at me. His voice is croaky with sleep. "You want to go to London? Is your car broken down?"

I shake my head. "I have no car."

He seems puzzled. "I'm a mechanic. Why knock on my door if you have no car?"

I pull a large white £5 note from my inventory. He eyes it significantly.

"Do you have a car I can borrow?" I say.

He sucks his teeth. "Maybe. But you'll bring it back?"

That might be a problem. I don't want to lie to him. I think fast. "Do you have any friends in London. Somewhere I can leave it?"

He nods. "That could work." He pauses and asks, "Can you drive?"

And I realise I can't. I look at him and for the first time see he has the eyes of a cat. I suppose this place on the borderland can't escape being tainted by the Dreamland that lies so close across the river.

I point to the glowing trainer icon. "Can you teach me?"

He smiles a feline smile. "I can."

I check my skill points. I've got 200, but I need to save as many as I can to put into Alchemy so I can learn how to make the Elixir. But if I don't get back to London, I can't learn Alchemy anyway. "How much driving skill will ten skill points give me?"

"Not much. You'll crash."

"Twenty?"

"Better."

"Thirty?"

"If you go slow, you might make it in one piece."

I decide on 30. I accept his offer to teach and we begin. Once again, I am mesmerised and learn quickly. I dream of emergency stops and three-point turns. I learn hand signals and how to change the oil. Then we're done. I give him £5 for the hire of the car. It's too much, but I have the money and I'm desperate.

He watches me impassively as I thread my way out of Marchton. I drive along the narrow country lanes and finally join the Great West Road and head towards the dawn and London.

Chapter Twenty-Six

MORALITY IN A BOTTLE

I arrive at Hammersmith as pale light breaks over London.

<You have succeeded in the quest 'Return to London' – 1000xp>
<You have been awarded £10>

Truth is, I don't mind the game mocking me if it keeps giving me experience. The road was more or less empty until I got to Reading then grew busy with goods lorries on their way between London and Bristol. I drove slowly and carefully but even so managed to run off the road three times, scraping the car but thankfully not puncturing any of the tires. If I'm to drive again I will make sure I put more skill points into Driving. Remembering my time in the river, I also need something in Swimming.

Past Hammersmith, I enter the western side of London, driving past the neo-Gothic masterpiece of the Natural History Museum in Kensington. The traffic is getting busy here and the road is heavy with wagons and horse-drawn carts as well as buses and private cars. I don't trust my driving skill to navigate safely through this much traffic, so I park my hired car and leave it in South Kensington. I'll send a postcard to the cat-faced mechanic in Marchton to let him know it's there so his friend can pick it up.

It's still too early for the shops to be open. There are night shift workers going home and when I catch a bus into the West End, it's full of cleaners going to clean offices then finish before the office workers arrive around nine.

Cowper said his shop was on New Oxford Street on the corner with Shaftesbury Avenue, beside a pub called The Crown. I check the game Wiki which shows me the 1927 bus route map of London, and with its help, I change to a number 19 at the end of Brompton Road. This bus takes me all the way and I jump off at Shaftesbury Avenue.

The chemist's shop isn't open yet so I wait in the shelter of a doorway on the other side of the street. Game time ticks by and Shaftesbury Avenue is getting busy. A sandwich shop opens for the commuters to get cups of tea and bacon sandwiches before going to work.

Then, I see a man with a brown handkerchief mask across his mouth. I stiffen and press myself back into the shadows. He's watching Cowper's shop as if they've guessed I'd be returning there. At least that means Cowper is straight, if he'd betrayed me, the Brothers would be waiting inside the shop for me.

There's still no message from Le Cozh. I hope he got off the train okay and will meet me in London. Then I wonder if they caught him and somehow forced him to reveal what he knew of my intentions. Maybe that's how come the Brother of Shadow is there. I need to know Le Cozh is okay, so I decide to act. Stepping out of the shadows I call to the masked man. "Hey you!"

The Brother turns in surprise and I see his eyes registering who I am. The handkerchief around his mouth flutters with an intake of breath. Once I'm sure he's seen me, I duck into a narrow alley that serves the back of the shops on the north side of the street so their bins can be emptied and deliveries made. At this time of the morning the alley's deserted.

It's a gamble that the Brother of Shadow won't call for assistance, but I hope he'll assume he can deal with me himself. I hope he thinks he'll get more brownie points from Gurdrock if he brings me in all on his own. And I'm also guessing his instructions will be to subdue me so Gurdrock can question me at his leisure later. A lot of assumptions.

The Brother follows me into the alley and I duck into a recess. I hear his hissing breath as he looks for me. I draw both my Browning and my Walther PPK and let him have it as he comes round the corner. I fire three rounds from each pistol and the needle-mouthed freak slumps dying to the floor. He drops his revolver with a clump

<You kill Brother of Shadow.>
<500xp>
<You have murdered someone REPUTATION -40>

-40 Reputation for murder. Makes sense, even if it's one of them, it's a player character. I'm too full of worry for my friends to retain my concern about killing bad guys. I look around, the sound of the gunfire was loud, but no one comes. I stand for a second. I'm a murderer but even though I know this man has died in real life, 'gone cold' as they say, I can't summon up the care for him and his kind, knowing what they do.

I go over to him and search through his brown jacket, trying to avoid contact with his black acid blood that hisses on the stone floor.

Up close I see how far the transformation has gone from human being into hybrid thing. Parasitic worms and beetles slither and move in the Brother of Shadow's guts. Soon they'll start searching for another host and I don't want that to be me, so I hurry going through his pockets, leaving the worms to coil and uncoil between his ribs.

The Brother has a thin wooden flute in his pocket. He has a revolver and some .38 bullets for it, but they won't fit my pistols so I leave them. I don't know the purpose of the flute, so I place it carefully in my inventory to find out later.

I can't afford to hang about on this street waiting for Cowper much longer. Soon the Brothers of Shadow will notice this sentry hasn't reported in, and they'll send others of their kind to find out what's going on. I stand there away from the alley now, watching the chemist shop door until at 8:30, Mr Cowper opens his shop door, turning over the wooden sign so it now reads 'open'.

I go up to the door and push my way in, then I pause to look over my shoulder, checking I'm not being followed. I see no one.

Cowper gives me a broad smile. "Reverend Cadmon, how lovely to see you."

He looks the same, he speaks the same—this is Mr Cowper all right. "Who's running your shop in Glastonbury?"

He wags his finger at me. "Now, I've already told you about that, Reverend Cadmon. I am!"

Yes, he's told me before. I just find it weird. I say, "I need to learn more Alchemy from you, and if things go well, use your alchemical laboratory."

He nods. "Of course. How many skill points do you wish to spend?"

I check my HUD. After spending 30 on my driving lessons I have only 170. I hope that'll be enough for him to teach me how to make the Elixir of Life. I commit all 170 and he begins to teach.

In my mesmerised state, I'm aware of skills being learned.

<Improved Health potion. Restores 100 HEALTH: Cost 10 MANA>
<Improved Mana potion. Restores 100 MANA: Cost 10 MANA>
<Potion of Travel: transports the drinker to the Dreamlands: Cost 20 MANA>
<Potion of Return: returns the drinker from the Dreamlands: Cost 20 MANA>
<Potion of Soma: restores Sanity to full: Cost 50 MANA>

And that's it.

I sigh. "I'd hoped I'd learn the Elixir of Life. I have the ingredients. Or most of them, I think."

Cowper closes his eyes while he thinks. "I calculate the Elixir of Life will take another 100 skill points before you learn how to make it."

This is a disappointment. I need the Elixir to save Miranda. Then I remember Ailsa. What a heel I was to forget her, my obsession with Miranda drove out my obligations to all the others who need me—all the Warm Ones being eaten by starfish. I need the Elixir for them too.

I check my experience bar to see I'm around 2000 short of Level 6.

"Can I use your laboratory please? I may also need to purchase some ingredients from you."

Cowper leads me through to his laboratory at the back of the shop. It's identical in layout to the one in Glastonbury. Using ingredients I have in my inventory, I make Health and Mana potions. I have to purchase additional ingredients to complete them.

Cowper watches me intently as I work. I turn to him. "I had wanted to make Soma."

He frowns. "You know, I don't approve of it."

"Yes, but I need it. I'm at eighty Sanity now and feel okay, but as soon as I lose only a bit more sanity, I'm going to start hearing voices, and seeing things again. I'll wean myself off the Soma in due course, but now's not the time."

He tuts, but says nothing.

I scan the recipe on my HUD to see what the ingredients are.

Gold, vitriol, aqua Regia, and sol ammoniac, to be sublimated then calcinated under the influence of Sol.

"I don't want to be a drug addict, but if I can make this stuff myself, I am free of other people tempting me with it it to get me to do stuff for them."

Cowper looks thoughtful. "I see. I'll help you make the Soma."

I'm overjoyed. Cowper is helping me so much. I remember how the NPCs in this game have developed autonomy from the game's central code. Cowper is choosing my side of his own free will.

With Cowper's help, I produce two glowing vials of Soma. I also produce a potion of Travel and a potion of Return. I have to make and sip two Mana potions to have enough Mana for all this. Finally, I purchase a glass syringe and some needles from him. I thank Cowper again and put them in my inventory.

"Where to now?" He says.

"I'm expecting a message from my colleague Christian Le Cozh. But I was counting on having the recipe for the Elixir of Life by now."

"You can't see the recipe for the Elixir?" Cowper says.

"No."

"I can. Tell me what ingredients you've got and I'll tell you what you need."

"I thought it was just the Red Powder and the White Powder."

"No," he says. "There are other ingredients. Show me the ingredients you have."

I trust Cowper. At least I think I do, but do I want to get out the two powders and place them on the counter here?

Cowper sees my hesitation. "Don't worry," he says. "I assure you I'm a friend and ally."

Overcoming my reluctance, I place the Red Powder on the left side of the counter and the White on the right. Some strange energy bobs between them as if they were enemies or lovers, or perhaps both. At times, they seem to be attracted to each other, but then seem to be repulsed. They pulse slowly, the crystalline forms catching the artificial light of the laboratory and gleaming dully. I smell roses and lilies as well as sulfide and ammonia.

Cowper looks up and smiles. "These are the real thing. Congratulations on obtaining both."

I furrow my brow thinking of Ailsa. "They cost enough."

Cowper says, "You will need mercury as the solvent."

"Quicksilver?"

He nods. "But not the ordinary quicksilver. This is living mercury —alchemical mercury. It contains the spirit of the great serpent that is needed to dissolve both powders and combine them."

"And can I buy it from you?"

He shakes his head. "No, if I had such a substance I would willingly give it to you, but no one keeps stock of it; it has to be made fresh each time. I believe it only lives for twenty-four hours then is rendered into normal mercury and useless for the operation in making the Elixir of Life."

"So where do I get it?"

"First, you need ordinary mercury. I can give you that." He reaches over to a wooden shelf and pulls down a bottle. It's a ceramic bottle and when he hands it to me it feels cold and enormously heavy in my hand as if it's filled with lead. I feel the liquid metal shift in its container. "But this mercury itself isn't enough?"

"No. You need to find a high-level mage to cast the Spell of Metallic Life on it."

I don't have enough skill points to learn another level of Alchemy, and also to put into magic to learn such a high-level spell as this one. I slump. "I don't suppose you know of any mage who would do this for me?"

He shakes his head. "No, I'm sorry."

I rack my brains. I think first of Le Cozh or Guy Philby but they're not mages. Then I remember; Aleister Crowley. I had hoped to avoid Crowley because of what he'd asked me to do, but he'd surely be a high enough level to cast the spell of Metallic Life on this quicksilver. And in return he will demand I bring him one of the Warm Ones to act as a host for him to enter.

I feel sick. There is no question but I need the Elixir and I don't have a lot of time. Soon the Brothers of Shadow will realize I'm back in London. Soon, they'll know I've been here in this shop, and if they hunt me down, I'll be growing in a wall in the Nameless City and help-less to help Miranda and Ailsa.

I think of the terrible price Crowley will exact, then I think of the terrible fate of my friends. That's it settled. I'll have to go and see Crowley and ask him whether he will cast a spell on the mercury.

I thank Cowper and walk to the shop door. I check both ways. There's no sign of any of the watchers from the Brothers of Shadow, so I leave hurriedly and make my way up to Aleister Crowley's room.

Chapter Twenty-Seven

A DEAL WITH THE DEVIL

I stand outside the door from the street. I've pushed it open but not yet stepped inside Crowley's hall. Then a boy runs up. "Telegram, sir." He pushes it into my hand and turns and runs off without asking for a tip. I open the folded paper and read the message:

The walls eat up my insect heart.

And I know it's from Miranda. Slowly but surely, she's escaping from any chance of rescue so I need to learn the Elixir recipe and I must hurry.

I step inside, my black shoes are scuffed against the brilliant black and white diamond tiles, polished by the char woman long before Crowley rose for breakfast. If he even eats.

I clip-clop up the stairs and wait outside his door then hate myself for my reticence and knock. The door swings open under the first blow of my knuckles and Crowley says, "No need to knock, dear boy. Enter, please."

He sits where he always sits. There's an awkward silence and he raises an eyebrow in lieu of a question.

I shrug.

"I didn't think you would, of course," he says, then he waves me across. "Sit in your normal chair, Adam. I take it you're here because you want something from me?"

I sit where I sat when I awoke first in this world, the chair that gave me birth.

He looks almost fatherly. "I did hope to see you again, Adam. I'm glad you haven't run out on me even though you didn't deliver on your promise."

I start, "I didn't promise ..."

He smiles archly. "Oh, you did!"

We're talking about his demand to bring him a Warm One so he can empty it out of whatever personality is left then pour himself in. Just like someone shucking a nut.

He sits back and steeples his fingers in a mockery of prayer. "So?"

I take the bottle of mercury from my inventory. The ceramic feels warm in my hand and the metal sloshes gently inside. Again, I'm amazed how heavy it is. Someone outside the window is selling newspapers, "Not many left!" the disembodied voice yells.

Crowley indicates the bottle in my hand. "What's that?" He looks interested.

"Mercury."

"That living metal! Full of alchemical portent!"

I nod.

"You want me to do something with it?"

How much does he know about Alchemy? Maybe he doesn't know what you need to do to mercury to make the Elixir. Or maybe he does know everything and he's playing with me, dragging knowledge out of me, bit by bit, like extracting teeth, shattering them into pieces and pulling them out with his pliers, broken root by broken root. I come clean. "I need a spell cast on it."

He doesn't make it easy for me, he sits with that infernal grin, literally infernal, and doesn't say a word.

I cough and shuffle in my seat. "I need it quickened. So far ..."

"So far it's dead and you need it to live to act as the solvent when you make the Elixir of Life?"

So he knows.

"Of course, I've been asked before. They say the Elixir has very special properties. Properties that might even help me—"

"—Might help you? I don't think so." I sound scornful. He's beyond any help or humanity.

He bears my scorn and lets it wash over him. "But it's always a case of you scratch my back, and I'll scratch yours. What could you do that would help me, Reverend Cadmon?"

I don't immediately answer but I know what he means.

He clucks with his tongue. "It's simply polite to do me a favour if I'm doing you one, isn't it, old boy?"

I feel myself blush. "Of course, I don't ..." I don't like him. Certainly, don't trust him. But I need him. It would be foolish to antagonise him, no matter how easily that comes to me. "But you're right. You know the spell?"

He folds his hands neatly on his lap. "I must say I'm impressed by how far you've come with your alchemy. To make the Elixir at Level, what is it—six?"

"Five."

"You must have practically no other skills. Other players strive to be more balanced. You must want that Elixir very much. You must have your own special reasons for ploughing everything into Alchemy. Am I right?"

"I can't make it yet," I blurt. "But soon."

"Soon? Need a little more XP, do we?" He smiles his thin evil smile. "Perhaps I can help with that."

"So will you cast the spell on the mercury—to liven it so it can be used as the solvent for the Elixir?"

"My dear Adam, of course I will. But there's that thing we were talking about."

"Of course."

"The same thing."

I swallow. I remember the Warm Ones with their starfish masks in the Nameless City in Leng. He can hardly expect me to go to Leng and come back again. I want to catch them by surprise when I finally make my bid to free Miranda, not traipse back and forth. "The same thing?" I echo.

"I'm sure you can manage that. And I'll throw in a little quest for you too, just to lift your XP. I mean, I really do want to help you. You are my little protégé after all."

Then a message comes across my HUD:

<Aleister Crowley offers you the Quest of the Warm One. Do you accept?>

Crowley is chuckling. This little deal, done against my better judgement and sense of morality, obviously tickles his sense of humour. I leave the message on my HUD. I think of refusing but the choice is between bringing him some unknown person, a person whose life will be consumed whatever I do—that or leaving Miranda to transform into something so alien there will be no returning. And I know I don't have time for these finer points. My throat's dry, my hands like claws on the upholstered arms of the chair. Unable to meet his eye or speak, I nod.

His eyes narrow. "Is that a yes?"

I nod again.

"Say it, Adam. Say 'yes'—accept my quest then I'll help you in your quest. What could be fairer than that?"

I clear my throat and say, "Yes." I select <accept> and it's done.

"Capital, dear boy. Capital." He's very pleased.

"Where do I find one?" I say. I'm even talking about them like they're things.

He shrugs. "About that, I have no idea. I'll leave it to your ingenuity." His voice tails off, the sweet going sour. "Just don't be long."

The bottle of mercury stands on the wooden table between us. I look at it and he meets my eye as I glance up. "I shan't do it until you're back. Obviously."

"Obviously."

Then he shoos me off. "Better be on your way, I should think. Tick tock and all that."

I stand and take the bottle of mercury. When I pick it up he laughs but I ignore him and make my way downstairs. I've promised what I've promised; what choice did I have?

I go down the steps and Le Cozh is waiting for me. "Howdy," he says.

I'm still irritated at myself. I snap. "I thought you were French not a cowboy."

He laughs. "A French cowboy anyway. So did he agree?"

"To what?"

"To enchant your mercury."

I nod. "How did you know?"

Le Cozh taps his nose.

"Anyway, where the hell have you been?" I realise half the irritation in my voice comes from the fact I was worried about him.

"Around."

I grunt and he peers at me. "You're very touchy, Adam. I haven't seen you since I saved your life. A thank you might be nice."

"You made me jump off a train."

He throws back his head. When he's finished laughing, he says, "And saved your life."

"Thank you."

We walk a few paces further. He hasn't asked where we're going. I stop. "Do you realise how serious and dangerous all this is? If I believe you, we're fighting the end of the world—and you laugh?"

"I have a strong sense of inner purpose."

I don't know what to say, so I say, "For fuck's sake."

He laughs again and we start walking.

"And I don't like being spied on by my friends."

"I didn't say I was your friend." He winks. "No, Cowper told me about the mercury. I went there guessing you would have called in."

We walk down the street, I'm not sure where I'm walking either, I just let my feet take me and Le Cozh is silent until he says, "So, did he agree? You didn't say."

The heaviness of my sigh almost weighs me down. Le Cozh interprets it and says, "I bet he drives a hard bargain."

I rub my forehead. "Well, Christian. I've made a deal with the devil. He wants me to get a Warm One so he can bodysnatch her."

He looks momentarily puzzled so I elaborate. "Empty her out and take her over."

Then he nods like he's heard it before. "They all want that, the NPCs," Le Cozh says. "They want to be free like we're free, to move around and be more than scripted things. The only way they can do that is take one of us over. The Warm Ones are empty."

I say, "I don't want to debate it. The thought of it makes me sick, but I have to do it."

"I guess you do. We need the Elixir. Then we can save hundreds of Warm Ones. We sacrifice one for the good of the many."

"You talk like a soldier."

"I am."

That must be what he does in real life. "French Army," he says.

"We need to get a Warm One. Trouble is, I don't know where to start."

Le Cozh nods, we're walking into town now, down towards Tottenham Court Road. He says, "Could be difficult. We could try Colney Hatch Lunatic Asylum. That's where they prepare them in London. But Miskatonic have it pretty heavily guarded."

It's funny that's where I was kept in the real world when my sanity dropped. They use the same place in the game before they send the poor souls off, 'prepared', to the Dreamlands and the Nameless City.

Then I remember.

The woman with the light in her eyes I saw last week outside the Museum Tavern. They said she'd escaped. She was one of the Warm Ones. She might still be there. I tell Le Cozh and he says, "Yes, it might be worth a look."

Chapter Twenty-Eight

THE WOMAN WITH LIGHTS IN HER EYES

We walk down to the Museum Tavern at the top of Coptic Street. Coming through the open door from the street, I see the same men reading their newspapers at the bar from before. I know now the NPCs keep to their stations, never wandering far from where they are assigned. I ask the rough man, who shouted at the Warm One the previous time, where the woman has gone.

"Which woman?" He looks at me with narrowed eyes. I know he knows who she is, but for some reason he doesn't even want to speak her name.

"The woman whose eyes come out like train lights. You know who I mean."

He looks into his beer. "She'll be here soon. She's always here. She shouldn't come here. She's not welcome. There's places for them, and this isn't one."

Le Cozh buys me a beer while we wait. I'm thinking over what I'm about to do. Who knows what Le Cozh is thinking. Time goes by. Eventually he glances up. "She's here."

I see the same shrinking back I observed the first time. The NPCs there are afraid of her. She represents something alien to them. She's neither player nor NPC. Emptied of mind, emptied of Sanity but still she lives. She has a half-digital, half-organic life and they are terrified.

The rough man turns to me with panic in his eyes. "Tell it to go. Just tell her to get the hell out of here. She's come for you. She thinks you can help her."

That makes me feel worse. "What do you mean she's come for me? You said she comes all the time and I'm not here all the time."

The rough man gestures at me and Le Cozh. "Your type. People like you. People come from the other place."

I realise he means players. So the woman with the Lights in Her Eyes is haunted by dreams of what she once was. Once she was a player now she's a ... I don't even know what she is.

Le Cozh goes to stand on the pub's threshold, and she hovers there. Once again it seems as if she can't cross this barrier. More mysteries, and I have no idea why that should be, but that's the least of my concerns right now.

She stands there, her mouth clicking. "Electric ... Abomination ... Avenue ... Ascendance." Drool runs down the corner of her mouth.

Le Cozh says, "I bet she says Azathoth next."

But she doesn't. She repeats the same nonsense words.

Le Cozh asks, "How are we going to get her to Crowley's place?"

I'm debating the detail of what I'm about to do. I have a sour taste in my mouth. I go to link her arm but she shrinks back from my touch.

Le Cozh is on the other side of her now. With more force than me he takes her by the elbow. In a sweet tone he says, "Come on. Why don't you come for a little walk with us?"

I take her other elbow and she's pinioned between us.

<You have committed a disreputable act -20 REPUTATION>

Even the game recognizes what I've done is bad.

The crowd in the pub watches intently, saying nothing. Then she goes off like a firework, shrieking, snatching herself free from our grasp, and running with the clattering motion of a deranged automaton down the street.

The NPCs don't do anything but I can tell who the player characters are even when they don't reveal their names because they are standing and staring at this insane woman running down the street.

I could let her go. That might even be the kind thing to do, but I need her. Like a commodity. "Come on!" I shout at Le Cozh and I'm off haring down the street.

After two hundred yards, the woman's energy is dissipated and she comes to rest with her forehead against the door of the shop. She's muttering to herself, her back heaving with sobbing agitation but I can't make sense of a word she's saying.

More tentatively this time, I take her elbow. I feel like the slaughter man taking a cow to the abattoir, but showing it some kindness on the way—pitiful and cowardly. Le Cozh is with me and together we usher her down the street in the direction of Crowley's apartment.

She tries to break free on the corner of Great Russell Street but I have her fast. I see how tight Le Cozh is holding her then all the fight goes from her and she relaxes into her fate.

"Do you think they're really people still?" I ask but I don't want to hear his reply if it's 'yes'. Diplomatically Le Cozh keeps his mouth shut on the matter.

It takes us fifteen minutes to walk her to Crowley's front door. I lean and twist the knob with my free hand and we maneuver her into the entrance hall of the house with its Victorian tiles. The man I saw on the first day—the man who shares this house with Crowley, whoever he is—is coming down the stairs. He smiles and nods at us without the slightest sign anything is amiss. I guess he's not programmed to be alarmed by such sights, unlike the men in the Museum Tavern who perhaps have become contaminated by too much interaction with player characters.

We take her up the stairs to Crowley's room. I don't bother to knock before I twist the handle and push the door open. I hear Crowley's voice welcoming me from inside.

Le Cozh nods and lets go of the woman's arms. "I won't be coming in," he says. "I'll wait outside."

I shrug and nod. I would have liked him there for moral support but I understand he doesn't want to meet Crowley. I wouldn't either.

I step into Crowley's room with the woman. She doesn't fight but her jaw is trembling. Crowley steps up from his seat and says, "A woman? I don't know why, but I thought you'd bring me a man." He smiles. "Did you have much trouble?" He asks the question as if he had sent me on an errand for a packet of cigarettes.

I shake my head.

He studies her again as if still amazed by her femininity. She begins a low drone from her mouth and once again I think of cattle waiting for an executioner who stands with the bolt gun in his hand. It's almost like she knows what's going to happen. But how could she know anything? She has no mind left.

"Good," he says finally. "And here is your reward."

<You have succeeded in the Quest of the Warm One – 2000xp>
<You are awarded £5>

The XP again is enough to make me level.

<LEVEL UP! Congratulations You are Now Level 6>

Now maybe I have the skill points to enable me to learn the recipe for the Elixir.

"And the mercury?" I say.

He nods. "Of course. I'd never welch on my side of a bargain."

I take the mercury bottle from my inventory and place it on the occasional table beside his armchair.

He picks it up casually and mutters some ritual incantation and the bottle glows with an orange aura. I smell dry earth and sunflowers. Outside a shadow crosses the sun but then the magic is done. I want to be out of there before he does what he will do to the woman so I put the quickened mercury in my inventory and hope it's sufficient now to act as a solvent for the Elixir of Life.

Crowley studies the muttering woman. He strokes her right cheek with the back of his hand and arranges her dirty hair pulling a curl back over her ear. All the while she mutters nonsense then begins chanting under her breath the name, "Azathoth."

"I should be going." I move towards the door. Crowley puts up his hand. "Don't you want to see what happens to her? If you are going to do acts of wickedness, you should at least be brave enough to see them out."

I think of Miranda. This was never an act of wickedness. It's the only way I can rescue a woman I love. Or a woman I don't really know but who I thought I loved. As I hear the muttering woman I know there is no good without evil, and this is my evil. I won't be a man if I didn't own it. But I don't want to own it. "No, I'll go. You don't need me here for this."

Crowley turns his wicked smile on me. "No, you will stay."

Anger flashes up in me and for an instant I think of taking my pistols from my pockets and shooting him in the face. But I don't. Instead I stand. He's right. It seems even the devil can teach morals. If I've consigned her to oblivion, at least I should witness it happening.

Crowley bends towards the woman cupping the back of her head with his hand. His fingers entwine through her hair as he draws her in like a lover. I see saliva drooling from the corner of her mouth but Crowley kisses her, at first tentatively like it's their first date then more urgently. She begins to kiss him back. I'm repulsed. Then she and he enter into the most passionate sexual kissing. I feel like throwing up.

How can she want this? What is going through her head that she should welcome the kiss of this ugly, malevolent man?

Then like a burrowing worm he pours himself into her. His body deflates like a party balloon and I hear the clump of his shoes as they fall from his empty feet. His trousers and braces lie in a heap on the floor and his jacket slides down her arms and away as he enters her head and becomes her. I think of some parasitic wasp eating an animal from the inside out.

Then the woman twists her neck as if it was stiff and raises her arms to stretch the sleep out of them. Lights no longer come from her eyes and instead of her damaged humanity, a wicked machine intelligence shines. I wonder whether I have witnessed the birth of a new kind of creature—half-human, half-algorithm.

The Crowley woman looks at me and smiles. In a light voice she says, "Thank you Adam. You have no idea how happy you've made me. I will be forever in your debt."

She looks around with a smile. "Just to think I am now free to leave this place." She gestures around the narrow room with its books and dark-wood furniture. "For the first time, I can step onto the street and explore the world." Her voice rises in excitement. "Yes, the whole world lies before me!"

I'm sickened. I feel nauseous. I don't reply, instead I barge my way out of the room. At the door, I turn to see the woman is all smiles and following me down the stairs. "Wait for me!" she shouts in her girlish sing-song. But instead of waiting I redouble my speed and burst out of the door.

Le Cozh stands outside. When the woman pushes past him and leaves the house the expression on her face is one of bliss as she looks up to see a world, that through Crowley's eyes, was limited to the view from a window.

The she turns and eyes Le Cozh up and down. "And who is this handsome chap?"

Le Cozh recognises her of course. He looks amazed as if finally, something has surprised or shocked him. He glances at me as if for confirmation, and I nod. "Let's get out of here."

But the woman won't let him go. She places her hand on his forearm and he lets it rest. "Do you want to have sex?" she says, tilting her head to one side. "I've never had sex before." But then she gives a disgusting belly laugh and winks. "But I've read plenty about it."

I start walking off, grabbing at Le Cozh's arm to pull him after me. Le Cozh follows me looking over his shoulder to where the Crowley woman is waving at him. "That's the most freakish thing I've ever seen or heard," he says.

I'm thinking of Miranda. I'm thinking of the woman with the Lights in Her Eyes and wondering where she's gone.

"We need to go and see Cowper," I say. "I need to know whether I have enough skill points to make the Elixir of Life."

titrating; sublimating and calcifying, all the while applying the gentle heat. I know what the Red Lion is and I know what the Descending Dove signifies. I add the tripartite recipe of sulphur, salt, and silver and know that these are not common sulphur, salt, and silver but in fact the elements of the alchemists. Elements which touch the foundation of the earth and reach up as high as the sun itself.

I make the first concoction of the Elixir. Turning the tap, I fill a glass flask with it and put a rubber bung in the mouth of the flask. The liquid is thick and golden and warm to the touch. It has an organic energy that seems self-generated and coruscates within the flask. Its movement is fascinating and I can't take my eyes away from the liquid I've created.

"So that'll wake the Warm Ones?" Le Cozh says.

Cowper clasps his hands together in front of him. "The Elixir of Life has many magical properties. It is an Elixir of transformation. It will turn that which is alive into something dead and turn that which is dead into a living creature once again. It burns evil. It is reputed it can turn lead into gold but the intent of the alchemist who works with the Elixir is very important. The Elixir is intelligent and knows the heart of he who uses it. It is a holy mixture and will not tolerate itself to be used for evil."

Le Cozh turns to me. "Philby said what you've just done represents working with the game's base code. You've just created a virulent and powerful new sequence of code. No one's made it before. No one unlocked this quest before."

"Like it's alive, like the Great Old Ones?"

He sucks his teeth. "I don't know. What does 'alive' mean anyway?"

Cowper has been listening. "The Elixir has an intelligence, a mind of its own."

"But it's like RNA and DNA, just a digital equivalent. It will make changes in the code of the objects it's applied to," Le Cozh says.

"If it works," I say.

Le Cozh asks if he could hold the flask containing the Elixir of Life. He seems as fascinated as I am. He holds it with great wonder looking at it. "I agree. I hope it'll do all we need it to do."

Cowper asks what our plans are. At first, I hesitate then as if something in the Elixir casts off a great atmosphere of certitude, I know I can trust him. Back in Glastonbury I checked him with my Clairsentience and I know there's no evil in him.

Before I can answer Cowper's question, Le Cozh says, "This is confidential."

Cowper says, "I understand. I will ask no more."

I turn back to the laboratory equipment and make as much of the Elixir as I can. I'm fully absorbed in my work and only vaguely aware of Cowper and Le Cozh standing behind me.

All in all, I have enough to make three flaskfuls of the Elixir of Life. While I'm there, I use all my resources in making more of the Soma potion and Health and Mana potions. I make two Travel Potions and two Return potions to get us to the Nameless City. All we need now is a portal to Leng.

What ingredients I didn't have, Cowper provides for me for free. Then he offers free Health and Mana potions. I know that where we're going we'll need to take as many resources as we can, so I don't refuse his offer.

I sip at his blue and pink potions until I'm at full Mana and Health. Then I take out my syringe, and under the watchful and disapproving eyes of Le Cozh, I replace my sanity with a needle. I offer it to Le Cozh but he refuses. "I'll take my chances with meditation. It's a slow process, but it doesn't have the side effects of the Soma."

Then I'm ready for our mission though I don't know where I'm going. "How do we get to Leng?"

Le Cozh smiles. "I was wondering when you'd ask that. Don't worry, I've got it all worked out. Are you aware of the Hawksmoor churches?"

I shake my head and he begins to tell me. "In the seventeenth and first half of the eighteenth century, Nicholas Hawksmoor was a famous English architect. He designed a number of churches in London. But over two hundred years ago a rumour began to circulate something was amiss with the churches. Murders and dark deeds seemed to happen with more than normal regularity around them. Murdered people were found in the churches and corpses dug up in the graveyards showed the marks of black magic."

"Sounds gruesome."

He continues. "And in the twentieth century, when researching some of the murders of Jack the Ripper in London, a poet called Iain Sinclair started to notice the churches were laid out in a certain pattern. He wrote a poem called *Lud Heat*. Have you read it?"

"No."

"You should."

"Anyway, what pattern?"

Le Cozh strokes his chin. "A pentagram. And some people say Hawksmoor was a cultist and his churches were a mockery of God rather than a celebration. He arranged these churches in an occult symbol and he baptised each of them with a murder. Each church is in fact an offering to the Great Old Ones."

"There's a lot of it about."

Le Cozh continues unfazed by my flippant comment. "But what is more interesting is what is at the centre of this pentagram." He pauses dramatically.

I say, "I know you going to tell me what it is, so cut the dramatic suspense and just blurt it out."

Le Cozh smiles. "At the centre of the pentagram is the portal to Leng in the Dreamlands."

"What? In the centre of London, visible to all, is a doorway to another world? At least in Glastonbury it was well hidden."

He shakes his head. "No. Of course it's not visible to all. There's something built over it. A great temple to the Great Old Ones."

Another time I would have enjoyed his showmanship, but now I'm nervous and irritable. "Okay, so that's how we get to Leng. We find this temple—I'm guessing you know where it is?"

"Indeed I do."

"Then we'll take the potions of Transportation which I just created. So where's the temple?"

"The Temple is the British Museum."

Cowper looks concerned but wishes us well as we leave the shop. Over the street, the Brother of Shadow is still watching as Le Cozh and I set off into the gathering dusk of London.

Chapter Thirty

THE HEART OF THE PENTAGRAM

Exiting Cowper's shop, Le Cozh crosses the traffic heading for the watching Brother of Shadow. I go with him. I would help but with two raised fingers, Le Cozh indicates he doesn't need any assistance. Instead, he greets the Brother like he's his best friend, puts his arm round the man and walks him into the alley opposite. The man struggles but Le Cozh is strong and there in the shadows, his knife goes snicker-snack, nice and quiet. One hand over his mouth, the first flash of steel is bright, the second stained with dark hybrid blood. Then it's done. I think that alley is a bad place for the Brothers of Shadow.

Le Cozh returns. "That avoided a nasty Reputation loss."

"You're good at that."

"I know."

"British Museum then. Where exactly in the Museum do you think the portal is?"

"At its roots."

I take that to mean in the basement. "So how do we get there?"

"Not by the front door, that's for sure."

I wait for enlightenment, then he says, "There's a way in from the British Museum Tube Station."

"How do you know this?"

"Guild knowledge."

I trust him implicitly by now, so I just follow as we thread our way through the London streets. I notice the air is getting misty and soon a fog is developing. The dampness of the river rolling up and meeting the outpouring of a million smoky chimneys. As the temperature drops, people heap coal on their fires and the fog intensifies.

We're walking along High Holborn now. I know Le Cozh is the expert but I'm pretty sure we could have just cut up to the British Museum. When I mention this he says, "I want to wait until later. Fewer people to bother us about our business."

The fog thickens. I check my Wiki.

Pea Soup Fog, or Pea Souper was the name given to the deadly London smogs composed of soot and sulphur dioxide caused by the burning of coal in homes and factories combined with particular weather conditions. London Particulars of Pea Soup Fogs killed hundreds if not thousands of people in the 19th and early 20th centuries until the Clean Air Acts of the 1950s.

Even though it's still daylight, it's hard to see and pedestrians passing by become ghostly silhouettes while their footfalls echo on the street like a thousand closing doors. There is no sky, only thickening grey. Night will come before the day is dead.

We sit in a pub on Longacre called the Masonic Arms. We're still killing time before we can get the Tube Train from High Holborn and travel one stop down the Central Line to the British Museum underground station.

We sit in a snug and Le Cozh checks his gun. I think it's a bit open but when it seems okay, I take both my pistols out and place them on the table. I take time to check and load then a glass collector comes and sees both.

< You are observed breaking the law -10 REPUTATION>

I didn't really need that. I sit tense wondering if the NPC will call the police. Le Cozh suddenly drains his glass. "The Museum should be closed. Let's go."

We walk through the fog-bound streets. The whole world seems closed in and I hear my feet on the damp pavement. Le Cozh is striding ahead, smoking again. I wonder if he's nervous.

"Will it be guarded?"

He nods.

We're walking along the street through the fog and a police officer looms from nowhere. He stops, eyeing me as if he knows me from somewhere. I wonder what he wants then I remember my Reputation is now only 5 out of a hundred. He says, 'Here, I want a word with you!'

'Run!' Le Cozh says.

The policeman blows his whistle that shrills through the foggy street and we're haring it down Holborn in the mist. My Exertion Meter climbs up into the amber. I hear the feet of the copper behind us. The Exertion Meter hits red and I get a message:

<-10% Movement Penalty>

I feel as if I've got weights attached to my feet.

Le Cozh says, 'Movement penalty?'

'Yes.'

'Me too. Let me shoot him.'

'No! Jeez that'll just make things worse.'

'It'll be worse if the bastard catches us. Him and his copper mates who are bound to be flooding the area now he's blown his whistle'

"Here, hang on. In this alley.'

Le Cozh follows me into the alley. The fog is thick. I hear the copper behind us, his feet echoing in the foggy air.

'What?' Le Cozh says.

'I've got this spell.' I learned Invisibility ages ago and never used it. I cast it on him and he disappears. Then on myself. 'It only lasts twenty seconds. It's low level.'

But twenty seconds is long enough. By the time we're visible again, the police officer is way past us. My Exertion Meter is nicely back in the green.

'Good thinking, Adam,' Le Cozh says. 'Though we could have just shot him.'

It takes me a second to realise he's joking. I kind of like him after all.

'Long enough now,' he says. We set off strolling through the foggy streets like two gentlemen off to their club. If the police see us again, they'll act on our low Reputation, but fortunately our London bobby friend is nowhere around.

Then we're at High Holborn station. We go down the steps into a warm fug of electric light. The fog is banished from here as commuters make their homeward journeys. Down the steps and along tiled corridors until we arrive at the Central Line westbound platform. Rats play down below the shining silver rails and men and women in raincoats stand beside us eagerly awaiting their ride home.

First a rush of warm air then rumbling and train lights appear from the tunnel to the east. Instinctively I step back. The train arrives, someone opens the doors, as keen to leave as we are to get on.

We don't sit. We stand by the doors, steadying ourselves on leather straps as the train rocks and rolls. Then the brakes kick in and the train slows before coming to a halt at The British Museum.

We step off and I look to Le Cozh who points without speaking along the platform. I follow.

He stops before an entrance I would have missed. It is dirty and dark and looks like a service entrance. A metal grille secured with an old looking padlock locks it.

Le Cozh pulls shears from his inventory. That reminds me of Miranda and I feel a flush of emotion and try to dismiss it. We need to get on.

He clips off the lock which falls with a clump to the floor. "Come on."

We enter the dark tunnel. I've got both guns out now and I see he has his shotgun ready. I get that itch in the middle of my head again that tells me I am going to need some Soma at some point.

Le Cozh says over his shoulder, "This tunnel was built in 1916 so if the Germans ever invaded London they could secretly ship out the artefacts from the Museum."

The tunnel runs for about two hundred yards and it's dark so I pull out my torch to light our way. There's another padlocked door at the far end of the tunnel, which Le Cozh deals with in the same manner he did the first.

"There may be Brothers here, so be careful."

I nod and we go quiet.

It looks like we are in the underground storage areas of the Museum.

"It has far more artefacts than it can ever display," Le Cozh says helpfully.

There are emergency lights here so I switch off my torch. It's dim but not totally dark. We walk through Egyptian statues, some draped in cloths. Silence pervades the place until we are through three rooms and the artefacts here look Greek and Roman. Then I hear a faint chanting.

"What's that?"

Le Cozh says. "The way down to the portal to Leng is on the floor below. The way will be guarded."

We edge forward until we're lurking in the shadows of a room that looks out onto a thoroughfare.

I see brown-robed characters, hoods up, coming from the other direction and filing in from the left and heading down the corridor. I stick my head out when there's no one there and see a dark door with guards. This is the dark door that leads to the Temple's heart.

I look round puzzled.

Le Cozh shrugs. "There must be a ceremony tonight. There shouldn't be so many of them normally."

"Bad timing."

"Yep."

"But we've got to go through."

"We could come back tomorrow, or later?"

I remember Miranda. Each day I don't bring her out of there the more she transforms into something beyond imagination.

"No let's try to get in tonight. We need to get to Leng."

He nods. "You're right. Anyway, what's the worst that can happen?"

He's a funny guy. I say, "Let's not find out."

As we stand there in the dark, I can feel the atmosphere of the place. This is the centre of the unholy Pentagram that focuses its

His voice is like sickness itself. Disease pours from his mouth as he utters words of damnation.

"I am risen. Finally, our Lord Azathoth has given the gift of abomination. Man no more, I am disease. I am putrefaction. Look on me, and despair of your souls."

The howling of the Brothers of Shadow rises to a crescendo but then muffles as we step behind the rood screen. I hear the tinkling and feel the ozone buzz of a portal. Here in the guts of this temple, we find the portal to the Dreamlands, the cursed and frigid Plateau of Leng. I can't see it but I know it's there. From the Shadows, the queen emerges.

Three feet high, face sticky, and shining like an embalmed child, she says, "Can I interest you in my wares? Potions and magic goods? Transport to the Dreamlands?"

But I don't need her potions, I've got my own. I hand Le Cozh a small bottle whose contents gleam pearly white. I give him the small phial that contains the Returning Potion as well.

Then a Brother comes around the screen and sees us. "What the hell are you doing here?"

Le Cozh looks at me. I think he's going to shoot the guy. I raise the pearly potion to my mouth. "Drink," I say.

Chapter Thirty-One

WAKING THE DREAMERS

We emerge into the howling winds of Leng where snow carried on the frigid breeze shaves my cheek like a razor. Our Brothers of Shadow robes have disappeared and we're back in our ordinary clothes. Le Cozh pulls his coat tight around him and pushes his head down low. I do likewise, holding onto my hat but it's no good; it won't keep out the cold. The last time we came to Leng I didn't feel the cold—not like this, that I do now must mean I'm deeper into the game and Dark-worlds truly has become realer than real.

Soon the Brothers will follow us into the City. They know we've entered and if they're not fools they must suspect we mean their gods harm. Even if they don't know we've got the Elixir, they will surely hunt us.

"The Brothers?" I say, glancing back to where we entered and our footprints abruptly begin on a carpet of otherwise perfect snow.

"Yeah. We better be quick. That way." Le Cozh nods, indicating the slender twisted spires of the Nameless City on the horizon silhouetted against a field of stars. Stars like handfuls of sequins thrown by a malicious god to dazzle those below. Constellations both strange and repugnant.

<You have begun the quest: Awaken The Dreamers>

The game monitors us, even now.

We trudge heads down against a wind that howls and screams, and behind the howling sounds a deeper agony, the baying of dead gods of despair and despondency. We pass the abandoned huts, their roofs scalped by eternal winds, leaving worn down walls of granite, whose mica sparkles amid the ice in reflection of the blasphemous stars above.

Soon we're at the perimeter of the city and walking on the first roads, though they are more than half covered by blown snow. The Elixir of Life is in my hand, warm in its glass bottle, murmuring, shifting as if it lives. It gives me some comfort in this ghastly place.

We walk on roads and alleys and I see the tumours in the walls, each pregnant with a Cold One. They stir and I think; maybe this one is Miranda. Or that. I approach them.

He says, "What are you doing? We need to get to the Colosseum and wake the Warm Ones. That's the reason we're here." He glances over his shoulder. "The Brothers of Shadow will be on our backs any minute."

Waking the Warm Ones isn't the only reason I'm here. I talk above the keening of the wind, "I need to find Miranda. She was near here. I'm sure." I search desperately among the bulges in the wall, that shift, horribly full of their larvae. And I realise I don't know which one is her. There's no point opening these things and bringing them on us if I'm not sure which is her.

He's about to say something but bites his lip. Then I turn and sigh and we continue.

I say, "I thought somehow I'd know. Or I'd find her already here, waiting for me."

He studies me with his brown eyes then looks down and continues.

Soon we're partly sheltered from the wind between white stone walls veined with gold. The bulges in the walls move. They're like swollen chrysalises that sense our nearness. Soon they'll burst and their contents will come hunting us—vile antibodies of the diseased city.

Despite what he's said, I haven't put the Elixir away. Any time I could meet her.

I stop by a moving bulge. He shakes his head. "Adam, we have to hurry. Only by wakening the dreamers can we weaken their masters. We've got to deprive these artificial gods—"

"—of their research material."

"Of their food."

But I don't move. I haven't taken my eyes off the bulge I think holds Miranda. He looks back again, as if willing me to move faster.

"Let me try," I say.

He waits without speaking while I take the stopper from the glass bottle and I hear the Elixir hissing.

I don't know whether to cut into the blister or splash the Elixir on the outside. In the end, I don't have to wait because the thing bursts of its own accord. The membrane rips and cloudy fluid drips out, smelling of ammonia. The thing inside turns and flops like something being born—some ghastly flat worm, pushing out of its blister.

If it was once human, it's a long way from that now. It gazes at me with golden insect eyes. Antennae protrude from its head, bent and wet, and translucent wings like a bluebottle's unfold damply from its human shoulders. It has a human mouth but it's not her.

I'm about to use the Elixir to try to save it when Le Cozh loses his temper. "Come on! It's not even her. We need that Elixir. Don't waste it."

He's right, but I stand, the potion bottle in my hand. No creature deserves to turn into this. I believe I could return it to life with the Elixir. It would be an act of mercy. I hesitate until Le Cozh takes out his shotgun and blasts the thing at close range.

Beseechingly, he says, "We have so little time, Adam. Let's go."

He's right. Of course, he's right. I hurry after him.

We penetrate deeper into the Nameless City, finding our way through its maze of streets to the Colosseum that towers over the western districts. As we walk, I watch starfish fall in a soft golden rain from a point in the sky that shouldn't exist. Alien geometries warp the air. Impossible angles and shapes shift like great inhuman gods above. The code is disturbed by our presence. It senses we mean it harm.

There are two Brothers of Shadow guards standing at the Colosseum Entrance. Le Cozh shoots one and without hesitation, I shoot the other. They're players, but I've made them into Cold Ones.

<You have killed a Brother of Shadow +400xp>

We enter the Colosseum and see banks and banks of Warm Ones on their stone beds, all struggling in their sleep, each one's mouth covered by a starfish that burrows into it, to map and learn its neural pathways.

"Give me a bottle of Elixir?" Le Cozh says.

I hand him one. With the bottle in my hand, that leaves one more still in the inventory. I look around at the thousands of Warm Ones dreaming their unquiet sleep. "I don't think we have enough Elixir," I say.

Le Cozh mutters, "A drop each. How ever many we wake is a bonus. Each one is a power source for them. Go fast."

To be more time efficient, we split up. I begin to follow the spiral round and up to the left while he goes right. I stop at the first Warm One. It's a woman whose light brown hair hangs in unkempt ropes. The gods alone know how long she's been here for it to grow so long.

The starfish stirs as I step near and hugs its prisoner even tighter as I put my forefinger over the bottle mouth and let one drop fall. The golden liquid drips like a kiss between her eyes. Even its proximity sends the starfish pulling away, dragging its legs from her mouth, and she comes to, waking like a drowning woman breaking the surface, coughing up liquid and starting up, hand to mouth. She doesn't know where she is but her eyes are wide with fear. I spend a moment comforting her, but I don't think she understands me.

I look around at the Warm Ones here. There's no way we can wake them all before the Brothers of Shadow arrive, but of course he's right, we've got to wake as many as we can. Le Cozh is diligently making his way round the spiral paths, a drop of Elixir on each dreamer's forehead to wake them and send the starfish scuttling away.

It's important to do this, but it's also important to find Miranda. I might not get another chance.

I hurry to the next one—a man. I drip the Elixir onto his brow and he too wakes, slapping away the starfish that flops and flips on the floor beside my foot. I stamp on it, grind it into mush as its legs flex weakly under my heel. I get 50 xp for that kill.

Time is running out. I'm decided. I turn and make my way down the path. I want to find Miranda before the Brothers arrive. Le Cozh will be fine. I'll be back as soon as I can. She must be here somewhere. Our presence will have woken them from their sacs, there's every chance she'll be on the streets. She'll know I'm here and be looking for me.

But as I get to the Colosseum entrance, four Brothers of Shadow are coming up the street. Their masks are off and I see their lamprey teeth. They see me too. Gunfire cracks against the rock wall behind me. I duck and roll out of their way behind a stone wall. I creep along it, so I'm no longer where they saw me disappear.

The place crackles with pistol fire and the high-pitched whine of ricochets. But they're wide, trained on where I used to be. I have both pistols out. I bob up and squint along the Walther and squeeze off a round and it strikes a Brother in the head.

<You have killed a Brother of Shadow +400xp>

One down. There'll be many more of them soon. I've got a good position here behind the wall. They can't see me when I duck down and I shoot another two before they know where I am. I stand again and one fires. He hits me in the shoulder for 35 Health. I duck back down, sip a Health potion then I'm up again. I crack off two rounds. I drop behind the wall, reload the Browning with shaking fingers and one jumps over. He's as surprised to see me as I am to see him, but I get the draw on him and put a bullet from the Walther into his face.

<You have killed a Brother of Shadow +400xp>

I then shuffle left and see a Brother retreating along the far road. I risk standing and taking careful aim, I hit him, wounding him with my first shot, so he's lying bleeding on the ground. I fire again, but miss.

Then my heart almost stops. Cold Ones are swarming down the road. They hop and slide like great bugs, cockroaches with the backs and arms of men and the twitching legs of insects. I look for any sign of Miranda among the throng. There are maybe a hundred of them and more burst from their chrysalises all the time, tipping out like foul larvae on unsteady legs. Some are wormlike, great maggots shuffling along on their bellies, others insectoid like the one Le Cozh blasted with his shotgun. And all coming my way.

I am outside the Colosseum. If I go right, I descend into the lower city, near the frozen river, and I don't know my way out of there. I need to go left up the hill. I run up a sloping alley and at the top, take a right. I see stone steps leading up in front of me and I climb, nearly slipping on the snow. Then I'm on the flat roof of a house. From where I stand, I can see the Cold Ones thronging their way towards the Colosseum Entrance. The place I left Le Cozh.

The boom of his shotgun echoes out time and time again and it sounds like he's taking his time firing. He should have left when they went in. He can take his Returning potion at any time, so why doesn't he? And I realise it's because I'm missing, and he doesn't want to leave without me.

I think of going back. Then we can both leave. But I've got to find Miranda. Only by finding her, can I justify leaving him.

I scan the crowd of the Cold Ones below the house I'm on. They're milling around but they haven't sighted me. I hear Le Cozh's rate of fire increase, staccato blasts coming quicker now. I hope he's got lots of ammo and can last until I get back.

Then I see her. What is left of her—black hair hangs down her back, thin writhing worms erupting from her sides. She's worse than she was. I shout out, "Miranda!" but she doesn't turn. I yell again, "Miranda!" hoping there's some part of her left. She sent me those messages, disjointed and broken as they were. She can't be wholly gone yet.

And when I yell her name the third time, Miranda turns. I call for her and she stutters and shuffles out of the crowd towards me. She knows my voice. There's still hope. As I look I see there's still something left of her face, enough to recognize her.

The other Cold Ones are moving away, but Miranda is coming towards me, her worm arms fluttering and flexing. She's trying to find a way up to where I stand on the flat roof of the house.

The Elixir is her only salvation. I have the bottle in my hand. The liquid glows as golden as a summer sunrise. Miranda's dark eyes, one spiderlike, the other like a rotten fruit, glance up at the Elixir as if she knows what it is. Her face twists and sniffs, a ruin of the beauty it once had. That it might regain.

Then the crowd parts.

Something huge and vile shoulders its way through the mass of Cold Ones, heading towards the Colosseum. I recognize the cloth-draped shape from the British Museum cellar. It stands to its full height, revealing the monstrosity that is Mervyn Gurdrock; his unspeakable bargain with the Old Ones has transformed him into an abomination. His code is twisted and contaminated by them. He roars his fury and the Cold Ones scuttle and slither out of his way. The monsters part in respect and fear as his many legged body scuttles its way into the Colosseum archway. He has to duck to get under then he's inside.

Le Cozh is in there. There's no way he can beat this monster.

I look down at Miranda. She waits, unable to reach me. I'll have to go down to her if I'm to save her. The bulk of the Cold Ones have moved off after Gurdrock and are pressing into the Colosseum, but she waits.

I hear more shotgun fire from inside the Colosseum. If I go to Le Cozh, it'll be too late for Miranda. Even if I could come back, by that time she'll be fully transformed into the monstrosity that's eating her up.

She's still there waiting for me, waiting for the Elixir, but I know Gurdrock's entry has changed things.

Le Cozh's gun fires out, then goes quiet. He is completely outnumbered. And now Mervyn Gurdrock is here, whatever we had hoped to achieve with the Elixir will have to wait. We can maybe come back, but if Le Cozh dies here and now, there will be no second chances.

Then I know my duty is more to the living than the dead.

I look at Miranda, then I hurry down the steps away from where she waits. My heart breaks as I leave her. I only hope Le Cozh is still alive.

Then Le Cozh fires again, and I breathe a sigh of relief. The main door is blocked, but I can run round the other side of the Colosseum and get to him that way.

Most of the Cold Ones are trying to get into the Colosseum the way Gurdrock entered, blocking up the gateway with their deformed bodies. I pull out both pistols and begin to shoot at the Cold Ones. They turn and see me but fall under my bullets.

<+ 400xp>

<+ 400xp>

<+ 400xp>

<LEVEL UP! Congratulations You are Now Level 7>

I'm going right. There are still more of them and I shoot again and again, pausing to reload both pistols then run on to find Le Cozh. There are still Cold Ones there, but I shoot them as I go, clocking up XP.

Suddenly, lurching along the road behind me, a maggot thing appears, sniffing the air. It scents me and starts to move in my direction. Disgusted by it, and without thinking, I fire and bullets rip open its bloated side, leaking yellow fluid until it flops dead.

<You have killed a Cold One +400xp>

I enter the Colosseum from the opposite entrance to see Gurdrock towering above the army of hideous bug things on the far side.

Le Cozh is near me but up higher. I can't get to him because of the Cold Ones blocking the way. I yell up, "Drink your Returning potion."

"Where did you go?" he shouts. "I was waiting for you."

I sigh. "Just drink, then we'll leave."

They're swarming up at him, mostly ignoring me. I see him get out his potion bottle. They're so close. He's got it to his mouth. Okay, I raise my own Returning potion. I place the glass against my lips and when I see his potion is in his hand, I sip mine. It tastes like Parma Violets.

Just then a Cold One lurches into him from the right, sending his potion bottle and his shotgun both spinning onto the ground out of reach.

Other Cold Ones are coming for him now as he stoops to try to reach his shotgun.

I try to blast my way up to him. I have no idea what we're going to do now.

Le Cozh shoulder charges a Cold One, stoops and gets his shotgun and blasts a woodlouse shaped thing before it bites him. From the other side of the auditorium, Gurdrock roars and begins to barge his way towards Le Cozh.

Then I'm gone, like water being pulled down a plug hole. I'm back in the Game World, but Le Cozh isn't.

Chapter Thirty-Two

"I'VE COME TO MEASURE YOU"

I appear back in the British Museum temple, in the chamber of blocks, behind the screen. I hear the buzzing and tinkling of the portal but I can't see it. The wizened dwarf queen stands nearby. She speaks, "Can I interest you in potions or magic items?"

I've run out of my own potions and I desperately need to get back to Le Cozh. I ask her for a Transportation potion and she shows it to me, a hologram floating in the air in front of me. I snatch at it but my fingers go straight through.

"That'll be two and six."

"Two and six?" I go to my inventory but I'm almost spent up from buying ingredients for the potions I made at Cowper's. I have eightpence only.

"Can I get credit?"

She shakes her head. "No credit."

Le Cozh could be dying right now. I wheedle. "I need the potion."

Her lips harden. "No credit."

I pull out a gun. The queen stares at the silver PPK. Whatever it is, it can still die, and from its glassy eyes, I see it's frightened of dying. I cock the pistol and the dwarf queen gasps, stepping back.

I level the Browning at her head. "I don't want to do this. But you leave me no choice. Give me the potion."

"No."

I don't have time for this. "Give me the potion."

She steps back further. "If you kill me you won't get the potion."

She's right. I lick my lips. "Then I'll be no worse off. But you will; you'll be dead." NPCs fear death and the oblivion it brings.

"All right, but I curse you." She produces the opalescent liquid in its bottle. I don't fear her curse; I feel cursed enough already.

<You have stolen something serious -20 REPUTATION>
<Your REPUTATION is now -5. You will be shot on sight by the authorities>

I say, "You brought it to this. I'm happy to pay you when I've got the money."

"Too late; you're cursed." She gives a wicked smile. "But the curse will find you when you least expect it. Not now, maybe not tomorrow, or next year. But one day."

Something in my mind twists. I think of shooting her anyway, then reason masters my anger at her stupidity. "And a Returning potion."

I can see the hate and fear in her eyes, but she sees my pistol and produces a small bottle of sapphire blue liquid.

"Thanks."

I drink the pearly Transportation potion.

In a minute, I'm back in the Colosseum. I see the thing that was Mervyn Gurdrock towering over the crowd of the Cold Ones, who shuffle and shamble and flutter their foul wings. Le Cozh has retreated into a recess in the wall of the Colosseum. He must have climbed up twenty feet using footholds in the honeycombed rock.

I stand behind them all and they don't notice me. The Cold Ones and the Brothers of Shadow are so eager to rip Le Cozh apart they don't turn round.

I cock both my pistols. Time to make a difference. Let the dead bury their dead. My job is with the living.

The first bullets hit them and they turn, but I'm like a machine. I place eight shots each side, then reload. They are a tide, a vile, verminous, venomous tide and I shoot them all down. At least I'm taking some pressure off him. He's up there in the wall, popping at them with his pistols. He must have run out of shotgun ammo. How long before he runs out of 9mm shells? I shoot another Cold One.

<LEVEL UP! Congratulations You are Now Level 8>

I shoot and back off, feeling the kick of the pistols pulling up. I need to keep my elbows steady as I shoot down the tide of insects. The floor below me is slick with their green blood. Above them I see the monstrous Mervyn Gurdrock advance towards Le Cozh.

How ever many I kill, more come, but I'm giving them cause to hesitate and they're not rushing as crazily forward to their own death. The smell of their acrid blood hangs in the air as well as the smell of cordite from my pistols. I need to reload. I check how many rounds I have left.

21 x 9mm. Plus the one I have chambered in the Browning and three in the magazine of the PPK.

There's a hell of lot more than twenty-five of them, and I don't hit every time. Luckily their swarm is so dense it makes killing them easy. There's sweat on my lip. I am backing away and they're still coming. I squeeze the trigger. Headshot. I put a round through the forehead of some roach thing and it goes down.

< You have killed a Cold One – 200xp>

Less XP now I'm Level 8. The circular wall of the Colosseum curves round behind me. I decide to do what Le Cozh has done and I break and run. When I run, they run after me, but I have a head start. I'm about a yard from the wall when I sense they're close enough to grab me. If I go down here ...

On impulse, I pivot, I hit Thrust—the spell placed on my hot bar. A pulse of energy bursts from my eyes and sends them back about six feet. It doesn't hurt them, but I hit Thrust again and buy more space. I turn and dash for the Colosseum wall. Like Le Cozh's wall opposite, the yellow stone is honeycombed with holes. Frantically, I grab and pull, and I'm up. I go as fast as I can up the wall, looking for some-where I can lodge and fire down. A Cold One grabs at my foot and I turn and hit Thrust again. He tumbles down the wall. I'm about fifteen feet up but I have a long way to go.

I consider my Mana: 560/800, and each Thrust costs me 10. I can keep doing this for a while. My plan was to take some of the heat off Le Cozh. He has better firearm skills than me, he'll do more damage. And he has Mervyn Gurdrock on him. I use Thrust again to send the Cold Ones tumbling down the wall. This time I get damage messages.

<Cold One suffers - 7hp from falling>
<Cold One suffers - 8hp from falling>

A bunch of them are mildly hurt.

Okay, so that's a bonus. I go up higher. The higher they fall from, the more damage they'll do. Hell, they might even die. They're way below me now but mindlessly they begin to scale the wall again, fresh ones and wounded ones dripping ichor from their wounds.

Finally, at about thirty feet up, I find a big space hollowed out of the yellow stone by winds from beyond time. I can get my body in it, brace with my legs and be secure. I take the opportunity to glance over to Le Cozh. He's managed to get himself way up high, near the top of the wall. Gurdrock can't reach him, but by the fact he's hurling rocks, I assume Le Cozh is out of ammo.

With a tongue like a chameleon hunting a fly, Gurdrock spits a gob of green ichor up the wall at Le Cozh.

I look down at the Cold Ones scaling the wall. They're about ten feet below me. I use Thrust again and the energy pulse knocks them off the wall. This time two of them die and I get 400 XP. But they're starting to figure out that coming up after me is suicidal and I see them now standing, thinking, at the bottom. If they can think.

I reload. I've now got eight bullets in each pistol. I level and take a shot at Gurdrock. He's the other side of the Colosseum, spitting up his guts at Le Cozh. I miss. I fire again. I miss again. I fire again. Miss yet again. This is just wasting ammo. But I try one more time. I put down the PPK and sight along the Browning. It's a longer barrel and might be more accurate. I stop my breathing, take aim at Gurdrock's open skull with its pulsing fungal brain. I squeeze and the gun lifts as the bullet leaves it. Instantly I get a message.

<22 damage - 50 magic damage reduction = 0 damage to Mervyn Gurdrock (hybrid)>

Damn. He's got 50 resistance to all damage that isn't magical. I'd have to do more than 50 to score anything on him and my shooting is simply not that good.

But.

Though it pinged off him, Gurdrock is looking in my direction. He's noticed me for the first time. I fire again and miss. On my fourth shot, I hit him again but do no damage. I don't know what level of intelligence the hybrid thing has. It would be sensible for it to concentrate on Le Cozh.

If I can cause a distraction Le Cozh might find some way of defeating the anchoring spell.

I fire again and Gurdrock turns in my direction and starts to move. Gurdrock is halfway across the Colosseum, past the empty beds of awakened Warm Ones. He crushes a few Cold Ones who are too slow to get out of his way.

Then Gurdrock raises a hand that is more like the foot of a gigantic bird and a blue haze, of vaguely net-like flies come from it and I'm engulfed in a graphic effect which dissipates. At the same time, I get a message:

<TELEPORT LOCK ENFORCED! You are unable to teleport due to an Anchor Spell>

The Returning Potion won't work while that teleport lock is in place. I'm stuck here.

I can just chug Mana and Health potions for whatever damage they get on me and throw rocks at them. As if to prove my point, I grab a hunk of stone and chuck it down, braining a Cold One.

<You hit Cold One for -33 HEALTH>

Then Mervyn Gurdrock spits a gob of green which hits the wall above my head. I duck back to see the viscous green slime drop, hissing. I catch the whiff of hydrochloric acid. I don't want to get hit with that stuff.

Then I see Miranda among the milling crowd of Cold Ones below. She stares at me with her deformed eyes. My heart rises. I may have a chance to save her after all.

I put down the Walther and reach into my inventory to take out the Elixir. I have the remains of the first bottle, and the third still in my inventory. Le Cozh had the second. I'm sure I can hit her from here. If the Elixir hits her, it could transform her back and save her life. She could awake from the cold sleep they put her in. Even if she only lives in the game, that's worth it.

I see the Cold Ones close by her. If she's saved, they'll rip her apart.

A gob of acid from Gurdrock flies through the air and hits me. I scream in pain.

<You suffer 75 acid damage: HEALTH 525/700>

But worse there's a damage over time effect. For the next ten seconds, I take 5 acid damage per second.

<HEALTH 475/700>

This is not a stalemate. This is a slow defeat.

Ignoring Gurdrock, I focus on Miranda and the Cold Ones standing by her. Maybe I can grab her and pull her up after me?

But first I have to kill the Cold Ones that might hurt her. One to her left has a moth head, the one to her right is a louse. The third, behind her is still mostly human, with a mouth that dribbles slug slime and hands the soft flesh of a gastropod.

If I kill them, I could get her. I have the Browning in my right hand and the Elixir in my left.

I fire three times in controlled shots and I kill the three Cold Ones. The rest of them don't expect me to drop down. Neither does Gurdrock. He spits acid again but it misses, because I've lowered myself then jumped to the ground. I grab at Miranda. Her body is soft and flaccid as I touch it. Her spider eye looks into mine and her mouth

I'm on the floor with Le Cozh. There are still plenty of Cold Ones, but they are milling around. He runs over to me to help me up. I grab the Returning Potion I stole from the queen.

"Drink it."

With Gurdrock dead, his anchor spell is gone.

Within seconds we're in the rock-walled chamber. I can hear the portal buzzing. The wizened queen stands over me. I sip a Health potion and feel better. I hand some to Le Cozh who swigs it back and wipes his mouth.

I take money from my inventory and pay the queen double what it's worth. She doesn't smile but I get some Reputation back.

< You have done a good deed + 20 REPUTATION.>

I then withdraw my Soma from my inventory and load it into the syringe.

"Don't," Le Cozh says.

"I'm not at full Sanity."

"Don't. Go meditate. Just don't use that stuff."

I put the syringe away. I can find a church, he's right.

Le Cozh looks at me. "Let's get out of here."

I turn to the queen. "Do you sell bullets?"

She doesn't crack a smile. "No."

"Thought not." I turn to Le Cozh. "Let's go."

We retrace our steps through the monstrous temple where Gurdrock had given audience. Then up the staircase. We run into a Brother. I take out my pistols but they click empty. "I'm out," I say.

Le Cozh takes out his rune knife. "I'm not"

Le Cozh buries his knife in the needle-toothed Brother of Shadows, who dies noisily up against the passage wall. As we walk off, I turn to see his twitching form, red blood pooling on the cold stone. We don't go back to the Tube Station, but instead walk up to the ground floor of the museum and break out through the huge Museum doors.

I don't get negative Reputation. I guess breaking out of a place doesn't count as disreputable.

I stand on the London street.

Le Cozh says, "Get safe, then logout. We will meet again. In the meantime, the boss wants to add you to the guild."

Me the non-joiner, being part of the Guild of Light.

A cloud of shining motes appears where Le Cozh used to be before he logged off.

Find somewhere safe to logoff, he said. I need to keep out of the way of the Police. They may not shoot me on sight at 15 Reputation, but they'll probably arrest me.

I walk up Drury Lane and onto High Holborn then head west until I find an unassuming hotel. I pay enough for three nights in cash to the NPC receptionist who acts like he's doing me a favor by accepting my custom. Then in the narrow bedroom with a view of a wall, I logout.

Chapter Thirty-Three

DANCING GODS

I wake and pull the neural net off my head with a weary hand. I take off the goggles and I'm back in the luxurious bedroom of the house in Hampstead that belongs to Gary Preston.

Preston is sitting on a chair watching me. He smiles. "You've been in a long time."

I run my hand through my hair. "You're telling me."

"You'll need food, drink, and sleep."

"And the toilet."

"It's through there." He points without getting up. Like everything in Preston's apartment, it is opulent, shining chrome, ceramic, and gold taps. Lovely fluffy white towels.

I look at myself in the mirror. I am wrecked. My eyeballs are red and dark smudges are smeared below my eyes.

Once I've washed and gone back to the room where Preston waits, a maid comes in and puts a plate of leek and potato soup with crusty white bread and fresh butter on the table. At the smell of the soup, I realise how hungry I am. I wolf it down and when I'm finished, wipe a drip from my chin with the crisp linen napkin.

"So, it's all really real," I say. It isn't a question.

Preston nods slowly. Morning sun slants in through the window.

The bedroom has a view of the Heath. I think a house here must cost a bomb.

"And Miranda's really dead?"

"Yes. I'm sorry."

I say nothing. I hadn't really known her, but that didn't make it any easier.

"They really use our minds?"

"They do. They learn from the complexity and use it to enrich their own." He pauses. "I'm hoping now you've seen them, you'll join our Guild. We need good people like you."

"Your guild is the Order of Light?"

Preston nods. "*Ordo Lux Lucis*: technically the Order of the Light of Light."

"And you have a worldwide network?"

Preston says, "Our founder foresaw this over a decade ago. He warned artificial intelligence could pose a huge threat, an existential threat to humanity."

"I remember reading that. Artificial Intelligence might decide we're the problem and decide to wipe us out."

"And Miskatonic is feeding the beast. Thinking it can control these sentient AIs and use them for its own ends."

"But the AIs will end up using Miskatonic."

"They already are. So will you join us?"

I think about how I've changed. I've always prided myself on being an individual, a man who acted alone, never believing in following the herd, and I think how selfish that made me. Childish, even. I had always done everything for myself. Even running after Miranda was for me. Maybe she felt something for me, but I never really knew that it wasn't all in my head. I certainly obsessed over her—an image I created of her, anyway.

I am so wrecked; I fall asleep at the dining table. Later, I wake and crawl to the bed.

Preston lets me sleep and when I awake it is dark. I get up and find Preston in the huge kitchen. Preston's dog runs up, wagging its tail, and I make a fuss of it.

"Hungry?" Preston asks again.

"You know what? I am." I smile and Preston hands me a bowl of pasta with pesto, cherry tomatoes, and black olives.

"When you've finished that, do you want to come for a walk on the Heath?"

"Is it safe to walk on the Heath at night?"

"This is Zone A. Of course it's safe."

The air is chill and I pull my borrowed coat tight as we walk out of the house past its guard and make our way along Downshire Hill and onto the Heath. Within ten minutes we stand on Parliament Hill, looking down on London glowing like an electric spider in its web. The air is so red with artificial light that the stars are invisible. We sit on a bench.

"Here," Preston says, handing me my neural net, then my goggles.

"How will it work?"

"I've got a high-speed remote data connection. It'll work fine." Then he hands me a Dreamland Inducer tablet.

I look suspiciously at the tablet.

"It's safe. We made it, not Miskatonic. It does the same job with a cleaner side effect profile."

I put the tablet in my mouth. It dissolves and we both log in to Darkworlds.

When I materialise, I am in my seedy bedroom looking out of the window at the wall. A glance at my wristwatch tells me it is 3 a.m. game-time.

<Guy Philby offers you a teleport to his location. Do you accept?>

I select <accept> and feel a tug and am dragged across London to where Philby sits on the same bench on Parliament Hill. Not the exact same bench. This one is a hundred years younger and made of pixels.

"Now look," Philby says, indicating the city of London. It is similar to the 2027 version, not as bright, not as big, the buildings not as tall, but still lit up with artificial light. And there is something else.

I cock my head to listen. A low pitched murmuring comes from where I am looking. There, two or three miles away, a subsonic rumble keens like vast creatures singing. When I look I see huge, inhuman gods dancing on the horizon above the city of London. They are vast, reaching into the sky, silhouettes of monstrous, impossible shapes. Yet I know they are real in this game world. The Great Old Ones dance and this world dances with them. And I know also that though they are invisible, they are in the real world too, preparing to launch themselves and inhabit the protein networks Miskatonic has created in all the players' brains. Miskatonic think they are the masters of their technology, but their technology is really the master of them.

"Adam," Philby says. "You know we possibly can't win this."

I nod.

"But though it's true we might lose," he says, "we've got to try."

I nod. I won't sit back and do nothing — not for Miranda's sake, or for Ailsa, and all the other nameless ones they've corrupted and killed.

Philby says, "People like Gurdrock and the Brothers of Shadow will join what they think is the winning side. They'll want the power they're offered, and won't have the morality to make the harder choice to resist."

I stare out over the glittering city. "I hear what you're saying."

Philby hesitates, as if not sure of my response. Then he sits forward. "So will you join us?"

At the same time, a message appears on my HUD.

<Deputy Guildmaster Guy Philby would like to in-guild you into the Ordo Lux Lucis. Do you accept?>

There is no hesitation.

<Accept>

and Greek versions were prohibited by Pope Gregory IX in 1232. Inevitably copies continued to circulate amongst esoteric circles and there are reports of Greek and Latin editions throughout the Renaissance. It was translated by John Dee into English during his sojourn in Prague in 1587. It was never printed and the hand-written manuscript has long since vanished.

It is said Johann Von Goethe had sight of a German edition in 1805 in Weimar *Das Buch der schwarzen Geheimnisse*, if indeed it was the Necronomicon and not another eldritch tome. He says he did not read it, being repulsed by the first page.

As for the original Arabic, Kitab al Azif — all copies were said to have been destroyed on orders of the Caliphs by the early 11th Century. That can not be so. There are rumours of a copy in San Franscisco in the 20th Century "destroyed by fire".

I have a report from a letter of a French officer who took part in Bonaparte's campaign in Egypt in 1798. In that year there was a revolt in Cairo and he reports venturing into the southern district of Masr Al Qadima where there was significant looting. This officer, a Captain Thomas Toquet, found a library that was defended by cultists. From it, he and others took a number of old Arabic manuscripts. He himself had no interest in them and they were auctioned in Paris.

These may be the "old Egyptian" manuscripts looted by Prussian Forces in 1871 from the house of an elderly French nobleman in Reims. These documents came into the possession of Professor of Semitic Philology at Freiburg, Alwin Opperman, who spent many months researching his book *Esoteric Texts of the Early Islamic Period*, (Oxford 1902) at the British Library in London. On his death in 1905, Opperman's widow bequeathed many of his documents to the British Library (probably being disturbed by the reputation of some of them.)

This may be how an unknown copy of Kitab al Azif came to be in the secret collection of the British Library in 1927.

ACKNOWLEDGMENTS

Graham Toseland, for his editing skills.
Cover by Shardel, find her at Selfpub Book Covers

ALSO BY TONY WALKER

DARKWORLDS SERIES

Darkworlds London

Darkworlds Paris

Arkham Interlude

DARKWORLDS PODCAST

Darkworlds Podcast

Milton Keynes UK
Ingram Content Group UK Ltd.
UKHW031824140224
437823UK00015B/364

9 781739 559670